PU...

"We could get ki... ar voice from the grou... ...anned woman in her thirties, ...olored jumpsuit.

Soto looked at her b... addressed the group. "You fought long and hard to be invited. Did you think it would be any less of a fight once you got here?" Soto looked at his watch. "We'll begin in thirty seconds."

One man took off his face shield and threw it down. "This is crazy! I didn't come here for this!"

"You may quit at any time," Soto said. "The rest of you will begin in twenty seconds."

Matt's heart thumped triple time to the countdown in his head. His entire field of vision shook with the intensity of his fear, but at the same time, he'd never felt so alive.

Matt glanced down at his Aurora University duffel bag. It contained his clothes, his diploma, and a single reminder of his childhood: a toy Imp Mecha, battered and worn by his passage through a dozen refugee ships. He'd miss the Imp, but he was now at Mecha Training Camp. There wasn't a single thing in the bag that mattered anymore.

Two, one, zero, he thought. *Better become a hero.*

"Go," Major Soto said.

MECHA CORPS

A NOVEL OF THE ARMOR WARS

BRETT PATTON

A ROC BOOK

ROC

Published by New American Library, a division of
Penguin Group (USA) Inc., 375 Hudson Street,
New York, New York 10014, USA
Penguin Group (Canada), 90 Eglinton Avenue East, Suite 700, Toronto,
Ontario M4P 2Y3, Canada (a division of Pearson Penguin Canada Inc.)
Penguin Books Ltd., 80 Strand, London WC2R 0RL, England
Penguin Ireland, 25 St. Stephen's Green, Dublin 2,
Ireland (a division of Penguin Books Ltd.)
Penguin Group (Australia), 250 Camberwell Road, Camberwell, Victoria 3124,
Australia (a division of Pearson Australia Group Pty. Ltd.)
Penguin Books India Pvt. Ltd., 11 Community Centre, Panchsheel Park,
New Delhi - 110 017, India
Penguin Group (NZ), 67 Apollo Drive, Rosedale, Auckland 0632,
New Zealand (a division of Pearson New Zealand Ltd.)
Penguin Books (South Africa) (Pty.) Ltd., 24 Sturdee Avenue,
Rosebank, Johannesburg 2196, South Africa

Penguin Books Ltd., Registered Offices:
80 Strand, London WC2R 0RL, England

First published by Roc, an imprint of New American Library,
a division of Penguin Group (USA) Inc.

First Printing, December 2011
10   9   8   7   6   5   4   3   2   1

For Lisa, who thinks atomic weapons are hilarious

"You are remembered for the rules you break."
— Douglas MacArthur, General of the Army,
United States of America

"Nobody is ever born into this world as a soldier."
— Rau Le Creuset, Elite ZAFT Commander,
Mobile Suit Gundam SEED

ACKNOWLEDGMENTS

Thank you to the following individuals. Without their support, this book would never have been written.

Pete Harris, who was my mentor throughout.

Matthew Cohen, who thought it would be a good idea for Pete and I to talk.

Lisa, and her unending patience and understanding.

MECHA CLASSES

Excerpted from Mecha Cadet Training Content
Version 4.1.a, 04.13.2316

PREMECHA

POWERLOADER: A simple, powered exoskeleton used for transport of heavy loads or augmentation of manual labor. Widely used across the Universal Union, Corsair Confederacy, and other Interstellar Governmental Organizations (IGOs). Typical height: 2.5–3 m. Typical weaponry: none.

MECHANICAL MECHA

RASCAL: An augmented PowerSuit, first used in combat at Pellham's Front (Union colony). Still used on many fringe worlds of the Union, as well as on independent Displacement Drive ships. Typical height: 3–3.5 m. Typical weaponry: 5–15 mm depleted-uranium rifles, cutting laser.

IMP: A large, tough Mecha design. Extensively used in both warfare and industry. Arguably the Mecha best known to the general public. Typical height: 8–8.5 m. Typical weaponry: 15–30 mm depleted-uranium rifles, cutting laser.

VILLIAN: The last of the fully mechanical Mecha, built entirely for warfare. Led Union Army to decisive victory at Forest (former Corsair colony.) Extensive armament; exceptionally rugged. Typical height: 9 m. Typical weaponry: 15–30 mm depleted-uranium rifles, cutting laser, guided missiles.

BIOMECHANICAL MECHA

ROGUE: First-generation biomechanical Mecha from Advanced Mechaforms, Inc. Rogues transformed Mecha into the de facto surgical engagement tool of the Universal Union in the victory at New Jericho colony. Limited transformational capability. Typical height: 8 m. Typical weaponry: 10 mm depleted-uranium rifles, pulsed fusion device, antipersonnel missiles.

HELLION: The standard second-generation biomechanical Mecha. Larger and more powerful than Rogue class. Neural buffering improves pilot usability. Good transformational ability; limited combinational ability. Typical height: 10 m. Typical weaponry: 15 mm depleted-uranium rifles, antipersonnel and guided missiles, pulsed fusion device, antimatter rifle.

DEMON: Planned third-generation Mecha with both excellent transformational and combinational ability. Much larger than Hellion class. Exponential power capability. Additional <REDACTED>. Typical height: 30 m. Typical weaponry: <REDACTED>.

PART ONE

EARTH

1

DISPLACEMENT

This is stupid, Matt Lowell thought, as the airlock cycled down to vacuum.

Bright red letters on the hatch read UUS MERCURY SURFACE-ACCESS PORT 3A — NO EGRESS AT DISPLACEMENT. And yet here he was, getting ready to go outside, with Displacement only minutes away.

Matt licked dry lips and took a deep, shuddering breath. Yeah. It was dumb. But he had to do it. This was his last day as a civilian. It was time to say good-bye to his old life.

The air-lock screen flashed bright red: AIRLOCK EVACUATED. But Matt stayed on the steel bench a moment longer. *You don't have to say good-bye like this,* he thought. *Go back inside and watch the Displacement from the viewports, like everyone else.*

No. He'd already slipped the digger a twenty for his ill-fitting space suit. And Displacement was close. He might not have time to unsuit and make it to the viewing deck.

Matt sighed and levered the air lock open. The surface of the UUS *Mercury* looked like any other Displacement Drive ship: dusty, brittle gray rock, punctuated by air locks, hatches, antennae, and reconnaissance towers. A converted asteroid. So much like the refugee ships he used to call home.

Matt slipped out onto the surface and tugged the lock closed. *Mercury*'s bridge rose against the short horizon, a shining metal cliff with bright-lit windows. Uniformed crew members gathered around colorful displays beyond the glass.

Matt's heart hammered. Could the crew see him? He shuffle-stepped behind the air lock, cursing the microgravity. If he moved too fast, he could build enough velocity for a one-way trip into deep space.

On the other side of the air lock, Matt crouched, taking big breaths of suit air that stank of recycled sweat and asteroid. He expected warning Klaxons to blare on his comms and blinding security lights to flare any second.

But nothing happened. Matt's thundering heartbeat slowed. On this side of the air lock, the brittle gray-white rock and dust of the UUS *Mercury*'s surface was unbroken. It was as if he were alone on a pristine asteroid, whirling through space.

Matt smiled. This was right. He needed to be here. It might be dangerous to be outside during Displacement, but it wasn't that crazy. Yeah, everyone had a story about an uncle who lost a hand or a head when the Displacement field went unstable, but when you pressed them, they'd waffle. You'd find the uncle had been standing on a five-meter scaffold, or hanging ten meters out on an unauthorized dock. If you stayed near the surface, you were pretty safe. Matt had done it a hundred times as a kid, lying on the rock and watching the stars change. It was the best view in the universe.

Beneath him, the UUS *Mercury* shivered slightly. Most likely the last of the heavy cargo ships arriving. Matt imagined the giant freighter nestling into one of *Mercury*'s titanic bays, and the steel doors grinding soundlessly shut. It wouldn't be long before Displacement.

He lay down on the surface. In the microgravity, it took several long seconds for him to settle. He put his hands behind his head, like he was relaxing on a beach in the sun.

But this beach was ash colored and frigid, under a pitch-black sky sparked with a million chill stars, and lit by a blue-green world covering a quarter of the sky: Aurora.

Only a few jewel-like city lights on the dark quarter of the planet showed the presence of humans. Even though Aurora was one of the oldest worlds in the Universal Union, it had never grown to the size of industrial giants like Geos or Eridani. It was a world dominated by Aurora University.

Matt's past three years had been spent on Aurora. It was the longest time he'd ever stayed on a planet. But even at a breakneck pace, even with his gifts, a degree in analytical business took time. He'd graduated summa cum laude with a half-dozen rich offers from the biggest corporations in the Union already in his pocket.

And on that same day, he also received an invitation to Mecha Training Camp.

Matt never had to weigh his options. Those employment offers were sitting in a trash can in his dorm room. His training camp invitation was inside his space suit, tucked in his breast pocket.

The UUS *Mercury* vibrated violently, sending Matt skidding over the dusty rock of the asteroid ship. He instinctively reached out and grabbed a large rock to stop his slide. No problem. Displacement would happen any second. They always docked the largest ships last.

The space suit's communications unit lit up with a bright red ALERT light. A scratchy voice filled Matt's helmet: "All personnel, prepare for Displacement in thirty seconds."

Matt imagined huge energies gathering in the fusion core of the UUS *Mercury*. But the energies were silent, buried deep in the center of the asteroid. He saw nothing, felt nothing.

The scratchy voice blared again: "Displacement in twenty seconds."

A sudden thought hit Matt. Maybe this wasn't dumb just because of the danger. He was breaking the rules of a Universal Union ship. What if they found out? Would it keep him out of training camp?

"Displacement in ten. Nine. Eight. Seven—"

He had no time to get back in the air lock and cycle it. Matt was committed, for better or worse.

As the last seconds sounded, Matt suddenly remembered a childhood countdown rhyme. What they used to say on the *Rock*, the Displacement Drive refugee ship that had been his home.

> *Five, four, three, time to flee.*
> *Two, one, zero, nobody's a hero.*

Above him, the sky changed.

Aurora disappeared. Earth filled Matt's entire point of view, its brilliant blue-white surface seemingly close enough to touch. The sun shimmered off waves in the oceans, and lightning flashed under cloud banks at the terminator between day and night. They'd Displaced directly into low Earth orbit.

Matt's veins thrummed. He'd made it.

Here and there on Earth's surface, splotches of gray concrete and sparkling glass marked sprawling cities. Broad highways traced spidery lines across the continent. It was like seeing close-up photos of Eridani, the first-settled and most-populous world in the Union. But unlike Eridani, many of the highways were broken and incomplete, as if they'd fallen into disrepair. Some of the cities on the night side of the terminator were only dimly lit or completely dark.

Matt frowned, gripped by sudden sadness. Earth was humanity's first home, but time had passed it by. In the Universal Union, everyone knew the opportunities were on Eridani in politics, or Geos in technology, or Aurora in academia. You could have a quiet, comfortable life on one of a dozen second-tier worlds like Fedora or Epsilon. Or you could try to make it big on any of twenty frontier worlds, as long as you didn't mind the chance of tangling with the Corsair Confederacy.

But Earth? Earth was an end. The only thing new on Earth was Mecha Training Camp. Or, more accurately, Bio-Mecha Pilot Candidate Training Facility No. 1, a Division of Advanced MechaForms, Inc., a Universal Union Exclusive Contractor.

As the clouds shifted, three huge lakes in a clover-leaf pattern came into view. Matt realized what he was looking at: the continent of North America. Which meant that the ancient state of Florida should be in the Southeast.

Thick clouds piled on Florida's eastern coast, and lightning flashed inland. Strange lightning. Green tinged, it shot horizontally through heavy mist.

With a start, Matt sat up straight. That wasn't lightning. That was a battle.

That's Mecha Training Camp.

Matt gulped, losing his breath in a rush of pure elation. That was where he was headed. That was where he was going to pilot a weapon powerful enough to be seen from orbit.

He watched green sparks arc through wispy clouds, crossing half the peninsula. *That was several hundred kilometers!* Were Mecha that fast? Mecha technology was the most carefully guarded secret in the Universal Union. Mecha didn't march in parades. Mecha specs and capabilities weren't released. Even the videos of Mecha taking out a Corsair terror cell in a sprawling frontier town were carefully edited.

Not that it mattered. They didn't need heroic video or over-the-top propaganda. An invitation to Mecha Training Camp was one of the highest honors in the Universal Union, given across both civilian and military ranks. In the words of Union Congressperson Tomita, it was for the "most exceptional individuals, so we may build the most irresistible force." Application to Mecha Corps began with an agreement to allow possibly decades-long surveillance and auditing of academic, military, or business records. From there, only a small percentage of candidates were chosen.

Matt stood up and shuffled back to the other side of the lock. He had a shuttle to catch and Mecha to learn. And he had the best reason in the universe to do it.

As Matt reached for the hatch, the air lock opened. Inside stood a figure wearing a crisp blue space suit. Across his chest, stark white letters read SECURITY. The man's black utility belt held a stun stick, handcuffs, and a bright orange Spazer gun.

Matt's stomach lurched, and he had time for one clear, resounding thought: *I am in deep shit.*

Then he saw the officer's face. His eyes were wide and darting with fear, his jaw set in a grim line. White-blond hair only partially hid a rash of acne on his forehead. He wasn't much more than high school aged.

They sent the new kid, Matt thought. But that was dumb. Scared people did stupid things.

As if reading his thoughts, the guard leapt at Matt. The kid came at him like a linebacker going full bore at a quarterback, but one important thing was missing: gravity. And this kid had just jumped hard enough to escape the UUS *Mercury*'s microgravity.

Matt saw the perfect chance to dodge his misfortune. All he had to do was step out of the way of the security officer, slip back in through the air lock, and get on his shuttle. It wasn't his fault the kid had decided to take a flying leap.

Matt stepped in front of the guard. He couldn't let the kid go. That jump might be a one-way death trip into outer space, or a fiery plunge into Earth's atmosphere.

The guard hit him like a hammer. Their helmets impacted with a resounding crack, and Matt's feet came off the ground. The young man grabbed desperately at Matt as they tumbled over the surface of the UUS *Mercury*, slowly gaining altitude. Blue Earth and gray asteroid wheeled in Matt's POV.

If the kid was frightened before, he was terrified now. His lips skimmed back over chattering teeth. Beads of sweat stood out on his forehead. He yelled at Matt, spittle spraying on his faceplate.

Matt cursed. It wasn't his problem if the kid didn't know how to use comms. Talking was pointless anyway. Their trajectory would take them close to the top of the bridge. With any luck, they'd hit it. That impact would sap their momentum and they'd fall back down to the surface.

It would be close. The bridge swelled in front of them. Inside, a crew member looked up from her screen, her mouth agape in surprise.

Matt stretched hard, but his fingers only brushed the edge of the bridge as they passed over it. That didn't do anything except make their tumbling worse.

"Hey!" Matt's comms crackled alive. The guard had finally found a clue.

Matt looked down. They were about ten meters off the asteroid and still rising. That was bad. That meant they probably weren't coming down.

Matt turned on his comms. "What've you got to throw?"

"What?" the kid's voice was high and screechy.

"Throw! Something to throw! To get us back down."

The kid shook his head. "I—I don't get it."

Matt sighed. "This is microgravity. We have to slow down, or we're going on a long trip in a space-suit spaceship." Matt felt along his own suit, hoping the digger had left an anchor. There was nothing. "We need to throw something in the direction we're going, or we aren't going to come down. Heavy things. Got anything heavy?"

The kid shook his head. "I— Uh, I don't know."

Matt groaned. They didn't have time for this. He pulled the stun stick off the guard's utility belt.

"Hey! You're under arrest!" the kid grabbed for the club.

"Let's save ourselves now and talk about that later."

The kid looked doubtful while Matt weighed the stick in his hand. It was heavy, but not nearly heavy enough to make a difference in the velocity of a 150-kilo mass. Unless he could launch it fast enough.

"Give me your belt," Matt said.

"Why?"

"Because you don't want to die."

The kid pulled off his belt. Matt looped it through the wrist strap of the nightstick and twirled it over his head, like a video of an ancient cowboy about to rope a steer. He'd have to release it at exactly the right moment. That would be tough. They were still tumbling over the asteroid's rough surface.

"Hold on," he told the kid. "And don't move."

Matt threw the nightstick. It rocketed out toward Earth, disappearing almost instantaneously into the brilliance of the clouds.

He'd timed it well. They were falling slowly toward the surface of the UUS *Mercury*.

The guard saw it. "How'd you know to do that?"

"I learned a thing or two growing up on Displacement Drive ships."

The kid nodded. He looked down at the surface, now only a few feet below them. They passed over a deep pit where a Rhino-class Union warship crouched. Dark gray and angularly utilitarian, it was intended for close-range combat in deep space. Lights glowed dimly through tiny, slit windows, deep-set under thick armor. Long gouges in its sides spoke of recent combat. Matt wondered where they'd been fighting. Some frontier world too insignificant to make the news? Or perhaps near one of the fleets of independent Displacement Drive ships?

It didn't matter. Battleships were single-purpose machines, whether they were slow Rhinos or fast Cheetahs. The decisive victories, the ones people cared about these days, came on the ground, via Mecha. Mecha were the only things that could protect the tiny number of habitable worlds in the Union without the wholesale destruction of nuclear weaponry. Even the Corsairs weren't insane enough to poison a valuable planet. Mecha were used when the fight mattered the most.

Matt and the kid grazed a rocky outcropping, spraying dust and rock chips in glittering, sunlit plumes. Matt pinwheeled his arms to change their orientation and dug his heels into the ground. More dust ballooned up as he brought them to a stop.

"You can let go of me now," Matt said.

The kid blushed and released him, taking two unsteady steps away. He grabbed for his Spazer gun at his belt. Of course, the gun and his belt were both gone.

"I still, uh, have to arrest you," he said.

Matt shook his head but said nothing.

"It's dangerous, what you did. Against regulations."

Matt could tell the guard that he'd been safe, that he'd done it before. He could remind him that he'd still be on an unplanned tour of outer space if it weren't for Matt. But all that didn't matter.

Only one thing mattered: Would this keep him out of training camp?

The kid found an air lock and escorted Matt down the passenger corridors to the security center. His Velcro-soled shoes scritched on the fuzz of the floor. Happy passengers dressed in bright tourist colors passed them with curious glances, heading toward their vacations on historic Earth.

The holo-posters in the hallways seemed to mock Matt. VISIT AMAZING WASHINGTON, DC, AND SEE THE FOUNDATION OF THE UNION CONSTITUTION one read, showing gleaming white marble buildings. ROME/ATHENS COMBO TOUR: SEE COLISEUMS, TEMPLES, CATACOMBS read another, which displayed fantastic ruins. DISCOVER ANCIENT CHINA: FORERUNNER OF TAIKONG LINGYO offered a third.

The security center was a large room carved directly out of the raw gray rock of the asteroid. Stainless-steel desks stood in rows, manned by blue-uniformed staff. On the far wall, a giant holoscreen streamed hundreds of video feeds from inside the UUS *Mercury*: docks, corridors, restaurants, rec rooms, bridge and command centers, even feeds showing the stony surface outside. Yellow icons floated over some of the feeds, calling out minor problems like lock malfunctions and suspicious behavior.

A large, red-faced man stomped up to meet them. He wore a blue uniform and an intricate badge that read UUS *MERCURY* SECURITY: LT A. HARPER.

"What the hell you think you're doing, kid?" Harper shouted at Matt. "Trying to get yerself killed? Trying to get Pete here killed?"

"I'm sorry, sir," Matt said. "I didn't mean—"

"You didn't mean shit!" Harper bellowed. Everyone in the room turned to look at them. "We saw you bribing the digger—we got you on the vid! You knew what you were doing. And you meant to do it."

"Look, sir. I really didn't want any trouble. I shouldn't have been out there, and I'm sorry. It's just, well . . . You see, sir, I've got to get down to Earth."

"Ha! Like hell you do!" Harper said. "Put Earth in your memory bank! You'll be a digger the rest of your life right here on the ol' *Mercury*!"

Matt's stomach flipped. His chance at being a Mecha cadet was flying away like a paper airplane in a zero-G hangar.

"But . . ." Matt trailed off. What could he say? How could he justify it? NO EGRESS AT DISPLACEMENT. Simple as that. Stupid.

"But what? What you gonna tell me I don't already know?" Harper picked up a glowing slate. "Rich kid from Aurora U thinks the rules don't apply. Well, money ain't a get-outta-jail-free card!"

"Sir, I'm not—" Matt's anguish made his voice crack. "Look, I have to get down there! I'm going to training camp!"

"I don't care where you—," Harper began, then stopped himself. "Wait. What did you say?"

"I'm going to Mecha Training Camp."

Harper went beet red. "You're a Mecha cadet?"

"Yes, sir."

Harper glared at Matt, his expression shading to purple. "You got proof?"

Matt nodded. He reached into his breast pocket and pulled out the laser-etched holographic invitation. Gasps erupted in the room around him. Pete leaned over Matt's shoulder to gape at the gilded e-sheet signed by Kathlin Haal, the Union's Prime.

Harper snatched it out of his hands and ran it under a scanner. All color drained from his face as he read the screen.

"You're a goddamn Mecha cadet," Harper grated low and rough.

Matt nodded, afraid to say a single word. Was that good? Bad? Would Harper tear up his invitation and laugh at him? Would there be more penalties from the Mecha division itself?

Harper thrust the invitation back at Matt. "Go."

Matt took the paper with numb fingers.

Harper nodded. "Get on the shuttle." Then he blew out a big breath, all his anger gone. "Go save the Union."

"Yes, sir!" Matt said.

"Just don't pull any dumb shit like you did here," Harper called after him.

Matt shook his head. No more dumb stunts. He smiled. He was a Mecha cadet, and the Universal Union needed him.

2

INDUCTION

Matt's invitation directed him down to UUS *Mercury*'s Auxiliary Shuttle Bay, where a small, delta-winged craft squatted. It bore both the Union's concentric thirty-star insignia and the logo of Advanced Mechaforms: the shadow outline of a Mecha crouched to jump.

The pilot was a young woman with short-cropped red hair. She wore a simple gray uniform with three silver stripes embroidered into the sleeve. On the front of the uniform was a single black bar reading L. STOLL.

Stoll scanned Matt's e-sheet invitation and nodded at the shuttle's hatch. Matt started when he noticed that her eyes were a bright violet color. Violet eyes were a signature of genetic modification, and genemod was widely hated in the Universal Union. It was a holdover from the Human–HuMax war 150 years ago, when the genetically engineered "superhuman" HuMax laid siege to the richest human worlds. They'd almost won, too. Only the formation of the Universal Union and the eventual eradication of every living HuMax had ended it.

She noticed his stare. "What is it, cadet candidate?"

"I, uh, I don't recognize your uniform," Matt lied. "I was trying to place it."

"Mecha Corps Auxiliary," she said. Her face was unreadable, her tone all business.

"Gotcha," Matt said. He tried not to steal a glance back

at her as he slung his duffel bag over his shoulder. Most genemods wouldn't openly display a hallmark like violet eyes in public. Was it just an Earth thing, or did it not matter in the Mecha Corps?

"Where is other cadet?" bellowed a voice from deep within the shuttle. "I am not wanting to miss opportunity!"

Matt jumped. Another cadet? He hadn't expected that. He virtually flew through the hatch.

In the cramped interior of the shuttle, a large man slouched on one of the four bare plastic seats. A loud, shiny shirt printed with floral patterns and a pair of white pants hung loose on this thick frame. Crow's-feet wrinkles nestled in the corners of his eyes, and his bushy beard was shot through with gray. A huge pile of matching leather luggage covered the seat next to him and spilled into the walkway.

"I not spent ten years struggling to miss cadet chance!" the man shouted, waving his invitation at Matt. "You see date and time? Sit in seat!"

Matt sat down and buckled himself in. "I didn't know there was another cadet on the ship."

The other man ignored him, his angry eyes fixing on Sergeant Stoll as she stepped in and pulled the hatch shut.

"HuMax pilot, you go now! Time ticking!"

Matt felt a quick stab of anger. She certainly wasn't HuMax, and she'd probably had her share of taunts, insults, and outright beatings growing up.

"Hey, did you choose your genes?" Matt said, struggling to keep his voice even.

The other man's eyebrows shot up in surprise. "I not genemod!"

"She didn't choose hers either. Her parents did. So why don't you stop trying to piss off the pilot?"

Out of the corner of his eye, Matt saw Sergeant Stoll turn to watch them. Her neutral expression didn't change.

"Oh, HuMax apologist, yes. They did not choose their genes either?" the bearded man said, coming off his seat, but the seat belt held him down.

Matt clenched his fists, thinking of his father. His own stories. His own secrets. "HuMax chose what they did, and for that they are monsters." His voice broke in anger.

The bearded man twitched a quick little smile, apparently satisfied.

"Some sense in you." He looked up at Sergeant Stoll. "Freaky genemod pilot, please be going now."

Sergeant Stoll didn't respond or change expression. She just ducked through the door to the cockpit and slid the folding partition shut.

Moments later, the shuttle's turbines spun up. Acceleration pushed Matt back in his seat. Through the small, thick window at his side, the raw stone of the UUS *Mercury*'s Auxiliary Shuttle Bay blurred past. Soon they were dropping toward Earth.

The other man looked straight ahead, his arms crossed, his jaw set tightly. Matt sighed. Even if the guy was an asshole, he should introduce himself. Hell, he might end up fighting next to him.

"I'm Matt Lowell," Matt said, holding out his hand. "I didn't expect anyone else from Aurora."

Silence for a while. Then: "Not from Aurora! Not rich boy with too much books!"

Matt nodded. Displacement Drive ships couldn't Displace any less than two light-years, or any more than twenty. That meant commercial ships had to hop from system to system in series, in a giant ring. This guy must have come from one of the worlds before Aurora.

"Are you from Eastern?" Matt asked. "Or Purchase?"

More silence. Finally, almost grudgingly: "Purchase. I am Serghey Anan."

"Good to meet you," Matt said.

"Now cease pretend interest, rich Aurora boy."

Matt sighed. Maybe wearing his blazer with the Aurora University crest wasn't the brightest idea. But it was warm and comfortable. And growing up he'd learned never to let anything go to waste. Not clothes. Not even food. Refugee ships were rough places. Everybody worked, even when they were eight years old. Sometimes Matt's job cleaning corridors didn't pay enough to buy dinner. Sometimes he'd get to mess and find one of his digger friends had been sent to the doc because of a crappy pressure suit. Sometimes his friends just stopped showing up at all.

What the hell does this jerk know? Sudden irritation boiled Matt's blood. Rich or poor, life or death, nothing should be taken for granted.

Matt forced his voice to be calm. "I'll leave you alone."

"Bah," Serghey said. He closed his eyes and made loud snoring noises.

As the shuttle fell into the atmosphere, a high whistling filled the passenger compartment. Streamers of superheated orange air flickered outside the window as the air thickened.

Florida swelled quickly as they dropped. Brilliant white clouds had moved in over the coast, covering Cape Canaveral, and the green Mecha lightning no longer flashed.

When the shuttle finally descended below the clouds, the Cape lay just ahead. Green Florida grass and scrub alternated with mud-brown wetlands. Stubs of old, blocky buildings protruded from the greenery connected by broken blacktop roads. Just below them, a sprawling mass of concrete covered the land like a kilometers-wide spider. The center of the expanse was stained black-purple with multiple rocket burns, and the fading number 99 was etched at one side.

Matt felt a sudden shock of recognition. Launch Facility 99. That was something they taught in human history. It was the first of the heavy launch facilities used by the United States after the discovery of the Displacement Drive. The First Expansion into space had started here, more than 250 years ago.

Farther off, the Atlantic shimmered like polished aluminum under the bright, overcast sky. At the edge of the ocean, spindly structures rose from overgrown cement pads, mottled black and red. They had to be gantries. Left-overs from the first days of the Space Race.

A shiver of pride passed through Matt, and he drew a deep breath. This was huge. Even though the United States was gone, as all nations were, its Constitution had formed the basis of the Universal Union's Articles of Unity.

But the farther they flew, the worse Cape Canaveral looked. Crumbling buildings overgrown with vines, black-top slumped into sinkholes, rows of dust-streaked tents, trenches gouged in the Earth, rusted heaps of old cars—it looked like the setting for a postapocalyptic game. Matt turned to get a better look, but it flashed past too fast as they touched down. Matt couldn't help wondering, *This is Mecha Training Camp?*

When Sergeant Stoll opened the hatch, the heat and humidity hit Matt like a slap in the face. He gasped in the thick air. His Aurora University blazer was an oven, and sweat instantly coated his face.

And there was the smell. Swamp rot over salt tang and seaweed, wet cement and the bloodlike scent of rust.

"Propaganda about perfect Earth," Sergey sneered, wiping his damp brow. Sweat had already stained the collar of his too-bright shirt. "All bullshit."

Matt nodded. Tourists liked to talk about how oddly "perfect" Earth was. The cradle of humanity! The best possible combination of gravity, weather, and environment! No other world came close! But to Matt, Earth was like the hydroponic gardens on the *Rock*, where sewage cooked by the solar concentrators fed the crops.

Matt grabbed his bag. Serghey looked around unhappily. "Where is porter?" he cried, looking at his mountain of luggage.

Sergeant Stoll ignored him and pointed across the runway to a group of people standing near the edge of the wetlands. "That's where you need to be." Her carefully neutral expression never changed.

Matt nodded and hopped out of the shuttle, trying to

avoid her eyes. Even though the sky was overcast, the ground gave off waves of heat. He took off his Aurora U jacket and carried it as he trudged across the runway.

Matt stopped five meters away from the group and put down his bag. There were maybe thirty people, standing singly or clustered in groups of two or three. A broad cross-section of the Universal Union, they reflected the Mecha Corps selection motto: "From the finest, the finest." The Union selected precandidates from school and public records. From there, if precandidates passed the initial mental and physical exams, they were put into a candidate pool and their achievements and actions monitored for up to ten years. The invitation to Mecha Corps could come at any time in that decade.

They ranged from kids dressed in the raglike attire of the hot frontier world Hyva to young men and women wearing smartly tailored business suits, to thickset men in casual T-shirts and jeans who were seemingly ready for a construction gig, to rail-thin spacers in refugee jumpsuits. Most of them were young, but a couple were older, in their thirties or forties, like Serghey. The entire group had a tense, pumped-up feel, like a group of diggers waiting to try out for the single spacer job. Everyone was trying to look cool while at the same time sizing up the competition.

Serghey panted up, dragging his beautiful luggage and muttering curses. Unlike Matt, he bulled his way to the front of the crowd, drawing bemused glances from the other cadet candidates.

As they moved out of the way for Serghey, Matt noticed one woman wearing fatigues. She also stood apart from the main group, crouching at the edge of the wetlands to peer intently across the sluggish water at the low rise beyond. Her long blond hair was tied back in a ponytail and shoved into the back of her fatigue jacket. Something about her exuded utter strength.

A blond guy wearing a blue striped shirt and carrying a navy blazer over his arm came to crouch beside her. He said something that Matt couldn't hear. The woman turned to look at him, her blue eyes like icy steel. Matt drew in his breath. Her face was like a fine art sketch, impossibly perfect and flawless. She stood, her full lips pursing as she studied the man. Even her baggy fatigues couldn't hide an amazing figure. Matt wondered what it would be like to unbutton her fatigue jacket, then quickly pushed the thought away. He wasn't here for that. He was here for the Mecha. To become part of the irresistible force.

But can't there be more than that? he wondered. For the first time since he got the invitation, the crushing loneliness of his life came down on him. He'd always been going at a dead run toward the next goal, toward the justice he needed because of that one day now so long ago. Matt shook his head. He couldn't forget that Corsair. He couldn't let it go.

Without saying anything, the woman walked away from the blond man, going fifteen meters down the banks of the wetlands. There she crouched, looking again out at the low rise.

The guy shrugged and looked back at the group, where two of his well-dressed friends laughed at his failure. Matt realized that everyone in the group was looking at the woman in fatigues. Who was she? She carried no bags, and she seemed far more intent and serious than the rest of the group. Could she be more than an invitee? Mecha Auxiliary? Mecha Corps?

The electric whine of engines swelled behind Matt. He turned to see an articulated High Mobility Land Vehicle and a large Land Transport drive up. Driving the HMLV was a man in a Mecha Auxiliary uniform. Next to him was a woman, also wearing Auxiliary gray. In back was a chunky, dark-skinned man in a sweat-stained T-shirt and gray uniform pants. Chiseled muscles stood out under his T-shirt. The two Auxiliaries went to the HMLV as the T-shirt guy hopped out of the HMLV and surveyed the group, hands on his hips.

The Mecha Auxiliaries came back with tarp-covered carts. The big man nodded at them and approached the group. Matt was closest to the three, and they stopped in front of him.

The T-shirted man took a bulky vest out of one of the carts and turned to Matt. On his T-shirt was a shiny metal name badge that read: G SOTO. Matt noticed that Soto's T-shirt had six stripes on it. A major's stripes.

"Put your arms out," Soto said.

Matt did. Soto draped the heavy black nylon vest over Matt and pulled it tight at his waist and solar plexus.

"Comfortable? Fit well?" Soto's dark eyes fixed on Matt.

Matt nodded, confused.

Soto did something to the vest. It vibrated, expanding around his upper body and arms to embrace him like a space suit. Matt jumped. Soto gave him a thin-lipped smile and put a scratched, pockmarked duraplas face shield over Matt's head.

"Don't take this off. It's bulletproof."

"Bulletproof?" Matt asked.

Soto nodded and handed him something else: a rifle.

What the hell? His fingers felt numb as he took the gun from Soto. It was amazingly heavy, and he had to grab it hard to keep from dropping it.

"This is an MK-1. Standard Union Army issue, deformable depleted-uranium rifle, 5-mm ultra-high-velocity rounds, clip of five hundred rounds. Used one before?"

"Nuh-uh. No," Matt said.

"That's okay. Safety's here. Trigger's here. Point at target, pull trigger. Easy."

"Uh—," Matt began, but Soto had already moved on to the next cadet. He repeated the same flak-jacket, face-shield, gun drill with the other guy, then moved on to the next.

A low murmur grew among the cadets. Groups of two and three formed, muttering about what was happening. One of them—the same blond man who'd approached the girl in fatigues—went over to Soto and the Auxiliaries.

"Sir, what are you preparing us for?"

Soto looked up. "Oh, you want to be next?" He took a flak jacket and pulled it over the man's head.

"Sir, is this a drill? We're only cadet candidates."

"Face shield," Soto said. "Don't take it off."

"Sir!"

"Gun. You know how to use it?" Soto's expression didn't waver.

The blue-suited man sighed and nodded. Soto moved on to the next cadet. Matt tried to hide a grin. Seemed like the blue-suited guy wasn't going to get any satisfaction from Soto either.

The woman in fatigues was last. She stood at attention and snapped off a salute. "Major Soto, sir!"

Soto gave her a grin. "Union Army?"

"Yes, sir! Private Michelle Kind, sir!"

"Regular army or reserve?"

"Reserve, sir! Earth has few regular positions, sir!"

"Hoo-rah, Earth girl?" Soto seemed amused.

Michelle's expression twisted angrily, but she still shouted, "Yes, sir!"

Soto nodded. "Then you know the drill, Earth girl." He handed her the flak jacket, face shield, and gun. Michelle shrugged them on. When the flak jacket molded itself to her hourglass figure, every man in the group drew in his breath.

Soto turned to address the group. "All right. Here's how we start. Live-fire combat."

The murmur in the group swelled to sharp mutterings and angry words. Soto spoke over them.

"Your goal is to make it across the stream, over the hill and through the swamp beyond. You will see the medical tents on the other side. Gunners will be stationed throughout your course, defending the position."

Matt was dumbstruck. Live fire? Combat? With real weapons? He hefted the rifle. Could he even shoot it? Could he point it at someone and pull the trigger? He'd never even held a gun before. He'd come here for the Mecha, not to be a grunt.

Muttering became cries of protest, echoing Matt's chaotic thoughts. Someone yelled, "What the hell is this?"

Soto raised his hands for silence. "If you talk, you'll miss critical info."

Choruses of "Shut up!" echoed through the group.

"In the medical tents are ten doctors. There are thirty-two of you. The first ten to make it through will have the most options."

The group went dead silent as Soto let this soak in.

"There are no rules beyond that. You may take your bags with you, if you wish to risk slowing yourself down."

Serghey groaned audibly.

"We could get killed out there?" asked a loud, clear voice from the group. It belonged to a deeply tanned woman in her thirties, wearing a sand-colored jumpsuit.

Soto looked at her but addressed the group. "You fought long and hard to be invited. Did you think it would be any less of a fight once you got here?" Soto looked at his watch. "We'll begin in thirty seconds."

One man took off his face shield and threw it down. "This is fucking crazy! I didn't come here for this!"

"You may quit at any time," Soto said. "The rest of you will begin in twenty seconds."

Matt's heart thumped triple time to the countdown in his head. His entire field of vision shook with the intensity of his fear, but at the same time, he'd never felt so alive.

Some cadets frantically dug through their luggage in a last effort to grab some prized memento. Matt glanced down at his Aurora University duffel bag. It contained his clothes, his diploma and a single reminder of his childhood: a toy Imp Mecha, battered and worn by his passage through a dozen refugee ships. He'd miss the Imp, but he was now at Mecha Training Camp. There wasn't a single thing in the bag that mattered anymore.

Two, one, zero, he thought. *Better become a hero.*

"Go," Major Soto said.

*   *   *

Cadets rushed into the water, splashing bright droplets into the gray sky. The loudest sounds were the slosh of feet and the panting of ragged breaths. One cadet slipped and went face-first into the murky water, his cry echoing in Matt's wraparound face shield.

Matt forced himself to push forward. What mattered was in front of him. The scratched duraplas of his face shield fogged in time with his exhales. The low hill ahead swam, as if in a fever dream.

Private Michelle Kind led the way. She ran fast, low to the water, as if she'd done this a thousand times before. The blond man in the blue shirt followed close behind her, grinning at her ass.

Matt pushed down a flash of anger. Following an Army reservist was smart. She knew what she was doing. She'd been ready. In fatigues. No luggage.

Matt ran harder to catch up with Michelle and the blond man. The water was up to their knees now, and Matt slipped and stuck in the soft mud beneath. Suddenly, one of his shoes was sucked right off his foot. He didn't look back. The only thing that mattered was getting to those tents.

Water sheeted his visor as Matt passed several laboring cadets. One of them was the deeply tanned woman who'd complained to Soto. Through the muck on her visor, Matt recognized the look on her face: stark, primal fear. Her mouth hung open, eyes wide and fixed forward. Matt wondered if she even knew where she was anymore.

Halfway to the low rise, Matt closed on Michelle and the blond guy. Michelle waded through the thigh-deep, thick water, but larger cadets now had the advantage. A tall, rail-thin kid passed Michelle, followed by a pale and muscular man. They pushed forward toward the gentlest part of the rise, where bushes gave way to short grass.

Michelle didn't follow. She veered toward a thicket of heavy brush, some of it taller than a man. That made sense. Better to come over the hill under cover than in the open. Matt and the blond guy both zagged behind Michelle.

Blondie looked back at Matt. His expression alternated between annoyance and a quick grin, as if acknowledging Matt's wise choice.

Michelle leapt from the water like a cheetah and disappeared into the brush. The blond man followed, but got hung up on the dense brambles. He cursed and beat at the bush. Matt ducked low as he emerged from the water. Thorns scraped painfully along his exposed foot, but he kept moving. He couldn't lose Michelle. She'd get him through this safely. He passed the blond guy and ran over the top of the rise.

Suddenly, Michelle was right in front of him. She'd stopped to look through the branches at the scene ahead.

Matt couldn't stop in time. He ran face-first into her strong shoulders. Michelle went sprawling on the thin carpet of leaves and grass. She rolled fast and came up on her back, pointing her MK-1 at him.

His hands came up in reflexive defense, his heart racing. His thoughts ping-ponged between gut-wrenching fear and intense excitement. She was beautiful. And she was pointing a gun at him.

"Idiot," she hissed. Michelle lowered her weapon and got back on her feet.

The blond man came over the rise at that moment. Michelle shook her head. "Two idiots."

"I'm sorry," Matt said.

Michelle's face twisted in anger. "No time." She pointed at Matt. "You. Go forward." She jerked her chin at the base of the hill, where the dirt disappeared into swamp muck.

Matt nodded and charged down the hill.

A sledgehammer hit him in the chest. Matt blew out the entire contents of his lungs in a single, bellowing whoop. He flew backward and landed on his butt in sticky mud, his MK-1 falling out of his hands.

I've been shot, he thought. The idea was oddly disconnected. Almost funny.

But Matt couldn't laugh. His chest heaved, but he

couldn't draw in any air. He strained as hard as he could and got only a thimbleful of oxygen down his windpipe. Matt's vision went purple as he felt a rising sense of panic. Had he been shot through the lung? He scrabbled at his flak jacket. Nothing had broken through, but there was a big divot on the left side of his chest where he'd been hit.

Live fire. Soto wasn't kidding. This wasn't a game. He could die.

Matt became aware of the crack of gunfire around him. To his left, where the brush petered out and the rise was its gentlest, he heard the cries of cadet candidates. Most of the fire seemed concentrated there. Only the odd bullet whizzed through the brush over to his position.

Matt sucked air with all his might and managed a shallow breath. It cooled his burning chest. His panic subsided. He was still alive.

Michelle ran past him, into the swamp. "Thanks," she said through a grin.

"Yeah, great move," the blond guy said, following her.

Matt pushed himself up. At the far edge of the wetland, maybe three hundred meters away, a small group of dirty gray tents stood. Between Matt and the tents were a couple of low rises, little islands in the muck. The remains of an old concrete road ran at an angle across the swamp, raised by sturdy pylons. Near the road, rusted carcasses of old cars dotted the swamp. They wouldn't provide much cover.

Michelle and the blond guy ran, doubled over, through tall grass. Bullets splashed in the water around them. Matt saw no muzzle flashes. Where the hell were the rounds coming from? The bushes by the tents? One of the mini islands? Michelle and Blondie ended up behind the stub of a rusted steel tube poking out of the ground like a vent, with gunfire ringing off the other side.

No time to think. Matt ran toward them. For an eternity, there were no shots. Then bullets dotted in the water ahead of him. Rainbows flashed in the air. Matt ran through them.

He joined the two others at the rusty tube. Michelle

flashed angry eyes at Matt. "Quit following me!" She turned to the blond guy. "Both of you!"

"Why?" Matt asked.

"Together we're more of a target," the blond guy said. "Anyone with combat training knows that."

"Then why are you following me?" Michelle snarled.

Blond guy grinned. "I like the view."

Michelle reddened, her jaw tightening.

The blond guy grinned wider and stuck out a hand. "Kyle Peterov, Eridani ROTC."

Michelle ignored his hand. "We should go around the edge, come in at the side of the tents. It'll be harder for them to target us if they're concentrating on the main mass of cadets."

Matt glanced back. Some cadets still hadn't crested the first hill. They looked over the rise with fear-glazed eyes as bullets sprayed mud. A few were fanning out through the swamp, heading for the cover of the road.

Michelle pushed Kyle. "You hear me? Go! Around the edge!"

Kyle nodded and went. Matt followed him. For long moments there was nothing more than the splash of the water and the thundering of his heart. A bullet hit the ground ahead of him. Kyle dove into a tangle of tall reeds for cover. He looked back in the direction they came.

"Fuck," Kyle said. "We've been played."

Michelle hadn't followed them. She was running full speed for one of the pylons.

Embarrassment burned Matt's face. He sprang from the reeds and ran toward one of the islands in the swamp for cover. A bullet splashed in front of him. Another whizzed past his leg so close he felt its warmth.

The gunner was hidden up on the island, and Matt was going to die out here before he ever got in a Mecha.

Matt yelled and raised his MK-1. He squeezed the trigger. The gun was like a jackhammer in his hands. Its explosive din drowned out all other sound. It drowned his thoughts. In that instant, it didn't matter if he lived or died.

Matt crashed into the brush of the island. Brambles tore his pants. He was almost on the other side before he realized the firing had stopped.

He looked back up at the smoking remains of an automated sentry station. Its sensor array was fractured, and its gun barrel twitched impotently.

Ahead of him was part of the old road. Huge blocks of concrete had tumbled into the swamp. Atop this ramshackle ramp, behind the remains of a rusted Humvee, Michelle crouched. She glanced at Matt. Bullets stitched orange dust from her Humvee cover.

Matt cut a zigzag path through the debris toward Michelle, his legs like pistons. He slammed into the Humvee as more rounds spanged its top. Michelle looked up at him. This time, though, her expression cycled between determination and grudging respect.

"There's a gun emplacement ahead," Michelle told him. "Shoot it."

"That's what I've been doing," she hissed. "I think this one is armored."

"Let's both hit it together."

Michelle ground her jaw, as if looking for a reason to disagree.

"Go!" Matt said, and shot from behind the Humvee. Incoming fire erupted from the bushes right next to the tents. Taking careful aim back at it, Matt squeezed the trigger and didn't let go. His ears rang so hard there was nothing else but the din. Out of the corner of his eye, he saw Michelle join him. Her weapon thundered next to his.

The bush disintegrated in a hail of shredded leaves. Dark armor glinted inside. It sparked and jumped in the hail of depleted uranium. Then it stopped firing. A puff of smoke curled from it, like the last exhalation of a dying man.

"Yeah!" Matt yelled, but he couldn't even hear his own voice.

Michelle said something. Her words were softer than a whisper, unintelligible. She tapped on the side of his gun, where the LCD readout showed 023.

He had only twenty-three rounds left. Twenty-three rounds, and a hundred yards to go.

He nodded. "Guess we'll have to make a run for it!" Without waiting for Michelle, Matt charged out into the swamp once again.

And through the splash of water, he saw something incredible: Kyle running full-bore ahead of him. He'd taken the opening that Matt and Michelle had created. Matt bit his lip, thinking how unfair it was.

As if to rub it in, Michelle flashed past Matt as if he were standing still. Her speed left him dazed. She closed the gap with Kyle. Matt struggled to get his burning legs to move faster.

Every moment, he expected a bullet to find his back, but the sentries were silent. He came close enough to see a doctor standing cross-armed in front of the tent.

Michelle sprinted past Kyle, who had started to limp as if with a strained muscle. His face contorted in pain, but he kept running ahead of Matt.

Matt reached the gravel walkway leading from the edge of the swamp to the tents, as Michelle ran past the doctor. The doctor called out in a loud, clear voice: "First!"

Matt slowed to a fast walk. *First?* She was first? It seemed like an eternity he'd been in the swamp. How could they not be last?

Kyle ran into the tent.

"Second," the doctor said.

Matt sped up and ran through the flaps, finishing strong.

"Third," he heard, behind him.

3

TESTS

The medical tents were huge, obsessively clean, and lit with the kind of actinic, perfectly white medical lamps that made everyone look sickly and pale. White-suited doctors stood at the sides of the tent, poking disinterestedly at slates or watching a tremendous wall screen playing Union Broadcasting Corporation news.

The main story was about an abortive Corsair attack on Portal, the newest Union world. Diagrams showed the Union Displacement Drive warship UUS *Ulysses* in orbit around the planet, as well as a dozen Rhinos and a smattering of Cheetahs. Talking heads yammered unintelligibly, but the upshot seemed to be that nobody had been hurt. There were no pictures of smoking cities, and no Mecha had been deployed. Below the main news streamed additional headlines: GEOTECH INDUSTRIES TERRAFORMING PRACTICES IN REVIEW BY UNION GOVERNMENT; ERIDANI FARMING YIELDS FALL—IMPORTS NECESSARY FOR CURRENT YEAR; ANNO SERVICES STOCK SPIKES ON NEWS OF MERGER.

"Congratulations!" said one of the doctors, stepping forward to grin at Matt, Kyle, and Michelle. He was a slight, dark-haired man in his early forties who would have been pale-skinned even if he weren't under the medical lamps. His name badge read: E. PECHTER, M.D.

Pechter continued before any of the three could talk. "If there were medals, you'd be wearing them." He shook his head sadly and gestured at a row of gurneys. "Unfortunately, all we have are these beds. Why don't you take a seat and let us have a look?"

"I'm not injured," Michelle told him.

Pechter nodded. "Well, don't you earn the gold star? You still need a physical. Up on the bed."

Michelle frowned and sat on the closest gurney. Kyle limped to the one next to hers.

Matt didn't want to move. After the surreal fight through the swamp, he felt floaty and strange, as if his brain had been disconnected from his body. They'd shot at him. Like some expendable army grunt. Why was he here? Was this really the highest honor in the Union, or was it all just a con job?

Matt gritted his teeth. He couldn't just up and leave. There was too much at stake.

"Hello?" Pechter waved a hand in front of Matt's face. "Earth to Number Three. Come in, Number Three."

"I . . . I'm—" Matt looked around. Everyone was watching him. The doctors. Kyle. Michelle.

"Sit," Pechter said.

Matt sat on the gurney next to Kyle's, not daring to look at him. Kyle must be smirking.

The doctor outside the tent flap peeked in at them. "Rush's starting," he said.

"Okay, let's get these sorted," Pechter said, motioning for the other doctors. They put away their slates and sauntered over, seemingly unconcerned.

Pechter took one look at Kyle's swollen ankle and frowned. "Bad sprain. Pretty good, coming in second with this beauty." He waved another doctor over. "Let's give him Accelerated Recovery."

Pechter looked at the divot on the chest of Matt's flak jacket. "Ooh, Purple Heart candidate," he said, bending down to examine Matt's wrecked jacket. "Well, not so fast."

"What do you mean?"

In answer, the doctor grabbed a slim metallic wand from

a nearby tray and used it to pry something out of the flak jacket. But instead of the shiny metal bullet Matt expected, it was a red, splattered glob of plastic.

Pechter waved the wand at Matt.

"Coward rounds. Like a paintball, but with a short-lifespan neural inhibitor that makes you feel, well, like you've been shot. But since it didn't make it through the jacket, we don't have to neutralize it."

Matt just stared openmouthed.

"You don't think we'd go and gun down the best and brightest of the Union, do you?"

Matt's guts seethed with amazement and anger. "You— you tricked us? Into thinking we could be shot?"

Pechter raised an eyebrow. "You'd prefer the real thing?"

Matt shook his head. *Of course not!* But . . . it was a helluva test.

They want to see who's really committed, Matt realized. Anyone with the right academics and athletics could fill out the prequalification forms for training camp. Anyone who passed that stage could accept the up-to-decade-long auditing and surveillance that might get you invited to training camp at any point during that ten years. But not just anyone could pick up a gun and charge in without hesitation. That's the test he'd just passed.

Pechter turned to examine Michelle.

"I don't need treatment," Michelle said.

"You sure?" Pechter said. "Do you even know if you're hurt? You juiced up, Earth girl? You're awfully fast."

Michelle's expression went rigid, but her eyes blazed hard and angry. "I don't need juice to beat these candidates, Doctor."

Pechter laughed and nodded at another doc. "Drug scan." He turned back to Michelle's glare. "Nothing personal. Just part of the job."

The doctor swooped in and took blood, then injected it into his slate. He tapped a foot as he waited for the results.

"Fourth!" called a voice from outside.

Matt turned to see another cadet run in. It was the older woman who'd protested before. She looked unharmed, but her breath came in loud whoops, and her eyes were wide and darting.

Pechter turned to her. "I'm sorry. No gold star for you. But we have a place to recline." He pointed at a gurney.

"Five! Six!" came from outside the tent.

The two kids dressed in Hyva rags came through the door. Neither was injured, though both were covered in mud to their knees. They sauntered in casually, as if the whole exercise had been an evening stroll.

"You see, Jahl?" one of them said. "I told you. Let the ones at the forefront take out the automated sentries. Note where they are, then walk right through."

"You're too clever for your own good, Peal," the other told him.

"Isn't that what they always say?"

Pechter stopped the duo. "Sit," he said, pointing at the gurneys.

"Okay," they said together.

"Seven, eight, nine," came the voice again. "Another dozen coming!"

Pechter nodded. "Rush hour." He turned back to the doctor who was running Michelle's drug scan. "Well?"

"She's clean," he said.

"Good," Pechter said. "You win."

"I win what?" Michelle asked.

Pechter grinned. "You'll be the first through the Mind Raze."

Pechter led Michelle and Matt through the curtains. Beyond them was a large area filled with a wide variety of diagnostic and treatment machines. Matt recognized the sleek, stainless-steel shapes of imagers and the hulking outline of robotic-surgery suites.

Kyle lay inside a bullet-shaped transparent tube Matt didn't recognize. Haze filled its interior, thickest around

Kyle's swollen ankle. He saw Matt and Michelle and smiled dreamily, his eyes glazed and faraway.

"He's out of it," Pechter said. "Accelerated Recovery is powerful stuff."

"I've never heard of it," Matt said.

"No reason you should have," Pechter said. "Though there's a rumor running around that Acc Rec is the reason the Eridani Tigers are doing so well this season." Pechter leaned in to add, "Eridani's Senator Kline has a lot of pull, you know."

Pechter led them back through another set of curtains to a small room where a single machine sat. This one didn't look like any of the others. It was formed of a single, flowing piece of polished dark metal, with complex curves like frozen flame. A reclining seat led up to a translucent cowl, just large enough to accept someone's head.

"We're supposed to call it the Neural Interface Assessment, but that's pretty boring compared to Mind Raze, don't you— Ah, er, shit. One sec. Be right back." Pechter ducked back through the curtains, like maybe he'd forgotten something.

Matt looked at Michelle. "Look, I think—"

"Stop it right there," Michelle cut him off. "Get this straight: we're not a team now."

"I never thought—"

"I'm not here to help you." She flashed bright, angry blue eyes. "I'm only here to become Mecha Corps—that's it. And I'm certainly not here to meet any guys."

And I'm not here to meet girls, Matt thought, but he kept his mouth shut. Her bravery, focus, and anger made Michelle that much more interesting, and he didn't want to piss off the beautiful Earth girl any more than he had already.

Michelle opened her mouth to say something else, but Pechter ducked back through the curtains again. Now he held a slate.

"Okay, Army girl, up and at 'em." Pechter nodded at the machine.

Michelle didn't hesitate. She climbed onto the seat and lay back. Pechter nodded and punched a control on his slate. The cowl dropped over her head.

"Ready?" Pechter said.

Michelle nodded.

"This is gonna feel weird. But at least it's quick." Pechter pressed a button on his slate. Michelle's face went blank. Not sleep-blank, but blank like death. Matt shivered as memories swam close behind his eyes.

Pechter's slate glowed green. He grinned and pressed a button. Michelle's lips twitched and her eyes flitted from side to side. She tried to sit up and hit her head on the cowl.

"Easy," Pechter said.

Michelle slid down in the seat and jumped off the machine before the cowl had finished retracting. She took a couple of steps away from it and hugged herself, as if chilled. Her gaze traveled from Pechter to the machine and back again.

"That was . . . disgusting," Michelle said.

Pechter nodded. "That's what everyone says! The good news is, you passed." He held up the emerald-glowing slate.

Michelle blew out a big breath and nodded.

Pechter turned to Matt. "You're next, rich boy."

Matt opened his mouth to correct Pechter, then stopped himself. Why did he care? Let everyone make their assumptions based on the way he dressed. Let them be wrong.

Matt got up in the seat. The thin padding covered hard metal, but it wasn't cold. In fact, it was almost uncomfortably warm.

"What kind of test is this?" Matt asked.

"I told you. Mind Raze. Or Neural Interface Assessment, if you want to be formal and academic-like."

"But what does it do?" Out of the corner of his eye, Matt saw Michelle watching intently.

Pechter sighed, as if Matt's question was the greatest burden in the universe. "It determines whether or not you can use the advanced brain-machine interfaces that are part of your training."

"So Mecha are run by mind control?"

"Ye— Oh, hell." Pechter looked away. "Lie back. I have to start the test."

"What if I don't want to?"

Pechter crossed his arms. "Like everyone says, you can waltz out at any time. It's a helluva honor just to be invited to training camp. No real shame in washing out. With all the data they have on you, I'm sure you'll still get lots of job offers from your daddy's rich friends."

"Then this test is required."

Pechter set his jaw. "That's right. And we're on a clock. Should I tell all the other cadet candidates who's holding up the line?"

Matt lay back. The translucent cowl descended over his head, blocking his vision. For a moment, the entire world was cool, blue-white light.

Then it went away and Matt saw nothing. He tried to move his head, but he couldn't see or feel his body anymore. His senses registered zero input, other than the sensation of space, as if he were floating in an immense, pitch-black room.

In the darkness, something moved. Something that scratched at the edge of his vision, ultraviolet and infrared. Matt wanted to run, but his body didn't respond. He was numb. He couldn't move anything, not even a finger.

The thing in the dark moved closer. Matt felt its presence, like static electricity in the desert, like a musty odor in an old room.

It touched him, and brilliant, acid pain cascaded through Matt. He tried to thrash against it. Every time he tried to move, the pain reached a new crescendo.

Relax, a distant voice whispered.

Matt thrashed again. Pain exploded. It was worse than the chemical nerve stimulation that refugee-ship police used to extract confessions. It was worse than anything he could imagine.

There is no pain in acceptance, the distant voice said.

Matt relaxed. Immediately, the pain stopped. The thing wrapped its static-musty embrace over him. Matt had to force himself not to struggle. It was like being smothered.

It pressed inward. Into him. Into his brain. Matt screamed a silent scream. Talons raked through his mind, scrambling his thoughts, rooting through Matt's cortex. Every neuron rifled, sorted, and cataloged.

And he heard that distant voice again. Now it bellowed throughout his body from his head to his toes. And it was overlaid with feelings: intense interest; ravenous hunger.

What are you? it asked. *What made you?*

Matt's thoughts turned backward. Toward his childhood. Toward his father.

Suddenly he was six years old again.

Matt ran ahead of his dad, down the long, dusty hallway deep below the surface of the planet Prospect. He was just back from another one of his Displacement trips from Eridani, and Matt was happy to see him.

The lab crew had strung bright phosphorus utility lights along the ceiling, but much of the hall was still draped in shadows. Rooms off to either side gaped like yawning mouths.

Matt didn't like the dark. Once, he'd found a skeleton in the shadows, slumped over the rusted remains of a mining laser. In the shaking light from his flash, it almost seemed to move. It had come back in his dreams, chasing him down endless halls that bent to no refuge.

"One hundred forty-one," Matt's dad called behind him. Matt grinned. The picture game. Dad was seeing if he could remember the image from its index number.

"A pink flower." The picture was vivid and defined in Matt's mind. Twenty-one petals, shot through with thin veins of white. A bright yellow center. An insect hovering nearby. "With a bee."

"Seven hundred ninety."

"An asteroid. Stars in the background." Matt tried to match them to constellations he knew, but couldn't. "Far away from Earth."

"Four."

"You, in a lab coat."

"Five thousand, one hundred ninety-three."

Matt frowned. That was a picture of a world a lot like Prospect, except the sand ran up to bright green water under a clear blue sky. "A world. With water."

"A beach on Eridani," his dad said. "Someday I'll take you to a planet with beaches."

Matt looked back at his dad. He was looking at the photo that Matt had just described on his slate. His face had that sad, faraway look he got whenever he thought about Mom.

Dad looked up and saw Matt. He thumbed off the slate and put it in the oversized pocket of his white lab coat.

"No more?" Matt asked.

His dad shook his head. "No more. I don't need to test you further. You remember everything you see."

"You don't?"

"No. Nobody does. Not like you."

Matt walked in silence for a while. His dad had told him this before, but it didn't seem possible.

Dad caught up with Matt and put a hand on his shoulder. "You haven't told anyone, have you?"

"No."

"It's very important you don't tell anyone. Your Perfect Record is a small gift. I wish I could do more. But it was difficult enough separating out that trait from the ..." He trailed off, then squeezed Matt's shoulder. "Just don't tell anyone, okay?"

"Like I can't tell everyone you're a secret agent for the Union."

Dad laughed. "I'm not a secret agent. The Union just trusts me to do some very important research for them."

"A secret agent."

Dad looked doubtful. "In a lab coat?"

"Secret agent scientist!"

Dad laughed. They'd reached his lab, a small room with walls covered in copper mesh. On stainless-steel tables were pieces of twisted wreckage. They were tagged with holo-floats calling out atomic maps and carbon dates, as well as compositional analysis and genetic sequences. Matt didn't know what they were at the time, but later on, reviewing his memories, he'd understood more and more.

His dad turned on the wall screen and leaned close to it. Cross-sectional views of Prospect's tunnel maze rotated on the screen, bright with false colors.

"Be careful what you bury," Dad said. "You never know what may bloom." He wore that faraway look again.

He was probably thinking about Mom, Matt knew. He'd never known his mother. She'd died in childbirth. Matt's Perfect Record didn't reach back to the womb.

Footfalls echoed from the hallway. A man brought himself up short at the doorway and darted wide eyes from Matt to his dad. It was Yve Perraux, the head of security for Union-Prospect Research.

"We have to evacuate!" Yve gasped.

Dad frowned. "I haven't heard the—" A warning Klaxon blared through the concrete hallways, cutting him short.

"Dad?" Matt said.

"Not now," Dad said. To Yve, he asked, "Corsairs?"

"Maybe." Yves eyes skittered to Matt. "Maybe worse."

"No," Dad said, toggling the wall screen to the security view. A number of multicolored dots descended toward the curved edge of a tan planet. They all converged on a single target: a green block labeled UNION-PROSPECT RESEARCH FACILITY I.

Their facility. Matt's guts clenched. He knew what Corsairs were from videos. They were the bad guys. They killed people. And they were coming here. What would they do then?

"Dad—," Matt began.

"Matt, sorry, but *not now*." Dad fumbled frantically with the mass-storage-system interface on one of the desktops. He slotted his slate down into it. Its screen showed it filling with data.

Dad pulled the slate out as soon as it was full, and typed in commands. Matt didn't know what they were at the time. Later, he saw they were instructions to wipe and reformat their entire data system.

"I'm scared," Matt said.

"Just a second, just a second. Gotta do this," Dad muttered. "Just a second; then we go. I promise. You'll see those beaches—"

The wall screen flashed a red warning dialogue. Even at six, Matt knew what it was. It was what happened when you wanted to make the data system do something that it couldn't.

Dad pounded a fist on the table, making artifacts jump. "No, no, no, no!" he chanted. He pounded out new instructions on the keyboard. More red dialogues appeared.

"They're already in the system!" his dad cried, turning to Matt with an expression of abject horror.

Matt's stomach rolled over and he felt his bladder loosen. He'd never seen his dad look like that.

Dad scooped up the slate, grabbed Matt's hand, and pulled him out the door. Matt's feet tangled in the hall. Dad swept him up and carried him, like he used to when Matt was a baby.

Dad came up short at the lift. It was still crawling its way down the thousand-feet-deep shaft. It had never seemed so slow. Dad pounded on the control panel.

"We'll make it," he said. "We'll make it." It was as if he were trying to convince himself.

Corsairs. A thousand images from the news came to beat at Matt: scruffily dressed men in armored spaceships descending on a new colony town, pelting the rough concrete buildings with explosives. A shaft on a Displacement Drive ship, filled with bodies. Flickering red lights at the edge of the Union, like torches outside a castle.

What if the Corsairs were already on the surface, waiting for them? Matt whimpered and squeezed his dad's hand tighter.

"We'll make it," Dad said.

Finally, the lift came. Dad slammed the door shut and pressed the button marked SURFACE a dozen times. With a groan, the lift began grinding upward.

"We will make it," Dad repeated, his voice cracking.

Matt remembered the security display and the dots. He remembered how fast they had moved. He counted out the seconds. The dots should have already reached them.

An eternity later, the elevator socked into its cage in the surface hangar. The outer doors of the building were open, revealing a dry, sandy landscape under a beige sky. Wind howled outside, and dust swirled into the hangar, driven by Prospect's seemingly endless wind. One of their three six-man Hedgehog transports rose into the sky outside.

The other Hedgehog sat on the steel-grate floor only fifty feet away, it's cargo door open. A Powerloader stood like a sentry outside the Hedgehog's cargo bay, clearly abandoned in the rush to leave. Its ready light still glowed.

Through his fear, Matt felt a strong pang of desire. Rex Cooper, the ops steward, had let him drive it once. Strapped in its battered steel-tube frame, he felt like a giant. Rex had to chase him around the hangar before Matt gave up the cockpit.

"See!" Dad said. "Close up the 'Hog, and out we go. We'll make it!"

The screaming rush of missiles echoed through the hangar. A brilliant flash came from outside, followed quickly by a rolling crump of thunder. The rising Hedgehog was gone. In its place, a dark transport hung in the air. Figures dropped from it.

Dad punched the EXTERIOR DOOR button. The steel doors began grinding closed, laboring through layers of sand and grime.

"Come on!" He dragged Matt toward the ship.

They didn't get far. Blue-white light flashed in front of them, and the doors buckled inward. Matt's eardrums compressed painfully. Then he was flying backward, sliding along the expanded steel grate as pieces of the door flew overhead.

Matt looked up. His dad lay ahead of him on the ground, his leg bent back at a crazy angle. Red blood stained his khaki pants. Dad tried to push himself up off the ground and hollered in pain. His leg rolled limply. Even back then, Matt knew it was broken.

Something inside Matt snapped. *Dad is hurt!* His dad! Dads didn't die, except in videos he wasn't supposed to watch. Matt wailed. It was a shrill sound, echoing off the metal walls.

Through the door, black figures came. One, two, three, a dozen. They wore scarred, bulky black space suits and carried short, deadly looking weapons with gaping barrels and well-worn magazines. Their visors were mirrored, concealing the troops' faces. They reflected only the steel girders of the hangar like a fun-house mirror.

On the suit helmets, Matt recognized the red, thousand-daggers insignia of the Corsair Confederacy. Back at the base circling Alpha Centauri A, he'd played Union vs. Corsairs with the kids. He never wanted to play as a Corsair. Never. He'd only play as Union. He wanted to bring people together. He wanted to save them. Why would anyone play as a Corsair? Hot tears streamed down his cheeks.

Matt's dad groaned and tried to stand again. It was a terrible sound. Matt shivered, his mouth dry. Even without his Perfect Record, he knew he'd never forget this day.

"We'll make it!" his dad said, dragging himself along the floor toward Matt. His limp leg trailed blood.

The approaching Corsairs looked at one another, as if in amusement. They didn't hurry. They just sauntered. As if nothing could stop them.

A red-hot dagger of anger shot through Matt. He didn't think. He just moved. He ran for the Powerloader.

He expected the Corsairs to yell or try to intercept him, but he didn't turn around to check on them. He had to get in the Powerloader. Fast.

He scrambled up the steel tube and threw himself in the seat, punching the control panel for the smallest operator. The hand grips and foot pedals whirred closer. He strained to reach them. Slipped in a foot pedal. Caught a hand grip.

The Powerloader jerked to life. Matt lost his balance and fell against the Hedgehog. The ship slid sideways on the steel grate with an incredible screech. Matt levered himself upright and finally dared to look.

The Corsairs had stopped to watch. One had stepped forward to the front and opened his helmet. He wore a thin, sarcastic grin. Flanking him were two Corsairs. Both pointed their weapons at Matt. Bright orange fusion flares glowed deep in their barrels.

It was over. There was nothing he could do.

Matt didn't care. In four shambling steps, he placed himself between the Corsairs and his father. He held out his big, steel-tube arms, blocking their way.

The lead Corsair laughed. "Should I shoot through you, child?"

"No!" Dad screamed. "Don't hurt him!"

The Corsair leaned down to look at Matt's dad through the frame of the Powerloader. "Then let's talk."

Silence for a moment. The wind howled louder outside, bringing the rattle and ping of sand against the steel walls.

"What do you want?" Dad's voice was a little more than a whisper.

The Corsair reached out a hand. "Your slate."

Dad hugged the slate closer to his chest. "Never."

"We already have most of your data. Give me the slate, and you and your son may go free, and you can continue your archaeological adventures with the Union."

"No."

"I don't like that word, 'no.' Wouldn't you like to run with your son on the beaches of Eridani?"

Matt jerked back, surprised. He heard his dad gasp. How did the Corsair know about that?

And suddenly, Matt saw exactly what would happen. His father was dead, no matter if he gave them the slate or not. It was how Corsairs worked. They weren't just boogeymen conjured up to scare kids like him. They were absolutely, totally real. They took everything. Even lives. Especially lives.

Matt screamed and charged at the Corsairs. Pistons fumed and pumped. His arms reached out to crush them.

But the Corsairs just watched him. Matt's Powerloader was powerful, but it wasn't fast. He bumbled toward the enemy, the two Corsairs with fusion rifles taking their time as they rose to track him.

"Don't hurt him!" Dad screamed. He took the slate and slung it low over the hangar deck.

It skidded to a halt a meter in front of the lead Corsair. He leaned down and scooped it up. "Thank you."

The Corsair nodded at the two with fusion rifles. "Kill the archaeologist."

Weapons swung toward Matt's dad. Matt dug in his heels and tried to put himself back in the line of fire. But the Powerloader's clumsy legs just wouldn't move fast enough.

The Corsairs fired. Bright orange fire exploded from their weapons, and his father disappeared in a blast of light.

Matt felt nothing. He was nothing. He was going to die like his dad. He knew that. In pure rage, he launched himself at the Corsair leader.

He expected to explode in a burst of orange fire. But he was just fast enough. He barreled into the Corsair leader with the three-ton Powerloader and drove him up against the hangar wall. Tears streamed down his face and spattered on the controls.

They were suddenly face-to-face. The Corsair was young, not much more than a teenager. He gave Matt a bemused grin and looked up at him with oddly calm eyes.

Odd eyes. One eye was bright violet. One eye was an intense golden color.

Matt gaped. That was impossible. Violet and gold eyes. HuMax eyes. But the HuMax were dead. Everyone knew that. The Union had been formed just to wipe them out, and that was more than a hundred years ago.

Matt remembered watching an entertainment video, late at night when he wasn't supposed to. It was set on Eridani after the HuMax invasion. Violet-and-gold-eyed people swarmed over the verdant colony, while nuclear mushrooms blossomed. His dad had come in and turned off the video, saying, "You don't need to watch stuff like that."

Something exploded on Matt's chest.

He flew out of the Powerloader cockpit and fell on the expanded-steel hangar deck, skidding to within ten meters of the Corsair troops. Smoke curled off his jumpsuit, and the acrid smell of burnt hair filled his nose. Fusion weapons swiveled to target him.

The Corsair leader pushed the dead Powerloader off himself with superhuman strength. *Like a HuMax,* Matt's terrified brain told him. *But he can't be.*

The front energy cell on the Powerloader gaped open, black and smoking from the explosion. But the Corsair leader's weapon was also twisted and broken.

He dropped it on the floor and came to examine Matt. His violet-and-gold eyes were heavy and unmoving, like lead. He looked at Matt for a long time.

Matt wanted to scream at him, *You killed my father. I'll kill you. I'll rip you apart. I hate you.*

But all he could do was stand there and tremble, tears streaming down his face as little sobs escaped from his lips.

Finally the Corsair leader smiled again. The chill, alien expression never touched his eyes. Those strange orbs didn't move a nanometer.

"Sometimes, courage must have its reward," he said.

He walked past Matt and joined his fellows. They sauntered out through the shattered hangar doors. Shortly, there was the scream of ramjets. A craft lifted into the sky.

Matt sat alone in the broken hangar. Slow realization crept over him, like a chill fog.

His dad would never return. A Corsair had killed him. *A HuMax Corsair.*

Chill turned to heat, and heat turned to rage. Matt stood up. He ran out into the sand. He wanted to leap up into the sky and chase the murderer down, smashing and burning everything in his way. But there was nothing he could do. He looked up at the blank yellow sky and screamed, without a sound escaping his lips.

"I'll find you!" Matt yelled.

Bright medical lamps glared down on him. He lay on his back on a warm, hard surface. White-suited doctors and gray-uniformed Mecha Auxiliaries leaned over him. Some of them winced or recoiled as if in shock. Matt realized he'd yelled out loud.

He was back at Mecha Training Camp.

On the Mind Raze machine.

Fresh, hot memory beat at his mind. Talons raking through his brain. That memory, that terrible memory, in full 3-D glory, brought back sharper and stronger than in even his Perfect Record. He'd lived the death of his father all over again.

That HuMax—that impossible HuMax. How they'd laughed on the *Rock* when he told them that. HuMax were extinct, they said. You're just a little kid, they said. You're too young to remember clearly, they said. Eventually, he'd stopped talking about it. Eventually, he'd started doubting even his own Perfect Record.

But he never lost the need for revenge. He would find that Corsair, no matter what it took, and courage would have another reward. One that might finally heal his terrible pain.

Matt scrambled off the machine, nearly falling. He took

several steps away from it. He drew in ragged breaths, almost panting.

"Are you . . . all right?" Pechter asked.

Matt realized the room was full of cadets too. Kyle stood with his arms crossed at the edge of the curtains. Michelle leaned against a tent pole on the opposite side of the room, watching him. Sergey sat on a bench, looking at Matt with bored eyes. The Hyva twins leaned over the shoulders of the Auxiliaries for a closer look.

"What happened?" Matt asked.

"Damn machine locked up. You've been out half an hour." Pechter's wide eyes alternated between the slate and Matt. "How do you feel?"

I feel like I just lost everything that ever mattered to me. Again.

"I . . . I'm okay."

Pechter shook his head. "Well, if that's true, you're holding up the line, rich kid. If it wasn't for you, we'd all be at chow."

"Is he out of interface state?" a voice said from Pechter's slate.

Pechter jumped and fumbled with the pad, then addressed it. "Yes, sir."

"What is his final test result?" said the voice.

"Passed. Though I have no idea how." Pechter gripped the glowing green slate tightly.

"Your ideas are not important," the voice said.

"What, uh . . . what should we do with him, sir?"

"Proceed as with any other passing candidate."

"Yes. Understood."

Pechter's slate displayed the END CONNECTION icon. He stood there, staring at it for a time.

"Who was that?" Matt asked.

Pechter swallowed. "That was the general manager, Dr. Salvatore Roth."

Matt started. Dr. Roth was the person who'd perfected biomechanical technology, the father of all modern Mecha.

Everybody knew that, but little more. His company, Advanced Mechaforms, Inc., wrapped itself deep in Union state secrecy. He didn't give interviews. He didn't do press tours explaining his technology. Armchair speculators loved to guess at Dr. Roth's secrets, when they'd never seen a Mecha at all.

"Why would Dr. Roth—," Matt began.

Pechter held up a hand. "Doesn't matter. The machine had a little problem. You passed. All is well. Gold stars for everyone. If we had gold stars." He turned to wave at Kyle. "You're next. Come on up!"

Matt wasn't ready to be dismissed. He got in front of Pechter. "How many times has it malfunctioned like that?"

Pechter looked away. "Not too often."

"Like, how many? An estimate?"

"Like, never," Pechter said, through clenched teeth.

Matt shivered. *Never.* What did that mean? Was it because of his father's gift? His Perfect Record? Did other cadets experience the same flashbacks he did, or was that something special? Was that why Michelle looked so disturbed?

Pechter pushed Matt aside. "Now, if you'll get out of the way, I can get on with testing."

Matt nodded and stepped away. Kyle took a seat on the machine and lay back. The helmet went down. Pechter's slate glowed green. Then, only moments later, Kyle stood up and looked at the machine uneasily, like Michelle.

Uneasy. Not screaming in vivid memory. Just like Michelle. What had happened to him?

They cycled through the cadets quickly. Nobody took more than a few seconds to complete the test. Everyone showed some degree of unease or revulsion when coming off the machine.

Until the sixth cadet. A thin woman in her early twenties, her hair still caked with swamp mud. She lay back underneath the hood. It came down over her, and her expression didn't change. When she stood up from the machine, she didn't recoil from it.

Pechter's slate flashed bright red.

"I'm sorry," Pechter told her. He motioned for the Mecha Auxiliaries to step forward.

"Sorry?" she asked, looking at the Auxiliaries who flanked her.

"I'm afraid you're gonna need another career," Pechter said. "If you don't make it through Mind Raze, you don't make it to training camp."

"What?" she said. The Auxiliaries clamped down on her arms. She struggled, but they held her.

"I'm sorry," Pechter said as they led her out of the tent. "I know it's hard to take. But it's an honor just to be here. I'm sure you'll still get plenty of job offers."

After Mind Raze, they were fourteen.

Matt's mind churned the simple arithmetic. Eighteen cadets lost the first day. Eleven washed out in the live-fire exercise. Seven rejected by the Mind Raze machine.

Arithmetic was better than letting his mind wander. He'd spent every moment of his life trying not to think about that day back on Prospect. He'd spent countless hours trying to trick his Perfect Record. Anything to erase that one memory. Anything to forget.

But the Mind Raze machine had brought it back, more vibrant than ever. Now all he could think of was that day, his father, and the HuMax Corsair. Matt clenched his fists.

That's why I'm here. To find and kill that man.

Dinner was Union Army Insta-Paks on mess-hall tables in the medical tent, under the watchful eye of the Auxiliaries. Michelle took hers and walked all the way over to the edge of the tent, where she crouched and ate.

Matt wanted to pick up his Insta-Pak and go over to her. But Michelle clearly wanted to be alone. And she wasn't why he was here.

Kyle grabbed the Insta-Pak next to Matt and headed toward Michelle. A flush of hatred nearly pushed Matt up from his seat, but he caught himself and eased back. That stuff didn't matter. At least, it wasn't supposed to.

Kyle crouched next to Michelle. She looked up, frowning. Kyle smiled and said something that Matt couldn't hear over the murmur of the other cadets. She shook her head, stood up, and walked away. Kyle stood there for a while, shaking his head and whistling. Then he came back and sat across from Matt.

"That's hot," he said, nodding at Michelle. She was now looking pointedly away from them.

Matt said nothing.

"Make no mistake," Kyle said. "That one's mine."

"Uh-huh," Matt said, pushing down his anger.

Kyle watched Michelle for a while longer, then turned to Matt. "So, what family are you from? Tortelli? Bryce?"

"Family?"

"You're an Aurora kid. I saw the blazer. Who's your family? We're the Peterovs of Eridani."

"Peterov, as in Senator Peterov?"

"That's Dad. Also have Secretary of Education, Undersecretary of Unity, a couple other UniGov staff members. You know how it goes—it's hard to keep track."

Matt closed his eyes. "I don't have a family."

"Are you part of the Fragmenting Phillips?"

"Nope. I'm a refugee. No family," Matt continued as Kyle tried hard to hide his shock. "I got into Aurora U on merit, not on connections. Just like I'll get through training camp."

Matt turned his back on Kyle and went to grab his own space by the edge of the tent. Kyle just sat at his table and kept smirking.

After dinner, the Auxiliaries led them to individual tents outside to bunk down. The overcast sky was deep charcoal black, devoid of stars. Far off was the sound of surf. Over everything was the stink of the swamp.

Alone in his tent, looking up into the dark, Matt's Perfect Record brought him back to that day on Prospect once again. He fought back his memories until he felt on the brink of sleep.

It was like Soto said. They had all fought so hard to get here. Why would they expect it to get any easier?

4

ASSESSMENT

The next morning, Matt woke to a piercing electronic squeal. He jumped off his cot, heart hammering.

Memory came slamming back in high-definition. He was at Mecha Training Camp. In a tent. Runnels of condensation ran down from its peaked roof. The air was chill and clammy.

On the bench opposite his cot, Matt's neatly folded clothes were gone. In their place was a light gray jumpsuit, with a small note reading *Wear these*.

Matt did. The jumpsuit fit as if it had been tailored to him. It bore only two decorations: the silhouetted Mecha logo of United MechaForms above the thirty-star cluster of the Universal Union.

Outside, the fog reduced everything to shades of gray and white. Other cadets had already emerged. Matt couldn't help looking for Michelle. Nor could he help appreciating how she filled out the Mecha Cadet jumpsuit.

"Hubba hubba," said a voice beside him. Matt jumped and turned. It was the two kids who'd worn the Hyva rags yesterday. Dark-skinned, with thick black hair and bright eyes, they looked young enough to be in high school. They both held slates that glowed blue-white in the morning's heavy air.

"You brought slates?" Matt asked. "Through the swamp?"

"A man must have priorities," said one of them.

"Like our beautiful Private Michelle Kind," said the other, nodding at Matt.

"She isn't important."

"You suppress your hormones too much, Jahl."

"And you play too much in things that don't concern us, Peal."

Peal crossed his arms. "Superposition and entanglement are essential qualities of many solutions."

"Which can also lead to chain reactions—"

Matt cut him off. "Wait. Who are you two?"

The two chuckled and gave Matt a little half bow. "Peal and Jahl Khoury, the Wunderkind Pair of Hyva."

"Or the criminal hackers of Hyva," Jahl told his brother.

Peal shook his head. "You're too hard on us."

"Merely realistic about how we might be remembered. However, you do have a point. They never did press charges."

Matt sighed. The two kids bantered back and forth as if he weren't even there. Just like the data geeks back on the *Rock*, his old refugee ship. He searched for a reason to break away.

"We noticed your incident with the Mind Raze machine," Jahl said.

"And overhead your altercation with the poster boy from Eridani," Peal added.

"We find you interesting," they both said in unison.

Great, Matt thought. *Geeks as friends.* "Look, I've got to—"

Peal didn't let him finish. "You should see the data we have on Earth girl," he said, flashing his slate. Michelle's photo floated amid a stack of Union Army and EarthPop records.

"Lots of data flying around training camp," Jahl said.

"More than meets the eye," Peal agreed, grinning.

Matt only half heard them. He was looking at Peal's slate. One piece of data was highlighted: a historic breakdown of Mecha cadets by Union planet. Eridani had sent thousands of candidates over the years. Most other core worlds were in the hundreds. The frontier worlds were in the double digits. At the very bottom of the list was Earth, with a single digit: 1.

Matt looked up. "Michelle's the first Mecha cadet from Earth, ever?"

Peal laughed and clapped his brother on the back. "I told you he's quick."

Another electronic squeal made the cadets jump. Two Mecha Auxiliaries appeared out of the mist. "Follow us," they demanded.

Peal and Jahl tucked their slates into their jumpsuits, and Matt had to struggle to quench his disappointment. He wanted to see the rest of the dossier on Michelle.

"Where is breakfast?" Serghey bleated. "And where is Mecha?"

"Old man's got a point," someone said, as they fell in behind the Auxiliaries. It was the sandy-haired woman who'd complained yesterday. She had that deeply tanned, leatherlike skin that came from living in a desert.

"What?" Matt asked.

"He may be an idiot, but he's right. I dunno about you, but I came here for Mecha. Ain't seen one yet." She looked Matt up and down. "I'm Ash Moore. From Keller."

"Keller? Lithium-mining Keller?"

Ash laughed and stuck out a hand. "Yeah. Surprised a rich Aurora boy'd know it. Armpit of the Union."

Matt gripped her hand briefly. It was like shaking hands with a Powerloader. A Powerloader with a wedding band. "Matt Lowell. And I'm not rich."

She waved a hand. "Everything's relative."

"You're married?" Matt asked, pointing at her ring.

Ash nodded. A strange expression flickered across her face for a moment and then she looked sheepish. "Yeah. They sent the invite near the end of my monitoring period. Things'd changed, but what can you say? No?"

The Auxiliaries led them out of the camp to a large personnel carrier. Matt ended up sandwiched between the Khoury brothers, facing Michelle. She looked pointedly out the back of the vehicle, avoiding everyone's gaze. The sun shone on her clear brow, outlining her strong nose and high cheekbones.

Kyle dropped down onto the bench next to Michelle, in a slightly too-small spot. She frowned and scooted away from him.

Leaning close to Michelle, he said, "I forgot to congratulate you."

Michelle said nothing for a long time. Finally, not looking at him: "For what?"

"For being first last night."

You asshole, Matt thought. He could hear the calculation behind Kyle's comment. Win her respect with praise. Be persistent, but not too clingy. Like a formula out of a book.

Michelle sneered. "You're just not that fast."

Some snickers came from the other cadets, and Kyle reddened.

The truck got moving with a jerk. They bounced over the cracked and broken concrete. Matt waited for Kyle to say something else, to keep laying it on thick. But he said nothing. Michelle watched the khaki-painted steel floor of the truck, her hands in her lap.

They passed huge concrete fields and old white-washed, tilt-up buildings, some fallen in with age. A breeze lifted the morning fog, revealing hangars squatting in the distance and a silvery bay stretching to the north.

"Are you really a refugee?" Michelle asked, breaking the silence.

Matt started. "Where'd you hear that?"

Michelle nodded at Kyle, who reddened again.

"Yeah." Matt nodded.

"Where?"

"The *Rock. Yellow Submarine. Far Side of Paradise.* Not that you know any of those names, I guess."

"*Yellow Submarine* Displaced here a couple years ago," Michelle told him. "I thought of going out on it."

"On a refugee ship?" Matt said, thinking, *Ship out on* Yellow Submarine? *She has to be kidding.* They ran scoop-ships down into gas giants to fuel their antique fusion generators. The whole ship was going to go up in a fireball one day. Matt had spent seven months there as team leader, and had taken a bump down to Second Digger to get onto *Far Side of Paradise*—and that ship wasn't any prize either.

Michelle sighed. "Better than here. Better than being a fun-times girl on a commercial ship."

Is Earth really that bad? Matt wondered. But he had to stop. She wasn't part of the program. He just nodded and said nothing.

Michelle broke the silence. "I'm sorry," she said.

"For what?"

"Thinking you were just another stupid rich kid." Matt glanced at Kyle, who winced.

The rest of the ride went in silence. They stopped in front of a low building the size of a city block, set at the edge of a narrow bay. Its galvanized exterior was streaked with white oxidized zinc and orange iron rust. A faded NASA logo, cracked and crazed with age, emblazoned the doors. Beside it was a simple stainless-steel sign: ADVANCED MECHAFORMS FACILITY 11B. North of the bay, green-white flashes lit the sky, followed seconds later by ground-shaking booms.

"First exercise," Major Soto said, nodding to the north.

Today, he wore a full Mecha Corps uniform, multicolored medal bars and all. Matt's Perfect Record matched them to a military awards guide. Soto's record was like a history of all the great Mecha battles. He'd been at Pellham's Front. He'd fought in Forest. He'd even been there for the recent attack on Hyva.

"Exercise with Mecha?" Serghey blurted.

Major Soto shook his head. "You aren't ready."

"Ready for Mecha!" Serghey whined. "Ready for breakfast too!"

"Exit shuttle's that way." Soto nodded back in the direction they came. "It'll have food."

Serghey's mouth clicked shut.

"Everyone inside," Major Soto said, as the roll-up doors of the building clattered open.

The interior was pre-Expansion industrial, like something out of a historical vid. Concrete floors and cinderblock walls under grainy *Mercury*-vapor lights. At the center of the building, tubular stainless-steel racks held what looked like floppy, translucent gray silicone suits. The racks stood in the middle of a large white square painted on the floor. Beside them were a half-dozen Auxiliaries, including Sergeant Stoll.

"Get in the square, strip, and suit up," Major Soto said. "Auxiliaries will help you with the fitting of the interface suits."

"Strip?" Michelle asked.

Soto nodded. "The exit shuttle's private, I hear."

Serghey was already there, taking off his clothes. White flesh and black hair clashed under the *Mercury* vapor lamps. Serghey grinned and turned to give everyone a full frontal. "Come in—spa is fine!" he said. Men cringed and women looked away.

Matt chose a spot near the racks of silicone suits and peeled down. He tried not to look at Michelle. He even succeeded for a few moments.

But he had to look. Her body, free of the jumpsuit, was perfectly proportioned, with just enough muscle to define her curves. Under the *Mercury*-style lamps, her skin almost glowed. The only mark on her was a small QR code on one shoulder blade: a Union Army ID tattoo.

Matt forced himself to look away. Nearby, Kyle was half out of his jumpsuit, staring at Michelle's backside. He saw Matt looking and gave him an exaggerated wink.

Matt turned to the silicone suits. Up close, the milky gray, translucent rubber was shot through with millions of hair-thin metallic threads. On the inside of the suit, the wires terminated in a galaxy of little silver dots, and converged at a thick, shiny nexus at the neck.

Matt had seen things like this before at arcades back on Aurora. Kinetic-feedback jumpers. It was what the university students wore when they were blowing off steam in an immersive game. But these outfits were on orders of a magnitude more complex. The arcade suits had dozens of wires, whereas here these suits had millions.

Matt pulled on the suit. Inside, its rubbery surface yanked painfully on his arm hair, his chest hair, his—

"Many cadets choose to shave," said a voice beside him. Sergeant Stoll.

Matt didn't look at her as he shoved himself the rest of the way into the suit, wincing.

"It could be worse," Matt told her, nodding to where Serghey cursed and grumbled as he struggled to get his bushy bulk into the suit.

"Zip up," Sergeant Stoll said.

Matt fumbled with the front of the suit. There was nothing like a conventional zipper, but the two open flaps jumped together, as if magnetic. Matt stood in the floppy silicone bag, sweating.

"I'll adjust the suit." Sergeant Stoll produced a small handheld device with a small screen and ran it down Matt's chest. The silicone flowed together and tightened. She did the same for his arms, legs, and back until the interface suit was like a second skin. Sweat dripped off Matt's forehead.

"It's hotter than hell."

"One moment." Sergeant Stoll took her handheld device and held it against Matt's chest. He felt momentary heat and looked down. Emblazoned on his right breast were two lines of black text:

M. LOWELL, C.C.
H091-031

"What is 'C.C.'?" Matt asked.

"Cadet candidate."

"We're not full cadets?"

"Not until you—" Sergeant Stoll stopped herself. "I've turned on the active cooling. The suit should be more comfortable now."

It was. Matt no longer felt like he was in a sauna.

"Until we do what?" he persisted.

Sergeant Stoll shook her head and went to help fit Michelle's suit. Matt tried again not to look. Once more, he failed. When her suit was adjusted, it left very little to the imagination. The dull gray silicone outlined a fantasy-poster body. Every man in the room stared at her.

Why is someone so gorgeous here? Matt wondered. *Why would she think about shipping out of a refugee rock? And how much determination had it taken to be the first Mecha cadet invitee from Earth?*

When they were done suiting up, Major Soto ordered them to the side of the building, where a dozen screens were set against the wall. Black squares on the floor marked a position in front of each screen. A thin gray silicone cable dropped from rigging overhead of each position.

He had them each pick a square and plug the silicone cable into their suits. When they did, the screen lit with a false-color body outline, painted in shades of green, yellow, and red. Matt ended up between Peal and Jahl. Sergeant Stoll and the other Auxiliaries went through and made adjustments to each suit on their slates, maximizing the amount of green. Strange sensations crawled up and down Matt's body as she did so.

"So Mecha are controlled through direct neural interface," Peal said.

"And accompanying feedback. Some of the interface is clearly kinetic," Jahl added.

"Or inductive," Peal said.

The Auxiliaries refused to comment.

When they were done, Soto had them play simple games on the screen, imagining the controls in their hands. The first was a piloting game where they flew over fantastic landscapes while trying to hit a precise marker. The weird part was that Matt felt the air rushing past his body, as if he himself were flying.

The next game was an interpretive game, where coordinates were flashed on the screen, together with "enemies" that would capture the cadet candidates if they couldn't calculate time and distance fast enough. Then a game where they got to fire on the enemies, but they couldn't control the trajectory. That one gave a nice jolt when they got shot. They drilled through the morning on the simple games, stopping only for nutrition bars.

One cadet candidate never got the hang of it. Sweat streamed down his face, and his little flying vehicle jerked and skidded across the screen. The Auxiliaries kept trying to tune his suit, but it stayed mostly yellow and red. During one break, he was escorted away by two Auxiliaries.

Matt was getting bored by the repetitive games when finally Major Soto stopped the exercise and ordered them to the back of the building. There the concrete floor sloped down to meet a dark pool of water. Sinuous, metallic forms bobbed in the artificial lagoon.

Matt leaned forward to get a better look. The machines in the pool were about six meters long, tapered on either end, and segmented like a worm. Their dark, polished metallic surface reflected the blue *Mercury*-vapor lamps and the light streaming in from the broken windows with funhouse distortion.

Major Soto kicked off his shoes, rolled up his uniform trousers, and waded down to the closest of the machines. He patted its front, and it wriggled like a puppy.

An uneasy murmur went through the cadets. The thing looked almost alive.

"Anyone know what these are?" Soto asked.

"Eels," Kyle said. "They're used for security in The Round on Eridani."

"Correct," Major Soto said. "In this test config, each Eel

holds three crew: pilot, sensor, and gunner. The pilot runs
the Eel. The sensor provides strategic feedback based on a
situation model. The gunner, well, shoots at stuff."

Nervous chuckles from some of the cadets.

"You will have only ten rounds of ammunition, so use it
wisely. Also, these test Eels use conventional lithium-fusion
reactors. Range is limited. You begin with ten percent total
power, which gives a maximum run time of five to seven
minutes."

"Where is charger?" Sergey said.

Soto ignored him. "Your objective is to reach a marker
defended by Auxiliaries. The marker is clearly specified in
the sensor array."

Matt nodded. Now all the games made perfect sense.
They'd been training for this.

"Let's get started." Soto pointed at Matt. "Pilot." Serghey. "Sensor." Ash. "Gunner." He keyed in something on
the Eel. A top hatch unfolded, revealing three cramped
seats, where they sat hunched over like speed-bike riders.

"Want pick better team!" Serghey said.

"Want being in Mecha Corps?" Soto snapped. "Shut up
and get in."

Serghey splashed over to the sub.

"Sensor in the middle," Soto said. "Pilot in front; gunner
in rear."

Matt waded into the water and met Serghey and Ash at
the sub. He climbed over the edge and dropped into the
pilot's seat. Water sloshed through a mesh grille underneath his feet. In front of him, a small display showed:

% MOTIVE POWER: 10%
COMPASS: NNE
VELOCITY: 0 KNOTS

"No looking at bottom downstairs," Serghey said, as he
dropped in place.

"Nothing worth seeing," Ash told him, jumping in.

"A fine view!" Serghey said, slapping his butt.

Ash laughed. "Keep dreaming."

Soto tapped Matt on the back of the neck. "Plug in."

Matt found the interface cable and snapped it in place. Suddenly, it was like he was nude in the water. He felt its chill currents and the hard concrete underneath. Matt imagined pushing the controls forward and the Eel nudged ahead.

"Not yet," Soto told Matt. "Now watch your head."

The top of the Eel folded down, shuttering them in darkness. Soto waved Matt out of the way, so Matt brought the Eel to the back of the pool. There, a short tunnel led to the murky green waters of the bay.

Outside, Soto pointed out another group of cadets: Michelle, Jahl, and Kyle. Matt felt a stab of jealousy.

"Is like game," Serghey said. "Marker clearly shown."

"This feels so weird," Ash said.

Soto counted out two more teams, having Sergeant Stoll take the gunner position to complete the third. When he was done, his voice crackled over the Eel's comms:

"Cadet candidates, begin assignment."

Matt shot through the tunnel and into the bay, feeling the water rushing past him through the interface suit. It was an amazing sensation, like swimming in the nude.

The murky water of the bay hid the detritus of centuries of spaceflight. Directly in front of them was a tumble of corroded, weed-grown cylinders. Areas of white paint still bore faded numbers and fragments of red and white stripes.

"Get it moving!" Serghey bellowed. "Not tourists!"

Serghey was right. Matt pushed forward. His speed climbed quickly: 10, 15 knots. Schools of dun-colored fish parted in front of them, revealing more wreckage. This time, it was an old Imp-class Mecha. The pilot's cockpit was smashed as if by a giant hand, and shards of Plexiglas had gone opaque with green algae. One arm was missing entirely; the other twisted and broken, with stubs of control rods and hydraulic cables protruding. Matt swallowed. It was just like the model he'd left behind.

"Keep pedal on it!" Serghey bleated.

Another Eel shot past them. Matt pushed forward as hard as he could. They gained on the lead Eel. Who was inside it?

"Are there comms to the other ships, Serghey?"

"Markers only."

How were they supposed to coordinate with the other ships? Maybe that was the point. Maybe this was more like something they'd experience at the end of a battle when a Mecha wasn't operating at full potential. The only coordination they had would be through Serghey's map and visual reckoning.

"Where are the other ships, Serghey?" Matt asked.

"And I am telling you why?"

"Dammit, Serghey!"

"You concentrate on drive; I concentrate on next meal," Serghey said. "Only one kilometer to marker."

"We're supposed to concentrate on getting everyone to the marker!" Matt said. "How can I do that if you don't tell me where the ships are?"

"Tell him, you dolt!" Ash said.

"Cafeteria zero-point-eight klicks—" Serghey's voice was cut short by the sound of a meaty blow. "OW!"

"Didn't like that one, didya?" Ash said.

"Woman, when we out, there will reckon," Serghey whined.

"Tell him!"

"No."

The sound of blows came from the back of the ship. Serghey screamed like a girl. Matt grinned, remembering the ship's layout. The way the Eel was constructed, Ash could reach his backside, but Serghey couldn't turn to reach her.

"Okay—telling, telling!" Serghey said finally. "One ship ahead, fifty meters. Two ships behind, one hundred meters approx. One ship to left, approx ten meters."

Matt looked left, where another Eel paced them. It

moved through the water with sinuous grace, looking almost alive. The slit window revealed a familiar face: Michelle. She gave him a quick grin and a thumbs-up. Matt did the same. She veered away, the slit window reflecting bright light from the surface.

"Zero-point-four kilometers ahead; zero-point-one below," Serghey said.

Matt pushed the Eel down toward the rocky bottom of the bay, still chasing the lead ship and cutting a way to get ahead of Michelle. His screen showed 7 percent power left, 40 knots. Maybe this would work. Maybe this would be easy.

Something sizzled by him, trailing bubbles. In the interface suit, its passage warmed his skin.

"Incoming!" Ash yelled, just as the first bullet hit them.

Matt yelled. They all did. Through the interface suit, he felt the bullet like a red-hot poker in the side. He didn't need an advanced display to show him where the Eel was hit.

A tremendous crack echoed through the ship, and Matt's body jerked in pain. They'd been struck again, this time near his viewport. A crack chased across the clear pane, dribbling water. Matt pushed into a steep dive.

"Position!" Matt yelled at Serghey.

"Marker is two hundred meters ahead and below."

Matt nosed them down farther. The water leak became a stream as the pressure increased. Ahead of them, the lead ship took fire. It convulsed like a dying animal. The blue-green murk almost hid six people in armored wetsuits armed with MK-1s, stationed all around a dark opening in the bay's rocky bottom.

"Enemies on screens!" Serghey yelled. "Suggest Devil Woman shoot now!"

"Shooting!" Ash screamed. There were two hard, reverberating bangs and the Eel rocked. Bubbles traced their line of fire. Both shots narrowly missed their targets.

"Aim at enemy!" Serghey yelled.

"I am!"

The lead Eel retreated from the battle, and Auxiliary fire converged on Matt's ship. Searing pain exploded all along his body. Ash screamed and shot four more times, but none of the rounds went anywhere near the targets.

Through the agony, Matt pulled back on the stick and retreated. Another Eel shot past him and entered the line of fire. Matt caught a glimpse of Michelle's face, teeth gritted in pain, as it passed.

Michelle's gunner fired wild, wasting eight rounds in rapid succession. One finally struck an Auxiliary, sending him spinning out of control. The rest of their opponents directed a steady stream of fire at Michelle. Her Eel writhed and convulsed.

Matt turned his Eel back toward the battle as another sinuous sub joined them. Now there were three Eels closing in on the Auxiliary gunners. And that's when he realized, *This is the only way we'll win it. With a concerted attack from every Eel at once.* He drove a wide circle round the other Eel and made eye contact with all the candidates in the other sub, and like the leader for all of them, drove his Eel into a hard plunge after Michelle. The other Eel followed on his wing.

"Shoot, Ash!" he yelled.

Rattling bangs from his Eel. Bubbles traced lines to the closest Auxiliary. Her weapon went flying and she tumbled through the water. Matt turned toward the next, but his viewport suddenly crazed. Chill water sprayed everywhere. Matt blinked in the salty mist and wiped frantically at his eyes. He squinted and pushed himself closer to the viewport, so he could see through a small part of it that wasn't cracked. The Auxiliary was changing clips on her MK-1.

Matt accelerated toward her.

"Ash!" he yelled, as the Auxiliary finally managed to snick a new clip in place.

"I'm out!" Her voice was a screech.

The Auxiliary raised her gun. Matt looked right down its

barrel. And he saw exactly what was going to happen. He wouldn't reach her in time. She'd fire, their viewport would cave in, and they'd be done.

An Eel shot in front of them, knocking the Auxiliary off her footing. She tumbled away into the murky water. Another Eel wiped out the last of the Auxilaries.

For a moment, Matt let the rush of victory take him. They'd done it. He whooped in delight as water sprayed in his face.

"Time for happy later," Serghey said. "Marker ahead, in hole. Is craft leaking?"

Matt laughed and shoved them forward. His display read:

% MOTIVE POWER: 2%

That was fine. That's all they needed. They slipped into the hole at the bottom ahead of the other Eels. Darkness surrounded them.

"Where's the marker?"

"Ahead, one hundred meters."

"A hundred meters?"

"Is what display indicates."

Matt pushed forward. Utter black closed in on all sides, shuttering his vision. He felt the Eel brush against rough rock through the interface suit, and the water got warmer.

What if there are more troops in the cave? What if this whole thing is a trap?

"Marker ahead, twenty meters," Serghey said.

Matt pushed forward. He had to trust the mission.

"Ten meters," Serghey said.

Matt scraped against something that didn't feel like rock.

"I don't know about this," Matt said.

"At marker!" Serghey said.

Orange light flared around them, revealing steel mesh all around. They'd driven into a cage.

"Shit!" Matt reversed hard. His sub flipped end over

end to face the three other Eels behind. Metal grating dropped, trapping all the subs inside. Matt's Eel bonged off the mesh.

"Fuck!" Outside the grating, a heavy metal door slowly fell, blocking the weak blue-green light from the cave entrance.

"What's going on?" Ash asked.

"We're screwed," Matt said.

"But that was marker," Serghey bleated. "Exercise did. We complete."

A rush of bubbles jostled the Eels. Matt slid sideways and bumped into one of the other ships. Michelle's frightened eyes looked back at him. He tried to move their viewports closer, but his readout read:

MOTIVE POWER: 0%

Bubbles cascaded upward. An air pocket formed at the ceiling and expanded rapidly downward. Soon, the four Eels were all sitting on steel grate grown over with moss in a chamber full of air.

The top hatch of Matt's Eel popped open, spilling sickly orange light on them. Matt unfolded himself from the pilot's seat and scrambled out onto the grate. Serghey, cursing, fell hard beside him. Other pilots and crew got out of their Eels, looking around in confusion. On either end of the cage were solid steel doors.

"Did we win or did we lose?" Jahl asked.

Matt almost laughed. He had no idea. Michelle paced beside her Eel. Kyle sat on the edge of the Eel cockpit, studying the walls of the cage.

An almost subsonic hum shook bits of sand and rock from the ceiling, tinking on the metal grate.

"Look," Ash said, pointing at the inner steel door. It rose slowly into the ceiling. It revealed a polished floor, reflecting bright blue-white light. Two strong, muscular legs stood in the middle of the floor. As the door rose higher, Matt wasn't surprised to see that it was Major Soto.

Behind Major Soto rose a miniature city, set under a brilliant blue sky. It was like something you'd see in the *Future Ideals of the Union* video. To one side, streamlined, graceful towers, connected by transit tunnels with bright-lit cars sliding like strings of pearls. Broad avenues carried gray-uniformed Auxiliaries and blue-suited Corps hurrying to their jobs. To the other side there was a broad blacktop training area, covered with markings like a giant football field. Eventually the blacktop area gave way to more natural rock, trees, and grass. In the natural area, concrete slabs simulated a town. They were heavily cracked and cratered.

Matt swallowed hard, trying to hide his awe. It was an underground city under a simulated sky. The sun streaming down on them was likely a small fusion reactor, riding rails set into the ceiling.

"Welcome," Major Soto said, "to the real training camp."

5

ENTRY

Two days on Earth. Two hours in underground Mecha Training Camp. Matt stood on his tiny balcony in Cadet Housing and looked out over the bustle of the city, drained and numb. Part of it was simple fatigue. Part of it was the beating he'd taken from the interface suit. And part of it was the incredible vista in front of him.

Cadet Housing looked right up one of the main avenues of the mini city. Auxiliaries and Mecha Corps hurried up and down the broad boulevard, beneath a fake sky that had faded to purple twilight and stars. The crowd moved quickly and purposefully, intent on their business. Almost everyone walked alone. The few couples kept a tense distance between them. Eyes locked forward, looking at something beyond the edge of the horizon.

Matt knew that look. Every refugee ship had its share of people lost in endless drudgery. Workaholics. Obsessives. Or those who lived only for the bar at the end of the day. Alcoholics. Addicts.

Love without joy, Pat had called it. Pat Osaki was boss of the gardens on the *Rock*, the Displacement Drive ship that had picked him up after his father's murder.

In contrast with the passersby, small, bright-lit signs advertised businesses centered around entertainment: JAKE'S TAVERN; IL TRATTORIA, A RESTAURANT; PENNI ARCADE ADVENTURELAND; REAL-SIM VIDEOTOPIA (FEATURING *CORSAIR RAIDER*

REVENGE 7 & TWO WORLDS: A LOVE STORY); SEACURSIONS & EARTH TOURS; MECHA CORPS SPECIAL SERVICES.

Above the throngs, big adverboards cast a garish light. The one closest to him ran a PSA on the Union's most-wanted Corsairs. Number 1 was represented by only a silhouette and a single name: Rayder.

Everyone knew Rayder, but few had ever glimpsed him. They called him the General in Shadows. He kept well-hidden, despite leading some of the most daring and direct raids on Union worlds in the past decade. Rayder loved high-profile targets. He'd recently destroyed an entire Universal Union Displacement Drive cruiser in a skirmish near Epsilon, deep inside the Union.

Matt's hands twisted on the chrome rail, remembering once again, all of a sudden, in vivid detail that last day with his father. That was more like a Corsair: strike at the edge of the Union, kill defenseless people for money you can get from black-marketing stolen tech, then run and hide. Corsairs were only loosely organized. If they couldn't fight the Union, they'd happily hit the Aliancia or the Taikong, or fight among themselves.

"Hey," a voice came up from below.

Matt looked down. Michelle stood on the balcony one floor beneath him, one room over.

"Hey, yourself," Matt called, telling himself, *You're not here for this.*

Michelle leaned on the railing and looked out over the city. After her first greeting, she seemed content to ignore him. The silence stretched like a challenge.

Matt was first to speak. "Have you ever been off Earth?"

Michelle looked back up at him, her expression suddenly grim. "Not even to orbit."

Instantly, Matt wanted to take her on a Displacement Drive ship. He wanted to lie out on its surface and watch the stars change with her. "What'll you do when you're out there?"

Michelle's face compressed in concentration, and she

looked at Matt for several long moments. For the first time, Matt thought she really saw him.

"You think I'll make it." A statement, not a question.

"Yes."

"Don't feed me bullshit." But her tone was neutral.

"I'm not," Matt said. Thinking of Kyle, of his calculating words.

Michelle swallowed and looked away. "Gotta get through this first."

"We will," Matt told her.

"You can't say that for sure."

Matt nodded. Three others had walked out after the Eels. There were eleven cadet candidates left. Only about a third of their original group. And they still hadn't gotten in a Mecha.

"Yes, I can. So can you."

Michelle nodded, but her expression went tight-lipped. She looked back out over the city. Matt let the silence stretch out. After a while, Michelle waved and went back into her room. Matt heard the door slide open and shut.

"Good going," said another voice beside him. Matt leaned farther out of the balcony to look. Ash was two doors down from him.

"Thanks," Matt said. "I think."

Ash nodded. "She's skittish. Got lots of walls up."

"I'm not . . ." Matt trailed off. He wasn't what? Human?

"Problem with the skittish ones: sometimes they don't get close enough to make the right choice. Y'know?"

"No," Matt said, laughing. "I have no idea what you mean."

Ash laughed with him. "Lotsa folks say that. Well, g'night." Matt heard the sliding door again.

After a while, he went back in. His room was tiny and severe. A single bed done in three shades of gray covers. Two bare shelves beside the bed. A table and chair built into the wall. There was a single button on the desk marked EMERGENCY COMMS.

Matt went to the door and twisted the knob. It didn't

turn. A small screen above the knob flashed bright orange words: ACCESS TO TRAINING CAMP SUBFACILITY IS LIMITED AT CADET CANDIDATE LEVEL. THIS ROOM IS SEALED FOR YOUR PROTECTION.

Matt nodded. Everything they'd been through so far made sense. Minimize the budget while weeding out the incompatible candidates. Invite the remainder into an exclusive club. Then ensure they can't do anything stupid if they got second thoughts.

Yeah. It made sense. It was also scary as hell.

What had he gotten into?

The next morning, Soto and the Auxiliaries made the cadet candidates put on their interface suits before transport through the city. The Auxiliaries and Corps on the avenues watched them pass with knowing smirks.

But when the transport pulled up to the blacktop practice field, suddenly it didn't matter.

On the field, five Mecha stood at ready. Five times the height of a man, they were made of something like black chrome, sculpted into fluid equations of power. Legs bulging with metallic muscle supported a massive, ridged torso pockmarked with shuttered, carbon-burned apertures.

Powerful arms serrated with razor-sharp protrusions terminated in skeletal talons that looked like they could rip through steel as easy as paper.

A spiked head with mirrored visor reflected the crawl of white clouds in the artificial sky above. They looked more alive than mechanical, more grown than made.

Matt shivered, his heart racing. *This is why I'm here.*

"Hol-ee shit," Ash said, jumping off the transport. Murmurs of appreciation rippled through the ranks of cadet candidates as they lined up in front of the Mecha. Michelle looked up at the Mecha in raw hunger. The Khoury brothers were silent, and even Serghey seemed at a loss for a dickish comment. Only Kyle seemed unimpressed. He stood with his arms crossed, his expression relaxed and almost a little bored.

"These are Hellion-class Mecha," Major Soto said. "They are not trainers or simulators. They are exactly the same as the front-line units."

Major Soto nodded at Sergeant Stoll, who held a small slate. She keyed a long sequence into the device.

The Mecha closest to them crouched down in a fluid, organic motion. Unlike a Powerloader or an Imp, it made almost no noise, save for a faint metallic squeak. The Mecha's chest unfolded along invisible seams and opened in six sections like a flower. One of the sections touched the ground, providing steep stairs up to the cockpit.

The cockpit itself was like nothing Matt had ever seen. There was no seat. The only thing inside was a simple body harness, fashioned of the same metal-veined silicone as their interface suits. The top of the harness formed a silicone cap, almost completely shot through with metallic fibers. The walls were plain metal, sculpted into organic forms and striated like muscle.

"In a Hellion, a Corps member is completely encased in the chest cavity. There are no viewports or windows, which provides a high level of protection in combat."

"How do you see outta it?" Ash asked.

"Nonphysical Projection, or NPP, provides a three-hundred-sixty-degree view from within the cockpit," Soto said.

"All screens, bad design," Serghey muttered.

Soto's eyes rolled heavenward. "Any of you have experience with mechanical Mecha? Imp or Villain class?"

Matt remembered his tiny cubicle on the *Rock*, where his model Imp-class Mecha had kept him company, Velcroed to the wall above his sleeping bag. Compared to the Mecha standing in front of him now, an Imp was laughably old-fashioned. But there were still a few on Aurora, loading and unloading large cargo shuttles.

Serghey and Kyle raised their hands.

"Powerloaders?"

Matt raised his own.

Soto shook his head. "Don't count on your experience. You can't run a Hellion like a mechanical Mecha."

"Principle same. No difference!" Serghey yelled.

"This isn't force feedback," Soto said. "The neural interface establishes a direct mind-body connection with the Hellion. It may take days for you to have fine control."

"I'm quick study," Serghey said, crossing his arms.

Major Soto nodded. "You'll get your chance soon. For now, let's talk sensors and weapons."

At the mention of weapons, cadets snapped to attention.

"First, the sensor arrays. If you've been in Union forces, you already know most of this. Standard visible light, with IR, radar, EM, light amplification, thermal, and compositional overlays. Sound with amplification, rectification, and augmentation. Detection of all known languages, automatic translation. Best you just run through all of those once in the cockpit; we've set aside time for that.

"Weapons are different. Standard handheld weapon is an MK-15, 15mm, depleted-uranium slug gun, strong enough to pierce a half meter of carbon-fiber/steel-laminate armor. The MK-15 is plenty for most everything. Corsair fighter on the ground, MK-15. Corsair transport on the ground, MK-15. Corsair in an Aliancia tank, MK-15; Corsair in a Taikong — well, maybe then you gotta move up to short- and medium-range ordnance. Those are your Fireflies and Seekers."

Major Soto pointed at the small apertures on the Hellion's chest. "Fireflies are small, semismart rounds closely coupled with the Hellion's sensor systems. Sweep the area, map the unfriendlies, send out Fireflies, and, bam, no unfriendlies. Or no slow ones, anyway." He pointed at the larger apertures near the Hellion's shoulders. "Seekers are larger missiles that have limited steering capability — think armored carriers and Taikong tanks."

"Second, close-quarter combat. Every once in a while,

you'll come across something that's really tough. Corsairs dig in, put up all the armor they got, you're not getting through. For that, we have the Close-Quarters Fusion Pulse, CQFP, or, as we like to call it, the Fusion Handshake." Major Soto gestured at the Hellion's hand, where a lampreylike aperture was visible on the palm. "Grab on, trigger the Fusion Handshake, and that's pretty much the end for whatever you're holding on to."

"Finally, we have the weapon of last resort." Major Soto nodded at Sergeant Stoll. A compartment unfolded from the side of the Mecha, revealing a dazzling, mirror-plated gun. "The MA-ZERO matter-antimatter rifle, or, as corps call it, the Zap Gun."

Some gasps and mutters from the cadets. Kyle continued to look unimpressed. *An act?* Matt wondered. *Or is he so high up in government, he's seen it all?*

"Don't use the Zap Gun unless you really need it. The Corsairs drop an entire battleship on you. You're out in free space and you're completely out of ammo. You're stuck on a rock with a fighter that has zero-permeability coating. Situations like that. The Zap Gun just makes really big things disappear. Forever. Got it?"

Matt grinned and nodded. How could any Corsair stand against that, no matter how superhuman?

"Finally, don't ever underestimate the power of a Hellion. We've disabled all weapons systems for the purpose of today's test, but even without them, Hellions are one of the most powerful machines ever created. Don't push it."

"No sufficient Mecha for all," Serghey bleated. "How we choose—flip coin?"

Soto nodded. "We go in shifts. Serghey, you can be in the first group." Soto pointed out four more cadets. Ash and Michelle were the ones Matt knew by name.

"Here's what you'll do," Soto said. "You'll get in the Mecha. You'll put on the neural interface and Mesh."

"What's Mesh?" Ash asked.

Soto's mouth twitched and his eyes darted sideways, as if

he were uncomfortable with the question. "It's the connection between you and the Mecha. No Mesh, no Mecha Corps."

Soto nodded at Sergeant Stoll. Mecha unfolded like gargantuan metallic flowers, and cadet candidates climbed inside. Soto went to each in turn, explaining how to connect their interface suits. Cadets fumbled with silicone cables and, one by one, the Mecha folded up again.

Nothing happened for a long time. Sergeant Stoll watched the slate intently. Matt caught a glimpse of a slice-'n'-dice video feed of the five cadets.

One of the Mecha suddenly moved. It took one wavering, uncertain step backward, swaying like a drunk. Some of the cadets laughed nervously, but Major Soto paid no attention to them. He seemed unconcerned about the Mecha toppling, but his jaw was still set, hard and grim.

What's he afraid of? Matt wondered.

The Mecha that Michelle had chosen stood and took several jerky steps forward, then stopped and opened and closed its hands, as if testing their function. Another darted forward and fell to its knees with a great metallic clang. Serghey's Mecha wrapped its long, skeletal fingers around its head and rocked back and forth. Ash's Mecha raised and lowered its legs smoothly, then did a juddering sprint around the rest. Matt laughed. She literally ran a circle around them.

Michelle watched Ash complete her circle, then took off in pursuit. The two Mecha headed down the blacktop field at a shambling run. Ash reached the edge of the field first, where the blacktop gave way to grass and concrete of a simulated town.

Soto told Sergeant Stoll, "That's enough. They don't have enough control yet." Stoll spoke to her slate, and Ash and Michelle started back to rejoin the group.

Serghey's Mecha started screaming. A high-pitched, ululating sound, half-animal, half-metallic. It ricocheted throughout the facility like a banshee howl. Serghey's Hellion clawed at its head, as if it wanted to rip it off.

Major Soto grabbed the slate from Stoll's hands. "Don't fight it!" he yelled at the device, trying to be heard over the rising squeal of agony. "Hit the release! Now!"

The Mecha's scream rose up and up, echoing from the one side of the giant city cavern to another.

"Think *emergency release*!" Soto's face was red and panicked. "Hit the physical switch!"

Sudden silence.

The Mecha twitched and went limp, its chest unfolding to touch the ground. Serghey slumped forward in the pilot's harness. Gray-brown puke dribbled down the front of his interface suit, and the sharp smell of stomach acid wafted over to the cadets.

"Fuck!" Soto ran up the steps and tore Serghey from his harness. Soto shook him like a rag doll, his face contorted in fear. Matt's guts did an uneasy twist. It was the first time he'd seen the major scared.

Sergeant Stoll joined Soto with the cadet. She showed him something on her slate and shook her head. Soto cursed and let go of Serghey. Only the silicone connection cables kept him from spilling out of the cockpit.

Sergeant Stoll spoke to the slate. The rest of the Mecha stopped twitching, formed lines, and opened up. Cadets blinked in the bright, simulated sun. They all stared blankly, as if interrupted from a deep sleep.

Matt couldn't stand it anymore. "Is he all right?" he called out.

Soto looked at Matt, then stepped back to address all of the cadets. "I'm sorry. He's dead."

Silence, like a lead hammer, dropped over the field. Peal was the first to speak. "Huh," he muttered. "I thought the assholes always lived."

Soto glared at Peal. Peal swallowed and said, "I'm sorry, sir. Jest is an inappropriate antidote to pain."

Soto looked across the cadets. Suddenly he looked ten years older, his eyes sunken and sad, deep-set in age-scarred sockets. "Very rarely, we have an extreme reaction to Mesh. I have to stress, these incidents are rare. We test extensively, but . . . it happens."

The wail of a siren swelled. A HMLV sped across the blacktop toward them, marked with the red cross of an ambulance.

"What do we do now?" Ash called.

Soto looked at her, as if seeing her for the first time. "Nothing. You and Earth girl passed already."

Ash blinked. "But he's dead!"

"Yes, and Corsairs look down jealously at the Union and continue to plot," Soto said. "And every day brave colonists die on frontier worlds."

Ash swallowed and said nothing.

Soto nodded, as if he'd come to a decision. "All cadets, out of the Mecha. Next group is up."

"What about us?" one of the other cadets in the Mecha asked. "We never got it working."

"You'll need additional simulation training," Soto said. "Medical will pick you up after the first Mesh is complete."

The ambulance arrived. Two Auxiliaries unhooked Serghey's harness and dragged him into the back of the HMLV. Matt felt a strange sense of disconnection. He'd come down with Serghey. It could have been him in there.

I could've died. I could still die.

"You," Soto said, pointing at Matt. Peal, Jahl, Kyle, and another cadet Matt didn't recognize filled out the group.

Kyle looked at Matt. "Good luck," he said.

Matt started. Kyle's eyes were serious and he sounded sincere. "Ah . . . good luck to you too."

"Luck and skill to us all," Jahl said, nodding at the other cadets.

It wasn't until Matt approached his Hellion that he realized *This is the one Serghey died in.*

Matt climbed into the Hellion. Inside the hatch frame a small metallic plate read:

UNIVERSAL UNION SPECIAL FORCES
ADVANCED MECHAFORMS, INC.
HELLION SN00183 REV A
"IMPULSE"

The cockpit stank of panic sweat and puke. Matt pushed away the thought of Serghey. He couldn't think about that. It didn't help. It didn't help one damn bit.

Inside the cockpit, silicone cables dangled, smudged with greasy handprints. The close-set walls were solid metallic muscle. Matt ran a hand along them. They were hard as steel but felt warm to the touch, as if the Mecha were alive.

Matt put an ear against the metal. He heard nothing except a faint ticking.

Even inside the cockpit there were no visible controls, just the webbed harness hanging from an anchor at the top. Matt got in the harness and pulled the straps tight. He slipped the silicone cap over his head and plugged the interface cable into his suit.

The forward hatch folded up in front of Matt. After a moment of complete darkness, the NPP lit around him in a 360-degree panorama. Matt blinked at the sudden light. The illusion was amazing. It was almost as if he were hanging in space over the concrete. Only the faint glints of screen light on metal hinted at the shapes of the cockpit beyond.

On the screen, an overlay appeared:

INITIATING PHYSICAL SYSTEMS: DONE
INITIATING WEAPONS SYSTEMS: DISABLED
INITIATING NEURAL MESH: DONE

As the word "done" flashed, Matt's world exploded. In a sudden rush, he fell into darkness.

Past a static-dusty thing, past a hail of voices raised in

pain, past the feeling of a grand hallway where unseen things churned and flopped—

Into something that felt like that last morning with his father. Something idyllic. Like the first kind words from Pat on the *Rock*. Like the first time he'd taken a drag of an illicit cigarette in a dump-and-dip frontier town. Like the first time he'd drunk vacuum-distilled whiskey. It was what Matt imagined killing that Corsair would feel like.

The painful tear of the interface suit fell away. He felt nothing but pure elation, pure power. He could do anything.

Matt opened his eyes. He was no longer inside the cramped pilot's chamber. He'd stepped through. He hung in space, suspended by his will, seeing the world only through the Hellion's eyes.

I would do anything to feel like this, he thought.

Matt raised his hand. The Hellion responded seamlessly. He marveled at every fiber of biometallic muscle tensing; he watched the perfect articulation of his fingers. There was nothing tentative about it.

He took a step. It was like a dream, perfect and fluid. He ran a short distance. His Mecha didn't rattle or shake. It fairly flew over the test court. It was amazing. Matt felt the chill underground on his metallic skin, smelled the sharp tang of the grass, heard the thrum and chatter of the city in the distance.

He glanced back at the others. Two of the Mecha took uncertain steps. One crouched on the ground. The last twitched and shuddered.

And Major Soto was staring at him. Straight at him, with an expression of openmouthed amazement. As Matt concentrated on him, the scene zoomed in and an overlay appeared:

SENSORY ENHANCEMENT MODE

In the sudden close-up, tags identified MAJOR GUILIANO

SOTO and SERGEANT LENA STOLL. It was like he was standing right in front of them.

As he watched, Lena's slate chimed. A voice barked: "What is that cadet's Mesh effectiveness?"

Matt recognized the voice. It was the same one he'd heard coming out of Mind Raze: Dr. Roth.

Sergeant Stoll looked right at Matt. "Candidate Lowell's Mesh effectiveness is eighty-seven percent," she said.

"Stable, resonant, or sliding?"

"Stable."

The slate chimed as the connection terminated. Stoll and Soto shared a glance. "He's the highest yet," she said.

Soto nodded. "Amazing."

A Mecha started to scream. Jahl's Mecha. It had never gotten out of its crouch.

Fear twisted Matt's guts. His POV snapped back to normal as he sprinted back to Jahl.

"Hit the release!" Major Soto said.

Matt knelt in front of Jahl and scrabbled at the hard metal of the other man's cockpit. There had to be some way to open it! Waves of fear and pain washed over Matt as Jahl fell deeper into reverse Mesh.

Of course! They were all connected. Matt felt all the cadets' panic, not just Jahl's. It fed on itself, spiraling up and up.

Matt's Mecha went dead. Matt yelped in surprise in the sudden darkness. Then his cockpit opened. Brilliant artificial sun seared his eyes.

In front of him, Jahl's Mecha yawned open. Jahl flailed at the control cables, then slumped forward in his harness.

Matt tried to jump out of his cockpit, but the harness held him back. Peal tore off his connections and charged up the stairs to his brother. Major Soto followed close behind. The two men pulled Jahl free by the time Matt reached them.

Jahl gasped and convulsed. His eyes were like black pools. Peal held him down until the seizure passed. Jahl tried to raise his head. Peal and Soto helped him stand and shuffle down to the blacktop.

"Is he okay?" Matt asked.

"He's alive," Soto said. "But he won't ever be Mecha Corps."

In the end, it was Matt, Kyle, Michelle, Ash, and Peal. They stood in front of Major Soto in their Hellions. Matt quivered in excitement. Despite the horror of the day, just being inside a Hellion was a wonderful feeling. He wanted to run up the sides of the city chamber, leap off, and swing from the buildings, charge up his weapons, raze an entire battalion of Corsairs.

"What are your orders, sir?" Michelle said. A comms icon appeared: CADET M. KIND → MAJOR G. SOTO: PUBLIC.

"Systems drills, reaction timing, and fine motor control exercises." Another comms icon lit: MAJOR G. SOTO → ALL. "You have a long way to go. Well, most of you do. Before that, half hour free exercise. Don't break anything."

"Yes, sir!" Michelle's Hellion snapped off a shaky salute. She spun and puttered down the field, calling, "Race ya!"

Matt laughed and gave chase. The others followed.

It was like nothing Matt had ever experienced. Just running across the concrete, feeling every impression in its grooved surface, was pure pleasure. No endless loop of Perfect Record. No muttering voices in the back of his head. In Mesh, he was free.

Matt flashed by Michelle. His ground-speed indicator rose quickly: 100, 200 kilometers an hour.

"Hey!" she yelled. Matt laughed and came to a skidding stop at the edge of the city chamber, where concrete pylons held back the native rock. Above them, the blue-green light of the Atlantic shone in through the chamber's transparent wall.

Michelle came to a stop beside him. "How are you so fast?" Michelle said, out of breath.

"I don't know." Matt frowned. Running the Mecha took no effort at all.

"You . . . aren't . . . even tired," Peal said through whooping breaths, as he clumped up to join them.

"No." Matt shook his head.

"Fricking Superman or somethin'," Ash said.

"Let's see how Superman fights," Kyle said, balling his Hellion's hands into fists and dropping into a boxer's posture.

Matt backed away. *The best way to win a fight is to avoid one.* That's what Pat used to say. Matt had used it to good effect in bars on Aurora, where bragging got heated and tempers flared. He'd always been able to talk the other guy down.

"Scared?" Kyle said, advancing. He moved jerkily, nowhere near as fluid as Matt.

"No."

"Then why are you running away?"

The women stopped to watch in that universal, hip-cocked posture that said *Boys will be boys.* Peal stayed off to the side, as if to say *I don't want any of this.*

"Cadet Candidate Peterov, stand down," Major Soto interrupted them over the comms.

"Yes, sir!" Kyle said, snapping to attention.

"All of you, come on back for drills," Soto said. "There's a time for this, but not now."

Matt jogged back with the others, wondering, *If not now, when?*

The systems drills consisted of Sergeant Stoll on a screen running them through the three major Mecha systems: comms, weapons, and sensors. It was all pretty straightforward, controlled by thought through the neural interface. Still, everyone had to run through it again and again.

Matt's Perfect Record picked it up immediately, so he turned his attention to the city and played with the limits of sensory-enhancement mode. There didn't seem to be much it couldn't do. He read the menus at Il Trattoria like they were in his own hands. He overhead conversations between anxious Auxiliaries as they talked about the pressure of their new schedules.

In the city, one building stood out from the rest: a sleek, mirrored monolith that twisted gracefully as it reached upward to touch the sky. At the top, glass balconies protruded, offering a vertiginous view of the city below. Matt zoomed in on the balconies and followed them up.

On the very top balcony, two men shook hands. Tags flickered over them in Matt's sensory-enhanced viewscreen. One man was DR. S. ROTH; FURTHER CREDENTIALS REDACTED. The other was CONGRESSPERSON S. TOMITA, CHAIR OF UNION ADVANCED TECHNOLOGIES COMMITTEE.

Matt felt a shock of recognition. Dr. Roth. Dr. Salvatore Roth. The voice on the slate. The father of modern Mecha. The man who'd asked about him.

Dr. Roth and Congressperson Tomita shook hands, but their expressions were set and grim. Matt's sensory enhancement brought him in at midgreeting.

"—san, it is a pleasure to receive you at our humble facility," Dr. Roth said. His voice was thin and reedy through the enhancement, but intelligible.

Congressperson Tomita frowned. "Spare me the pleasantries. And spare the suffix as well. Japan was three hundred years ago. We're all Union now."

"I only want to make your visit as productive as possible."

Tomita shook his head. "Productive for you, or for the Union?"

"For both of us."

"You know we have grave concerns about your procedures and outcomes. You are deviating significantly from standard military training. Many feel there should be more oversight, including Prime Haal," Tomita told him.

Dr. Roth nodded. "The new obedience, physical, and psych tests have led to only a single death in first Mesh."

"It is still a death!" Congressperson Tomita hissed. "How many are actually usable?"

"We have over ten percent full-capability"—the audio dropped out momentarily—"on first Mesh. With additional neural conditioning, we expect to drive final full-piloting candidates into the twenty-percent range."

"Terrible numbers!"

"Much higher than the two to five percent previously."

Congressperson Tomita said something lost in the garble. He finally came back with, "—leadership believes the nature of your biomechanical—"

"The Union believes they need more Mecha pilots." Dr. Roth cut off Tomita, his voice guttural and deadly. Then he softened. "You are within grasping distance of wiping out the scourge."

Congressperson Tomita nodded, but he didn't look at Dr. Roth.

"Would you prefer Rayder take another colony world?"

Matt started. *Another* colony world? Rayder had already taken a Union world? That never hit the news.

"Of course we must continue the campaign," Congressperson Tomita said.

"Good," Roth said. "I am delivering on my objectives. Now you must deliver on yours."

Congressperson Tomita looked up at Dr. Roth. Heat-distortion of the image made his face into a writhing mask of pain. Audio garble ate his words.

When the audio came back, Dr. Roth was talking again: "—or you won't get the Demon you most desperately crave."

6

WITHDRAWAL

The next morning, Matt's head felt like it was stuffed full of knives, and the shrill alarm was like someone pushing them deeper into his skull. He groaned and reached to turn it off. Even that slight movement sent crescendos of pain through his entire body. His digestive tract roiled and churned, filling his mouth with bile.

Sick. Great. What new torture did Major Soto have planned for them today? Even the thought of getting in his Hellion again did nothing to rouse him.

When Matt finally levered himself up, he noticed his door screen had changed. It now read: OPEN: STANDARD CADET PRIVILEGES. RETAIN ACCESS CARD AT ALL TIMES.

Matt forced himself to shuffle to the door. A thin slot at the top of the screen held a small card, engraved with a realistic hologram of his face. It read: MATT STANDFORD LOWELL. MECHA CADET. INDUCTION GROUP 715.

Cadet? No longer cadet candidate? Matt managed a weak grin. He'd piloted a Mecha. He was a full cadet now.

He flipped the card over, where it displayed an interactive map of the city, with the following tag: REPORT TO CADET HOUSING CAFETERIA.

Matt retched at the thought of food, but he followed orders and went down to the cafeteria. There, a smattering of men and women wearing gray cadet uniforms sat in groups of two or three. Some looked up when he walked in. *Fresh meat,* their smirks said. One guy nodded at an empty table, where a small, hand-lettered card read CADETS, GROUP 715.

Matt went to the table and sat. He didn't want to get anywhere near the food. His head radiated pulses of pain as he slumped in a seat.

Above him, wall screens showed a live session from the latest Union Congress on Eridani, while a scrolling ticker reiterated the important points. Unicrats had maintained their slim margin over the Freecycles. Augmented Union Services were promised for outlying colony worlds. Talks proceeded with Percy's Folly, an independent world considering Union membership after repeated Corsair attacks.

In an inset close-up, a talking head was jabbering Unicratese: How immensely valuable every habitable planet was, no matter how far toward the edge, or how young its charter, or how marginal its ecosystem. How Unification under standardized laws and practices promoted stability and growth, and how any other policy encouraged factions like the Corsairs.

"Did you get the number of the monster truck that hit me?" a familiar voice said. Matt jumped. It was Michelle. She slid into a seat and put her head in her hands.

"Monster truck?" Matt asked.

Michelle looked up at him. Her normally rosy complexion was pale, and dark circles nested under her eyes. "Old Earth expression. You know, 'Don't let the door hit ya where the dog shoulda bit ya'? 'Easy as pie'?"

Matt shook his head.

Michelle sighed. "I forgot you aren't a real silver-spoon type. They're all into Earth culture."

Matt suddenly realized what she'd been saying. "You're sick, too?"

"More like a hangover."

Things clicked into place in Matt's aching, slow brain. *Hungover. We are hungover.*

"From the Mecha?" he asked.

Michelle looked up, surprised. She nodded. "It *is* a helluva rush."

Matt remembered the intense feeling of Mesh. Now just thinking about it made his agony fade. Maybe that's what he needed—to get back in the Mecha. A strong pang of desire shot through his body.

"Do you think we'll pilot Mecha again today?" Michelle asked.

"Not a chance," said Peal, dropping into another seat. His dark complexion had an almost greenish cast, and his black hair stuck out in big spikes.

Michelle's expression went from hunger to annoyance in an instant. "Why not?"

"It's clear the neural interface is physically addictive," Peal said. "Party line is that it's only mental, though."

"How do you know that?"

Peal extracted his slate and waved it at them. "If it wasn't physical, they wouldn't have extensive documentation on the treatment of MUNS, or Mecha Utilization Neural Syndrome."

"You're hacking training camp?" Matt asked.

Peal nodded, looking smug.

"Is that . . . uh, safe?"

"I don't think it matters," Peal said. "This city is a roach motel."

"Roach motel?" Matt said.

Michelle nodded. "More old Earth slang. It means, 'It's a trap. Roaches go in, but they don't come out.' "

"What does that have to do with—," Matt began. More memories fell into place. The empty-looking cadets and corps. The throngs of Auxiliaries.

Peal nodded. "They're pushing real hard for Jahl to join the Auxiliaries. Really hard."

Michelle looked horrified. "And if he doesn't?"

Peal shrugged. "I don't think he's going to disappear or anything cloak-and-dagger. But I wouldn't be surprised if he ended up with a job on a colony world that makes Hyva look like Eridani."

"What about you?" Matt asked.

"Everything has an angle." Peal waved his slate and tapped his head. "You just have to figure out what it is."

Matt didn't know what to say. What were they up to now? A sudden memory of the conversation he'd overhead yesterday came back to him unbidden.

"There's a lot of stuff going on here that we don't know about," Peal said, through a grin.

Ash slipped into a seat next to them without a word. She put her head down on the table and groaned.

"And a rousing 'good morning' to you too," Peal said.

"Screw you," Ash grumbled.

Peal just laughed. Ash flipped him off.

"What a fine group of cadets we have here!" boomed a familiar voice—Major Soto's. He wore uniform-casual again: Corps pants and tight-fitting T-shirt with major's stripes. Beside him stood Sergeant Stoll, looking impossibly crisp and perfect in her Auxiliary uniform.

Michelle sat up straight. "Good morning, sir!"

"Can it." Soto pulled up a chair to the head of the table and sat in it backward. "I know how you all feel. Like shit. The good news is, we'll run a dozen laps of the city now."

The silence was so total you could hear a pin drop. Ratcheting laughter came from a group of cadets at another table. Peal went even greener.

Soto chuckled. "I'm joking. You aren't in any shape for that."

"What about—," Michelle began.

"And you're in no shape to be running Mecha," Soto said, talking over her. Michelle sagged, defeated. Matt knew exactly how she felt.

"Who're we missing?" Soto said, scanning the table.

"Cadet Peterov, sir," Lena said.

"When he gets here, let him know it's a free day."

"Free day?" Ash asked.

"Yes. Congratulations, cadets. You earned it."

Matt felt a rush of pride. He sat up straighter. They all did. Even Ash lifted her head off the table and gave everyone a wan grin. They were cadets now.

"Free, of course, is relative," Soto said. "If you're up to it, I'd recommend the Strategic Archive, where you can review Mecha battles and deployment, or Mecha Interface Training, where you can improve your fine motor skills—"

"Found it last night," Kyle said, walking up. Except for the bags under his eyes, Matt had to begrudgingly admit that Kyle didn't look that bad off.

"Last night?" Michelle asked.

"Yeah, I've got to catch up with Superman." Kyle nodded at Matt.

"Does it work? Does it feel like being in a Mecha?" Michelle asked, leaning forward.

"I got my Mesh percentage up by nine points. But, no, it doesn't feel like being in a Hellion. I can show you, if you'd like."

Michelle nodded eagerly, a spark in her eyes for the first time. "Yeah. Please."

Under the table, Matt clenched his fists. *And there she goes with the golden boy. So easy for him.*

When Soto had gone and they'd choked down some food, Kyle stood up. "I'm going back to Interface Training. Who's coming with me?"

"I'll go." Michelle said.

Ash shook her head. "I'm goin' back to my room."

"I'm working." Peal poked at his slate.

Michelle and Kyle looked at Matt expectantly. Matt held up his hands in surrender. "I think it's the Archive for me."

He watched them leave, thinking, *You've just blown it.*

Maybe he had. And maybe that would have to be okay.

The Strategic Archive was a long, broad room full of privacy screens in the Mecha Corps Administration building two doors down from Cadet Housing. Matt's access card granted him BASIC LIBRARY RIGHTS, according to the screen.

Matt found it pretty amazing. They had video and transcripts from every major Mecha battle from Pellham's Front and New Jericho to the present day, together with battle strategies describing how to deploy Mecha for typical situations: a single Mecha with low-power rounds and extra Fireflies to go into a colonial city to take out a single terrorist with no casualties; a two-pronged drop from orbit with fast land assault on a ground space port held by a Corsair force, using Aliancia mortars and tanks; coordinated multidrop assaults with Mecha Flight Packs designed for planetary occupation.

Mecha could fly? Matt didn't know that. He found a long list of Mecha Augmentations (Hellions), including Flight Packs, High-Speed Ground-Maneuverability Units, Ballistic Deployment and Recovery, High-Dexterity Auxiliary Arms, and much more. Videos showed the Hellions melting and reforming around the packs to form a seamless biomechanical unit.

There were also files clearly marked off-limits to him, such as Merge (Multiple Units) and Merge (Advanced).

Still, Matt was enthralled. Before he knew it, the afternoon was gone, and the artificial sky had shaded to purple twilight. He yawned, grabbed his access card, and headed back to his room.

Matt didn't feel tired at all, but he lay down on the bed just for a moment. Being horizontal helped quiet the last of his pounding headache.

When he woke, the artificial sky was full night, and the door-screen clock read 22:14. Matt dragged himself out to his balcony and looked out over the city. The adverboards were playing feel-good scenes from a new colony world, with smiling Union officials surveying a bleak, storm-wracked landscape.

"About time!" Michelle called up from below.

Matt leaned over, expecting to see her on her balcony.

Instead, she stood in the middle of the little park that fronted Cadet Housing, her face a white oval in the chill city light. "Can you let me in?" Michelle asked.

"Let you in?"

"I didn't take that—what was it?—access card."

"How could you miss that?" Matt asked, without thinking.

Michelle put her hands on her hips. "You gonna help or not?"

"Yeah, hold on!"

Matt went down to the lobby, wondering, *Where has she been? In Interface Training this whole time, or somewhere else?*

When he opened the door, Michelle darted in and headed for the elevator. "Thanks!"

"How are you going to get in your room?" Matt called after her.

Michelle's face went slack. "Shit."

They went up in the elevator together and tried her door. Of course, it didn't budge. Matt scanned through the help menu on his access card. There wasn't any info about lost cards or live services.

"I guess I get to sleep in the hall," Michelle said.

Matt grinned. "Not necessarily."

Michelle shook her head. "Don't even think about inviting me into your bed—"

"What are you, sixteen?" Matt asked. "I just figured you could swing down to your balcony from mine."

Michelle started, then looked at him incredulously. "What are you, twelve? Hang off the side of the building?"

"Beats sleeping in the hall."

Michelle looked at Matt for a long time, as if trying to see if his offer was a trick. Finally, she nodded.

Matt took her up to his room and carded them in. She stepped into the cramped space gingerly, as if expecting to step into a disgusting bachelor pad.

On the balcony, Matt looked down. It seemed like she

could just drop down on the one directly below his room, then swing around the privacy wall to reach her own.

"Yeah. Let's do it." Michelle climbed up on the slick chrome railing and turned around. She took one step down onto the lower rail, then turned and looked down. Her arms quivered.

"Are you sure—," Matt began.

Michelle lost her grip.

Without thinking, Matt reached out and grabbed her arm. Wiry muscle worked under the coarse gray fabric of her jumpsuit. Michelle's hand grabbed his upper arm and her fingers dug in.

"Just hold on." Matt drew her up, thankful for the years he spent in high-G centrifuges. If he were a typical refugee, he wouldn't have been able to lift her.

Michelle got her feet under her and climbed back over the rail, backing away quickly on shaky legs.

"I'm sorry," she said, hugging herself and pacing. She wouldn't look at him.

"No reason to be sorry," Matt told her. "You're tired. It was just a slip. Everyone slips."

"You don't!" Sharp, angry.

Yeah, Matt thought. *I'm chased by every terrible, perfect memory, I'm hell-bent on revenge that won't bring my father back, and I'm gonna screw up my chance with you before it ever gets started. I slip all the time.*

"You didn't go to Interface Training because of Kyle." Michelle's words were a statement, not a question.

Matt tried not to react.

Michelle sighed. "I don't know why you two are so oil and water."

Kyle. That cocky face. That expression that said, *I've never been hungry a day in my life. I've never had to work for an instant. I've always been able to pick and choose my ROTC and classes and tutors so they are all perfectly balanced, the same way I'll pick my women and the same way I'll choose my job.* Kyle had never woke up smelling the sewer stench of a Displacement Drive garden. He'd never spent sixteen hours a day digging tunnels for months on end. He'd never had to sit behind a half-broken Taikong depleted-uranium slug gun when they came close to a frontier world with an interesting slant on negotiation.

"You guys are both good," Michelle told him. "If you worked together—"

"We're nothing alike!" Matt snapped.

Michelle drew back and crossed her arms, saying nothing. The silence stretched out, a terrible vacuum. Matt had to fill it.

"I watched my dad die," Matt said, each word wrenched from his heart. It was something he'd never told anyone. "A Corsair killed him."

A HuMax, he thought. But he bit down to stop the words. HuMax didn't exist anymore. Everyone knew that.

Michelle opened her mouth, then closed it. "You're telling the truth, aren't you?"

"Yes. I am." The memory of that day cascaded behind his eyes, the curse of his Perfect Record. He wanted to tell her more, tell her everything. Maybe that would salve the pain.

But Michelle spoke first. "I'm sorry. I thought . . . I thought I had it worse than anyone."

She told him about life on Earth. About the devil's choice: work for Earth First, the monolithic preservation society that made its real money through scams like Bordeaux wine and Blue Mountain coffee, neither of which existed anymore. Or ship out in a hospitality job on a Displacement Drive ship.

Matt knew all about hospitality jobs. The young, dead eyes. It wasn't a way out. It was just another trap.

She told him about Earth First. That's what had consumed her parents. Her mother could recite the timeline of middle-American wallpaper from 1950 to 2050; not just major trends but specifics and technologies, both passive and active. Her dad was one of the top coffeehouse scholars on the planet, having written several thousand-page tomes on the business practices and rise and fall of the American coffeehouse during the late twentieth and early twenty-first centuries. So utterly focused, so completely consumed that they hadn't even noticed when she left for Mecha Corps.

Matt pushed himself up on the lowest railing. His foot slipped and he came down hard. He stumbled forward, into Michelle. She caught his arms. She smelled of something tropical and exotic. Close, so close. Inches away. Her eyes, wide, on his.

"See?" he said. "Everyone slips."

She didn't push him away. Matt looked at her for what seemed like an eternity. She looked back at him, her wide eyes softening. It was as if she wanted to be kissed.

Matt leaned down.

Michelle suddenly pushed him away, hard. "No."

Matt stepped back. "I'm . . ." He started. *I'm sorry.* No. He wasn't sorry. Given the chance, he'd do it again. "New plan. I'll open your door. Meet me down there."

Without waiting for an answer, he dropped down onto the balcony below and swung across to her room. Thankfully, the sliding door wasn't locked. He opened it and went to the front, where her access card still glowed. He plucked it out and opened her door.

Revealing Kyle. The man stood outside in the hall, mid-pace. For a moment, he didn't realize who he was looking at. Then Kyle's expression compressed in anger. "What the hell?"

"He's just helping me get in my room," Michelle said, coming down the hall, fast.

Kyle's eyes darted from Matt to Michelle and back again. He grabbed Matt's collar and dragged him out into the hall. "Helping how?"

"Helping, like you're helping by going back to your room," Michelle said.

Kyle blinked and let go of Matt. "What?"

"This is over. Thank you, Matt." Michelle plucked her access card from Matt's hand, eyes flashing. She pushed past him and slammed her door, rattling its frame.

Kyle looked at Matt, his rage slowly being replaced by amusement. He laughed.

"Game, set, match. We both lose."

7

BREAKTHROUGH

The next five days were an endless slog ripped straight from Matt's worst visions of the military: hours of dexterity exercises and simple weapons drills in the Hellions, dry firing at targets set up on the far side of the blacktop. MK-15 targeting. MK-15 firing. MK-15 reloading. Firefly targeting. Seeker targeting.

Matt mastered every exercise and drill in minutes, then spent the rest of the time mindlessly pulling the trigger and enjoying the rush of Mesh.

That was one thing he'd never get tired of. Mesh. He couldn't get down to the field fast enough every morning. Forget breakfast, forget working out, forget wondering if Michelle and Kyle were out to dinner last night, spending the first of their thin Mecha cadet paychecks.

It was all about getting in the Mecha, plugging in, and getting that first giant rush. That I-can-do-anything feeling. The others wanted it too, staring intently at the Hellions until Soto came out and opened them up.

Like addicts, Matt thought, remembering Peal's words.

But Matt didn't care. Not really. Every time he got in the Mecha, all his doubts washed away. He was perfect, all-powerful. He could do anything.

It got more interesting when Soto ordered them out to the simulated city. All around rose towering concrete blocks, pockmarked with bullet spall and carbon burns from previous battles. Between the simulated "buildings," sheet-metal outlines of ground cars and an occasional battered Aliancia tank shell provided surreal cover.

Above the concrete city hung a glass-and-steel control room. Matt's sensory enhancement brought details into sharp relief. Major Soto, in full Mecha Corps uniform, stood on an elevated stage, pacing and glaring down at the Mecha as he spoke. Below him, five Auxiliaries sat at consoles in front of ranked screens. Matt recognized only one of them: Sergeant Stoll.

"First, ground rules," he said. "Even though we're using only fluff rounds and popcorn Fireflies, there will be no shooting at any targets other than those in the mock cityscape. No shooting at the control tower. No shooting at Training Camp City. Not even as a joke. I repeat: do not test it.

"Second, structure. If you've been reading up on Corps command structure like I suggested, this shouldn't be a surprise. Sergeant Stoll is your acting controller for this exercise. You will follow her instructions precisely, to the letter, and without hesitation. If she says stop, you stop. Understood?"

"Understood, sir." Michelle's voice quivered in anticipation.

"Yes, sir," Kyle snapped off.

"The rest of you, sound off! Understood?"

Everyone did.

"Okay. Here's what you're going to do. Go through the city, shoot the unfriendlies. It should be pretty clear who they are. If you're good at that, we'll step it up."

Matt's screen changed to show a new flag:

WEAPONS SYSTEMS (BASIC, REDUCED POWER): ENABLED

Matt's screen also showed a grid layout of the mock city. His position was highlighted with a Mecha icon and a tag:

CADET M. LOWELL. The other Mecha didn't appear on the grid display.

A new comms icon flashed: SGT. L. STOLL → CADET M. LOWELL.

"Cadet Lowell, you will deploy to the location indicated and clear it of the enemy." On his screen, a dotted line appeared, connecting him to a spot deep in the cement jungle.

"What about the others?" Matt said. "Ma'am?"

"They will receive separate instruction, cadet."

"Mecha versus Mecha, then?" Matt asked.

"You will address Sergeant Stoll as 'ma'am' or 'Sergeant,' " Major Soto's voice boomed, his comms icon lighting.

"Sorry, sir. Sorry, Sergeant Stoll."

Major Soto's comms icon remained on. "To answer your question, ask yourself: Why would we fight Mecha versus Mecha? No other IGO has Mecha."

"What happens when they do, sir?"

"Then we will beat them as well. Until then, Mecha fight tanks, not other Mecha."

Matt headed toward the position indicated on the grid map. Through the Mecha, he felt the rush of the chill underground air and the brush of tall grass on his feet. His trot turned into a run. He punched a concrete block as he passed. Shockwaves vibrated up his arm, and a car-sized piece of the block shattered.

Lena's comms icon flared. "Cadet Lowell, please refrain from any unnecessary destruction of simulated property."

Matt reached his designated position at the end of a long corridor formed by towering cement slabs. Alleys between the blocks gave plenty of cover for approaching enemies. Behind him was a large open area, punctuated only by low dirt berms and concrete bunkers.

Matt ducked behind the edge of the simulated building at the end of the avenue. Were they going to funnel his enemies down the street, hit him from behind, or both? And what would they look like? Tanks?

A flicker of movement down the long road caught his

eye. He jerked his MK-15 to ready and pulled the trigger. The gun bucked like a jackhammer. Rock dust flew from the edge of the simulated building nearest the movement.

"One civilian death," Sergeant Stoll intoned, sounding disappointed.

"Civilian?" Matt looked again. The street was now populated with casually dressed people. Some strolled near the cement-block buildings, stopping to peer into nonexistent shop windows. Some sat on benches in the middle of the broad avenue. Some wore suits and hurried purposefully down the street.

And one lay, crumpled but bloodless, where Matt had fired.

"Holographic projections?" Matt asked.

"Of course," Sergeant Stoll said.

Matt turned to look behind him. The broad, open area had become a park. Parents and their kids played among the ditches and bunkers.

"Why?"

"We sharpen the knife edge between life and death," Sergeant Stoll said.

"What does that mean?"

"It's an old Mecha Corps motto. Pre-biomech. It means, among other things, 'Don't kill civilians. There's no excuse for that.'"

Matt nodded. "Unlike the Corsairs."

"Unlike the Corsairs," she echoed.

Matt opened his mouth to speak as slugs slammed into his Mecha's head. Matt yelled in surprise, echoes of the sudden pain reverberating in his body. He whirled. Nothing in front of him. Nothing behind him. Where had the rounds come from?

Oh, shit, Matt thought. *Of course.*

He looked up. Clinging to the side of the building was a spiderlike robot. Its face was a black gun barrel. The barrel blurred and Matt's screens flickered off for a moment, while a deep stab of agony seared his eyes.

"If those had been full-powered rounds, your optical sensors would be nonfunctional for at least one hundred sixty seconds," Stoll's voice told him.

Matt didn't answer as he ducked and rolled, bringing his MK-15 up to target the robot. It scuttered quickly around the side of the concrete monolith, out of his sights.

No doubt waiting for me to poke my head around the other side, Matt thought. He sprinted down an alley and circled around the back of the simulated building.

There it was! Pointing the other way, waiting for him to appear on the other side. Matt blew it off the side of the building, grinning at the little metallic squeal it made.

He didn't have much time to be smug, though, as a hail of bullets spanged off his backside. Matt whirled to see a half-dozen of the little robots, some on the ground, some halfway up the side of the concrete blocks. His Hellion's arms blurred as the MK-15 made short work of them. Matt laughed as the gun pounded in his hands. Mesh was great, but this was even better.

Two more spider robots peeped out from behind a building, far down the alley. Matt almost killed a pedestrian, but stopped himself at the last moment. He sprinted down the alleyway at the robots.

As he passed a side street, something whizzed at him from the park. Something bright. Matt only managed to turn partway before it exploded against his side with a brilliant flash and a spear of pain. His Hellion tumbled to the ground and slid within a couple meters of a simulated couple kissing on a bench.

"Ouch," Matt groaned. The first hot twist of anger made him flush. How was it fair to snipe at him with a bunch of unfeeling automatons? Bring on the Corsairs! He'd make them feel some pain.

Matt stood and charged down the side street toward the simulated park. Amidst the spider robots, simulated families threw balls and pointed at nonexistent birds. Perfect cover. Or so they thought. Matt's MK-15 barked in precise little bursts, perfectly controlled by his dextrous Hellion talons. Spider robots squealed and fell dead.

This was easy. As easy as the weapons drills—

A living carpet of spider robots crested the low hill at the center of the park and came at him, fast. Matt sprayed his MK-15 as the ammo counter cycled down to zero.

"Fireflies," Sergeant Stoll told him.

Of course! Matt slapped his head. That was stupid. Fireflies. That's what they were for. He brought up the targeting overlay and mapped for best dispersion. It'd be close on the civilians, but the robots were coming fast.

Matt triggered the Fireflies. Pure white brilliance shot from inside him, briefly blinding him. A thousand tiny explosions reverberated through his Hellion as the robots melted to slag.

"Civilian casualties," Sergeant Stoll said. "Three, five. Six total."

"I had to do it!" Matt said. "They'd be all over me—"

"Don't argue with your controller, cadet!" Soto bellowed.

Matt slumped. The concrete-block city suddenly seemed like the most desolate place in the world.

"Never kill," Sergeant Stoll said, her words measured, almost soft. "Unless there's no other choice. Or else we'll be the same as them."

Matt shivered, thinking of his father.

Thinking of that Corsair.

Later that afternoon, Soto had them work in teams of two and three to take on bigger scenarios, like destroying an artillery trench at the edge of the city and faking out an Aliancia tank when one Mecha was out of ammunition.

Matt got to work with Peal and Michelle on one exercise where they had to work through a nest of spider robots, a sniper with shoulder-fired Mini Seeker missile support, mined streets, and finally a tank.

Michelle had actually gotten faster than Matt. Where he

had the precise control to target, shoot, and move on to the next, she could sprint across a broad avenue without taking a round in her Mecha at all. The machine almost blurred as it passed. Matt shook his head in amazement. At the same time, a small angry voice asked, *Training with Kyle?*

Peal was uncanny at predicting exactly when and where the spider-robot swarms would strike. He was so good, Michelle accused him of hacking the system. But it ended up there was an even more bizarre reason for his prowess.

"Entangled computing," he told them. "Jahl and I got the implants as kids. The computing network is part of us now."

"Isn't that illegal?" Matt asked.

"Not illegal. Simply unsupported. In the words of the Union, 'Maintaining technology at this level of complexity is too difficult in a low-density, distributed state; therefore, it is beyond the warrants of life and fitness inherent in our Articles of Unity.'"

"You colonists are crazy," Michelle told him.

"As are you, Earth girl."

Michelle just laughed. "I don't have any deep, dark secrets. What about you, Matt?"

A chill shivered through Matt, and he stopped dead still. His Hellion almost overbalanced and fell forward. He forced himself to start walking again.

"Nothing like that," he said finally. Which was technically true. His secrets were a lot deeper, a lot darker. The silence stretched out. Matt sensed they were waiting for him to say something.

"Enough chatter," Sergeant Stoll broke in on all their channels.

Matt breathed a silent sigh of relief.

Soon, a tank came into view. Matt raised his MK-15.

Fighting never felt so good.

Next, Matt and Kyle got paired on something that looked really simple at first: take out a single Taikong tank.

This tank wasn't a crawling shell, though. This was the real deal. Or real enough. When Matt stuck his head out of an alley, the thing damn near took it off with a well-placed shell. Fragments of concrete showered down on them, and the booming report echoed through the city.

"Shit. That's real ammo," Kyle said.

"Wanna try it yourself?" Matt asked.

Kyle's Hellion shook its head. His Mesh had gotten a lot better; his Mecha now mimicked his bored slouch, cocky walk, and snappy salutes almost perfectly. Still, he was trying. Matt had to admit he didn't seem to be just a silver-spoon kid there for a thrill.

Instead, Kyle tried circling around to the other side of the tank. Matt watched Kyle's tag move through the city grid on his NPP. But the moment he poked out his head, the tank almost took him out too.

"Damn thing's fast!" Kyle said. "New plan. I say 'Go,' we both jump out, and the one it isn't targeting takes it out. Fireflies. Full burst."

Matt bristled at Kyle's presumed command, but it was a solid plan. "Ready."

"Go!"

Matt jumped out. The tank's short turret whipped around toward him as Kyle stepped out of his alley just a moment later.

"Oh, shi—"

That's as far as he got. Matt's world went red in electric pain. He fell backward, thrashing. On his screen, a bright-red warning flashed:

CONTROL NEXUS FAULT

"Controller, what's wrong? Ma'am!"

"You were hit in our right-side upper Control Nexus. A known Hellion weakness."

Matt pushed himself up off the ground as Fireflies exploded from Kyle's Hellion, painting laser-bright trails to the tank. They enveloped it and the tank disappeared in actinic fire.

Matt tried to stand, but he couldn't keep his balance. He managed a few shambling steps, then stopped, gripping the concrete wall. His Hellion felt broken and clumsy.

"What's wrong with me?" Matt said.

"Your Control Nexus needs time to regenerate," Sergeant Stoll told him.

Matt finally noticed the tag in his screen:

CONTROL NEXUS FAULT: REGENERATING. 15 SECONDS.

But he had other problems. As the smoke from the Fireflies cleared, Matt realized, *That tank is still alive.*

A shell exploded right next to him and his Hellion hit the ground. All he could do was thrash. He couldn't get up again.

"Get in close!" Kyle yelled. "We have to hit its sensors with the MK-15 rounds as hard as we can."

"I'm down!" Matt cried. "Control Nexus fault."

"Come as fast as you can!" The chattering reverberation of MK-15 fire came from Kyle's direction. Matt twisted to look as the tank swung to target Kyle. The tank's targeting seemed uncertain; it narrowly missed the other Mecha.

Finally, a chime sounded. Matt's screen displayed the words

REGENERATION COMPLETE

Matt whooped and ran to help Kyle. His MK-15 barked a hail of slugs at the tank as the turret spun in confusion.

"Good! It's done!" Kyle said.

Matt grinned. He was healed and he had a weapon full of ammo.

"Stop firing your weapon!" Kyle yelled.

Matt jumped, the barrel of the MK-15 came up, and

slugs peppered Kyle. Even though they were light rounds, ripples deformed Kyle's Hellion as he fell backward. Sparks shot from its visor.

"I'm blind!" Kyle bit out. "Idiot! What's wrong with you?"

"I'm sorry," Matt said.

"You're an idiot. A hundred seconds of regen."

A little coal of anger glowed in Matt. "It was an accident."

"I bet it was," Kyle growled.

Silence for a long time. When Kyle finally spoke, it was to both Matt and Major Soto. "Major, I never did get to see how Superman fought. What do you say, sir?"

Soto's voice crackled over the comms: "I say it's stupid. But if you want to spar, have at it. No weapons."

"Got it, sir. Cadet Lowell, you have twenty seconds before your ass kicking."

"I don't want to fight."

"Scared?" Kyle said, standing.

"No."

"Then why are you backing away?" Kyle's Hellion dropped into a boxer's posture, hands clenching into fists. Matt swallowed. He'd never boxed.

Matt put up his hands in imitation of Kyle. He stepped forward. *How bad can it be?*

Kyle's Hellion's fist came up, blurring fast, and Matt's vision fragmented. The blow was like a sledge in his stomach. Dust flew out of his joints and he fell backward on the ground. The entire cockpit rang like a bell.

Matt scrambled upright as Kyle leapt at him, spraying chunks of dirt behind him.

The two Mecha met with a resounding clang. Matt raised his arms to ward off a hail of blows. Kyle switched to an uppercut and caught Matt's Mecha right on the chin. He fell on his back, skidding along the rough practice field.

Matt sprang at Kyle, his anger rising. He wasn't going to lose to this high-born asshole!

At the last moment, Kyle turned and crouched. Matt's momentum carried him over Kyle. Kyle grabbed him in midair and threw him to the ground. Matt's Hellion let out a metallic groan as Matt got the wind knocked out of him.

Kyle jumped on top of Matt and pinned him with a headlock. The feedback through his suit was suffocating. Matt flailed on the ground, trying to find purchase.

You don't wanna be on bottom, Pat said. *Don't stay down. Break a bottle over his head—anything.*

Matt pulled his legs up under him and pushed as hard as he could. Kyle bucked with him and his grip slipped. Matt pushed again, hard. The two Mecha flew five feet in the air. Kyle came down on Matt like an anvil. But in that moment, Kyle lost his grip on Matt's neck. His long fingers spun and whirred, trying to find a grip.

A bottle . . .

Matt pried a broken hunk of cement out of the dirt and brought it up fast on Kyle's head region. There was a deep metallic bong as the rock exploded to dust. Matt rolled out from under Kyle and quickly retreated.

Something fell from the sky. It landed between Matt and Kyle, shaking the earth under their feet. A Hellion. A Hellion with wings. Jet exhaust streamed from bulking apertures on its back, burning Matt's Mecha. Its tag read: MAJ. G. SOTO.

"You guys suck," Soto said. "How about a real fighting lesson?"

"Yes, si—," Kyle began, but that was as far as he got.

Soto's Mecha moved, blurring by fast. Kyle's Hellion was suddenly on the ground, writhing in pain.

In one jump, Soto was on top of him. His Hellion's arms flashed like obsidian spikes.

Matt got up and charged Soto's back, but Soto flashed out of the way at the last second, hurling Matt over his shoulder to land face-first on Kyle's Mecha. The entire simulated city rang with their impact.

Soto stood with a foot on the two downed Mecha, laughing. "Think you're hot? You're still babies."

Matt felt rage blossom in his mind like a nuclear flower. Except it wasn't just his anger. It was Kyle's dark thoughts about his father, standing over him like a tower, telling him, *You will never let a lesser man beat you.*

Wait. What was that? Was that real?

Are the Mecha connecting them somehow? Connecting their thoughts?

And there was something else. A buzzing, almost electric sensation wherever he touched Kyle's Mecha. He didn't know where his Hellion ended and Kyle's began. As if they could come together. As if they could work together. As if they could . . .

Merge.

Like the Flight Pack. But with two Mecha. Matt's thoughts echoed like a coin dropped down a pipe. They *were* sharing thoughts.

Matt's reached out and took Kyle's arm. Like a dream, his Hellion's arm dissolved and melted into it. Suddenly, Kyle's thoughts were bright and sharp: *No, no, no! Do it by myself! Stop it!*

Like drops of mercury, their Hellions flowed together. Reflective muscle bunched and coiled. Their arms grew larger, stronger. Legs expanded. Cockpits reformed. It was so much more amazing than Mesh.

Matt opened his eyes. He was dimly aware of mirrored muscle catching glints of light beyond the NPP, but it didn't matter, it didn't matter at all, it wasn't just him, it was both of them and Soto was yelling at them to stop it. It was too soon, and it was too dangerous.

The thing that stood on the practice field was two times the mass and size of a Hellion. Obsidian and fire, it towered over Major Soto's pristine Mecha.

Soto screamed at it. "UnMerge now! That's an order! Acknowledge, cadet!"

Soto's words were so far away. Unimportant. Instead, he chose to run toward Soto. The giant Mecha took a few jerky steps as Kyle's thoughts reverberated. *No, no, don't. Not now. Please let's just listen to him!*

Soto's Hellion pounced, driving spikes deep into the Merged Hellion's Control Nexuses.

Matt screamed in agony, and his consciousness snapped out into complete whiteness.

When he awoke, he was back in his Hellion . . . and Kyle was back in his.

They sat on the ground opposite Soto's Flight Pack–equipped Mecha. The major stood in his open cockpit, looking down at them, expression cycling between disgust and awe.

Matt wasn't surprised when everyone steered clear of him in the cafeteria, or when they ran through their exercises with him gingerly the next day, as if expecting him to try to absorb them too.

What did surprise him was Major Soto showing up on the doorstep to his tiny little apartment, dressed Mecha-casual, and looking profoundly nervous.

"May I come in?" Major Soto asked.

Matt stood openmouthed for a moment. Then: "Of course, Major."

Soto went and took the seat in front of the tiny desk. His eyes skated off Matt's face to dart around the room, as if he were looking for something to comment on. Of course, there was nothing, not even Matt's old Imp model.

Matt couldn't let the silence stretch any longer. "Sir, if this is about the unauthorized Merge the other day, I've been reading up on it, and I'm sorry—"

Soto laughed. " 'Sorry,' he says."

"I don't understand."

"You're sorry. For one of the most amazing feats I've ever seen." Soto shook his head. "It takes a full Mecha Corps member—not a cadet—months to learn how to

Merge a Hellion with a Flight Pack. To Merge two Mecha, it takes the better part of a year."

Matt stood stock-still, staring.

"It seemed natural, sir."

Another laugh. "Natural. Okay."

Matt waited for Major Soto to speak. When he did, his mouth pulled down into a deep frown. "We have an opportunity for you."

"You don't seem happy about it."

Soto eyed Matt, his face still grim. "We're already running too fast and loose." He sat back in his chair and sighed. When he looked at Matt again, new respect showed in his eyes. "We've been lucky because most of the old Corps are military. So far. But this is no way to run training. Roth knows it, but this is his game, so we play by his rules...." Soto trailed off. He stood back up and paced, visibly uneasy.

"What's the opportunity, sir?" Matt asked.

"Running a full First Exercise. Up on the surface. Hellion with real ammo, weapons fully enabled, realistic assignment."

That's what I saw coming down from the Displacement asteroid, Matt thought. *Those green sparks flying through the clouds. Visible from space.* He shivered with excitement.

But why was Soto so rattled?

"Sir, if you were in my position, would you take it?"

Soto turned to fix Matt with a steady stare. "At your age, of course I would. Now I'm old enough to say, 'Whoa, that might be a bit much a bit too soon.'"

Matt nodded.

"But I'm not the one who's being asked," Soto said. "Only answer that's worth a damn is yours. So, what's it gonna be, Superman?"

8

EXERCISE

The next day, Matt's Hellion rode the rails up from underground Training Camp City to stand alone on the surface.

To his right, an amber sun bloomed over the steel-colored Atlantic, backlighting the black bones of the long-dead launch platforms. Behind him, the rust-stained block of Mission Control squatted. Inside, bright blue-white lights glared through slit windows. He imagined Sergeant Stoll sitting at her console and Soto brooding over her. In that moment, he saw everything as a whole, as if from outside himself.

It was a haunting, powerful scene: the fluid chrome of his Hellion set against the ruins of the birth of human spaceflight. Power rising from the Earth once again.

Every cell in Matt's body resonated with excitement in the infinite confidence of Mesh. Soto was wrong. This wasn't too fast. This was going to be easy.

Easy as pie, Matt thought, remembering Michelle's words.

"Transmission garbled. Repeat." Sergeant Stoll's comms icon popped to the fore of Matt's NPP.

Matt felt his face go red. He didn't realize he'd spoken out loud. Then he grinned. "Easy as pie."

"Easy as what?" Sergeant Stoll asked.

"Pie."

"Pie, as in the ancient American dessert, or pi as in the irrational number?"

"As in the dessert."

Silence for a time. Matt imagined Sergeant Stoll's brow furrowed in silent rebuke.

"What if it isn't?" she asked.

"Isn't what?"

"Easy."

Matt laughed. He was in a Hellion, high on Mesh. He'd Merged before any cadet should be able to. *Everything* was easy.

"Enough team-building crap," Major Soto's voice came through the comms. "Are you ready, Cadet Lowell?"

"Yes, sir!" Matt couldn't help coming to attention.

"Yes, sir," Stoll said.

"Cadet Lowell, your assignment today is to recover Universal Government ambassador hostage Petra Novograd from Corsair Confederacy Attachment Seventeen."

Data streamed onto Matt's viewscreen. Attachment 17 was one of the more violent splinters of the Corsairs. They did the usual piracy thing, but seasoned it with a side of sadism. According to Matt's display, they were located in the town of Cochran's Cove about one mile to the north. Their offensive and defensive weapon profiles both read UNKNOWN.

"Do you understand the situation, cadet?" Sergeant Stoll said.

"Yes, Sergeant Stoll," Matt said.

"Your assignment is to recover the hostage with zero civilian involvement," Stoll told him. "Acknowledge assignment."

"Acknowledged, ma'am." In the darkness of his Mecha, dim glints of metallic muscle twitched in anticipation.

"Begin assignment."

Sweating in his skin-tight silicone control suit, he lifted one foot and felt the giant Hellion respond. Around his tiny Mecha pilot's chamber, biometallic muscles flowed and clenched.

And Matt's lips curled up. *Easy as pie.*

He turned his Hellion north. Gleaming leg muscles tensed, and suddenly he was gone, parting the morning mist like a juggernaut.

They had Cochran's Cove set up like any of a hundred dump-and-dip towns on any water world on the edge of humankind's expansion outside of the Union. Easy to dump your cargo in the muddy bay, and great to dip your overheated drive in for a quick cool-down and reprovision. Matt had lived for days or weeks in a hundred towns like it, gagging from the reek of dead fish cooked by the waste heat of ships and freight.

The outskirts of town were built from the detritus of space: shells of old drop cans, silo containers, end-of-life solar panels, pop-up Insta-tents. The town proper was the grim, poured-cement architecture of lowest possible price, pocked here and there with artillery fire.

From one of the taller buildings, the thousand-daggers flag of the Corsairs fluttered, bloodred on white. The Corsair ships—and Matt's hostage—were undoubtedly in the bay. That meant Matt had to go through the town. Where the Corsairs could have entire battalions hidden.

As Matt sprinted into town, the crack of AK-47s split the damp dawn. Matt grunted as depleted-uranium bullets spattered off his Hellion's skin. They were a small annoyance. He was too high on Mesh; every thought turned seamlessly into action, every movement a sensation of ecstasy.

It was amazing. The painful tear of the suit had fallen away. Matt was only peripherally aware of the thrusts and jabs he made with his arms and legs, and of the flowing and bunching of the biometallic muscles in the dark around him as the Hellion responded to his commands. He was no longer inside the cramped cockpit in the Mecha's chest. He'd stepped through.

Now the itch of the bullets was joined by the dull pain of heavy artillery. Matt winced as shells struck the Hellion's chest and arms. But it was still a distant irritation through the pleasure of Mesh.

A smartshell flashed at him, and Matt's arm suddenly flared with acid-dipped pain. He screamed in frustration as the giant biomech lurched and fell against a pockmarked building. Matt thrust with his half-dead arm, trying to regain his balance, but he couldn't get up.

CONTROL NEXUS FAULT, his screen read. The countdown to regeneration began: 42, 41, 40 . . .

He flailed on the ground. More smartshells appeared on his viewscreen, dotted lines of destruction arcing at him from the bay. They closed the distance, flicker fast.

"Reposition," Sergeant Stoll said.

"Trying!" Matt said. The smartshells arrowed at him.

At the last moment, Matt crouched and sprang blindly. His Hellion crashed into another building and flailed helplessly, but the missiles impacted harmlessly on the tarry road.

A new, bigger group of smartshells appeared on Matt's screen.

Matt levered his Hellion upright, sweat dripping from his forehead. His viewscreen counted down seconds—30, 29—to complete healing, but he didn't have time to wait. He couldn't risk another wild leap either. The missiles blazed at him—and this time they'd surely calculated his maneuverability.

Fireflies, Matt thought. His mapping algorithms flashed to the fore, but Matt ignored the screen. *There. There. There.* He could feel the enemies.

Tiny Firefly rounds, white-hot and semismart, sprung from his Mecha's chest, flashing toward the artillery. For a moment, Cochran's Cove burned brighter than midday, all the color leached in the radiant light of the Fireflies. Matt had momentary glimpses of terrified holographic faces before the Fireflies extinguished the artillery gunners forever.

His kill list scrolled four names and reported the all-important status: NO COLLATERAL CASUALTIES. Even more important, the regeneration chime sounded. Matt sprang to his feet.

"Easy as pie," Matt said.

Sudden heat flared in Matt's chest, doubling him over. Through slitted eyes, he saw the source of the attack: a tank. His screen tagged it as TAIKONG X-6/LASER PLASMA CANNON.

Matt danced forward. "Okay," he said. "Let's play."

In three long jumps, Matt crashed down on top of the Taikong tank. It cranked its laser cannon toward the sky, but the tank was painfully slow. Matt reached down with a skeletal hand, picked up the Taikong, and shook it like a rattle.

Two more tanks rounded a rough stone building, lasers blazing. The Hellion's biometal glowed in the lasers' attack. The pilot's chamber was suddenly a convection oven. Matt felt his exposed skin crisping. But he never flinched. Flexing the Hellion's muscles, he crumpled the tank and threw it at the other two. The Taikong wreckage struck the ground and spun, taking laser fire and spraying molten orange metal. The tank struck one of the others. Both went up in a brilliant burst of fire.

But the last Taikong kept coming. It was different from the others. It gleamed like Matt's Hellion, though its flanks didn't ripple with biomechanical muscle.

The Taikong's laser tracked Matt as it sped forward. The dull red threads turned bright yellow. Matt pushed through waves of heat and grabbed at the tank, but his Hellion's fingers only scrambled for purchase on its slick surface. Matt tore at the tank's laser cannon. It came off in a burst of plasma and sparks. Matt glimpsed the faces of the white-painted men inside the tank—eyes wide, mouths open in a scream.

Matt took the tank in both hands and held it. He felt something welling up, something that felt very, very good and that strained for release. A low rumble built within his Hellion's core. Blue waves of force exploded from both of its palms. The tank blazed white and vaporized.

Seconds later, the dull boom from Matt's Fusion Handshake echoed back from distant swamplands.

Matt hung limp, for a moment drained by the power of the Fusion Handshake. He hadn't even known it was enabled. He hadn't thought. He'd just . . . imagined it.

"Cadet Lowell, update situation," Sergeant Stoll said.

Matt panted and said nothing. *Easy as pie, and fun like nothing else.*

"Update situation!"

Sergeant Stoll's tone was urgent. Matt looked up—

—right into the eyes of an Imp-class Mecha, painted with the thousand-daggers insignia of the Corsairs.

Matt froze. Corsairs didn't have Mecha. Nobody had Mecha except the Universal Union. For several long moments he remained openmouthed, unable to move.

But Imps were ancient. His toy Imp had been hugged to sleep for a dozen years while he dreamed of the day he might drive his own. But Imps were pure mechanical tech. Not much more than overgrown Powerloaders. Nothing like his Hellion.

The Imp lumbered at him. It was almost comically slow, but then it managed to slam into him with a force like a billion-ton cargo freighter. His Hellion's feet came off the ground. Matt gasped, the wind knocked out of him. For a moment, Matt wanted to laugh. He was flying through the air in the arms of a childhood toy.

The Imp shoved his Hellion through the side of a concrete building, sending metal desks and wall screens and filing cabinets and office chairs flying in every direction. Boulder-sized chunks of the building showered the Mecha. Matt glanced the kill list, which showed NO COLLATERAL CASUALTIES.

Then the Imp started trying to pull Matt's arms off.

Matt screamed. A high and pure note, echoing in the tiny pilot's chamber. His Hellion's muscles tensed around him, writhing in sympathetic pain. Matt pushed frantically at the Imp, but the old Mecha was strong. Immensely strong.

But he wasn't going to get beaten by a toy. Matt couldn't

get his hands together for a Fusion Handshake, but maybe he could use an RCM. He triggered the missile, then wondered . . .

What'll happen when it explodes between us?

BOOM. The Hellion's chest cavity rang like a bell, and Matt's vision went blurry.

But the Imp was off him and reeling. Matt shoved it backward and triggered his Fireflies. They scorched out the Hellion's torso, enveloping the Imp.

But the Imp stepped through the brilliance, seemingly unhurt.

Matt didn't think. He rushed. Speed was his advantage. The Imp barely moved before Matt had his hands around its head. Matt looked down into the dark eyes of the old machine and softly said, "Good-bye."

As he triggered the Fusion Handshake.

It was awesome. It was ultimate power. It was the end of all things. Matt shivered in delight. The ancient Mecha went purple with heat.

But it didn't disintegrate.

Matt had a single moment of complete and utter shock. The Fusion Handshake *ended* things.

An icy hand twisted his guts, and a rough and terrible voice whispered in his ear, *This isn't just an exercise. This is a test.*

A potentially deadly one.

The Imp reached for him, and Matt ran.

Toward the bay. Toward the Corsair ships. That was the only way he would complete this mission. Run in, smash and grab, get out. He had to stay away from that hellish Imp. It could have any mods, any weapons.

It could kill him.

Matt heard his own breath loud in the cramped pilot's chamber. He felt his sweat, suddenly freezing, between his skin and his interface suit. He remembered his first thought about this exercise: *easy as pie.*

Matt laughed. His Perfect Record only went so far. He could do a drill once and remember it forever, but this wasn't like that. This was unpredictable. *This is something I have to figure out.*

Buildings streaked past him, and the Imp fell behind. Through a gap in the buildings, he saw a patch of dirty water. The bulbous shapes of three Corsair ships squatted in the middle of the cove.

There! Get there, get the hostage, and get out. Speed was the key. Speed would do it.

Pain flared in Matt's back. Suddenly, he was flying headlong. Muddy dirt road passed beneath him. He splashed to a stop at the edge of the moat. Through his kinetic-feedback suit, the water on the Hellion's biometallic skin felt oddly soothing, like a warm bath.

He'd been shot. On the wraparound viewscreen, a dotted line traced the Imp's missile that felled him; the screens told Matt both his left and center nexuses were compromised. Damage to its muscles made them feel partially numb, like scar tissue.

He flailed in the water, trying to rise. But the Hellion's balance was shot. Even a random leap was out of the question.

Matt's viewscreen showed a large Corsair transport flanked by two smaller fighters. The transport was spinning up its ignition drive for launch. Steam rose from the boiling water around it.

Matt thrust with his legs and managed to flip the Hellion over. The Imp scuttled toward him, a slow-motion death.

Only a single chance clawed at the surface of his mind. "Zap Gun," Matt whispered.

A compartment sprung open in the Hellion's side. Thin fingers drew forth the Zap Gun, bristling with potential destruction. The thrumming tension of the weapon's antimatter heart permeated his senses. So warm. So comforting. So—

"Antimatter weapons are not recommended—" Sergeant Stoll's voice, her icon glowing on the screen.

But her voice was drowned out by the throb of imminent power. Matt raised the weapon and sighted.

"—for close-quarters combat." Stoll said.

She's right, Matt told himself.

But it was a fleeting thought, lost behind a tiny voice that gibbered *Easy as pie, easy as pie,* or another voice, not his own, that defiantly hooted in laughter and detached amusement. And as the Imp lumbered closer, something so primitive and ancient it shouldn't even be in space, let alone be able to withstand the blast of a Fusion Handshake, Matt also had to wonder, *What other surprises does it have for me?*

He pulled the trigger.

The air ripped apart. For long moments, there was nothing but the Zap Gun's brilliance. There was no Cochran's Cove, no Mecha Corps, no training camp, nothing but matter being furiously converted into energy.

The Zap Gun's beam touched the imp, sparking hundreds of shards of blazing, spinning, mirrored light. Where the shards touched nearby buildings, glass shattered and concrete flowed in red rivers. Rebar flashed to vapor, and contents blew to dust. For a moment, the Imp stood as a black outline against the spectacle, and Matt had time for two coherent thoughts.

—damn it, zero-permeability coating, damn it, damn it—
and

—the whole town is burning, the whole town is burning—

before the Imp simply blew away like the last fragile embers of a fire.

His kill list lit with words that gripped his stomach in a painful vice: COLLATERAL DAMAGE: 1 CIVILIAN CASUALTY.

Of course. The Zap Gun should never be used in a town. It was too risky. Of course someone would get hurt. Of course someone would die.

"Mission failure," Sergeant Stoll said. "Terminating."

"No." Matt's voice was low, almost a growl.

"Cadet, your mission is terminated." This time Major Soto.

"No!" It didn't even sound like him.

Sergeant Stoll, slow, commanding. "Cadet Matt Lowell, your mission is terminated. Return to base."

"No!"

"Cadet Lowell, this is Major Guiliano Soto. You are ordered to return to base. Acknowledge your orders."

For a moment, it seemed like a good idea. For a moment, Matt saw himself acknowledging the order and going back to the base. But then the desire to compete and be the best tugged at him again.

"Orders acknowledged. I will return to base when my assignment is complete." He wasn't going to lose to an Imp.

Behind him, the Corsair transport rose in a column of steam and shimmering fire from the bay. The afterburn of its orbital rockets sizzled on Matt's back.

Voices yelled, but he was done listening to them. It was time to finish the mission. Do the impossible. Easy as pie.

As if in response, Matt's regeneration chime sounded. Matt stood.

One of the Corsair fighters screamed toward the sky, following the cruiser, making Matt think, *All I need to do is fly.*

Matt thrust into the cove, splashing great white sheets. When the water was deep enough, he dove straight down. His Hellion's hands came together and changed form. His head tucked in. His legs came together and joined. Suddenly, his Hellion was something like a cross between a shark and a submarine.

Matt shot at the remaining fighter like a torpedo. For a moment, he saw its pilot looking back at him, eyes blank behind his helmet. Other crew members tried to swing weapons toward him as talons sprung from the Hellion's fingertips to pierce the fighter's skin. Instantly, Matt felt something like a bond with the fighter, as if it were . . . something he had known for a long time. A friend.

"You will not Merge with unauthorized components!" Major Soto's voice thundered out of the comms. "Emergency abort! Cut power!"

Matt reached deeper within the fighter, seeking its core, whispering to its simple-minded computer control. A strange thought, sudden in its intensity: *Merging is universal. Merging is what all things wish for.*

Matt's Hellion melted into the fighter, veins of his living metal running deep within the dumb alloy, rerouting, reconfiguring, and regrowing. Merging. Changing.

The thing that rose from the bay wasn't the fighter anymore. It wasn't the Hellion either. More than anything, it looked like a bat. A spiky black, metallic bat with fusion-tipped fangs.

Somewhere deep inside, Matt hung in his control suit, pressed close against pulsing metal muscles, not hearing Lena's commands or the curses of Major Soto. There were only two things: the Corsair freighter ahead of him, spewing overheated nuclear exhaust as it raced toward orbit. And the insignificant peninsula of Mecha Training Camp, falling away below.

"Come on, come on, come on," Matt muttered, lost in Mesh, unaware he was muttering, unaware that he wheezed painfully in the thinning air, unaware of the sweat beading into icicles on his forehead.

Something happened behind him. At first just a feeling. A tremor of incredible power. It coursed through Matt's mind.

The merged Mecha sensed it. His POV swung sickeningly as sensory enhancement kicked in. The screens zoomed down through the haze of the atmosphere to focus on Launch Facility 99. Matt started, dimly remembering his ride down in the shuttle. Less than two weeks ago. It seemed an eternity.

The broad concrete expanse of Launch Facility 99 split in two, revealing a grand cavern almost completely full of water. Rippling shadows of brilliant lights and black scaffolding enveloped a barely visible red shape.

In the scaffolding, something moved. Something like a Hellion, its mathematically perfect curves shaped into a brilliant equation of Armageddon. This beast was twice the size of a Hellion, and its rippling metallic skin was tinted bright red. As if it didn't have to hide. As if nothing could hide from it.

Then, with an eardrum-compressing boom like a close-range energy grenade, the thing leapt from the pit.

A fiery speck rocketed at Matt.

Another surprise, he thought. No time to think about it. The escaping Corsair freighter was close. Close enough to touch.

Matt's razor-sharp hand prodded at an engine pod. Matt clenched his fist, feeling the exquisite pleasure of tearing metal. The cruiser sang back at him, wishing to Merge. The whole Corsair freighter listed sharply to one side as an engine sputtered. Matt had one glimpse of the curve of the earth against black sky speckled with stars and time for one coherent thought: *Oh, shit.*

The Corsair ship tumbled out of control, and Matt was stuck along for the ride. Earth and black sky strobed sickeningly as they whirled.

Matt closed his eyes and thrust his hands deeper into the ship. It wanted to Merge. If he completed the Merge, he could save himself.

Something hit him hard. For a moment he spun even faster, seeing nothing. Then the earth steadied beneath them. Clinging to the scarred hull of the freighter was a giant red Mecha. It was easily three times the size of his Hellion.

Even in the depths of Mesh, Matt's mind gibbered: *This isn't an exercise. This isn't a test. Someone is playing with me.*

Hot rage exploded, and Matt lunged at the red Mecha.

Before he'd moved a yard, the giant machine closed the gap and grappled with him. Matt tried to twist out of its grip. But it held his arms seemingly without effort.

Then it ripped off one of his arms. Matt squealed. He'd never felt pain so intense. His vomit spattered on the floor as his left arm fell useless at his side.

The red Mecha pulled off his other arm. In the tiny pilot's chamber, the noise Matt made didn't even sound human. He surged against the confines of the pilot's chamber, went rigid, and passed out.

As the mock Corsair freighter fell toward earth, the red Mecha ripped chunks of living metal off Matt's merged Hellion fighter. It revealed an egg-shaped mass of shining muscle, the remains of the Hellion's pilot chamber.

Green Florida coast grew close, swelling fast.

With a mighty rip, the red Mecha pulled the metallic egg from the Corsair and made a sonic leap. Leaving behind a speed trail of crimson, it shot upward just as the Corsair impacted murky swamp. Billows of steam rose golden in the morning sun.

Matt awoke in the swamp. His head pounded like after a night of doing shots of vacuum-distilled space whiskey. He squinted and raised a hand against the low sunlight.

His hand protruded from the ruptured sleeve of his interface suit.

What happened?

Matt pushed himself up, slipping in a tangle of silicone and dead, hardened biometal. A giant red Mecha towered over him like a skyscraper.

The Corsair. The exercise. Memory crashed back like a twenty-pound sledge banging into an anvil into his head. Every dumb move, every stupid mistake. *Easy as pie.* And his Perfect Record meant it was etched in his mind forever.

"Ah, shit," Matt said.

"Such eloquence," someone said. Someone familiar. Matt blinked against the sun and saw Dr. Salvatore Roth. The man on the balcony with the senator. The voice on the slate. Now standing over him. He was tall and slim, with a hard-chiseled, craggy face as immobile as granite. Dark pupils fixed on Matt, looking through him with no hint of emotion.

Matt realized Dr. Roth wore a control suit like his own. And that the chest panel of the red Mecha was open.

"You . . . your Mecha . . ." Matt asked.

Dr. Roth cocked his head to one side, but his expression didn't change.

"What kind of Mecha is that?" Matt asked, licking his cracked, bleeding lips.

Dr. Roth looked back at the towering red giant, as if seeing it for the first time. For a long time, he said nothing.

Then: "Demon class. Entirely new. I must admit, it was satisfying to finally test the least of its functional modes."

Matt nodded. In that moment, his only thought was primal: *I want.*

"I hoped for a more auspicious debut." For the first time, Dr. Roth's tone was judgmental.

Matt flushed. Nothing could change what he'd done.

"Which brings us to the key question. You killed a simulated civilian. You refused to obey a direct order from your controller. You disobeyed your commanding officer. You Merged with an unauthorized craft. Is there any possible reason you should still be a Mecha cadet?"

Matt looked down. Panic overwhelmed him. He'd never pilot a Mecha again. His dream . . . that Corsair . . .

But Dr. Roth waited, his expression unreadable, as if expecting an answer. A justification.

And there was no way that was a normal exercise, or even a test.

Matt squared his shoulders. "Yes."

"Yes, what?" Dr. Roth's expression didn't vary a millimeter.

"I should be a Mecha cadet. Because I did it. I did something nobody else could do."

Dr. Roth nodded just once. "Exactly."

Matt fell back exhausted in the stinking swamp, streaming tears of joy. He'd done it. He'd left it all out on the field that day. And he'd won.

Paramedics rushed up, bending over Matt. One of them scanned him with a little monitor and frowned at the readout. Another came back with a stretcher. Strong hands lifted Matt.

"Take him to the lab," Dr. Roth told them.

"Not the hospital?"

Roth shook his head. "No. The lab."

Matt frowned. *What does that mean—the lab?* Why would they take him to the lab? What was Dr. Roth going to do to him? Matt struggled against the paramedics. Rough hands held him down.

A hypo-spray descended, and Matt's world faded to black.

PART TWO

"Today we may say aloud before an awe-struck world: We are still masters of our fate. We are still captains of our souls."

—Winston Churchill

"One man's magic is another man's engineering."

—Robert Heinlein

9

DISRUPTION

Who are you?

The thought was like a whisper in the darkness, echoing down a long rock tunnel. Sharp memories of the dark corridors under Prospect beat at Matt.

Where did you come from?

The same whisper, stronger, more urgent. The feeling of chilly steel talons raking through Matt's mind. The smell of mildew. The prickle of static. Like the Mind Raze machine all over again.

Like the first time he got in a Hellion.

What has been done to you?

No longer a whisper. Loud, grating, like a steel sheet sliding across a rough-hewn stone floor. Far away, he felt himself thrash against his restraints.

Restraints?

Matt struggled through the darkness. Shadowy shapes coalesced and gained form. He oscillated in that strange place between dream and reality, sucking a void on one side and the chrome rails and crisp sheets of a hospital bed on the other.

Beyond the bed, cold blue-green light outlined hulking humanoid shapes.

In bed? In a hospital? What was wrong with him?

Memory came crashing back. His flight in the Hellion. Meeting the Demon. Dr. Roth's orders. He wasn't in a hospital. He was in Dr. Roth's lab. Matt convulsed, held down by straps at his wrists and ankles.

His heart pounded triple time as his vision cleared. He lay on a simple chrome gurney, clad in an interface suit. Beyond the bed, Dr. Roth sat in front of a panoramic NPP display. It showed an outline of a human body shot through with brightly colored tendrils. Most of the threads glowed brilliant yellow. Orange and red skeins twisted through the spine and brain. Small specks of green and blue sparkled at its extremities.

But the colorful screen paled in comparison to the wonders beyond. Black metal latticework framed a hundred-foot-tall transparent wall. On the other side, dim bluish lights illuminated a gigantic red Mecha: the Demon. The Mecha wavered as if through heat waves, and haze in the chamber made the vision seem almost dreamlike.

Not haze. Water. The chamber was full of water. And it was huge. Other shapes hulked in the distance, individual details hidden by algae and sediment.

More Demons hidden? Matt thrilled at the thought. *Or some other Mecha?* A powerful desire gripped him. What other wonders did Dr. Roth have in store? When would he unveil them?

Dr. Roth swiveled around to look at Matt. "Interesting. A notable resistance to forced neural interface. Let's try this again directly. Who are you?"

"What?"

"It's a simple question. Who are you? Answer it."

Matt shook his head. None of this made any sense. But what could he do? "I'm Matt Lowell. Mecha Cadet Matt Lowell. Why am I here? Where am I?"

Roth came to the side of the bed and bent over Matt. Roth's irises were dark, almost the same color as his pupils, and his eyes were oddly immobile, as if they were made of lead. His entire expression was so alien that Matt had to tamp down an instinctive revulsion. He forced himself to meet Dr. Roth's stare.

"I know you are more than just another cadet. What has been done to you?"

Matt shook his head, fighting panic. Did Roth know he was genemod, or whatever it was, exactly, that he was? In the display, purple skeins flashed and twisted through the body. Roth turned to study it, his expression unchanging.

"I—," Matt began, then closed his mouth, remembering more of Pat's advice: *When caught in a big lie, tell a small one.*

"I don't know," Matt said. That was true enough. He never knew exactly what his father did to him. He looked up and noticed the body outline shaded more into cool greens and blues.

"How is it that possible?" Dr. Roth's mouth twitched, a millimeter of amusement.

"I'm a refugee," Matt said. Also true.

"We know that the independent Displacement Drive ship the *Rock* picked you up from an unspecified world when you were six years old. Which world?"

Matt's heart skipped a beat. "I don't know."

The skeins twisted violent red-purple. "I know you're lying," Roth said, glancing at the screen.

Matt didn't know what to say. Should he just come out and tell Roth everything about his father?

"If you want to have any chance to pilot the Demon, I suggest you cooperate. Which planet?"

Desire, hot and intense, spiked through Matt. He couldn't help staring at the red Mecha beyond the wall.

"Prospect."

Roth's eyebrows darted upward. "No wonder they didn't record the visit. What did they do to you on Prospect?"

"I've already told you, I don't know. I know I'm different, but I haven't figured out exactly how. I'm still . . ."

"Growing into yourself," Dr. Roth said, nodding. He went to the screen, muttering into a voice interface and bending close to examine images that rushed by. When

Roth came back to the edge of the bed, he gave Matt another fractional smile.

"Matt Stanford Lowell, son of Dr. Oscar Stanford and Pia Lowell. Your father was part of the Union research team lost on Prospect. So, what gifts did your father bestow upon you before he was lost?"

Matt gulped. It didn't matter anymore. He would never run a Mecha again. No matter what Roth said, he was out of the program. He had to be.

"I assure you, I have no interest in discarding a prodigy such as yourself," Roth told him. "What sort of gifts?"

"Perfect Record," Matt said, a bit confused. Was Roth too curious about him to set him adrift?

"What is that?"

"I remember everything."

"And?"

Matt shook his head. "And nothing."

"Nothing?" Roth looked incredulously at Matt's cool-blue body image. "Nothing that you know of, perhaps? How deeply was your father involved with HuMax technology?"

"HuMax technology?" Matt shook his head.

"Don't prevaricate. Surely you know Prospect was a former HuMax settlement."

Matt's mind whirled. HuMax technology? Was that what his father was really doing? The "special things" the Union trusted him to look into? Was he digging into the history of the HuMax? Was that why the Corsairs—and the HuMax Corsair—had raided them?

"My father . . . was an archaeologist." Matt sputtered.

"I already know that, cadet. What happened on Prospect?"

"Corsairs." Matt's body image gyrated wildly in bright reds and yellows.

"How is it that you survived?"

"I took a Powerloader. Went at the leader."

Dr. Roth laughed, a cold, mechanical sound. "How perfect for a Mecha prodigy." He sat back, seemingly satisfied.

Suddenly, huge chunks of Matt's past fell into place in his mind, a seamless whole. That HuMax had been real. He was just posing as a Corsair. He'd been after the HuMax data his father uncovered.

But the HuMax were extinct! Everyone knew that!

But maybe the histories were wrong. Maybe some of them had survived. Which would mean that his father had been killed by a genetic Superman, a real monster.

Matt clenched his fists. Corsair or HuMax, it didn't matter. He'd find him and have his revenge.

And even as Matt's mind whirled, he couldn't take his eyes off the Demon, floating behind the transparent wall like a red specter. It almost seemed to be grinning back at him. He'd pilot that. He'd master it.

And he'd use it to make that Corsair pay.

Matt stumbled out of Dr. Roth's lab into the underground night. He stood at the edge of the darkened city. Purple-black clouds wreathed a sliver moon in the projected sky. Discreet red CLOSED signs glowed below the bars and restaurants. A few couples leaned on each other as they staggered down the street, barking drunk laughter. Matt's access card read: 3:12 a.m.

Matt trudged down the street toward Cadet Housing. Not a single light glowed there. Matt's legs were shaky and uncertain, and his head swam with fatigue. Probably like the rest of the exhausted cadets, but much worse, thanks to Roth's poking and prodding. All Matt wanted was a bed and some sleep.

Halfway to Cadet Housing, he passed a couple bent over the light of a phone. The screen's glare painted their faces stark and cold like death. Tinny voices shouted on the screen. The couple shared terrified glances, then took off.

What was that about? Matt wondered, turning to watch

them. He shrugged. It didn't matter. All he needed was sleep.

A lone man wearing a Mecha Corps uniform ran down the avenue, slate held out in front of him. On it, nuclear fireballs lit his face with orange actinic light.

Lights flicked on in the buildings around Matt. One, two, five, then a dozen. Cadet Housing lit up, every window blazing. Cadet shadows moved jerkily behind the sheer curtains.

Matt's access card shrilled. He fished it out of his pocket. The screen read: CORSAIRS STRIKE GEOS. YOUR BRIEFING AT: CADET HOUSING CAFETERIA. ASSEMBLE IMMEDIATELY.

Corsairs? Geos? It must have been a mistake. Geos was on of the Union's primary worlds. There was no way the Corsairs would hit the Union's core. How could they bypass the planetary defenses, the Union warships? It had to be just an exercise.

Still, Matt ran.

When he reached the cafeteria, it was already three-quarters full of screaming and crying cadets. Blinding orange-white flashes strobed from wall screens over the kitchen.

Matt pushed forward until he could see. The flashes were mushroom clouds. From low orbit, they bloomed like toxic flowers over the cities Moore, Heisenberg, and Woo. Three flashes, three great cities erased.

"That was Heisenberg!" a cadet cried. "My mom is in Heisenberg!"

The image cut to scenes of cities in ruin, suburbs burning red like hell under a halo of black smoke. Geos' sun hung like a dim, iron-red disk in the midst of the boiling clouds. Brown-gray dust coated the orchards beyond the city, casting everything in shades of ochre. A newscaster wiped blood from her eyes and pushed back dirt-caked hair. She opened her mouth to say something, then broke down sobbing.

An inset of the Universal Union Prime, Kathlin Haal,

appeared on the screen. Her face was thin and drawn with
anger. She promised aid from the Union and vowed retribution on the Corsairs who'd struck the world.

This wasn't an exercise. The Corsairs had hit Geos, and
they'd hit hard.

A terrible anger swept over Matt. He felt himself flush
in hate. He wanted to do only one thing: get in the Demon
and smash every Corsair in the universe.

A pair of hands grabbed Matt and turned him around. It
was Michelle. Her hair stood out in crazy sleep spikes, and
her eyes were sunken from lack of rest. Her rawness made
her the most sympathetic creature he'd ever seen.

She grabbed him and hugged him hard, just for an instant. "You're back! We were worried!" She nodded behind
her where Kyle stood, looking at their embrace with smol-
dering eyes.

"Back?" Matt said. "What do you mean?"

"You were gone for three days."

Three days? The room swam. How long had he been under? What had Dr. Roth done to him?

But he couldn't think about that. Not now. Not with images of destruction streaming on the screens above.

"What's happening?" Matt said, nodding at the news.

Michelle shook her head.

"Someone nuked Geos," Ash said, joining the group.
She nodded at Matt. "Welcome back, kid."

"It's not nukes," Peal said, slipping through the crowd
with his slate held high. "There's no radiation. It's—"

"Displacement Drives," Matt and Peal said in unison.

"What?" Kyle grabbed for the slate.

Peal clapped Matt on the back. "Good deduction.
There's hope for you yet, refugee."

Matt nodded. It made sense. Displacement Drives
weren't hard to implement; only costly in terms of energy.
Drill a Displacement Drive into a bare asteroid, and pop it
into a gravity well to build velocity. Then pop it into orbit
aimed at the planet. The kinetic energy released would be

similar to that of atomic weapons, but there wouldn't be any radioactive cleanup. It would take a ton of planning to coordinate a simultaneous attack, but it was doable.

"Displacement Drives! What the hell?" Kyle snorted.

"The logistics are exceptionally complex, but it's absolutely possible," Peal asserted.

"They're getting smarter," Matt said.

"And more powerful," Kyle added.

No one spoke up, all in silent agreement.

Major Soto pushed through the crowd. At the front of the room, he muted the screens and called for order.

"Listen up, cadets—," Major Soto started.

"What's happening, sir?" Someone cut him off.

"Is it Rayder?"

"Get me in a Hellion. I'll take 'em out!"

"All of you shut the fuck up!" Soto thundered. "I'm not here to give you a full briefing, and I can't take questions. Here's what you need to know. First, Corsairs have struck Geos, using asteroid bombardment via Displacement Drive. Casualties are upwards of five million. Second, you should all expect accelerated training and deployment. Third … this is make-or-break time. We perform, and we're the heroes of the Union. The kind they put in history records."

And if we don't perform, it won't matter, because there might not be any Union to make the records, Matt thought. *If the Corsairs could hit us on Geos, the Corsairs could win.*

"That is all. Cadets, dismissed."

Among some grumbles, cadets moved toward the door. Matt continued watching the images of Geos on the screen, until Soto turned it off.

Matt turned to leave and saw something that sliced at him like a blade: Michelle and Kyle leaving together. Michelle leaned on Kyle, as if for comfort. Kyle had his arm around her waist, and she wasn't trying to shake it off.

Three days. He'd been gone three days. Not long.

But long enough for the world to change.

* * *

"Get up!"

Another terrible dream. Matt grabbed his covers and wrapped them tighter around him.

"Cadet Matt Lowell, get up!" Something tugged on his covers, hard. He tugged back.

"You are ordered to get up, cadet!" That angry voice again. Matt decided to open his eyes.

Bright sunlight streamed into his little Mecha Cadet Housing dorm, splashing Sergeant Stoll's face. The shadows made her look even stranger than usual.

Surprised, Matt let go of the covers. Stoll immediately yanked them off him. He was glad he didn't sleep naked.

"Your access card has been on alert for ninety minutes," Sergeant Stoll said. She flicked the buzzing device at Matt. It read, REPORT FOR MEETING, ADVANCED MECHAFORMS TOWER, ROOM 1248.

Matt groaned, his body still heavy as lead. Was it from the lingering effects of his Merge and rush to orbit, or was it from the rigors of Roth's tests? Matt didn't want to think about that. How much did Roth know about him? And, more important, what had Roth done to him? Matt didn't want to dwell on that disconcerting thought.

"A meeting?" Matt got up and headed toward the bathroom.

"You don't have time for that. Put on a clean jumpsuit."

Matt did as told and followed Stoll across the city. She walked ahead of him at double-time pace, not emotional enough to be angry, but clearly not happy.

In the Advanced Mechaforms Tower lobby, Sou Tomita grandstanded on a wall screen showing the Union News Network. The same Sou Tomita he'd seen talking to Dr. Roth. Matt paused for a moment to watch.

"Mark today's date," Congressperson Tomita said. "We will look back many years from now and say, 'This is the day the Corsairs began to fall.'"

"Come on," Sergeant Stoll said, stopping to cross her arms.

"Another minute won't kill them."

On-screen, Congressperson Tomita continued. "This day, the Universal Union invokes Constitutional Clause 13: Full Survival Measures. Yesterday's attack on Geos goes beyond any raid. It was a precisely planned and maliciously executed act of war, perpetrated by a force that would be considered a standing army in any state. For this reason, we are suspending budget oversight to provide our Mecha forces with the resources necessary to meet this threat—"

Sergeant Stoll grabbed Matt's arm and pulled him along. She was surprisingly powerful.

"What's your genemod?" he asked. "Strength?"

Stoll looked away. Finally, she said, "Of a sort."

Matt's face burned in embarrassment. "I'm sorry. For being so direct."

Stoll shook her head. "Why should you be? At least here, I'm valuable."

"What do you mean?"

"Mecha Corps embraces all advantages, no matter history or prejudice," Stoll recited.

Matt nodded. She was referring to the genemod paranoia that still resonated in the older generations within the Union. *Humans must stay pure,* they said. *Genemod leads to HuMax,* they said.

But parents will always try to give their children advantages. That's why, despite the prejudice, genemod was slowly coming back. Stoll's parents had probably tried their best to conceal the violet-eye marker. To make her undetectable but still special. Much like Matt's own father wanted for him.

Was that why he felt a distinct bond with her? Was that why he defended her from the start? They hadn't spoken much at all, but their engineered heritage implicitly united them.

She showed Matt into an elevator, punching the button for the twelfth floor. Room 1248 was a typical conference room: piano-black table, comfortable gray leather chairs, great view of the underground city beyond. Five people already sat at the table: Michelle, Kyle, Ash, and Peal were in a little cluster on one side, and Major Soto sat on the other. The air in the room was tense and electric, like a show just before it's about to begin.

"About time, coma boy," Peal said.

"Shut up," Major Soto said in his clipped, familiar refrain. Peal's mouth closed so fast his teeth clacked. "Take a seat, cadet."

Matt did as told, and the door opened. Dr. Roth walked in and took a seat beside Soto. The major's lips compressed into a thin line. He leaned away from Dr. Roth, as if he found the other man distasteful.

"Dr. Roth!" Kyle said, standing and holding out a hand. "It is an honor to finally meet you."

Dr. Roth stared down at Kyle's hand until he pulled it away. "I allow for physical contact only at specific times. But thank you for your gesture."

Everyone shifted in their chairs or found something else to look at during the awkward exchange. Roth didn't seem to notice, remaining basically expressionless.

Allow for physical contact? Matt thought, imagining all manner of invasive probes during his lost three days under Roth's supervision. He resisted an urge to pat himself down, looking for scars or other signs that he'd been tampered with.

Major Soto cleared his throat. "We've brought you here because of what happened on Geos. Does anyone have family there?"

Head shakes from the cadets.

"That's good news. Due to the attack, the Union is planning a radical offensive on the Corsairs."

"Was it Rayder, sir?" Peal asked.

Soto frowned and nodded. "But there's no official confirmation. There won't be. There was only limited ground activity."

"Ground activity, sir?" Matt asked, leaning forward. "Did they get surveillance video?"

Soto shook his head. "All video is classified, even at my level."

The room dropped into uncomfortable silence for a time. Ash broke it finally. "Why'd they do it, sir?"

"We don't know. A show of power as a prelude to demands, I'd expect. But there's been no credible Corsair faction to step forward and talk terms."

"Geos' most-advanced research labs are located in the three cities destroyed, sir," Peal said.

"Mecha technology?" Matt asked.

"No," Dr. Roth broke in. "They obtained no Mecha technology in the attack. Geos is not an active area for my Mecha research."

Peal frowned. "What were they after? What did they get?"

Major Soto held up a hand for silence. "We don't have all the answers. I promised yesterday that your training timeline would be moved up. This is a lot bigger than that."

Soto nodded at Dr. Roth.

"At this moment, Congressperson Tomita is introducing our latest Mecha, the Demon, to the Union," Dr. Roth said. At one end of the table, an NPP sprang to life, showing the huge red Demon towering over a black Hellion.

The cadets sat rapt, staring at the hologram of the huge new Mecha. In direct comparison, the Hellion seemed only half-formed, incomplete. Like a child's toy.

"Is that image to scale?" Peal asked.

"Yes," Dr. Roth said. "A Demon is thirty meters tall, and commensurately more powerful than a Hellion. However, that is not its most distinguishing feature."

Peal nodded.

Matt kept waiting for cadets to turn and stare at him, but nobody did. They didn't know about his adventure with the Demon, he realized.

"More significant features are in-built flight functionality, exceptional transformational capability, and exponential power increase when merged."

Soto broke in. "The Demon is the core of the Union's planned offensive against the Corsairs. An irresistible weapon for an irresistible force. The stated goal is no less than the complete elimination of the Corsair threat."

"Wouldn't Hellions suffice, sir?" Kyle asked.

Major Soto's jaw set grimly. "I don't make the decisions."

"And why are we here?" Matt asked.

Dr. Roth's heavy eyes fell on him. "To be the hope of the Union. I invite you cadets to become my Demonriders."

Matt's heart raced, and he felt momentarily light-headed. That same powerful need rushed through his body. He would absolutely do it, become a Demonrider. In that moment, Matt knew this path was what he was born for. His father had given him one hyperskill, and it got him this far. Now he had the chance to become one of the greatest pilots in the history of humankind. That would be up to him, his guts, and ability.

Kyle frowned and spoke up. "Why not use experienced pilots?"

Matt turned to him. He wasn't getting swept away in the excitement, and he was asking all the right questions. Matt had another moment of begrudging respect for his fiercest rival in the class.

Major Soto nodded vigorous agreement, glaring at Dr. Roth.

"Unlearning neural responses is an unresearched and dangerous challenge," Roth said. "Experienced Hellion pilots like Major Soto are deeply channeled by the Hellion interface, which is an impediment to learning the Demon. Perhaps a fatal one. I don't yet have enough data. I haven't had enough pilots to test."

Soto sat with his hands clenched, his entire attitude saying, *Just give me a chance.* But Matt couldn't shake the feeling that it was guinea pigs that Roth was really after. Lab rats hooked on the rush of Mesh. But for Matt the possibilities were too great to hesitate. *Revenge and glory first; ask questions later.*

Dr. Roth turned his attention back to the cadets. "You cadets have not yet been deeply affected by your Hellion experience, and you are the most advanced among your induction group. I expect you would make an exceptional team."

"I accept, sir," Michelle said first.

Always the most hoo-rah out of the lot, Matt thought. Always surprisingly beautiful and brave. But maybe she was like him, making the decision simply to run away from her past, to escape her dead-end future on Earth. Even in that way, they were aligned. Matt started to speak up, but he was beaten to the punch by Kyle.

"I'm in too, sir. It's a daring plan, but one we need to carry out for the sake of the Union."

Kyle and Roth both turned to Matt expectantly. Matt nodded, for some reason feeling a bit sheepish, "Yeah, I'm in too."

"No," Peal said.

Everyone swiveled, shocked. Peal blinked and blushed in the sudden examination. "I believe I can serve the Union much better as a Hellion pilot. I also would like to stay here with my brother."

"A noble half-truth," Roth said. "Retain this one as backup. Reassign both family members to Mecha Base."

Now everyone looked to Ash. She plucked at her lip, her eyes darting back and forth.

"We require a minimum of four components," Dr. Roth said.

Major Soto broke in. "Cadet Moore, we understand your special circumstances. We can arrange communication with your family, if you feel it necessary."

Ash nodded. "I thank you for that, sir. But I don't have to ask anyone's permission. I know what they all would want me to do. I'm in."

"Good. We're done," Dr. Roth abruptly said. He stood and left the room without another word.

Soto sighed. "You don't know how much I'd give to be in

your boots, cadets." Matt caught Soto's stare, and he could see he meant it. He was yearning for this mission.

"What does it mean, reassigned to Mecha Base?" Peal asked.

"It means you're still going to the same place they all are," Major Soto said while gesturing at the other cadets.

"And where, exactly, is that?"

Soto grinned. "You'll find out soon enough. Tomorrow we ship for Mecha Base, and believe me, it ain't a hospitality cruise."

10

BASE

Against the blue backdrop of Earth, the Displacement Drive ship UUS *Ulysses* looked more like a battleship than a converted asteroid. Except for a few rocky outcroppings along its equator, almost none of the asteroid remained. Everything else was hidden underneath human-made structures: squat buildings with tiny, slitlike windows; giant dish antenna arrays like impossibly perfect craters; huge swathes of battle-scarred steel armor; swollen gun emplacements; and even the carbon-lined pits of reaction jets.

Matt pressed closer to the tiny window of the shuttle to get a better look. Yes, those were fusion-reaction jets, the kind you'd see on a large freighter. That meant *Ulysses* had its own maneuvering capability. It was no immobile rock, completely dependent on its Displacement Drive. Matt marveled at the thought of an antimatter generator core large enough to move an asteroid. That was almost unimaginable power.

At the same time, a small voice asked, *Where is the balance between the power of the Union and the power of Dr. Roth? The* Ulysses *is impressive, but is it anything more than a giant Mecha transport?*

And Congressperson Tomita had just given Dr. Roth carte blanche. How did that change the balance?

But those questions were academic. Matt had too many more personal and pressing issues surrounding his future survival in combat and advancement through the Corps. What was it going to take to master the Demon? Did he have what it took? And should he tell everyone what happened on his first exercise in order to seek out advice?

And what about Michelle? She sat in the front row of seats directly across from Kyle. They'd been talking about their exercises for the entire shuttle ride. Apparently, they'd both been able to rescue their fictional ambassador. But they never mentioned the Corsair's Mecha. Did they even come up against one, or was that a surprise reserved for Matt?

Stark jealousy twisted at Matt's guts as he watched Michelle and Kyle talk on and on with gestures, grins, and playful touches. Michelle's hair floated free in zero g. She tried vainly to pat it down, as if she were trying to impress Kyle. Matt gripped the arms of his seat and tried to tell himself it didn't matter.

"Grab that any tighter, you'll break it off," Peal said, nodding at Matt's white knuckles.

Refusing to comment, Matt turned pointedly to look out the window. Guns on the Rhino-class warships surrounding *Ulysses* swiveled to track their shuttle. They passed by one close enough to read its insignia: UUS *Renegade*.

On the side of the *Ulysses*, a gray metallic expanse of armor split and retracted, revealing a pitch-black cavern the size of a city. The shuttle carrying the cadets advanced inside.

Coming out of the sun dazzle, Matt gasped. The *Ulysses* was almost completely hollow. Warships of every imaginable configuration berthed on every surface of the giant cavern like stalagmites of death. Rhino- and Hedgehog-class battleships. Cheetah-class fighters. Even a hulking Elephant-class troop transport.

And, among the ships, Mecha. Hundreds of them. Hellions, mostly. They stood dark and menacing, reflective surfaces like obsidian in the dim space. There were empty foot clamps along the floor for hundreds more.

Michelle and Kyle had fallen silent, each pressed against their windows, looking at the Hellions. Did they feel the same desperate pang that he did, the same uncomfortable need to get back in the cockpit?

The shuttle rotated toward an expanded-metal deck, where four giant red Mecha stood. Their Demons.

Up close, the Demon was a seamless personification of power. Bright red and mirror-smooth, its lines were more spiky and angular than the Hellions. Hundreds of apertures clustered along its sides, and striated metallic musculature flowed over its body. Serrated ridges ran down its upper arms and across its back. Its legs trifurcated as they joined the torso in three strong attachment points bulging with muscle. In comparison, its head was tiny, with a mere slit of a visor and two tiny protrusions, like horns, on top.

Only one Demon was complete. The three remaining Mecha swarmed with people in space suits. Biometallic skin was pulled back to expose mirror-finished sinew and muscle, glowing with fiber-optic data. One Demon's visor was open, exposing an array of conventional sensors grouped in support of four organic-looking orbs that looked uncomfortably like the eyes of an insect.

As their shuttle docked, Matt finally got an idea of the true size of the Demon. It was the height of a ten-story building—bigger than virtually every structure in Aurora University, bigger than anything Matt had seen outside of natural caverns in the *Rock*.

"Holy moly," Ash said, whistling. "We're gonna pilot that?"

"Reconsidering?" Peal asked.

"Not a chance, kid." Ash's voice was confident, but her eyes were wide.

Sergeant Stoll came down from the pilot's seat and opened the air lock. Chill air rushed in, bringing the familiar stale-rock-and-steel scent of a Displacement Drive ship. Matt sighed. In a lot of ways, this was like coming home.

They floated down a spotless steel corridor, though an

auto-security booth manned by a regular Union Army private. Michelle stayed close to the handrail, her eyes wide. Matt understood. This was her first time in zero g. Looking down a long hallway was a lot more disconcerting than being strapped in a small shuttle. She was probably fighting the vertigo that everyone got the first time out.

"How're you doing?" Matt asked.

Michelle's eyes flickered to meet his then went forward again. "Okay. It's—"

"You'll get used to it," Kyle said. "Keep your eyes fixed on one point; that'll help."

"Thanks," Michelle said, swallowing.

Preempted again, Matt thought

Once through security, Sergeant Stoll handed out new access cards. They showed a complex maze of tunnels and halls, most of which glowed bright red and RESTRICTED. The only green traces led to QUARTERS, MESS HALL, and UTILITY DOCK.

"Quarters?" Ash said, frowning at her card. "On a Displacement Drive ship? How long are we gonna be in here?"

Matt started. He hadn't even thought about that. It took only minutes to charge a Displacement Drive. You could Displace from one side of the Union to the other in a few hours, even with a maximum Displacement of twenty light-years. The only reason passenger ships took days to make the transit was the time it took to load and unload passengers and cargo. This wasn't a civilian ship. It wouldn't have those delays.

"How many Displacements are we doing?" Matt asked.

"Many," Sergeant Stoll told them.

"How many, ma'am?" Peal asked.

Sergeant Stoll shook her head. "I'm sorry, cadets."

"But we don't need to know," Peal finished her thought.

Stoll turned and led them down the hall. Matt followed the rest of the group. Michelle and Kyle floated ahead of him, talking in low tones. Michelle seemed to be doing better. She glanced back at Matt once, and her eyes weren't bugged with fear. He gave her a thumbs-up, and she grinned. That was a good sign. Some people had an impossible time getting used to microgravity, and you never knew until they were up in orbit. With his life spent on refugee ships, Matt had seen all sorts. Michelle seemed to be on a good track.

Each cadet got a tiny, individual cubicle constructed entirely of stainless steel. The only soft thing in the room was a thin mattress and tie-down webbing for sleeping. A wall screen showed a montage of Union News: images of Geos' bombardment combined with earlier video of Corsair skirmishes. On the bottom, a continuous scroll ran: A STRONG UNION BEGINS WITH U. UNION AND CORSAIRS AT WAR! SUPPORT YOUR UNION: ENLIST TODAY.

Matt turned off the wall screen. With the TV off, deep in the *Ulysses*, the only sound was the hum of the antimatter core.

Matt cursed silently. It *was* like coming home. A home he never liked being in and never wanted to return to. All he needed was his Imp Velcroed above his bed to complete the picture of a past he fought so hard to escape from.

The next morning, Matt found the group in the mess hall. Peal and Jahl sat at one table. Ash, Michelle, and Kyle sat at another. Velcro pads on the seats kept their coveralls stuck down, and magnetic strips on the tables ensured their gloopy Insta-Paks (micro-g/zero-g rated) didn't fly off. Matt shook his head and dug a spork into something that was supposed to be eggs and gravy, amazed at how much effort they put into making everyone behave as if there were gravity.

In an independent Displacement Drive ship, they'd have tables stuck everywhere—on the floor, on the ceiling, on the walls. Or it would be a free-for-all with nothing but handrails.

Crew wearing Union Army and Mecha Auxiliary uniforms filled out the rest of the attendance in the mess hall, but overall the crowd was thin. Union Army and Mecha

Auxiliary kept to their own tables, sneaking glances at each other from time to time. Neither group paid the cadets much mind.

Which makes sense, Matt thought. Roth and Tomita wouldn't tell the Union their fate was in the hands of newbie cadets. They were operating under a veil of secrecy about who was piloting the mighty Demons and where these savior machines were being stored before deployment against the enemy. Everyone in the Union could hope the plan to crush the Corsairs would work, but they didn't need to know the specifics. To the Army and Auxiliaries, Matt and his group were probably just another batch of raw cadets moving on to Mecha Base for some exercise.

Along one wall of the mess, a tiny strip of window looked out over the metal surface of the UUS *Ulysses.* The stars winked into another pattern as Matt watched. Another Displacement.

Matt took the table with Peal, who was reunited with his brother, Jahl. "Seventy-six," Peal said.

"Seventy-six Displacements? Since the first one you remember?"

"Till I stopped counting last night. If I calculate it out, based on average charge time, we've Displaced one hundred ninety-eight times since leaving Earth."

Matt nodded. If they were going in a straight line at maximum Displacement, that put them four thousand light-years away from Earth. He craned his neck to look out the slit window. None of the constellations were recognizable.

If they aimed an infinitely powerful telescope at Earth right now, what would they see? The pyramids being built? Lost civilizations in South America? The speed of light seemed almost laughably slow.

"What happened to you?" Peal asked Matt.

Matt shook his head. "When?"

"When you disappeared."

Matt hesitated, since he still hadn't figured out what to

say. Was there an angle? Everything was moving so fast. His Perfect Record was no help in deciphering his lost days in Dr. Roth's lab.

"We already know some of it," Jahl said. With a shock, Matt realized he wore the Mecha Auxiliary uniform, with a single stripe. "Unexpected orbital excursion in First Exercise, unprecedented capability, et cetera."

"It's great to see you again too, Jahl."

Jahl nodded in appreciation of the acceptance.

Peal was laughing. "We don't know about a tenth as much as we should. They clamped down on you hard after we pulled those summaries."

"A few tantalizing phrases were all we got," Jahl added.

"Enough to know you're probably the real reason Roth is creating this Demonrider program," Peal chortled.

Jahl shook his head. "Which makes no sense, since Hellions clearly could be used for a blanket Corsair assault, if we believe the public-capabilities assessment."

"Unless the Corsairs are more powerful than the public brief," Peal said. "Which would explain the extensive nonaccessible data on them."

"What nonaccessible data?" Matt asked, leaning forward.

Jahl chuckled. "If I knew, then it wouldn't be nonaccessible, would it? Though you probably could help us piece it together."

"I don't know what I can tell you," Matt said. "What I *should* tell you."

"We're friends, right?" Peal asked.

"Yeah, sure."

"Then between you and me, probably nothing."

Matt stopped himself before speaking. Was Peal playing mind games to get the info, or had he decided it would be better for his brother and him not to know any more?

For a while, the only sounds were the constant generator hum and the low murmur of voices from the Union Army and Auxiliaries. A smaller group of Mecha Corps in full blue uniforms came in, glanced at the cadets, then took their own table far in the back.

"I saw the Demon," Matt told the brothers. "It had to come into orbit to get me."

Peal's mouth dropped open. "How'd you get to orbit in a Hellion?"

"I Merged with a Corsair fighter."

For long moments, the two brothers only stared at each other. Finally Jahl held up a hand. "That's enough. This convo is already flagged, and I don't need them compiling any more data on me."

Laughter from Kyle and Michelle's table made them all turn and look. Michelle grinned and waved at them, as happy as Matt had ever seen her.

Peal said softly, "You were gone, therefore washed out, therefore there was only one logical choice. Or so I suspect."

"You don't understand women," Jahl said.

"And you are such a gigolo," Peal shot back, rolling his eyes.

Matt stirred the glop in his Insta-Pak. "I don't know if I want to know any more, anyway."

Jahl turned to Matt with a measure of compassion. "She may have fallen into orbit, but you can boost out of it."

Matt looked over at the other table. Michelle stared out the window, oblivious to his gaze. But she did look remarkably comfortable. As if she would never want to be anywhere else. Her first time off Earth and under such duress. She was handling herself with uncanny class. How could he not be a little jealous?

"The real question is whether or not we'll survive the boredom on the way to Mecha Base," Jahl said.

Jahl was trying to change the subject. *Fine*. He'd go along with it.

Matt pulled out his access card. "Well, we could go to the utility dock, whatever that is."

"What?" Peal grabbed the card out of his hands. He

frowned at it and showed Jahl, who shook his head. "Look at this. Wonder kid gets to go somewhere we can't."

"What do you mean?"

Peal showed Matt his access card. The only green areas were the mess hall and his quarters. No utility dock.

Matt took his card back, his fingers numb.

"Sounds like it's time for you to do a little exploring," Peal said.

The utility dock turned out to be a large, pressurized space adjacent to the UUS *Ulysses'* landing bay. Steel shutters covered its observation windows. Red NO ADMITTANCE indicators glowed next to the shutters.

Matt stopped at the air lock. Its door screen showed nominal air pressure inside the dock. So it was technically safe to enter, but did that mean he should just barge in?

A powerful vibration rattled the air-lock handrail, and a metallic buzz filled the air. A series of sharp bangs followed, echoing through the chamber. Matt lost his grip on the rail and had to grab for it again.

Then the buzzing morphed into a keening ululation that was all too familiar: a Mecha scream.

Matt swiped his card and shot through the air lock. Inside the utility dock was a thrashing Demon. Thick alloy shackles at its right wrist groaned and bent, pulling head-sized mounting nuts off their secure bases on solid-steel deck.

Another tug and the Demon's forearm popped free. It whistled through the air only meters from Matt and carved a bright gouge in the stainless wall. Matt caught the inner handgrip and ducked back into the safety of the air lock.

He risked another look. The Demon's heels beat thunderous metallic music on the steel floor. Its free arm clawed at its own chest, as if in agony. Strips of red biometallic metal flew. It was tearing itself apart.

What the hell is happening? What should I do? The air-lock's comms panel read SECURITY HOLD.

With a final groan, the Demon tore off a roof-sized piece of its chest. Red biometallic shards, gray optical cables, and blobs of clear fluid flew outward, spinning wildly in the microgravity. The Demon gave a final convulsion and lay still, its visor rolling over to look at Matt.

A body drifted above the Demon. Tiny and gray with death in its interface suit, it was clearly a pilot.

Matt shoved off the air lock and flew above the Demon. He intercepted the pilot, and his momentum carried them both toward the walls of the dock.

The pilot was soaked with sweat, his just-starting-to-gray hair slicked back as if with pomade. His mouth hung open, his face slack. Matt jumped in recognition. It was Major Soto.

Matt felt for Soto's pulse. It was strong and fast.

"Major Soto?" Matt asked.

Soto didn't respond.

They reached the far wall. Matt pushed off and guided them back to the air lock. He reached it in time to meet Sergeant Stoll and an Auxiliary carrying a zero-g stretcher.

"What happened?" Matt asked.

"You should not be here!" Stoll snapped as they started strapping Soto to the stretcher. "Go back to your permitted area."

"I am permitted, ma'am." Matt showed her his access card.

Sergeant Stoll shook her head. "They're all fools."

"Who is, ma'am?"

Sergeant Stoll pressed her lips together and looked away.

"Damn it, what's going on here?" Matt yelled.

"I shouldn't tell you anything," Stoll said. Then she softened. "That's not entirely accurate. I don't know what to tell you."

"Tell him the truth," Soto croaked. All three snapped to look at the major. The whites of his eyes were bloodred, and one side of his face twitched spasmodically.

Stoll sighed. "Major Soto is using his authority to self-train as a Demonrider candidate," she said.

"Training authorized by Dr. Roth," the major croaked.

"He'd be happy to see you die, as long as he got his data!" Sergeant Stoll snapped. Her face registered a brief moment of surprise, as if she'd never expected to be so frank.

Major Soto managed a coughing laugh. "I'll pilot that Demon, and it won't be the last thing I do."

But it just tore you out of its pilot chamber, Matt thought, looking at the floating debris. The Mecha had tried to destroy itself to get rid of him. Why would a machine reject its pilot? That wasn't like a machine; that was like . . . something alive.

Soto coughed again. Bright red bubbles of blood flew in the air, drifting off into microgravity.

"Get him to the infirmary," Sergeant Stoll said. She and the other Auxiliary pulled the major away.

When they were gone, Matt pushed off and floated up to the Demon. The hole in its chest exposed gleaming bunches of metallic muscle, intermittently flickering optical fibers, and strands of wet, dark-red fibers that looked almost organic. The pilot's chamber interior was featureless and dark.

Matt reached out to touch the Demon's chest, half expecting it to come to life again. The beast was entirely still, but its metal flesh was warm. Like an animal's.

Like a living thing's.

Matt shivered. What were the Mecha, and why had they granted him access? To see Major Soto fail?

Or maybe . . . to bond with it?

Mecha Base was a hidden place buried in bedlam.

Matt knew the moment they arrived. *Tick. Tick-tick. Ping! BANG! Tick.* The mess hall crackled like an old Geiger counter, punctuated every few moments by a deeper *BOOM.*

Matt's Perfect Record took him back to the time the *Rock* had Displaced into the edge of a planetary ring. It sounded something like this. Of course, the *Rock* wasn't armored. Back then, every ping or tick was followed by the sharp hiss of air jetting into space and the shouts of repair crews rushing to patch the damage. They Displaced out as soon as possible—right into orbit around a planet held by the Corsairs. The tribute they asked was a small price to pay for their lives, but the *Rock*'s citizens had been forced to half rations for the next six months.

But why would the *Ulysses* Displace into a ring system? Matt hurried to the slit windows, followed closely by Peal and Jahl. The rest of the cadets weren't around.

Above the pockmarked armor of the *Ulysses'* surface, the velvet darkness of space was replaced by layered, brown-red clouds of dust, like a sunset sandstorm on Prospect. Far off, a pinpoint of brilliant blue-white light glowed, haloed with sun dogs.

POCK! A pebble bounced off the armored deck just outside, leaving a ten-centimeter divot. That explained the ticking. It also explained the beating the *Ulysses'* armor had taken in the past.

"Perfect," Peal said in a reverential tone.

Something rose over the *Ulysses'* horizon, and Matt gasped. It was the largest structure he'd ever seen in space: an asteroid fifty times the size of the UUS *Ulysses*, covered by massive scaffolding supporting spalled, pockmarked armor shields.

In the shade of the armor, two Displacement Drive ships nestled within. Both were built to the same insane level as the *Ulysses*, with thick armor, heavy guns, and maneuvering thrusters like a battleship. Sunlight glinted off an armored protrusion on one of the ships, highlighting its name: UUS *Vulcan*. The other ship's bridge was hidden in darkness, its name unreadable.

Based on the size of the Displacement Drive ships, the

giant asteroid had to be at least ten kilometers in diameter. Not a single light shone on it, but the black barrels of heavy weaponry poked strategically from its surface, and swarms of space-suited humans, small as dust motes, surrounded the Displacement Drive ships.

A large rock glanced off the asteroid shields, soundlessly spinning off into space. Matt swore he saw the scaffolding flex.

Peal grinned. "Perfect location."

"You know where we are?"

"Unless I'm mistaken, we're in the middle of a solar system in the process of formation. Most likely within an agglomeration of matter that will someday condense into a planet."

"Why?"

"Where else would you hide the most strategic military base in the Union?"

Matt stared, openmouthed.

Peal shrugged. "It's not like this mud will condense into a planet overnight. There are undoubtedly orbits here that will be stable for decades. The trick is finding them—"

BANG!

"—and not getting destroyed when the condensation takes place."

Matt nodded. "So why is this perfect?"

"First, there's no reason to ever look here. Extrapolating travel time and number of Displacements, we're at least eighteen thousand light-years out. Beyond the edge of the Union. Maybe even beyond the edges of the First Expansion. What's out here? Nothing."

"Unless they're aliens."

Peal gave Matt a don't-be-stupid look. "Video-melodrama aliens don't exist."

"What about Centauri B?" Jahl said.

Peal crossed his arms. "Floaters? They're just plants."

"They sing."

"Pattern making isn't necessarily intelligence," Peal told him.

Matt nodded. Even though there was a lot of alien life, it tended toward the simpler end of the spectrum: seaweeds, mosses, grasses, simple flowering plants, scaled reptiles and amphibians. Some of it was even recognizable by human standards. Some was just downright strange. But it wasn't like humans had to worry about getting eaten by the alien equivalent of saber-toothed tigers, or dying of some alien plague. The worst humanity had encountered were some funguslike organisms that grew in the warm, moist environment of the human lung. But even the fungi didn't grow well in an alien host. It took years to die of Green's disease.

And humanity didn't have to worry about war or trade with another intelligent species. The universe was empty and quiet. It was one of the things his xenology professors on Aurora argued about constantly: Why were there no other intelligent species? There were dozens of theories, shading from scientific to theological, but none of them had ever been proven.

Of course, when you went digging into whys, you ended up with a lot of them. Why didn't Displacement Drives work on ships of less than a billion metric tons? Why did they only work in a range between two and twenty light-years?

"Second," Peal said. "Who's going to pay attention to a system that doesn't even have planets? It's worthless. Not even a gas giant to dive into for volatiles."

Matt nodded as Michelle and Kyle joined them at the window.

"What the hell?" Kyle said, pressing his face against the pane.

"Please do not interrupt the lecture," Peal said. "Third, even if you dropped into the system for a quick look-see, what are you going to find? Nothing. You're not going to take chances Displacing into the mud. Not without armor like this tank. Even if you did, what would you find? Nothing. Unless you're right on top of the base, you'd never see it. Absolutely perfect location."

"What the hell is he jabberin' about?" Ash said, rubbing sleep out of her eyes.

Peal was all too happy to explain it again. Matt tuned them out as they neared the asteroid.

The moment the *Ulysses* reached lee of the shields, the Geiger counter ticking stopped. In the darkness, details emerged: a giant wall of metal set into the side of the asteroid, punctuated by air locks. The comforting glow of light from hundreds of windows.

And a giant insignia, etched a hundred feet tall into the metal: MECHA BASE.

Inside Mecha Base, the first stop was Colonel James Cruz's private quarters. Intricately patterned carpet provided grip for the cadets' Velcro soles. Rich wood shelves held protective racks for ancient books. The colonel, a man in his midsixties with charcoal-gray hair and a slim, ascetic face, squatted behind a mahogany desk. Whip-thin, he gave the impression of wiry, tense muscle wrapped in a crisp uniform that only barely held him back. His chest carried many colorful bars.

Colonel Cruz waved the cadets to soft leather chairs with discreet lap belts. Sergeant Stoll and Major Soto remained standing.

"So this is the hope of the Union," Colonel Cruz said, his eyes piercing each cadet in turn. He didn't sound happy.

Stoll and Soto stood rigidly at attention and remained silent. Matt waited for Ash or Peal to say something dumb, but they remained quiet as well.

"You realize this operation won't remain secret for long," Cruz said. "As soon as you fire up the red skyscrapers, jaws will wag. And Corps members get jealous."

"We understand, sir," Major Soto said.

Cruz blew out a breath. "I still say go in with a full battalion of Hellions. Unfortunately, I am not the sole decision maker in the Union."

"No, you aren't," said another man as he slipped in through Colonel Cruz' office door. He was fiftyish, chunky, just starting to go gray, and dressed in a severe gray suit with a small Union star pinned to the lapel.

Matt jumped with the electric shock of recognition.

"Yve?" Matt asked. "Yve Perraux?"

The new guy turned to look at Matt. For a moment, a flicker of unease passed over his face, but he hid it in a broad smile. "Matt Lowell? I heard the name, but I never thought it could be Matt from Prospect."

Matt couldn't do anything except stare. Yve Perraux. Head of security on Prospect. The guy who that fateful day warned his father the Corsairs were coming.

"How . . . did you . . . get all the way out here?" Matt asked, thinking, *How did you survive?*

Yve glanced away before meeting Matt's eyes. "I could ask you the same thing."

"Care to explain the connection, Mr. Perraux?" Colonel Cruz cut in.

Perraux snapped to attention. "I worked with Matt's father on Prospect. Union Advanced Research Labs."

Cruz's eyes widened. "UARL. Understood." He turned to Soto, Stoll and the cadets. "Mr. Perraux is the Universal union liaison to Mecha Corps and the Biomechanical Technology Group."

Yve smiled at them all. "That's a fancy way of saying I'm the guy on the ground who gets to keep an eye on Dr. Roth for the Union."

Colonel Cruz grumbled, his words too low to be intelligible.

Yve turned to Cruz. "It also means I'm the guy who talks sense to the Mecha strategic leadership."

Cruz's jaw clamped down, and he didn't say anything for several beats. When he spoke, it was as if he were struggling to keep his voice calm and reasonable. "I still insist Hellions are less risky than new, untested tech with raw pilots. If we hit him right, we have the lever to force a deal."

"Work with the Corsairs?" Kyle spoke up with his steady and proud voice. "Sir, I have a hard time with that."

"You're putting words in my mouth. Deals can be unilaterally devastating."

"I'm sorry, sir," Kyle said.

"And what would you have us do, out of curiosity?" Cruz asked.

"Wipe them out, sir. All of them."

Colonel Cruz shook his head. "You're young. So young. Listen close. The Corsairs aren't just people. They're an idea. They're the Freecycles with cutlasses, the Aliancia with atomic weapons. You can't wipe out an idea. You can only hope to turn it sour."

"There are other considerations as well," Yve said, sharing a long look with Colonel Cruz. "Odds for a decisive victory are much higher with the Demon-led strategy. Without that pivotal victory at this point in this conflict, there is the possibility the Corsairs could be forged into a single power block."

"And if that is the case," Colonel Cruz said, "God help us all."

Yve Perraux begged off as soon as they were out of Colonel Cruz' office, telling Matt to look for him in the Decompression Lounge after his commanding officers put some exercises with the Demon under his belt.

Matt's access card glowed almost entirely green. It was easy to see the path to the Decompression Lounge, a small space next to a red-colored area labeled MECHA HANGAR. Only half of Mecha Base asteroid was tunneled out; its far half showed completely dark.

Matt wanted to head down to the Decompression Lounge immediately, if only to silence some of the voices ricocheting around in his head. What, exactly, had his father been working on? How did Yve manage to get away? And what was he up to now?

But Soto warned them, *Go exploring, expect to get hazed. Or worse.* Mecha Base was already buzzing about the arrival of giant new Mecha, and everyone throughout the vast base was chattering, wondering who'd get first crack at them. Nobody was guessing it would be the newly arrived cadets.

Matt made himself go down to his quarters. He was so intent on following the green lines on his card that he almost bumped into Michelle. He grabbed the corridor rail and squeaked to a stop not a meter away from her.

Michelle stood by a pair of the tiny windows, her face painted in the orange-red light of the dust clouds outside. She wore a curious expression, as if joy and sadness warred in equal measure in her mind.

"I never thought I'd see anything like this," Michelle said finally. Her voice was soft and far away.

The slit window revealed dazzling, layered, orange-brown clouds. Diffuse sunlight made individual pebbles and rocks glitter like metal chips. Far-off flashes arced in the clouds of dust and gas. Matt gasped as he saw a clearly defined lightning bolt slash through the murk.

"Lightning?" he said.

Michelle shrugged. "Jahl said it wasn't surprising. Something about the friction and static electricity and power density in the dust cloud."

"Our encyclopedic brothers; so many factoids between the two of them," Matt said. They both burst out laughing.

"I'm sorry," Michelle said, turning away from the window to look up at him. Her face was so close. Matt leaned down toward her.

Michelle pulled back and turned away. Matt silently cursed. They both looked out at the maelstrom for a time, while rocks ticked off Mecha Base like rain.

"Sorry about what?" Matt asked, finally.

"For—," Michelle began, then started again. "If it seems I've been avoiding you. I—I didn't think you'd come back."

"Neither did I."

Another silence fell. Matt searched for words, but couldn't think of anything. What could he possibly say to her?"

"I'm jealous," Michelle told him.

"Of what?"

"Stoll says you're the prodigy. The way she talks, we wouldn't be here except for you."

Matt's face burned with embarrassment. "What does she know?"

"I know she likes you."

Matt said nothing. There was nothing to say. *I had my chance,* Matt thought. *And I blew it.*

Michelle turned and put a hand on Matt's chest. He hoped she couldn't feel the thundering gallop of his heart. "Look, I want you to know, since you're the best pilot we have—"

"You can't say that."

"Yes. I can. And I want you to know that I'll do everything I can to make this the best team possible. Whatever it is between us that we're figuring out has to wait. There's war first."

She was echoing what he had been telling himself since he first saw her that day in the marsh: *This isn't why you're here. You have more important things to do.*

Still, something irked him. "What about Kyle?"

She laughed. "For a richie rich, he turned out not to be so bad. He's easy to be around."

"Easy?"

"He's helped me get through this. I'm not like you. It's not so easy for me, and everything is so sped up now. In that meeting back there, I really wanted to say, 'No, not yet. Let me be a Hellion pilot instead.' But I just jumped up and said, 'Yeah!' You . . . I'm afraid with you and me, it'd be like that—"

"Like strapping into a new Mecha?" Matt finished for her.

Michelle nodded, saying nothing. She turned back to the window. He wanted to put a hand on her shoulder. But that would be wrong. The time had passed. They were as far away from each other as Earth and Mecha Base.

"Not exactly a romantic place," he said, looking out on the collapsing planet.

Michelle pulled herself closer to the glass. "No," she said, softly. "But it's the perfect place for a Demon."

11

DEMON

"Aaah, gross!" Ash cried.

Matt grinned. It was one thing to know the Demon used a new magnetorheological gel-suspension system to protect the pilot during extreme maneuvers. It was another thing to get into the Demon's cockpit and slither past blobs of snotlike slime clinging to the biometallic muscles. Small globules floated in the middle of the cockpit, dropping slowly toward the floor in Mecha Base's microgravity. The Demon's cockpit was tighter than a Hellion's, and it contained no harness. There was a single connector for the interface suit and cap, and a complex face mask made of opaque plastic.

Matt's body slid past the ID plate. This one read:

ADVANCED MECHAFORMS, INC.
DEMON SN00000 REV 0
"GENESIS"

Serial number zero? Was this the Demon Dr. Roth had rode into orbit around earth? Somehow that was more unsettling than getting into the Hellion Serghey died in.

Matt shook his head. It didn't matter who piloted the Demon before him. He'd ride it all the same.

He plugged himself into the interface-suit connection and tentatively put the mask over his face. It was completely smooth inside. How was he supposed to see out? He shrugged and pressed it on. Warmth flared on his cheeks as the mask bonded tightly in place against the cap. Metallic-tinged air filled his lungs. For a moment, he was alone with the hiss of the respirator and the thudding of his own heart.

Then the display lit, and Matt's eyes widened. It was as if he was seeing the entire dock from a new vantage point, one that was a thirty meters above the deck. The Demon's viewpoint.

He turned his head, and his POV shifted fluidly. The mask display was much more realistic than NPP. The only thing that indicated he wasn't seeing the scene firsthand were the data overlays that tagged every item in the dock: serial numbers of Hellions and Rogues, service dates for the same, names and ranks of Auxiliaries.

Matt grinned. "Nice." In his mask, the comms icon lit: DEFAULT: DC M. LOWELL → ALL

More icons lit. A sudden cacophony of voices. "Nice?" "What's he talking about?" "The visual interface, I think."

A new icon lit: SGT. L. STOLL → ALL.

"If you have not yet fitted your visual-interface mask, please do so now. We are closing hatches and hardening the suspension gel."

Wet warmth touched Matt's ankles and slowly spread upward. He looked down reflexively, but saw only the De-mon's chest and the expanded-metal floor of the dock.

Stoll continued, her voice oddly tense. "I will serve as controller for this introductory exercise. Colonel Cruz, Mr. Perraux, and Major Soto are present as observers. Dr. Roth will give the mission brief."

Sergeant Stoll's icon went dark, replaced by: DR. S. ROTH → ALL.

"You have two goals today." Dr. Roth's voice was flat, almost bored. "First, Mesh. Meshing with the Demon is more challenging than with the Hellion. Your Hellion ex-perience will not be a guide. Recall you were chosen over many more qualified pilots specifically for this fact. Malleability is key."

Malleability? Matt wondered. What was Dr. Roth molding them into?

"Second, following successful Mesh, you will move to general exercises. If there is capability, we will begin training for fourth-order Mesh."

"Fourth order?" Ash asked.

Seconds ticked by, long enough for Matt to wonder if Dr. Roth would answer. Finally, Roth said, "Each Merge increases the power of the Demon's configuration exponentially. Two Demons square power output, three cube it, and four raise the total output to the fourth power. Each Merge also enables additional operational configurations."

The warmth reached Matt's neck, and it felt like slimy wetness touching his exposed skin. He shuddered. What happened if his mask failed? Did the Demon have failsafes, or would he drown in the tiny, dark pilot's chamber?

"Will we Merge with flight components, Dr. Roth?" Kyle asked.

"No. Unlike the Hellions, there are no external components. Note the thrusters along the aft side of the Demon."

Sergeant Stoll's icon lit again. "Please note that all weapons systems will be enabled for this exercise. Use them with extreme care."

Matt's gaze went to an overlay in his POV, listing out
WEAPONS SYSTEMS:

FIREFLY
SEEKER
HANDSHAKE
ZAP
X

"What's the X weapon?" he asked, smiling at the notion of the button.

"It is not enabled in the base configuration," Dr. Roth said, his voice hardening.

"But what is it?" Matt insisted. Roth was like an insane toymaker. He'd know that X would be too tempting for them to resist, but he'd put it in there anyway. Just like he knew you didn't put the Union over a barrel—but look at him; he had Tomita begging for more. What was the secret of his magic technology? What was he hiding?

"It is an antimatter matrixing weapon capable of distributed annihilation of multiple targets," Dr. Roth said. "It is only enabled in Merged configurations, as it can be destructive to the Demon."

Only in Merged configurations, Matt thought, disappointed. But even their base weapons were insanely dangerous with inexperienced pilots and with all the rock and gas flying around them. Why didn't Roth just turn them all off? The most logical answer was also the most frightening: because they couldn't.

Because they rushed the Demons through to completion. Because Roth's ideas and execution were faster than safety precautions could keep up with.

He didn't want to know the whys anymore. Maybe not ever. He was a Demonrider, and he was in the most powerful piece of fighting gear in the known universe.

The ooze rose past Matt's forehead. He felt momentary pressure; then everything fell away and he couldn't tell where his body ended and the Demon began.

There was now tactile feedback. When the air lock opened, Matt felt the remaining air rush past his skin. When the powered cargo loaders came to drag him out, their serrated metal grips were cold on his arms. The coupling between man and machine was much more complete than with the Hellions.

The loaders parked the Demons near the edge of Mecha Base's armor. The maelstrom churned and flashed outside. Swirling bits of dust and rock glittered in the sun. Beside him, the soft light of the sun made the other Demons glow.

"Beginning full Mesh," Lena said.

A new tag flashed in Matt's POV:

INITIATING NEURAL MESH: COMPLETED

As the word COMPLETED flashed—

It was like embracing an atomic explosion. Matt opened his mouth to scream, but nothing came out.

This isn't real, isn't real, isn't real! Matt's thoughts ricocheted, rising toward a shrill panic.

Far away, something like scratchy laughter broke the silence. A thing that smelled of dust and crackled like static gibbered in the darkness. Rusty talons reached out for him, clawing though his mind.

No! Matt thought, recoiling. The thing laughed and pulled him closer.

No, no, NO! he thought. Each thought like a hammer blow. The thing fell away. His mind sped from thought to thought.

How had he ever felt any pain? This was wonderful!

Matt laughed. Meshing with the Demon was more than a high. It was the perfect feeling of well-being distilled into its essence. This was how he'd wanted to feel his entire life. Weightless. Carefree. Like a perpetual Sunday morning. He wanted to spend his life in here.

Senses came back to him. He hung suspended in the lee of Mecha Base, watching wan sunlight make the dust and rocks sparkle like diamonds. He was completely present, completely there. There was no difference between his body and that of the Mecha. The rush of energy, power, and strength reverberated through him, thrumming with more life and consciousness than he ever thought possible.

Matt raised a hand and flexed it. The Demon's sharp, precise fingers flashed in the light of the young sun. He was ready. And in that moment, he knew: *I can do anything!*

Matt grabbed the edge of Mecha Base's armor and hurled himself out into the maelstrom.

In the hail of dust and rock, Matt's Demon automatically adapted. His arms fell to his sides, merging with his body to form a continuous, streamlined shape. His legs flowed together. Matt's Demon was now a giant red shark looking for prey.

Inside, the ping and tick of hundreds of rock fragments filtered through the suspension gel. Matt laughed at the tickle of smaller grains and winced as larger shards stung. Tags floated in his vision, identifying dangerously large pieces of rock and the different kinds of spiraling gasses. A conic of the maelstrom showed increasing density down by the protoplanet's core, where space rocks had ground smooth like river pebbles in a constant ebb and flow of tide with gravity.

Let's see what's up above, Matt thought, exhilarated in the wonder of exploration. He'd never felt so free!

Brilliant white matter-antimatter jets flared on his backside, rocketing his Mecha up through the dust and gas. Redbrown clouds gave way to the blackness of space.

Icons flashed in his POV:

**DEMON 00002: "BERITH": MICHELLE KIND —
FULL OPERATION
DEMON 00003: "ASTAROTH": ASH MOORE —
FULL OPERATION**

More data overlays tagged the stars. The sun closest to him was labeled 09-428A.56.182.10. The orange cloud of condensing matter below him was labeled 09.428A-02-(FORMATIONAL). Other stars were tagged with their names. The only one he recognized was Rigel: 10,870 LY MEAN DISTANCE.

Rigel was almost nine hundred light-years from Earth. Which meant they were nearly twelve thousand light-years away from humanity's first home. Matt shivered. The brilliant pinpoints of light seemed so distant, so incredibly unattainable. Space itself was quiet, like 3:00 a.m. on a frontier world, where nothing and nobody was moving. Anything could happen.

A comms icon flickered: K. PETEROV → ALL.

"Help." Kyle's voice was soft, almost a whisper.

Kyle? In trouble? A sudden thought overwhelmed Matt, amazing in its intensity: *He deserves it! Let him struggle!*

But it wasn't Matt's thought.

Get off me! Matt yelled in his mind. Again, something recoiled from him, receding far away into the darkness.

Michelle's comms icon lit. "Kyle, are you all right?"

"It's too close," Kyle's voice quavered in fear.

"What's too close?" Michelle asked.

"I don't know!" A scream.

Matt powered back down into the maelstrom. In his POV, tags identified Mecha Base and the rest of the Demons. All three still huddled under the protective armor. Kyle's Demon was doubled over, twitching. Its tag read:

DEMON 00001: "RAMIEL": KYLE PETEROV— OPERATION ENABLED

Matt jetted to a stop in front of Kyle, briefly lighting his Demon with dazzling antimatter exhaust. Kyle reached out as if for help. Whimpers came through the comms.

Dr. Roth's words came back to him: *It's more challenging than Meshing with a Hellion. Don't expect your previous experience to be a guide.*

Matt gritted his teeth. He knew what Kyle was cowering from. It was the same thing he was barely controlling.

"Push it away," Matt told him.

"No! I can't! It's . . . like something alive—"

Finally, Dr. Roth broke the silence. "Figments of your own mind. Subconscious feedback is a by-product of the Demon's enhanced neural Mesh. Cadet Peterov, you have thirty seconds to complete Mesh."

Matt grinned. Suddenly, he knew exactly what to do.

"You aren't going to let me win this one, are you, Kyle?" Matt gloated.

"What?" Kyle's voice, suddenly sharp.

"I've already flown the Demon. Hell, I've been out of the dust cloud. I've seen the sun. It's easy. Easy as pie."

Kyle growled.

"I mean, come on. Next you'll let me steal your girl."

With a roar, Kyle's Mecha rocketed at him. Matt's screen showed new status:

DEMON 00001: "RAMIEL": KYLE PETEROV— FULL OPERATION

Kyle barreled into Matt, raking the Mecha's sharklike form with his long claws. Matt rocked from the impact, but Kyle's sharp-bladed fingers only scrabbled for purchase on Matt's seamless hide.

"Okay, Kyle, that's enough. You're fully operational."

Kyle kept clawing at him, growling unintelligibly. He brought his hands together in a familiar gesture, and brilliant yellow warnings lit on Matt's screen:

FUSION HANDSHAKE ENABLED

Oh, shit.

Matt slithered out from Kyle's grasp just as the shockwave hit. Expanding ripples of fusion power roiled the dust and gas. Matt and Kyle went spinning away in opposite directions.

"Cadet Peterov, cease weapons use immediately!" Stoll yelled, angry as all hell.

Kyle's Demon lit attitude jets and stopped its spin. For a long time, it didn't move. Finally, its visor snapped up to fix on the other Mecha.

"Sorry. I—I lost control," Kyle said, through a ragged breath. "I've got it now."

"It's all right," Matt told him, as he stopped his own spin. "I know what you were fighting."

"Thank you," Kyle said, softly. His comms icon read K. PETEROV → M. LOWELL.

Matt turned his own comms to the private channel. "You'd do the same for me."

"Of course," Kyle said, his voice strengthening. "We're Demonriders."

They started with basic piloting exercises, diving deep within the gas clouds, down to the core of the protoplanet. Building-sized chunks of rock churned within a hailstorm of smaller boulders, hidden in a fog of pebbles, dust, and gas. Huge shapes rolled out of the mud like juggernauts, passing within meters of the darting Mecha.

Each Demon had become a streamlined, sharklike shape. Each slightly different, as if reflecting the rider inside. Matt's was the sleekest and most pure. Kyle's was covered by swept-back spines, like a porcupine. Ash's was long and narrow, a pure thunderbolt of energy. Michelle's was shapely and smooth, but her arms were still separate from her body. She used them to push off a caroming ball of rock, changing direction in an eye blink.

"Michelle, did you do that deliberately?" Matt asked.

"Do what deliberately?"

"Keep your arms out to push off rocks."

"I didn't really think about it."

Matt decided to try it himself. He shot at an asteroid-sized chunk and imagined vaulting off of it like a pole-vaulter. His arms separated from his body, and one of his fingers transformed into a long, thin pole. The pole touched the asteroid and bent. Matt felt it shivering as tension mounted. He slowed, stopped, and then rocketed forward from the force stored in the pole. As he shot off the rock, the pole and his arms melted back into his sides.

Matt laughed like a maniac. It was incredible! He raced through the mud, caroming off house-sized boulders.

A skyscraper-sized rock loomed in front of him. Matt yelled and hit the thrusters, but it was too late. He crashed right into the asteroid.

The Demon's pilot chamber reverberated, and Matt gasped for breath. His viewpoint spun. Arms appeared and flailed. White-hot jets blasted to regain his balance.

Two asteroid-sized rocks came right at Matt, threatening to crush his Demon between their bulk. Matt fired every thruster full on, trying to get away. But the asteroids clapped together behind him, spraying his Demon with shards from the impact.

Matt flipped over and put his hands out in front of him, triggering a Fusion Handshake. The shock wave vaporized the sharp rock fragments and pushed him back like a rocket.

"Hell, yeah!" he yelled. This was the best feeling in the world.

"Enough play," Dr. Roth's voice cut in, his comms icon lighting in Matt's POV. "Sergeant Stoll, have the cadets begin their exercises."

They were asked to play a coordinated game of hide-and-seek, deep down in the core. Hiding in the dark, caroming off giant asteroids, weapons lighting the darkness. For a short time, it was like being a kid on Prospect again, playing Union and Corsairs. Set against the most mind-blowing backdrop in the universe.

Suddenly, Matt's backside exploded in heat and fire. He screamed loud enough to rattle his face mask. Bright light blinded his rear sensors. He whirred around and caught a glimpse of a tiny metallic sphere whizzing by him.

"Weapons drones," Sergeant Stoll said over the comms. "Consider them adversaries."

Matt grinned. So it *was* Union versus Corsairs! Again, the feeling that he was born to do this came over him.

Bright laser light flashed behind Matt and Ash yelled in pain. Matt turned and triggered Fireflies. A short burst annihilated the silver drone.

"Thanks, kid," Ash said.

"No problem."

It was amazing, like being let loose in a zero-g arcade with unlimited credit. Hell, with artillery! The drones would hide behind rocks and attack in small groups. As soon as Matt and the others learned to anticipate them, it was easy to dispatch the drones. He rushed ahead of the others, a hell storm of annihilation.

"Leave some for us!" Kyle cried.

Matt laughed. He'd do it all! No need for the others! He plowed through clouds of drones, and Kyle, Michelle, and Ash followed.

Matt pulled back from a cloud of drones rounding an asteroid and let the others take them on. Michelle and Kyle tumbled through the drones, clumsily shooting in little bursts. Ash barreled right in, cutting a swath straight through.

I'm still better than them, Matt thought. Another alien thought. He pushed it to the back of his mind.

"They hit me side-on, but there wasn't any Control Nexus fault," Kyle enthused when the sky was clear.

"Demons don't share that Hellion weakness," Dr. Roth told them.

How comforting, Matt thought.

"Enough of the drones!" Kyle yelled. "Send Hellions. Let's have some real action."

"No," Dr. Roth said. "From what I see of your progress already, you'd kill the Hellion pilots instantly."

The Decompression Lounge was a small space carved out of the solid rock of Mecha Base. Along one side, a floor-to-ceiling wall of glass looked out over the Hellion docks, where dozens of Mecha stood at ready. A polished aluminum bar ran along the opposite wall, with a pressure door behind it that opened on a small kitchen. Matching minimalistic aluminum tables and chairs were anchored to both the ceiling and the floor to maximize the available space, like they did on an independent Displacement Drive ship. Still, the modest crowd stuck mainly to the "down" side of the bar, seemingly reluctant to give up their illusion of gravity.

Matt grabbed a handrail just inside the Decompression Lounge, surveying the crowd. It was mostly men and women in Mecha Auxiliary uniforms, with one trio of Mecha Corps captains talking about the "giant new red Mecha." They only glanced at Matt as he entered. The news about the Demon pilots must not have made it out yet.

On one of the inverted tables, a single man in a dark gray suit sat with an empty coffee bulb, staring out over the Hellion docks. Yve Perraux.

Matt launched off, flipped over, and stopped himself at the seat opposite Yve.

Yve looked up at him, his brown eyes tired, almost resigned. "I figured I'd see you sooner rather than later."

"I've been busy."

"I know. Training seems to be going well, from what I hear. Dr. Roth almost smiled."

Matt laughed, but quickly sobered. Roth might be an odd duck or an insane toymaker, but he was also one of the most powerful people in the Union.

"I didn't think . . . I didn't think you survived back on Prospect," Matt said, to fill the silence. "I didn't think anyone made it."

Yve sighed. "I never expected to see you again either."

Silence for a time. Matt's mind raced. *I saw your transport blow up,* he wanted to say.

And even if Yve had made it to orbit, it wasn't like there would be a Union Displacement Drive ship waiting for him. He'd have to wait for pickup. He certainly didn't go out on the *Rock*. Did he throw in with the Corsairs?

"What happened to you?" Yve said finally.

"A refugee ship picked me up. The *Rock*."

Yve nodded, his face crumpling into a deep frown. "I'm sorry."

"What about you?"

Yve's expression cycled from sadness to ironic humor. "Like many things your father worked on, I can't talk about it. It's cliché to say, I know."

"My father was working on HuMax technology."

A surprised nod. "I didn't think you knew."

"How long has the Union been working on HuMax technology?"

Yve drew in a big breath. "For a long time now. But only very carefully, and in very limited terms. That's all I know. I wasn't much more than a grunt when I worked with Dr. Stanford, and I'm on the Mecha side now."

"Why?"

Yve fell silent. For a long time, it didn't seem like he'd speak. Then, "The HuMax were monsters, but what they created . . . they were far beyond us. The Union chips at the edges of their accomplishments. So do the Corsairs and the Aliancia and Taikong."

"So is Mecha tech HuMax?"

"Ha!" Yve barked a quick laugh. "No. Don't even say that. Dr. Roth is the genius behind BioMecha, and he makes sure everyone knows it."

Matt slumped back in his seat.

"And, you know, this doesn't have to be an interrogation session," Yve added. "It's good to see you. Put your feet up. Have a drink."

"I'm sorry," Matt said. "It's good to see you too. I've just been running so fast, I don't have time for anything."

Yve nodded. "There's a ton of pressure on all of us. There are still plenty of colonels who'd send all the Hellions we have to every known Corsair location and try to end it that way."

"Then why don't we do that?" Matt asked.

For a moment, a flicker of unease chased across Yve's face. "Coordination of a massive Hellion effort is difficult. Perhaps impossible. They're spread out all across the known universe. Plus, our faster-than-light communications are extremely limited."

"So they'll bet it all on the Demon?"

"Yes. Theoretically, a Merged fourth-order Demon configuration is unassailable. It's the strategically correct solution."

"But you can't send the Demon everywhere at once," Matt said.

Yve's eyes darted away and locked on Matt. His gaze was suddenly cold, calculating. "No. We can't. But we can use it for a decisive demonstration or three. And we can be ready when—if—the Corsairs who hit Geos strike again."

So we're a symbol of what the Union can accomplish; the ultimate weapon, Matt thought. *And bait.*

"Geos was Rayder, wasn't it?" Matt asked.

Yve clenched his fists, then nodded. "You'll never hear that through the media, but yes. It was."

"So you need to hit Rayder."

"Yeah," Yve sighed. "But that's the problem. The location problem. We don't know where he is. They don't call him the General in Shadows for nothing."

"I heard Rayder also took over a colony world."

Yve jumped and looked hard at Matt. "Where'd you hear that?"

"From Dr. Roth."

"Ah." Yve waved a hand. "The frontier is more fluid than the average person knows."

"But Rayder, he actually took over a Union colony?" Matt pressed.

A nod. "Yes."

Matt sat silent for a time, letting that sink in. Yve continued. "Rayder is the most pressing issue. The Unicrats don't want chatter about the Union's vulnerabilities getting out. Ending Rayder would be a great propaganda win for them."

Familiar faces floated up to join them at the table: Sergeant Stoll and Ash.

"What's wrong with you guys, hanging upside down?" Ash asked.

Matt, Yve, and Stoll shared an amused glance, the look of people who'd spent a long time in space. "Everything's relative," Sergeant Stoll said.

"I don't know if I can eat like this," Ash said, looking down at the Hellions in the dock.

But when the food came, Ash didn't have any problem tucking it in. Soon she was completely oblivious, happily showing off little holograms of her kids to Yve, who smiled a politician's smile and nodded in all the right places.

How political is he? Matt wondered. *What, exactly, does he know?*

And what, exactly, will the Merged Demon become?

12

MERGE

Any thoughts of what the Demon might become was lost in
the tedium of Merge training. First, Soto and Stoll had
them all don interface suits and head down to a room full
of screens for more tuning. Matt's suit glowed a brilliant
grass green as strange electric sensations passed through
his body. The others showed splotches of yellow and red,
which stubbornly refused to go away as Sergeant Stoll
worked on each of them with a handheld controller.

Finally, she pronounced them as good as they would get.
Ash's suit still showed a large yellow area over her chest,
and Michelle and Kyle had yellow veins running through
their arms and legs. Soto and Stoll had a brief conversation
about "reducing Lowell's interface efficiency," then apparently decided against it.

Matt was happy with that. He didn't want to lose touch
with the Mecha. He couldn't let the others hold him back.

When they were finally done with suit tuning, they had a
whole day of Mesh optimization inside the Demons themselves. Matt drifted, bored, as the others tried to get their
efficiencies up above seventy percent, while his hovered in
the low nineties. He hoped they'd be done with it soon, because the news media was getting shrill about the Corsairs.
His Perfect Record played back images from his wall screen
that past night:

Interviews of grim-faced survivors on Geos, who looked

determinedly at the cameras and vowed to rebuild. A long line of young men and women standing in front of a Union Army recruitment center, many of whom had given up their university careers or stepped out of research labs in order to enlist. Their eyes burned bright with fiery anger.

On the screen spun diagrams of Union forces and Corsair territory, while Congressperson Tomita talked about the "irresistible strategy" the Union would use to wipe them out. Images of the Demon flashed on the screen like icons.

But there was no mention of Rayder. No talk about the colony worlds, hanging so close to the red haze of Corsair territory. No far-off blip showing the location of Mecha Base. The news was less than a thumbnail sketch of what was really going on, more theater than reality.

But that's what it has to be, Matt thought. *The Union must have the force to take on the Corsairs.*

As I must have the strength to take on my father's murderer.

Finally, they moved to Merge training just outside Mecha Base. From Dr. Roth's private Demon dock, the four giant Mecha debarked into the shadow of the giant armor shield, staying out of sight below the main Displacement Drive ship dock.

Even then, space-suited dust motes jetted over the horizon to stare at the Mecha as they worked. In sensory-enhancement mode, Matt saw their tags: some were simple Union Army staff, some Mecha Auxiliary, and some Mecha Corps. Even Colonel Cruz appeared to gaze at them once, briefly. The public comms reverberated with speculation about who the Demon pilots could be. Some of them even guessed that it might be the new cadets, but it was quickly dismissed.

Matt frowned. The hallways of Mecha Base would be less secure from now on.

Matt waited impatiently, edgy on Mesh, as Sergeant Stoll

ran through the last systems checks. The maelstrom beneath him beckoned; he wanted to dive deep down into it and carom off the bouncing asteroids, like they'd done the other day. He wanted Michelle to follow him. He wanted to embrace her—

Finally, Stoll's voice barked out of the comms. "We're beginning first partial Merge drill. Please follow instructions from Dr. Roth carefully."

Dr. Roth's comms icon flared. "Candidates, note the 'partial' and 'drill' aspects of this exercise. After further assessment, we have decided to approach Merge in stages to avoid potential imbalance between the components. Due to this, you will descend only to Stage Blue as indicated on your overlay. The intent is to familiarize you with the Merge experience."

Come on, let's get started, Matt thought. His Demon's hands twitched impatiently.

"Begin by forming a circle with your Mecha and taking your partner in hand," Dr. Roth said.

Matt reached out to take Michelle's hand. Michelle's talons meshed with his. Something like a mild electric buzz passed through him. Ash reached toward him. He took her hand. Kyle completed the circle. The buzz grew in volume and resolved into something like voices.

No. Not quite voices. Thoughts. Muttering and brittle, like wind-blown leaves.

Kyle was tired. Even fresh in the cockpit, his breath came fast and ragged. He was scared because the Demon was such work for him.

Michelle's thoughts were of Matt, how he helped Kyle last time. Distance echoed inside her, distance from Earth, distance from her estranged family.

Ash's thoughts bounced like marbles in a can, sharp and loud. Images of her husband and her sons flashed by like pictures in an album, overlaid with a sense of panic.

Come on, Matt thought. *This is easy. This is what happens in Merge.*

Everything's so easy for you. Michelle's thoughts came, fast and warm. *You're the natural. Superman.*

Matt looked down and saw that his Demon's hand and Michelle's flowed together like two droplets of mercury Sparks of optical fibers shimmered and sparkled on the edge of the Merge.

Sudden surprise from Michelle collided with anger from Kyle. But Kyle's anger was muted, diffuse. He was irritated about the Superman comment, but he was more mad at himself for failing to be the best, failing to live up to his family's expectation.

Matt blushed. If he could tell what Kyle was feeling, everyone could probably see right through him. If they wanted, they'd know everything. His father. His Perfect Record. His real reason for joining the Mecha Corps.

I accept you, Michelle thought.

Yes, you're all right, Ash thought.

Kyle's thought didn't resolve completely, but Matt heard something like: *I can't hate you so much now.*

Matt's arm Merged up to the forearm.

"Good. Merge stable. Stage Blue achieved," Sergeant Stoll's voice came through the comms, distant and jarring.

Their minds opened like windows. Suddenly, everything was laid bare. There was something they were heading for. Some distant unity where everything would be all right.

The unity flickered. Waves of fatigue passed over Matt. They'd never reach it. It was too far away. Every step felt like he weighed a thousand pounds.

What's wrong? Michelle thought. Her fear reverberated through Matt's mind.

I don't know, Matt thought, straining forward.

It has to be all of us, Michelle thought. *Kyle's tired.*

Then get him moving! Matt thought over a sudden spike of anger. He pulled forward as hard as he could. Pain flared sharply in his arm. In his POV, the cool blue stage indicator flashed orange-red.

"Unbalanced Merge," Stoll said. "Abort exercise."

"No!" Matt said. "I can do this!" He thrust forward again as hard as he could. Agony cascaded through his arm and into his chest. Michelle and Ash yelled with the pain.

Stop it! You can't do it by yourself! Michelle called in his mind.

Help me, Matt told her.

I am! You're too strong!

"Abort exercise now, cadets! Acknowledge orders!" Stoll's voice was harsh.

Acid thoughts swirled in Matt's mind. He could do it! If they didn't hold him back! Just a little more! He almost didn't see the stage indicator, now mottled black and red.

Please stop, Michelle said through waves of pain.

Yeah, please, Ash added.

I can't. Please, no more, Kyle thought.

Through one final, brilliant flash of rage, Matt groaned. *So close! So little to go!*

But they're right, a little voice told him. *Stop. Stop now.*

Matt sighed. That was right. He should know that. You didn't leave your teammates behind.

His arm peeled away from Michelle's Mecha, becoming separate once again.

"Exercise terminated. Return to dock," Stoll's voice barked.

Three more days; twenty more attempts at partial Merge. Every time, they got a little better at maintaining their balance.

Stoll added their Mesh effectiveness readouts to their screens, so they could see how they were doing in real time. Matt's bounced from the high 80s to mid-90s. Everyone else's was spiky. Michelle was most consistent, usually in the low 80s. Kyle would jump from the 70s to the low 90s. Ash's numbers went from high 60s to mid-80s.

Every evening after their exercises, Soto would get into one of the Demons and try his own hand at it. Matt watched one of the sessions, where Soto's Mesh effectiveness hovered at 38 percent. Sergeant Stoll stood in the hangar, frowning down at the numbers on her slate.

"Is that bad?" Matt asked.

"Twelve points below activation threshold," Sergeant Stoll said, not looking up.

Peal and Jahl entered the hangar.

"Is the major trying to kill himself again?" Peal asked.

"He's getting better," Stoll told him. "Stable Mesh, but below activation threshold."

Jahl leaned over the slate to peer at Major Soto's cockpit image. "Come on, Major! You know how many Mecha pilots had great careers with effectiveness in the low fifties?"

"Trying," Soto said. "It's just . . . intense."

Is Soto scared? Matt wondered. *What can I do to help?* He thought of Yve, so easy to talk to. What would he ask?

"Where are you from, Major?" Matt asked.

A long breath. "Nuevo Leon."

"You're Aliancia?"

"Not really," the Major said, his voice firming. "My parents joined the Union when I was four. I grew up on battleships. *Prometheus*, mainly."

"Because of the Corsairs?"

"No." After a pause, Soto continued: "There are a lot of people in the Aliancia that don't fit well with their charter of 'nonviolence, by individuals or groups.'"

"'It is one of the central mysteries of the human universe how a libertarian nation was formed from predominately Latinate roots,'" Matt said, quoting his Union History class on Aurora.

"Thanks, professor," Soto said sardonically.

"Yeah, that's from Aurora U."

"The Aliancia is a reaction to the Union," Soto said gruffly.

"At least the Aliancia is peaceful."

"They have to be. For all their words, they know the Union could crush them at any time. They'd be much better off if they'd just join the Union."

"The Corsairs don't seem to care."

Major Soto made a noise like a snort. "The Corsairs are vicious dogs that need to be put down. And that's no professor talking. That's me, based on seventeen Mecha battles."

"What's it like, fighting the Corsairs?" Matt asked.

"Like I said. Pack animals," Soto growled. "They don't care if they live or die. If they're losing, they'll crash their ship into your Displacement Drive battleship. If they're overwhelmed, they'll leave suicide troops behind."

"Why do it?"

"They're sharded. Some are drugged into being berserkers; some are promised eternal life from plundered Union labs; some just kill and maim for the fun on it. The one thing I know is this: carry an Aliancia banner, and that's fine. Carry a Taikong banner, and that's okay. Run up the Corsair banner, and you deserve only one thing: to die." Major Soto's voice became ragged and rough toward the end of his speech, dripping with emotion.

But his Mesh effectiveness stood at 55 percent. Soto's Demon raised one hand jerkily and flexed it, as if wondering at the simple action.

"Holy hell," Jahl said. "It worked."

"What worked?" Peal asked.

"Talking him through it."

Soto's Demon's arm quivered and fell back to the dock with a crash. On-screen, his Mesh effectiveness had fallen to 45 percent.

"Damn!" Soto said. "I had it. I had it right there!"

Stoll stared at Matt, then stopped to study her screen. "Yes, and you'll have another chance at it. For now, abort."

"I can do it again!" Soto cried. "Just a little more. Please!"

"Out, Major," Sergeant Stoll said, voice firm.

Soto exhaled theatrically, but the screen went blank and the Demon's chest opened like a pupil. Major Soto emerged, trailing globules of goo. As he joined the group, he clapped Matt on the shoulder.

"Thank you, cadet," he rasped.

Matt straightened. "You're welcome, sir."

"Now, if you can just do the same with your teammates."

"What, sir?"

"Work with them," Stoll added, her intense violet eyes fixed on Matt. "Help them through the Merge."

"I am helping them!" Matt cried.

"Carrying them on your shoulders isn't helping," Soto told him.

Matt's face flushed with embarrassment. "I—I don't know what else to do."

"Do what you just did here," Major Soto said. "Be a friend."

Matt hung in perfect Demon darkness, feeling the warm magnetorheological fluid wash up his body. His heart thudded hard enough to echo in his eardrums. Random thoughts flashed through his mind like rockets: *Why am I doing this again? Genesis—what is Genesis but a beginning? Do Demons start at zero, or is mine special? You should stop and get out now.*

But of course he wouldn't stop. He couldn't.

I need the Demon, he thought. *I'm hooked.*

"We'll continue as before," Sergeant Stoll's comms icon flared. "Partial Merge. If stable, we'll move on to full Merge."

Matt took Michelle's hand as Ash and Kyle completed the circle. This time, there was time only for a single burst of incoherent thought, like static on an old-fashioned communicator.

The three Demons melted and reformed up to the shoulders. For a moment, Matt lost all sense of self. Then that incredible feeling again, beyond any high. He felt himself rise, as if on a giant wave. A wave he could command.

He shoved forward toward the brilliant light of full Merge.

Wait, Kyle thought. *You're leaving me behind. I can't go as fast as you.*

Instinctive rage arced through Matt, but he pushed it down. Instead, he thought, *I'll bet you never said that on a football field back in Eridani.*

Kyle's thoughts juddered into sharp new forms. *Actually, I did,* he thought. *I was never that fast.*

You don't have to be the fastest, Matt told him.

But it's so easy for you. I'll never have it that easy. I never had it that easy, Michelle thought.

Easy is nothing, Matt thought, sending her images of the hydroponic farms on the *Rock. Determination is what you need. You have that, don't you?*

Michelle rocketed forward as Ash joined them. *That's a thought I can get behind,* she told them, thinking of long days in the dusty mines of Keller.

"Mesh stable below Stage Blue; entering Stage Green. Partial Merge balanced. Begin full Merge, cadets."

The Demon flowed together and re-formed into a streamlined new shape. This was like a slim arrowhead, fashioned to plunge into the heart of evil. Bright red and almost two hundred meters long, it bristled with fusion pods and exhaled white-hot antimatter energy. Simple, streamlined arms held close to its side, it combined the characteristics of both battleship and Mecha.

Matt gasped. For the first time, he saw what the Merged Demon could be. Not just a battleship, but a battleship with the power of a hundred and agility greater than the fastest fighter. Or it could be an armored ball, nearly impregnable. Or, on a world, it could stride through cities like a flaming giant, laying waste to everything in its path, or plucking a single person out of a crowd with immense precision.

"Excellent!" Sergeant Stoll exclaimed, surprised and breathless. "Merge complete in Stage Green. Exercises will be as follows—"

"No exercises!" Kyle's voice was high, ecstatic. "Fun!"

"Cadet Peterov, obey your superior officer," Major Soto broke in.

"No! She's nothing! I'm everything!" Kyle yelled.

Oh, shit, Matt thought. A suffocating blanket of elation and desire washed over him. Kyle's thoughts. Matt gasped for breath. Michelle cried out. Matt felt her terror.

"I did it!" Kyle cried. "I'm not weak. I'm not tired—"

"Abort Merge!" Sergeant Stoll ordered. But her voice was tiny, distant, lost in Kyle's exultation, Michelle's fear, and Ash's pain.

Pain? Pain from Ash? Matt reached out to her in his mind. Waves of agony and fear lanced through him. Something clawed at Ash. Something hungry.

The Merged Demon shuddered. Blinding flashes of Ash's life came to beat at them:

A tiny baby wearing a face mask held close against a warm chest, as hot desert sun spilled yellow over jagged, barren cliffs. A child running to the cover of shade, his skin shading from pink to red in the yellow sun. A man, smiling kindly, his callused hands like sandpaper. A city like an oil refinery, shimmering in stainless steel and complex piping, ugly and utilitarian. A ring and a wedding and long days of decision and offers and Displacing and always trying for Mecha Corps, even though she knew she would never make it, even though the very thought was insane. And then the invitation. *Please report to Earth.* The feeling of indescribable joy, of discovering her life again. Her husband, trying to smile, trying to be happy for her. Crying children. The moment at the space port where she'd put her bag down and turned back to them, knowing she couldn't do it, knowing she couldn't get on the shuttle. Seeing them waving her onward. Tears, yes, but tears of joy. Her quivering hand as she picked up the heavy bag, almost dropping it. Her entire life laid bare. Every image overlaid with feelings of sickness and dread, until Matt felt physically ill. He forced down his rising gorge. Throwing up into his respirator in a canister filled with gel would be a terrible way to die.

"Abort now!" Stoll yelled, voice cracking. "You're entering Reverse Mesh!"

A chill hand twisted Matt's guts. Reverse Mesh. He saw Serghey, slumped over in his harness.

Blinding, searing pain wiped Matt's coherent thought. Ash's memories winked out, one by one. Her scream reverberated, almost ultrasonic. Memories vaporized, as if in front of a wall of atomic flame. Memories twisted and distorted, turned in on themselves. The acid pain of leaving. A sharp pang of mourning.

The Merged Demon's arrowhead shape twisted and bulged, losing its former mathematical perfection. Biometallic muscles rippled and flexed. Suddenly, it wasn't a battleship or a Demon. It almost looked like a wild animal. A wolverine, curled in on itself in a fit of self-destructive rage. A mouth with fusion fangs formed at the front of the Merged Demon. It ripped at its own armor, flashing antimatter brilliance and leaving long, blackened scars on the shining red metal.

Matt screamed from the pain. It wasn't just Ash. It tore at all of them.

"I did it!" Kyle's voice, high and screechy. Suddenly, Matt *was* Kyle: privileged son of a Union Senator, living a life where everything was planned, everything was calculated. He went to the right schools, he played the right sports, he hung out with the right people, so he could be one of the Just and Right people guiding humanity to new heights.

But hidden deep in those thoughts, some dark thing twisted the meaning of "right." It rode Kyle like it rode Ash. And Kyle pressed ever harder down on Michelle. Matt sense her gasping breaths.

In his mind, Matt reached out to Michelle. The waves of Kyle's hate and pride hit him full force. He rocked back, reeling.

"Abort, abort!" Stoll screamed. Such a tiny voice. So easy to ignore. She seemed to be saying something about defenses.

Mecha Base's guns swiveled to lock on the Merged Demon. A new warning flashed in Matt's POV:

HEAVY-MATTER WEAPONRY DETECTED.

Dead. We're all dead, he thought wildly.

"Final warning!" Sergeant Stoll yelled. "Abort Merge now!"

Michelle's pain pierced Matt's heart. Something was on her now. A thing of spikes and shards, a thing that tore at her very being. Memories from Earth cascaded through his mind: at home in a rare quiet time, looking out over the Florida swamp, with the evening sun warm on their necks, just content to be there.

A sudden thought. If he couldn't conquer it, maybe he could cut off its power.

UnMerge, Matt thought, and pulled away with all his might.

There was a noise like thunder and a terrible tearing agony. Matt imagined his limbs ripped from his body.

The Merged Demon went rigid and split into four pieces. Three quickly re-formed into standard Demon shapes. One hardened into a hulking humanoid shape covered with ridges and spikes. Kyle. Kyle's Demon.

"Good!" Sergeant Stoll's voice was ragged. "Cadet Peterov, release Mesh now!"

"No!" Kyle's voice warbled, only partially human.

Kyle turned on the others. Apertures opened on the spiked Demon's chest. Fireflies flashed. Matt's chest rang with the impact, and he cried out from the pain. Ash's Demon tumbled, ending up tangled in the struts holding Mecha Base's armor. Michelle's Demon shot away into the maelstrom. Kyle chased her down.

"Cadet Peterov, release Mesh now!" Soto yelled. "That's an order!"

Matt flung himself after Kyle and Michelle. The tickling pings and patter of the maelstrom's rocks and dust were almost comforting. Michelle had transformed into a familiar, streamlined cruiser shape, but Kyle's Demon retained its strange, spiky, humanoid appearance.

Kyle's Demon fired Fireflies again, and brilliant explosions sent Michelle tumbling. She recovered her balance and thrust deep down toward the core.

Matt enabled his Fireflies and fired. White-hot explosions bloomed on Kyle's backside, sending him spinning. He caught himself on the edge of a large rock, glanced back once at Matt, and then dove down after Michelle again. He quickly closed the gap.

"Kyle, stop it!" Matt screamed. "That's Michelle!"

Kyle turned on Matt and fired a cloud of Fireflies. Matt launched a Seeker. Destruction flashed in front of them. Giant, house-sized rocks vaporized. Matt felt their fragments like pebbles on his metal skin.

"Fun!" Kyle laughed.

"Play later," Matt told him firmly.

"No. Play now!"

Michelle stopped and fired. Kyle flew right into her Seekers, and his scream echoed in Matt's ears. Kyle's Demon went limp and caromed off one of the big asteroid-sized chunks of rock. For a moment, its spikes sagged, and it almost regained a standard Demon shape. Then the spikes and ridges rose again.

When Kyle rose, a compartment opened on his side. He drew forth a weapon Matt knew all too well: the Zap Gun. The difference was that a Demon's Zap Gun was at least five times the size of his Hellion's Zap Gun.

"Big fun!" Kyle's voice was loud, childish.

"Disable antimatter weaponry immediately!" Soto yelled.

"I refuse!" Kyle giggled. "Sir!"

"Using antimatter weaponry in the protoplanet's core could cause enough damage to destabilize Mecha Base's orbit," Stoll recited, as if dazed.

Matt's world suddenly went white. Searing chunks of molten rock battered him. His Demon spun wildly. He grabbed for purchase and stopped himself on an asteroid. He blinked in amazement, catching his breath. A wide swath of matter was simply gone. Rocks, asteroids, dust, gas. He could see all the way up to a pinprick of black sky.

Another flash. Matt heard Michelle yelling incoherently. White-hot fire engulfed the wheeling asteroids of the protoplanet's core. House-sized boulders ceased to exist. Entire asteroids were consumed. Against the brilliant backdrop, two tiny black pinpoints danced.

Two of them. Michelle was still alive. Matt pushed his Demon as fast as it would go. He felt it change shape, becoming a streamlined, needle-slim spike to weave through the cascading rock and gas of the core.

"Michelle!" he called.

"Here," Michelle gasped. "Still here."

Matt pushed toward Kyle with all speed. The spiky Mecha swelled in front of him. Its Zap Gun swung toward Matt. Matt had a momentary glimpse down the gaping barrel—

He collided with Kyle's Mecha, sending it spinning. But Kyle still held his Zap Gun.

Matt launched Fireflies. Kyle's Mecha, laughing, stepped through them. He launched Seekers. Kyle dodged effortlessly and brought his Zap Gun up again, aiming it at Matt's chest.

Matt flung himself at Kyle, grappling with him. If he could get a grip on the gun and use his Fusion Handshake, he could end this. He hoped.

The two Mecha whirled in the dust and gas. Matt's grip kept slipping off the spiky Demon's irregular surface. He could keep Kyle from using his Zap Gun, but he couldn't bring his hands together for a Fusion Handshake.

An asteroid-sized rock hit them hard. Matt's viewpoint wheeled sickeningly. Kyle's crazed laughter filled his ears. "Fun, fun!"

Michelle launched Fireflies. Matt barely felt the pain as they engulfed both Mecha. He was beyond that. His whole world was Kyle.

Kyle triggered his Zap Gun. It cut a blinding swath

through the core. Asteroid-sized rocks flashed to nothingness. Matt could see the orbits of the other rocks changing, and remembered Lena's words: *It could destabilize Mecha Base's orbit.*

He had to end this. Now. Matt reached for his own Zap Gun.

"Cadet, no!" Sergeant Stoll yelled.

"I have to." Matt felt an electric thrill as his hand closed around the Zap Gun. He drew it forth. It almost seemed to be alive, humming with death.

Kyle saw. He struggled to bring his own weapon around.

Matt put his Zap Gun to Kyle's gun arm and fired.

For a moment, the only sound was Kyle's nearly ultrasonic scream. Kyle's arm and Zap Gun were outlined in black, like a cartoon sketch. Then they simply blew away, as if they had never existed.

Kyle's scream ended. His Demon returned to its standard form, minus one arm.

"Kyle?"

No answer.

Michelle came to join Matt. "Kyle, are you all right?" she cried.

No answer.

Michelle's Demon shook Kyle's one-armed Mecha, then bent over him, as if crying. It was an amazingly human gesture, one that looked profoundly alien when acted out by a thirty-meter-tall biomechanical machine. Matt shuddered.

"Kyle!" Michelle screamed. She whirled on Matt. "You killed him!"

She came at him, thrusters flaring. Matt let her bowl into him. He didn't even feel the impact. He wanted to tell her, *But he was trying to kill you.*

Or was he? Kyle should have been able to kill them easily. But he hadn't. Matt shook his head. He didn't know what was real anymore.

"Return to Mecha Base immediately!" Major Soto barked. "This exercise is over. Done. Got it?"

"But Kyle's dead!" Michelle cried.

"Cadet Peterov is alive," Sergeant Stoll said, sounding tired. "If he is incapacitated, assist him back to base. You will refrain from any weapons use. You will not attempt to re-Merge. Acknowledge these orders."

Michelle stopped grappling with Matt. For a moment, her visor was the only thing in his field of view. It reflected the rust-colored dust and gas of the protoplanet, as if in sync with her own internal turmoil.

"Kyle's alive?" Michelle breathed.

"Yes," Stoll said. "Acknowledge your orders."

"Acknowledged, ma'am," Matt told her.

"Yes, ma'am," Michelle echoed. Without waiting for Matt, she hugged Kyle's Mecha tight and shot upward toward Mecha Base.

Back at Mecha Base, Ash's Demon was already clamped down into the dock. Its red metallic skin shone smooth and perfect, in stark contrast to Matt's carbon-burned Mecha and Kyle's one-armed Demon. *Lucky Ash,* Matt thought, as the cargo loaders clamped him down. She'd missed the insanity.

The insanity. Matt's guts twisted in sudden reaction, and he doubled over. He'd shot an antimatter weapon at a fellow teammate. If he'd missed by just a few thousandths of a degree, Kyle would've been vaporized. He could have killed him.

But there wasn't anything else he could do, right? He had to stop Kyle. He'd gone rogue. Like a Corsair.

Matt waited impatiently for the magnetorheological fluid to drain. As soon as the cockpit opened, he yanked off his face mask and leapt out of the Demon. Michelle hovered near Kyle's Demon's chest, watching as Auxiliaries in gray jumpsuits dragged him from the cockpit.

Kyle sputtered and opened his eyes. His eyes were bloodred and his gaze darted from one face to another as if they were the strangest thing he'd ever seen in his life. He was like a man who had been on a weeklong bender; he had no recollection of where he'd been or what he'd been doing.

Michelle launched herself at Kyle and enveloped him in her arms. Kyle looked confused for a moment, then returned the embrace.

Matt fought sudden anger. *That should be me, damn it!*

One of the Auxiliaries put a hand on Michelle's shoulder. She jumped, then looked embarrassed. She let Kyle go.

"We have to take you to the infirmary, cadet," the Auxiliary told Kyle.

Kyle shook his head. "Not a chance."

"Cadet—"

"No," Kyle said. "I'm fine."

The Auxiliary shook his head and backed off, his hands up in defeat. He glanced at Matt and Michelle. "Are either of you injured?"

"No," Matt and Michelle said in unison.

"How are you mentally?"

"I'm fine, sir," Michelle told him, squaring her shoulders.

I could have killed him, Matt thought. His fingers trembled. "No problem," he lied.

Matt's Perfect Record fed him 3-D visions of the worst of the Merge. That terrible thing scratching at his mind. Kyle's red-hot hate. Ash's vibrant memories, fading to nothingness.

Ash's memories. Matt's mouth went dry.

"What about Ash?" he asked.

The Auxiliary hung his head and looked away. "Reverse Mesh," he said, in a low, rough voice. "She's dead."

13

QUESTIONS

In the pilot's chamber outside the Demon Dock, two gray-uniformed Mecha Auxiliaries were already packing away the contents of Ash's locker. They worked quickly and efficiently, not speaking, their lips set in hard lines.

Matt watched, numb, as they carefully folded Ash's gray Mecha Cadet jumpsuit and slipped her long, tarnished steel chain and wedding band into a pocket. One of the Auxiliaries fumbled with a razor-slim folio of holos, and they went spinning away in the microgravity. Matt caught glimpses of the brighter-than-life images: a blond boy, about nine, holding up a blurry slate covered with mathematics. A shaggy-haired man wearing dust-caked LithiChem mining coveralls and holding a tiny baby. A sandy-haired boy, maybe four, standing next to a craggy, ochre rock backdrop. The man in the overalls grinned like he couldn't imagine a more perfect place in all the Union.

Matt blinked back tears.

Ash Moore was dead. Mom. Wife. Colonist. Union citizen. Believer. Mecha Cadet. Demonrider candidate. Dead.

But people die, Matt told himself. Serghey. His father. Every twelfth digger on the *Rock*.

This was different, though. They'd been Merged. Everything Ash experienced, he felt. He saw her life cut away, piece by piece. He'd experienced her final moment of terror and diminution. Her *ending*.

A tiny voice called in the back of his mind, *Is this all?*

Matt slumped. For the first time, the path to his future blurred and doubled. What did killing the Corsair mean if it killed everything he believed in to accomplish it?

"I'm sorry," Michelle said, coming to lay a warm hand on Matt's shoulder. Out of the corner of his eye, Matt saw Kyle stiffen.

"It's not your fault," Matt said. *It's mine,* he thought. *If I'd helped everyone, she might be here today.*

"It's not your fault either," Kyle said, coming up to put his own hand on Matt's shoulder.

"I pushed too hard—," Matt began.

"Shut the fuck up," Kyle said. "We all pushed hard. You can't blame yourself for this. None of us can. Not if we ever want to do it again."

Matt straightened. Of course they'd do it again. As many times as it took. But he said nothing.

Kyle filled the silence. "My mother. She did that. Blamed herself." His voice, sandpaper rough, was almost inaudible. The Auxiliaries cast furtive glances at him as they blanked out the name on Ash's locker and headed for the exit.

"For what?" Michelle said.

"My brother. He had . . . special needs," Kyle's voice rose, his mouth twisting in grim irony.

"What happened?"

"Kent's in an assisted-care home on Eridani. Mom . . . she killed herself ten years ago. One of those things where everyone says, 'I never saw it coming.' But it was on a day when Kent was at the house, and the bathroom she did it in looked out over his playground."

Matt squeezed his eyes shut but remained silent. What could he say?

Michelle gathered them both into a tight hug. She squeezed them together and didn't let go, even as they left the floor in the microgravity. Matt opened his eyes, watching little drops of her crystalline tears float up and away. "We'll get through this. We have to."

Soto and Stoll entered the room. "Cadets, I'm sorry I'm late. I had to deal with—" The big man stopped short, gaping at the three embracing cadets.

"If you'd like, I'll come back later."

"It's all right," Kyle said, pushing away from them. Matt and Michelle drifted away to grab handholds on the tops of the lockers.

"We can understand if you need more time—"

"I need a drink," Kyle said, his voice quavering.

Soto nodded. "I could join you in that."

"I'm coming too," Michelle told them.

Stoll held up a hand. "The word is out about the Mecha Cadets being the Demon pilots. It might be better to maintain a lower profile."

"Lena, please."

Sergeant Stoll blinked. "Yes. You're right."

All eyes turned to Matt. He looked back at them, knowing exactly what would come next. The only question was who would say it.

"You coming?" Michelle asked.

On the way to the Decompression Lounge, the long, curved passageways of Mecha Base seemed to stretch into infinity, grim metallic corridors leading to an uncertain future. Matt couldn't shake the Perfect Record of Ash's death, playing over and over again in his mind. Every passing Mecha Corps seemed to be glaring right through him, judging him on the death of his teammate.

"Good job, Demon boy," one of them said finally, coming up from behind to pace them. He was a blond-haired kid not much older than Matt, wearing his Mecha captain's uniform with a single Hellion pilot pin.

Another young Mecha Corps captain came up to join the first man. His nametag read N. SANJIV, and the blond kid's read J. PELLETIER. "All the pretty boys," Sanjiv said. "Whose daddy did you have to know to get the Demon jobs?"

"Stand down, Corps," Soto called out.

"Sir, just expressing our opinion, sir," Pelletier snapped. "Completely nonphysical."

"I'd rather be physical," Pelletier said, bouncing off the handrail to pass close by Michelle, almost touching her. "Don't kill this one next, guys."

Michelle took a swipe at Pelletier and missed, spinning into the center of the corridor, out of reach of the handrails. Sanjiv and Pelletier laughed and launched themselves at her.

Matt gritted his teeth and kicked off to meet them. He imagined punching Pelletier in the face as hard as he could. He could almost feel the explosion of hot pain as his knuckles caught teeth and rivulets of blood sprayed in the microgravity.

But he didn't get more than a couple of meters before Stoll rocketed past him and grabbed the two men.

"Hey!" Sanjiv yelled. Stoll flipped in midair and brought them around, crashing their heads into the hard ceiling. The two men struggled against her, but she held them away without effort.

"Fucking strength genemod!" Pelletier yelled.

"Assaulting a superior officer!" Sanjiv called, looking at Soto.

"I don't see anything," Soto said. "I don't think Mecha Base surveillance will either."

Pelletier and Sanjiv slumped.

"You kids gonna be good?"

"Yes." Sullenly.

Soto nodded at Stoll, who let the men go. They gave her a final glare and shot off down the corridor.

"Damn greenies," Soto said. "Let's see how they feel when they lose one of their squad."

"You've lost teammates?" Matt said, thinking of Soto's long rows of color bars and all the Mecha battles he'd fought.

Soto's eyes suddenly went veiled and faraway. "We all do. It's one of the things that keeps us together."

* * *

In the Decompression Lounge, it took a couple of drinks of Earth-style, vacuum-distilled vodka before any of them spoke.

"What now?" Michelle asked.

For a while, the only sound was the hiss of the ventilators. Sergeant Stoll and Major Soto exchanged an unreadable glance. Finally, Major Soto said, "I don't know."

"You said you've had teammates die ..." Michelle trailed off.

"In combat. And—" Soto looked away.

"And what?"

"It's an expression." Soto sighed. "It's what we say when someone can't use Mecha anymore."

"Can't use it anymore?" Matt sat up straight.

"You know how it feels," Soto said. "Using a Mecha uses you up. It's a high. You get used to it. Then you get to need it. Then the Mesh doesn't ... work anymore. Suddenly, it's gone. It disappears on you. It can take years, sometimes decades, but it happens. When you can't use a Mecha anymore, you're ... dead. Or at least that's what we call it."

Matt shivered. Is this what he had signed up for? To be burnt out by a machine?

"All Auxiliaries are dead," Stoll added.

"You were Mecha Corps?" Matt asked.

Sergeant Stoll shook her head. "No, I never made it through the training. But I'm still dead, by that definition."

"What about you?" Kyle asked, nodding at Soto. "How have you kept using Mecha for so long? How can you use a Demon?"

Soto smiled a wan sad expression. "I was a damn good pilot. Almost as good as Lowell, Mesh-wise. I conserved my time in the Mecha, reserved it for battle. Plus, I've become a damn stubborn old man."

"How long do we have?" Michelle asked.

Soto shrugged. "Years. Decades. Who knows? But the

Hellions' neural buffering made them easier to take. The Demon—it seems more like a Rogue. Rough stuff."

Michelle nodded, her eyes wide. Matt knew she was going through a lot of the same feelings they all were experiencing, but she managed to put on such a consistently brave face.

"My first partner died in a Rogue," Soto offered to the group. "I felt the whole thing," Soto said. "That was back when we went in pairs. It was on Forest. The Corsairs had taken Amazon, the capital, and we were going in to rout them out—you know, spare the civvies and save the princess, all that shit. Except in this case it wasn't a princess; it was a mean old governor who'd gone Corsair on us, and he'd had a dozen Aliancia tanks waiting on the main approach to his palace. They unloaded on us . . ." Soto trailed off, his eyes going misty in memory. "Took out both my Control Nexuses, but got Jim right on the edge of the cowl. Drove a biometallic shard right into his eye. Felt the whole thing like it was my own. When I stopped screaming, our second partners had arrived. They turned it to our advantage. I ripped that one tank apart, the one that shot Jim. I pulled the men out like they were meat. I shredded them . . ."

"We felt it," Matt spoke up. "Ash."

"It was like she was being . . . deleted," Michelle added.

"Not deleted. Shredded. Ground away," Kyle's voice was low and slurred. His gaze was loose, unable to fix on anyone in the group.

"You should be in Accelerated Recovery. You're descending, my friend," Soto said.

"Been worse than this," Kyle slurred. "Been worse in ROTC. Been worse in school."

Soto chuckled. "Somehow I doubt that."

"It's true!" Kyle asserted. His head bobbed and almost hit the table.

Soto got out of his seat and nodded at Sergeant Stoll. "Come on. Let's get him to the infirmary."

"Don't need it," Kyle slurred. But he didn't struggle as Stoll helped him out of the chair.

"I'll come with you." Michelle started to rise.

Soto held up a hand. "No. You need to rest." A glance at Matt. "You do too."

"Yes, sir," Matt said.

Still, neither Matt nor Michelle moved to leave. Soto, Stoll, and Kyle floated toward the exit. Soto shot them a final glare from the door, but didn't say anything else.

Silence ticked by for a time. Michelle looked out over the Hellions in the docks, black chrome figures subtly menacing in the dim light. "I feel . . . hollowed out."

"You'll feel better."

Michelle banged a fist on the table. "Maybe I don't want to feel better! I don't want to forget about this! And I don't—I don't know what to do."

"What do you mean?"

Michelle's eyes jittered around as her mouth worked soundlessly. Finally she managed, "Mecha Corps was my dream. My ticket off. Now I get here, and I'm going to have my life sucked out by some machine?"

Matt nodded, remembering his earlier thoughts. But it didn't matter. He'd do anything to annihilate his father's murderer. He needed that new memory, one to play over and over again.

How far are you willing to go to get it? a little voice whispered. *How much are you willing to lose?*

"Everything," Matt said.

"What?" Michelle asked.

Matt shook his head. That wasn't entirely true. Not anymore.

After a time, Michelle sighed and stood up. "I think Soto's right. Time to pack it in."

"I'll walk you back to your quarters."

A head shake. "No need. Finish your drink."

Matt looked at the drink bulb in his hand. It was still half-full. He put it down on the sticky-mat holder.

When he looked up, though, Michelle had already pushed off for the exit. She never looked back at him.

The next morning, a loud chime from Matt's door screen pierced his Mesh hangover. He groaned and went to open the door.

Outside was a burly Mecha Auxiliary. His nametag read K. SU, and he wore sergeant's stripes. "Demonrider candidate Lowell?" he asked.

"Yeah?" Matt realized he'd only half-finished putting on his gray Mecha Cadet uniform. He shoved another leg into the loose coverall.

"Please accompany me." Sergeant Su gestured at the corridor.

"Why?"

"Mission debrief."

"What mission?" Matt echoed.

"Demon Merge, attempt twenty-one, failed with casualties," Su said, reading off his slate in a monotone.

Matt jumped. *Twenty-one attempts. Failed with casualties.* That didn't sound good. That didn't sound good at all.

"What're they going to do?" he asked.

Su shrugged, looking bored.

Matt pulled on the rest of his uniform and followed Su deep into Mecha Base. Here, the periodic ticks and pings of the micrometeorites from the maelstrom fell away to a smooth and absolute silence, like the deep interior of a refugee Displacement Drive ship during those long times when the drive was idle.

Su stopped in front of a door with a screen that read: CONFERENCE A: OCCUPIED. He gestured for Matt to go in first.

It was a room out of one of those cheap legal dramas they produced on every refugee Displacement Drive ship in the Union. Functional white plastic chairs. Morguelike stainless-steel tables arranged in a hollow square. On the near side of the tables, three chairs were anchored. On the far side sat four grim-faced men: Colonel Cruz, Major Soto, Dr. Roth,

and Yve Perraux. Colonel Cruz and Major Soto wore im-
maculately pressed gray uniforms, crisp and perfect and
decked with colorful bars. Dr. Roth wore a white lab coat
over a rumpled black coverall, as if he'd been pulled away
from some critical experiment. Yve wore a dark blue pin-
striped suit with the Union star on its lapel.

Major Soto looked up as Matt floated in and nodded at
one of the seats on the other side of the table. Matt sat, his
fingers numb, his mind racing with questions: *Are we going
to be charged with something? Is this the end of my career in
the Mecha Corps?*

"Where are the rest?" Colonel Cruz snapped.

"On their way, sir," Su said, behind Matt.

Matt sat and waited. The four men never spoke. They
just stared into space, as if afraid to meet each other's
gazes.

The door creaked open and Matt turned to look. Michelle and Kyle floated in, accompanied by another Auxiliary. They took the seats flanking Matt, neither saying
anything. Kyle's lips were compressed, and his face was
pale and shiny with sweat. It was clear he hadn't completely
recovered from his Demon misadventure, even after Accelerated Recovery.

"Let's proceed," Yve said. "Due to the nature of this de-
brief, we've been authorized to use FTL communications.
I'm bringing in Congressperson Sou Tomita, Chair of the
Union Advanced Technologies Committee."

The wall screen behind the four men lit up, and a watery,
bit-rotted image of Congressperson Tomita looked down
on them. He didn't look happy. Not at all.

When he spoke, though, his words were soft, almost
kind. "Cadets, let me begin with my condolences on the loss
of your teammate. Losing even a single Union citizen is a
terrible tragedy."

"Thank you, sir," Michelle said softly.

"The rest of what I have to say is less pleasant. First, let
me summarize, so our facts are in order: To date, there have

been twenty-one Demon Merge attempts. Twenty of these were only partially successful."

"They were intended to be partial Merges, for training—," Dr. Roth cut in.

"You'll hold commentary until the end of my summary, Dr. Roth," Congressperson Tomita said, clearly relishing his small triumph over Roth. "The one full success—if we can call it that—was unstable, with a dead pilot and injured cadet as its results. Is this an accurate assessment of where we stand right now?"

Matt shifted in his seat. The Velcro scritched under his uniform, loud in the still room. He couldn't refute anything Tomita had said. His head throbbed in Mecha hangover, and bone-deep fatigue sat on him like a boulder. At the same time, though, a powerful need resonated through every part of his body: *I need to get back in the Demon. If I get back in the Demon, everything will be better. I can get my balance again.*

Dr. Roth said nothing for a time. Finally: "An accurate assessment."

"We were led to believe the Demon Merge would be accomplished much more expeditiously," Tomita said.

"I expected to be farther along, yes," Roth said, glaring at Matt. Matt returned the stare, anger warring with fear. *Is it my fault? Did I push them along too fast?*

"This isn't a trial," Tomita said mildly, though his eyes were angry slits. "We are here to find solutions and consider alternatives. Any day, any second, Rayder could attack us again. We must be ready with a unified defense. We've requested that the pilots be here so we can better understand the challenges of Demon Merge and the causes of such a spectacular failure."

Roth shook his head. "The cause is clear. Our data shows that the individual with the lowest effective Mesh, Cadet Moore, received resonant gross feedback from the neural interface, resulting in an unstable Merge."

Congressperson Tomita turned to look at the three cadets. His image briefly blurred off the screen, and his voice slurred to unintelligibility. After all, this was a feed coming to them from twelve thousand light-years away. When he came back, they were still able to get the gist. "... personal experiences. What happened, cadets?"

Matt shared a look with Michelle and Kyle. What could he say? Other than the truth?

"At first, it was the best thing you could ever imagine," Matt said. "Merge is like Mesh times a hundred. It's all the same, uh, feelings ..."

"The Mesh high? You don't need to use euphemisms," Tomita said.

"It's more intense," Matt said. "It's almost like the De-mon is something else—a person, looking at you, challeng-ing you. And it's more than that too. You can also share the thoughts of your teammates as you walk through that gate."

"So, you feel as though you experienced Cadet Moore's death?" Tomita asked.

"Yes," Matt said, shuddering. Once again he felt her ter-ror, sharp and hot. The shining faces of her children. The feeling of being taken apart, piece by piece.

"It was like she was being peeled away," Michelle of-fered.

"Was there an obvious trigger? Something that caused it?" Tomita leaned forward.

Matt looked at Kyle. He'd refused the exercises. *Fun, fun.* But was that it? No. More likely Matt pushing them too hard.

Tomita saw the direction of Matt's glance. "Cadet Pe-terov. You refused a direct order for exercises. Do you be-lieve that had anything to do with the unstable Merge?"

Kyle turned to glare at Matt, his eyes suddenly murder-ous. Matt shook his head. He hadn't said anything. Was a look enough to give it away?

"No, sir," Kyle said. "I believe it was a result of the un-stable Merge, rather than the cause."

"Then why did you run after the Merge dissolved?" Tomita pressed.

Kyle shook his head. "I don't know. Continuing instability from the failed Merge?" But his eyes flicked over to Matt again.

"Doubtful," Dr. Roth said. "Cadet Peterov's Mesh effectiveness was high and stable during his pursuit."

"No other insight, Cadet Peterov?" Tomita asked.

Kyle looked hard at the screen, his face paler than ever. He wiped sweat from his brow. "None, sir."

"And you, Cadet Lowell?" Tomita turned to Matt. "Why did you disobey a direct order to stand down with your antimatter weapon? Was that also Merge instability?"

Matt sighed. "It's the only weapon that could stop a berserk Mecha holding a Zap Gun."

"So this was a calculated decision," Congressperson Tomita said. "Not a whim of Mesh high?"

"If I hadn't done it, we'd still be down in that mud. With at least two of us dead."

"Kyle wouldn't have killed us!" Michelle cried, glaring at Matt.

Tomita stared at Matt for a long time, as if daring him to drop his eyes. "You did enough damage down there to accelerate the course of the planet's formation."

"I know. And I'd do it again," Matt said, trying not to look at Michelle, but wondering if she was stealing a glance at him.

"You'll keep doing it until you destroy us all," Colonel Cruz muttered.

Tomita nodded. "Our colonel poses a valid question. Cadets, how far will you go to Merge the Demon? Far enough to endanger Mecha Base?"

Matt sat silent, as did his companions. There was nothing they could say.

Tomita continued. "Have you learned enough from your last encounters to ensure our safety?"

Matt started to speak, then cut himself off and looked

down. Remembering the rush of Mesh and Merge. His first exercise, running out of control to orbit.

Michelle and Kyle stayed silent too.

Tomita's image flickered again, accompanied by a burst of static. When he came back on, he was nodding. "I'll take your silence as a negative."

Tomita turned to address Dr. Roth. "Dr. Roth, do you care to comment on the failures to date, and any plans you have to improve upon the Demon's Merge capability?"

Roth frowned, visibly bristling at Tomita's criticism of his Mecha. "The Demon's Merge capability is flawless," he began. "However, this project was of significantly greater complexity than anything attempted previously. Upgrades to the biometallic architecture raise the level of neural interface needed. A Demon's neural interface is significantly more advanced than a Hellion's, which means it will take more time to master."

"So your strategy of using raw cadets perhaps was not the best plan of attack?"

Roth crossed his arms. "It's the only plan. Major Soto's experiences with the Demon are on record; we have cycled ten other willing Hellion pilots through the Demon with even more dire results, including two deaths."

"So we keep running these pilots until they too die?" Tomita said.

"I can deploy a thousand Hellions with a thousand skilled pilots anywhere in Corsair space tomorrow," Colonel Cruz cut in. "I don't see how Rayder can stand against that."

"How many thousand-Hellion maneuvers have you deployed, Colonel?" Dr. Roth spat.

Cruz blinked. "None, but it's a simple scaling—"

"It is not simple scaling. With every additional layer of control, the possibility for failure increases, as does Mecha capture. And that is leaving aside the location problem."

Cruz grit his teeth and said nothing.

"Location problem," Matt said, remembering Yve's words.

Dr. Roth nodded. "We cannot simply assault Rayder surgically, because we have not located his base of operations. So we must be ready with overwhelming force when Rayder appears next."

What planet might be hit before this is over? Matt thought. *Aurora? Earth?*

"Colonel Cruz, I appreciate your enthusiasm," Congressperson Tomita said. "It's an admirable trait in a Union citizen. However, you must accept that there are many valid reasons why a mass Hellion offensive isn't the best approach, even if we know Rayder's location."

"There's nothing a battalion of Hellions can't take on!" Cruz asserted. "Congress is being a bunch of scared old ladies."

Tomita only nodded mildly. "You must also accept there are considerations beyond your purview."

Cruz ground his teeth. "I hate this cloak-and-dagger crap." He sat back in his chair and glared sullenly at the other men.

"If I may answer Congressperson Tomita's question," Roth said mildly.

"What question?" Tomita asked.

"About whether we would continue to use these components"—Roth nodded at the pilots—"until death."

"Go on," Tomita said.

"The answer is no. I am bringing in another team, as well as a backup team, on the UUS *Ulysses*, when it is back from Earth."

It felt like Matt had been punched in the gut. "You can't do that!" he cried.

Dr. Roth turned to give Matt a neutral look. "I absolutely can."

"You're kicking us out?" Michelle asked, her voice hollow.

Roth shook his head. "I had excellent expectations, given your early results. Unfortunately, you've proved to be useless as Demon pilots."

Useless? Matt thought. Searing-cold defeat and blinding rage warred in him. "No!" he wailed.

"We can do it!" Michelle yelled.

Auxiliaries moved in to flank the three cadets.

"I apologize for Dr. Roth's unfortunate choice of words," Congressperson Tomita said. He turned to Roth. "However, I do concur with your overall assessment, Doctor. Ensure the new cadets are ready when they disembark, and let us all pray they'll be ready when Rayder strikes next."

14

DECONSTRUCTION

Sergeant Su escorted the three cadets down the hall. Matt's Mesh hangover pounded at his head even worse than before. Almost as bad as the first time. A thousand thoughts ricocheted in his head: *Gotta find a way to try again, talk to Soto. Can Stoll do anything? Who else can I talk to? Can't stop now; gotta get back in the Demon.*

"It was you," Kyle said as they neared the end of the long corridor.

"It was me what?"

"You. You broke the Merge. Made us fail." Kyle's voice was low and urgent.

"Kyle," Michelle said, laying a hand on his arm. "You don't really think that—"

Kyle shrugged away from her touch and glared at Matt, his eyes narrowing in anger. "I heard your thoughts! Your dad. His killer. Your stupid, petty revenge. That's all you fucking care about."

Matt was so shocked he couldn't speak.

"It has nothing to do with the Union. Or Rayder. You're chasing some ghost," Kyle said, his voice rising. "You don't even know if the man is still alive! You put that ahead of us, and you broke the Merge. You killed Ash!"

"Cadets," Su warned.

Kyle floated up to hover over Matt. "What do we do now? What does Michelle do now?"

Rage lit in Matt. *I remember someone going crazy, but it wasn't me,* he thought. Matt clamped his jaw tight. It took everything he had not to launch himself at Kyle.

At the same time, he remembered their time together in their pilot's chambers yesterday and the stories they shared. Why couldn't it always be like that?

"Kyle, I'm all right," Michelle said.

"No! You're not! None of us are. What do we do now?" Kyle's voice spiraled up and up, screeching.

"Cadets, last warning," Su said, his hand on his stun stick.

But Kyle got right up in Matt's face. "How will you make it up to us? Merge wrecker!"

Su pulled his stun stick. "Cadet, stand down!"

"Why? Can't you see? He ruined our damn lives!" Kyle screamed, his eyes jittering from Su to Matt.

Su brandished the stun stick. "Come with me. You need treatment for Mesh fugue."

Kyle blinked, his eyes losing some of their angry sheen. "I—I don't understand." He backed away from Su.

Su advanced on Kyle. "We can make this hard, or we can make this easy."

Kyle lashed out at Su. At the touch of the stun stick, he crumpled, limp.

"Kyle!" Michelle cried, going to him.

"Stand back, cadet," Su said, slinging Kyle over his shoulder. Michelle nodded and pulled herself away.

"Where are you taking him?"

"Infirmary," Su told them.

"Mesh fugue?" Matt asked. "There's a treatment for Mecha hangover?"

Su shook his head. "Not so much a treatment. Just tranquilizers. But at least he can sleep through the worst of it."

"Maybe that's what I need," Matt said.

"Not a chance," Su asserted. "This is only for when it gets real bad. The tranquilizers they use . . . sometimes they work, and sometimes they make it worse."

Matt looked at Michelle. She returned his stare with wide eyes, then shot off down the hallway without a word.

At the residential block, Matt stopped. Why was he going back to his cell like a drone? He was just going through the motions.

A storm raged in his mind, maybe a side effect of Demon Merge. No thought lasted more than an instant. Every emotion peaked and crashed in seconds, only to drive to another peak. He was unsettled to the core.

You're chasing a ghost. Kyle's words.

Kyle was right. He was chasing a ghost. He didn't even know if his father's murderer was alive. Or if he was really HuMax.

Yve worked with Dad on Prospect, digging into HuMax technology. What does he know about it?

Matt went to the Decompression Lounge to look for Yve, but the bar was nearly empty in the early morning, except for two guys wearing dirty coveralls and sucking on big bulbs of ale. Diggers coming off shift.

As Matt waited for Yve, his Perfect Record took him back to Prospect. It all came back to the HuMax. The way his dad was the only one allowed in the inner lab. The interlocks on all the data access in the outer lab. How all the other researchers orbited around his dad, their bodies held in awkward tension. As if they were scared of him. As if they knew something of what they were researching and knew it was wrong.

HuMax. HuMax technology.

All the histories read the same. HuMax were created as the logical endpoint of human genetic research. Instead of simply being smarter or stronger or more intuitive, or gifted with better endurance or longer life, they were all of the above and more. Able to live on the most hostile frontier worlds, they were a boon to humanity in the early days of the Expansion into space, after the discovery of the Displacement Drive. It was a rugged universe, and only a handful of worlds were fit to live on. HuMax spread far and fast, quickly establishing colonies on the most challenging worlds. Prospect had been one of their colonies.

Then they turned on unenhanced humans and tried to wipe them out. And they came close. The histories showed ruins of the capital on Eridani after the Human–HuMax War; only twisted girders and shattered stone remained, as far as the eye could see.

But we were supposed to have killed them all, Matt thought. The Human–HuMax War was nothing less than genocide. It was the defining event of the Union, when humans came together to forge their destiny.

But no history talked about the HuMax's superior technology. No recent articles even hinted that the Union was studying HuMax tech, unearthing the past.

What had his father been doing? What had he found?

Matt shook his head. That stuff didn't matter. What mattered was his father's murderer. He might be chasing a ghost, but what was the best way to find it? To become a Mecha pilot. To Merge the Demon. To take out all the Corsairs. He could do it. He just had to convince them to give him one more chance.

When it was clear Yve wasn't going to show, Matt went down to the Mecha Corps staff office to look for Soto. The Corps there gave him scornful looks. News of their failure must have traveled fast.

Soto was there, strapped down in an aluminum chair in a cubicle maze of offices. He looked tired, defeated. He listened to Matt plead for another chance, then shook his head. Nothing he could do. Decision from the top. It wasn't just their team's loss. It was Soto's as well. Soto had been ordered to cease his Demon training.

And, looking in Soto's bloodshot and angry eyes, Matt wondered, *Is he blaming me?*

Matt went to the far end of Mecha Base, following the maze of tunnels down to Dr. Roth's lab. On this side of the base, the corridors gave way from smooth steel to rough, plasti-coated asteroid rock.

Roth's lab was marked by a simple stainless-steel air-lock door bearing an inscription:

ADVANCED MECHAFORMS, INC.
AUXILLARY RESEARCH UNIT—MECHA BASE
SECURE AREA: ENTER CODE FOR ACCESS

Matt stared at the keypad displayed on the door screen. What could he tell Roth? That he was willing to do anything to try Merge again, not just for selfish reasons, but also to beat back the constant Mesh hangover? He had to get in the Demon again to make sure he didn't end up like Kyle, in nightmarish withdrawal?

But there was more than that. Even over the pounding of his Mesh hangover, Matt realized that he needed to make it up to Roth for the team. For Michelle.

The door screen changed to a head shot of a thin woman wearing a white lab jumper. Her blond hair was cut short, almost a crew cut. She studied him with violet genemod eyes.

"Cadet, this is a secure area," she said finally.

"I'd hoped to talk to Dr. Roth. I'm—"

"Cadet Matt Lowell. Yes, cadet. We know who you are."

"Can I see him? Dr. Roth?"

The genemod woman shook her head. "Dr. Roth is occupied. Please return to the main part of Mecha Base, or I'll call security."

Matt nodded. Of course. Roth wouldn't just be sitting behind a desk, waiting to talk to him. Roth probably wouldn't want to talk to him at all. Matt could only imagine what he might say. *You did what nobody else could do: killed an entire team.*

Despair covered Matt like a suffocating blanket. He had gotten so close to making it! He'd gone so far; he'd done so much. But in the end, he'd failed.

Matt woke to the soft glow of his wall screens. They showed him images of Geos, of protests on Union core worlds, of ranks of Mecha being prepared for battle. People picketed for the Unitarians: THE TIME FOR ALL-UNION IS NOW! ELIMI-NATE THE MENACE! EVERYONE UNITED! UNION FORWARD, UNION ALWAYS! The tone of the news was clear: the time for debate and dissent was past. They wanted to wipe out the Corsairs and everything else that stood against the Union, whether it be via Demon, Hellion, or even old-fashioned, world-destroying nukes.

Matt reached over to turn the screen off, and a hand reached out of the dark and clamped down on his arm. A chill rocked through his body.

Matt yelped and looked up. Standing over him was Kyle, wearing a hospital gown. His wide eyes seemed to dance in the soft light of the wall screen. In one hand, Kyle held a scalpel.

"You're not going to hurt us anymore!" Kyle said, slash-ing with the scalpel. Matt dodged and put up a hand. The blade cut deep into his palm. It stung hotly as his flesh split. Black drops of blood flew and spattered on the wall screen.

Matt brought up a leg and kicked Kyle as hard as he could. He might have felt like his life was over, but he wasn't ready to be killed. Least of all by Kyle.

Kyle flew away. His head hit the steel bulkhead with a loud boom.

The force of his kick pushed Matt down on the bed, which now sprang up and launched him toward Kyle. Kyle grabbed for a rail, found one, and turned to wield the scal-pel again.

Shit. Matt whirled his arms to bring his legs around. The flashing scalpel buried itself in the sole of his shoe, nicking his foot. Matt felt warm blood spread.

Matt brought around his other foot into Kyle's face. Kyle yelled in pain and slashed with the scalpel again. Pain and warmth spread on Matt's leg. Matt flailed away. He needed a weapon. Now.

"Don't run away!" Kyle screeched.

Kyle launched himself at Matt again. Long shadows cast from the screen light put Matt in the pitch-dark. Matt found the door. Pulled. It opened.

Kyle hit the edge of the door with his head. Howling in pain, he slashed blindly with the scalpel as blood poured from a gash on his forehead.

Matt slipped out into the hallway, blinking in the bright light. He pushed off, hard, down the hall. Kyle came after him. Matt trailed globules of blood as he flew down the corridor. He stayed close to the railing so he could pull himself along. Each time he moved up, he left behind a bloody handprint on the dull metal. His slashed hand had started to throb.

Where can I go? Matt shot into the Decompression Lounge. There was nobody in the room, and the bartender was asleep, floating in midair.

"Hey!" Matt called. The bartender's head snapped up. His eyes widened as he saw Matt's bloody state.

Kyle shot into the room. With great, dumb luck, he just happened to be on a collision course with Matt. His crazy eyes were focused on only a single thing. He held the scalpel out in front of him, ready to kill.

Matt stopped himself against the far wall. He crouched down, getting ready.

"Got you!"

When Kyle was a meter away from him, Matt pushed off as hard as he could. Kyle's eyes tracked him. He didn't notice the steel bulkhead.

Kyle hit the wall full force, making it ring like a bell. He bounced off, his eyes dazed, the scalpel drifting from his open hand.

Matt grabbed a handrail and reversed course toward Kyle. He kicked the scalpel out of the way.

Kyle blinked, then caught hold of Matt's ankle. His grip was amazingly strong. Matt kicked at him, but the man climbed up his leg until he reached the slash wound on Matt's thigh. Kyle dug a thumb deep into Matt's muscle.

Matt screamed and tried to break free. Kyle grinned up at him like a lamprey. He pushed his thumb in harder.

"Your fault . . . your fault . . . your fault," he chanted.

The pain was intense, unbearable. Matt felt the room receding away. This was how it was going to end. Killed by a teammate because he didn't work well with others.

Mecha Auxiliaries barreled into Matt and Kyle out of nowhere. Two grabbed Kyle, while another used a towline to bring him back to the wall. One of them gave Kyle an injection. Kyle slumped, slack.

"How . . . what . . ." Matt said. The room was fading again. There was no pain. Everything seemed distant, faraway. He saw dark bubbles of blood floating in the air.

He saw that the Auxiliaries had two stretchers.

It wasn't until later that he realized one was for him.

15

FRAGMENTATION

Matt flexed his hand, staring at the smooth pink scar that was the only trace of his late-night encounter with Kyle. Accelerated Recovery had mended his wound in just a few hours, as he lay in a happy state that felt just a little like Mesh.

"Are you going to Kyle's send-off?" Michelle asked.

Matt snapped back to reality. He was standing outside his tiny room in a long residential corridor. Michelle had come up to him, without Matt noticing at all.

Kyle's send-off. Major Soto had offered Kyle a new assignment as a Mecha Corps Hellion pilot, on a recon mission to the edge colonies. An easy job. A milk run. Matt saw the derision in Major Soto's eyes, even as the older man struggled to make it seem like the best thing in the world.

And maybe it was for Kyle. Maybe that's what he needed. Time to heal.

"I don't know," Matt said.

"He's not going to try to kill you again."

"It's not that."

"And he doesn't really hate you. Or blame you. That was whatever the Demon had been doing to him since he got here. Join us."

Matt shook his head. What would he do? Where was his offer? Soto had suggested waiting for the second round of Demons, after the new pilots Displaced in next week. But that was chancy. Would Roth even let him have another chance?

"Come on. It's starting soon," Michelle encouraged.

Matt and Michelle floated down the corridors in silence. He wanted to say something, but he couldn't think of anything. It was almost a relief when they reached the Hellion docks. They went through the open hatch and into the vast space. There, six men stood on a low stage in front of six gleaming Hellions. In front of the stage were rows of chairs.

Strong hands grabbed Matt and swung him around. Matt flailed and turned. It was Major Soto. His foot was casually hooked into the dock railing, and he grinned at Matt. Beside him hung Peal and Jahl, their expressions unreadable.

"Just making sure you're not still looking for payback," Major Soto said.

"He's not," Michelle said, coming up behind him. "I made sure of it."

Soto studied Matt. "No. You're okay. Sit down, have fun, enjoy the pony show."

"You don't think Kyle should go?" Michelle asked.

Soto shrugged. "I just deliver the offers. He accepted." He looked over toward the stage, where Kyle stood in full dark-blue Mecha Corps uniform. The two silver bars of his captain's insignia glittered on the dark gray fabric. His chest was free of other ornamentation. At a glance, he was the recruiting poster come to life.

Until you gave him a closer look. Under the uniform his body seemed hunched from fatigue, and the skin around his eyes was sunken as if after a long sickness. Worst of all was the expression in his eyes. No spark burned there. No joy. Kyle was a robot, hollowed out and empty.

"It's best for him," Major Soto said finally. "He does a good job, gets out, goes back to Eridani, does the Senator thing. This is just a checkmark on a long list of stuff he has to do. Just hope he has his shit together enough to do this one mission right."

Soto then turned back to address Michelle and Matt. "Too bad we couldn't keep you together," Soto said. "I would've gladly been your fourth."

They took seats up front. Michelle waved at Kyle, and he came to the edge of the stage to say hello. He turned first to Matt.

"I'm sorry," he said, offering Matt his hand.

Matt took Kyle's hand and gripped it hard. What could he say? *It wasn't your fault? Apology accepted?* Nothing seemed right.

"Come back soon," Matt said finally. "It'd be good to be a team again."

"You bet," Kyle said. But his eyes darted away.

A few more people drifted in, unfamiliar Corps and Auxiliaries. *Most likely friends of the other Hellion pilots,* Matt thought.

After a short time, Colonel Cruz came out and lined the men up, each under their towering Hellions. He praised each Hellion pilot in turn, highlighting their accomplishments during their training. He even said a few words about how Kyle had put his Demonrider candidacy on hold to lead new Mecha Corps members in a show of force on important Union worlds.

"Picking up the laundry," Jahl whispered.

"Shut up," Major Soto hissed.

Michelle watched the ceremony intently, her eyes fixed on Kyle. She bit her lip, as if seeing Kyle's fear and uncertainty. But she also made furtive glances at Matt. He saw her looking out of the corner of his eye.

He wanted to let her know he'd help her get through whatever came next. She was staying strong, and he admired that. He'd make sure both of them made it to the next level, whatever it might be.

When the ceremony was over, the six pilots got in their Hellions and were towed out to the waiting Displacement Drive battleship, UUS *Atlas*.

Michelle watched them go. She blew out a big breath, as

if in great sadness. Matt put a hand on her shoulder. "He'll be back."

Michelle shrugged off Matt's hand. "Don't say that," she said.

"Don't say what?"

" 'He'll be back.' You don't know that."

"I'm sorry," Matt said.

Michelle shook her head, shoulders slumping. "Just don't say stupid things. You don't know what's going to happen. You don't even know what's going to happen to us."

"Join the illustrious Mecha Auxiliaries," Jahl said, chuckling.

"Or continue your training as Hellion pilots," Peal added. "After all, Colonel Cruz says the past is the future!"

Matt nodded, but neither of those options had any appeal. He couldn't imagine being Mecha Auxiliary, even in Intelligence, like Jahl. He'd never have a chance to find that Corsair. It would be a comfortable, dead-end life, just like being an analyst for a terraforming corporation.

As for working in a Hellion after piloting a Demon, that would be like marrying the best friend of the woman you loved.

"It ain't over till it's over," Soto said in a rich, voice-over tone. "And I don't see any fat ladies singing yet."

"What are you talking about?" Matt asked.

Michelle snorted. "More old Earth sayings."

"They're not just sayings," Soto said. "It's not over. It's a pause. Wait till the other pilots fail, and then Roth will give us another shot."

"You think so?" Michelle asked, crossing her arms.

"Anything can happen." But Soto looked away.

The next week, Michelle went back into the Hellions. Not as full Mecha Corps, like they'd offered, but into advanced training for Merge. Matt watched in the Hellion docks as she worked with the Corps on Merging with Flight Packs first. Her first few tries resulted only in half-finished Merges, with shining antimatter jets gleaming below the incomplete dark-*Mercury* hide of the Hellion. She tumbled out of the cockpit, exhausted, to watch as a more experienced Corps person got in to complete the Merge—in mocking irony, it happened to be Sanjiv. The Hellion seemed to be sneering at them as Sanjiv completed the Merge.

Eventually, Michelle mastered the art of Merging with the Flight Pack, but she got hung up again when it was time to Merge the Hellions themselves. Now Sanjiv and Pelletier were both apologetic.

"It takes years to learn this," they said.

"Not for him," Michelle said, nodding at Matt. "He did it back on Earth, a couple weeks into cadet training."

"Oh yeah. Funny," Pelletier said. Sanjiv laughed too.

On the dock later alone with Matt, she asked, "Why don't you try it?"

"I'm not ready," Matt said. And that was true. But he'd have to make his decision soon. Cruz had given them a week's leave to recover and choose their course. They could go on to Hellion piloting or stay in the Auxiliaries.

Neither of which worked for Matt. He tried to see Dr. Roth and plead his case, but Roth seemed to be avoiding him. So he spent his time camped out in front of Yve's office or watching Michelle or sitting and poking at a slate in the Decompression Lounge, looking for a lever to use on Roth.

But Roth was like the HuMax. All the histories read the same. They started a decade ago, when Roth's Advanced Mechaforms had revolutionized Mecha technology. Before that, Roth's CV included a short stint at a conventional mechanical Mecha manufacturer a dozen years before he founded Advanced Mechaforms. His bio noted only "independent research" during those years. There was speculation he had gone to the Taikong during that time, due to some travel records that took him to the edge of the Union. But swapping allegiances between the different IGOs was insane; it was rumored that the Taikong implanted you with track-and-kill devices using FTL technology, and defecting from the Aliancia might involve you in a duel to the death, if you ever met another citizen of that realm.

Roth's technology was equally shrouded in mystery. The only thing accessible to Matt was an assessment of bio-metal versus composite armor, confirming the dramatic superiority of biomechanical technology. The only thing interesting was a small notation after tests involving a *Nuclear Annihilator (Enhanced Output)*. A sidebar noted: *Biometallic mass damaged beyond regenerative capability; refer to Appendix C for analysis of resulting new form.*

But Appendix C was classified, so Matt was left with his own speculation about what new form the Mecha may have become.

Eventually, Matt caught Yve in the lounge. Yve was sitting at his customary upside-down table, without even a drink bulb in front of him. As if he were waiting for Matt.

"Hey," Yve said, as Matt came up to him.

"Are you avoiding me?"

Yve shook his head. "Usually a more subtle approach is best. Like 'Hello, stranger.' "

"Have you?"

"If I were, I wouldn't be here now," Yve said, running a hand through his hair.

"I have to talk to Roth."

"So you talk to me?" Yve smiled.

"You're the oversight, aren't you? Maybe you can talk some sense into him." But Matt knew Yve was right. He was just looking for someone, anyone, to talk to.

Yve let the silence stretch out. "Are you going to go for the Hellion corps?"

Matt clenched his fists. That was the real question, wasn't it? That's what he had to decide. And if he got right down to it, why wouldn't he? He'd be able to hunt down his father's murderer just as well in a Hellion as in a Demon.

If Matt could ever figure out how to hunt him down at all. Officially, the Union never had any presence on Prospect, so all the records were locked away. Matt remembered more about Prospect than any screen could tell him, and he still didn't have enough to go on. Just the Corsair insignia and that memory of the Corsair leader with HuMax eyes.

"I've got my own location problem," Matt said.

Yve's eyes widened fractionally. "In regard to what?"

Matt shook his head. Yve wouldn't help him if he knew about his insane quest. He probably wouldn't understand it. He'd say something like, *Why are you wasting your life on a ghost?*

"Would you take the Hellion offer?" Matt asked.

Yve frowned. "I've talked to Dr. Roth. About you. I've reviewed your records. And I know Roth wants to find a way to, ah, use you."

"What does that mean?" Matt asked.

Yve shook his head. "I'm not entirely sure. Perhaps a Demon that's designed to be leader controlled, rather than shared-Merge controlled. Maybe something else. I know he has more ideas on the drawing board."

More ideas on the drawing board. Matt leaned forward, licking his lips. A shade of that old Mesh compulsion rose in his mind: *Yes. More. Back in. Cockpit.*

Yve's slate shrilled. He flipped it open and looked at it. All expression disappeared off his face.

"I have to go," Yve said.

"What's the matter?" Matt asked.

Yve's hand convulsed on the slate, snapping it closed. His eyes stared off into the distance. He looked like a dead man.

"Yve?"

Yve kicked off the table and shot for the exit. Matt thought about following, but before he could move, his thoughts were interrupted by Peal and Jahl. They rocketed into the lounge at what must have been thirty kilometers an hour, to make a hard landing on the stainless-steel wall. They flipped up to where Matt was sitting on the roof and caught themselves, breathless, on the edge of the table.

"You have to see this," Jahl said.

"Everyone has to see this," Peal added.

"Yes. You're right. Coupling to the lounge's wall screen."

Shouts of "Hey!" and "What happened!" came from the patrons as the bar's wall screens flickered and went black, showing only a single crimson insignia in the center. The insignia was similar to the Corsair's thousand-daggers standard, with one significant difference: in this design, a single, large center dagger was orbited by a hundred smaller blades.

"... stand by," the wall screen's speakers boomed. "Please stand by. Please stand by ..."

"I didn't mean *we* had to show everyone," Peal said.

"This transmission is happening on every world in the Universal Union," Jahl said. "Simulcast across the FTL network and transmitted by local satellites. They're just waiting for enough people to pay attention."

"They?" Matt asked.

"Corsairs," Jahl said.

"Rayder," Peal added. "He's stepping out from the shadows."

Matt's stomach flipped over. No wonder Yve had retreated at full speed. But what were they planning? Matt used his slate to send a message to Michelle's access card. COME UP TO DECOMP NOW.

COMING, she sent back.

The transmission's chanting stopped. The screen cut to a grainy, bit-rotted FTL image of a man dressed in a uniform bearing the a version of the Corsair insignia with a single dagger. He stood in what looked like a simple, spare office with windows that looked out over a dark city beyond. His hair was dark, almost blue-black. His face was angular and intense, as if carved from a block of granite by an inspired sculptor. And his eyes—

One was violet and one was gold.

"I am Rayder," the man said.

Matt rocked back with the force of recognition. His

body burned, as if immersed in a sun. A storm of insane rage built in him. But through the storm, one thought screamed:

Rayder is the Corsair who killed my father!

He hadn't been chasing a ghost. The man was real. The HuMax were real. The greatest evil alive was the man he'd sworn to kill.

All of his success—in life, in school, in the Mecha—it was all suddenly meaningless. He was a fool, lazy and confused, letting Ash's death consume him, letting Kyle's antics enrage him, letting Michelle distract him with the possibility of love. He should have never wavered from his childhood purpose for an instant.

On-screen, Rayder smiled at the camera. It was the smile of a snake, a grin without a shred of humor. "I address you today first to make a simple demonstration."

The screen changed to show a battle diagram. A Union Displacement Drive battleship, the UUS *Atlas*, floated over a green planet tagged CANTARA.

A new Displacement Drive ship appeared, this one tagged RAYDER 1. A second Displacement Drive ship popped into the frame, tagged RAYDER 2. Dozens of battleships swarmed toward the UUS *Atlas*. Shards of the UUS *Atlas* flew off into space, and a haze of fighters converged on the Union ship.

Stats began scrolling from the *Atlas*. Damage reports. Defenses mobilized. Time to charge the Displacement Drive. Deployment of internal troops. And, perhaps most important:

FIGHTER DOCK COMPROMISED
MECHA DOCK COMPROMISED
NAVIGATION COMPROMISED

The screen changed again as everyone in the Decompression Lounge watched breathlessly. Matt was aware that other cadets and Auxiliaries had flowed into the bar to watch the show, but that was unimportant. His brain resonated with only one thought: *Rayder killed my father.*

The Union's most wanted is my boogeyman.

Now surveillance video showed a Mecha dock. A dozen Hellions stood, bolted down to metal mesh. Raw stone rose above the Mecha. A large control tower extended out of the stone. The glass walls of the control tower had shattered, and a woman hung impaled on the shards. The external air lock was open, showing glimpses of fighters and plasma explosions.

Three space-suited figures shot across the screen toward the Hellions. Tags identified them: CAPT. KYLE PETEROV, LT. PAULA VORJOY, and LT. BENE ROSSBARD.

"Kyle," Michelle called out, echoing the screen in utter surprise. Matt looked up. She'd come to hang by his side.

Kyle reached his Hellion as a heavy cargo ship roared in through the air lock, thrusters full on in heavy braking. The interior of the cavern briefly lit as bright as day. Kyle held tight to the edge of the Hellion's cockpit as he was battered by the ship's exhaust. His two companions went tumbling out of the frame.

Space-suited troops poured out of the cargo ship. Some headed through the control tower, deeper into the ship. Some went to the main air lock.

And one group went toward the Hellions. Led by a single man, they moved with calm purpose, as if their actions had been scripted. They wore Rayder's single-dagger version of the Corsair insignia.

As Kyle pulled himself into the Mecha's cockpit, the Corsair in the lead raised a pistol and shot. The round hit Kyle in the upper arm. Air and blood fountained in a pink jet out of Kyle's interface suit. Kyle sagged, barely maintaining his grip on the Mecha cockpit. He dragged himself in. Another bullet glanced off the Hellion next to him.

The screen changed to show a cockpit view of Kyle. His face was white and his eyes were bloodshot as he slapped a patch on his suit. The hissing stopped and he pulled in great breaths, whooping through the microphones.

As the cockpit closed, Kyle strapped himself in and brought his hands up to his helmet, ready to remove it and plug into the Mecha's neural networks. He mouthed something as the cockpit folded up.

Something stopped the cockpit from closing. Kyle cursed and struggled with his straps. A hand reached down toward Kyle. The screen suddenly went dark.

The screen changed viewpoint again. The Corsairs had lodged a scaffoldlike device between the sections of the Mecha's cockpit, holding two of its pieces open. The lead Corsair scrambled into the cockpit.

The screen went back to Rayder, who spread his arms to his audience, as if embracing them. "You see our power now. We can take any Union warship. We can smash any Union planet, as we had our revenge on Geos. We now even hold your Mecha technology."

The camera panned to focus on Rayder as he paced. "But that is what I've had to do to level the field. Your Union would never seriously consider what I propose, if it wasn't for the threat of the same violence they hold over every Corsair."

"Subliminal influencing technology detected," Jahl said. "Filtering signal."

"My offer is simple: it is time for the Union to choose a new Prime. I enter my candidacy, provided that all votes from all Union worlds, frontier and core, are counted alike."

"Elect me Prime, or die in fire," Soto ground out, coming up to join the group.

"Elect me Prime. I will move the Union forward. And in time, I will show you what the Union hides in its labs. I will reveal how the Union has been lying to you all these years."

Rayder continued. "Has it chafed you that the Union hides its greatest advancements in secure labs? Have you wondered if there is something more than longevity treatments and pervasive computing? There is."

Rayder stopped to gesture outside at the city beyond his window. The camera's focus changed to look out over it. When it snapped into focus, Matt gasped.

Carbon-darkened spires reached for the sky. Ruined buildings slumped together, like drunks holding each other for support. The stubs of elevated walkways projected from the buildings, arching over broad avenues that glittered with frost. Some structures spilled green-tinted light out onto the streets. Some were sheared off to reveal complex crystalline machinery. Huge squares hosted the fallen remains of monumental architecture. One was nearly intact. It showed a man and a woman looking up toward the stars, their gazes intent and piercing, even in ruin.

"10,956," Matt said in sudden realization.

"What?" Michelle asked.

"That photo. My Perfect Record. My dad." Matt spat. The ideas were too big. His father had shown him that image. He'd seen that sculpture and that city.

Did that mean his father had been there? To the world where Rayder was broadcasting from?

It made sense. There had been times when Dad was away on Displacement Drive ships for weeks at a time, while Matt stayed behind on Prospect. Was one of those trips to Rayder's world, where he'd taken that image?

"10,956," Matt breathed. He remembered that one clear as day. A perfect match for the scene outside Rayder's window.

Was the location of that world what his dad was trying to hide from Rayder all those years ago? Or had Rayder already been there—and he'd attacked his dad on Prospect as retribution?

Either way, it all fit together.

All he had to do was remember what his father was working on. Then he'd have the answer he needed—and the answer to the Union's location problem.

Matt searched his memories, letting his Perfect Record take him back to those far-off times. Tears streamed down his cheeks as he had a picnic with his dad on the hot surface of Prospect, during one of the times the near-constant wind died down. As he watched a video of Geos and Eridani, but not the Geos and Eridani he knew. These planets had rings. Spindly and thread-thin, they arced across the night. Something they'd lost in the HuMax war, his dad told him. They'd lost a lot of things.

He remembered the last time his father came back from his Displacement Drive jaunts. He'd been tired, withdrawn. Fighting with the Union, he said. Fighting with himself. But then it'd been Matt's birthday, and there'd been cake, and Matt hadn't thought about it anymore.

Matt searched the days after that last trip, remembering whirling star charts on the screens at night, seeing anew how his father had handled those gleaming HuMax artifacts with a thoughtful expression, as if he knew how precious and dangerous the objects were that were now in his possession.

But the star charts were of known worlds, not of uncharted planets with shattered cities. And his dad had spent most of his time in the sealed lab. Matt wasn't allowed in there. Nobody was allowed in there. Dad had hidden too much.

Try as he might, Matt couldn't put together the location of Rayder's home world.

But if the data could be recovered from the lab on Prospect . . . if there was any chance, however small . . .

Matt tore himself out of the seat and rocketed at the exit. He had to find Yve. And this time, he wouldn't take no for an answer.

Matt's headlong plunge led first to Yve's office, where a Mecha Auxiliary explained that Yve was out. Matt jumped over her desk and opened the door to Yve's meeting room. No Yve. He turned to find Peal, Jahl, and Michelle waiting behind him. They must have followed from the lounge.

"Gotta find Yve," Matt told them, heading for the door.

"He's in Cruz's office," Jahl said, peering at his slate. "But you shouldn't—"

Matt didn't wait to listen. He rocketed out of Yve's office and down the corridor to Cruz's quarters. In the anteroom, armed Auxiliaries snapped to attention and went to block Matt as he shot into the room. Matt flipped over, caromed off the floor, flew over their heads, and hit Cruz's office doors. He pulled on the latch without effect. The door screen read: MEETING IN PROGRESS.

"Hands up, cadet!" bellowed one of the Auxiliaries, over the snick of his MK-1 safety release.

Matt gave the door one last tug, then turned. One of the Auxiliaries held his weapon pointed at Matt. The other covered Michelle, Peal, and Jahl, who'd just entered the anteroom.

"I have to talk to Yve Perraux!" Matt said, raising his hands.

"Turn around," the Auxiliary said. "Hands on your head!"

Matt groaned, frustration building in him like a pressure cooker. "I know how to solve the origin problem!"

"Last warning! Turn around!"

Slowly, Matt started to turn. If he could get a good kick-off from the doors, he might have a chance . . .

"Please let me pass," a familiar voice said behind Matt. He turned to see Dr. Roth, standing expressionlessly on the carpet.

"Turn around!" the Auxiliary said. "One moment, sir, until we secure the prisoner—"

"Dr. Roth," Matt said. "I know where Rayder is!"

Roth's eyebrows rose just a millimeter. "I suppose you have the universal stellar coordinates memorized."

"No! But my father knew. He found it. That's what Rayder was after. Rayder killed my dad."

"Turn around!" the Auxiliary bellowed.

But Roth laid a hand on the man's arm, his eyes widening with intrigue. "Let me talk with him."

Roth fixed his eyes on Matt. "Your father. The Union researcher on Prospect. How could he have possibly determined Rayder's location?"

"The view behind Rayder in that video today matches an image my father showed me," Matt began. "That must be the data he was trying to hide when Rayder came—"

"And you are in possession of this data?"

"No, I just remember a picture. But if we went back to Prospect, maybe we could recover it." Matt's wild gaze found Jahl and Peal. "Sergeant Khoury could recover it!"

"Stand aside," Roth said finally, addressing the Auxiliary.

"Sir, I don't recommend—," the Auxiliary began.

"Stand aside and open the door."

The Auxiliary gulped, lowered his weapon, and opened the door. Yve and Cruz were in heated conference with Congressperson Tomita on the screen.

"—tried the Mecha long-range destruct," Yve said. "But there's no confirming pulse."

The two men fell silent and turned to stare at the opening door. Roth walked in, his Velcro soles scratching on the carpet, motioning for Matt and the others to join him.

"Of course the Mecha destruct didn't work," Dr. Roth said. "Rayder is no fool. He would disable the function first thing."

"You tried to destroy the Mecha?" Michelle spoke up. "What about Kyle?"

Roth ignored her. "Gentlemen, we have new information. Cadet Lowell may have the answer to the location problem."

Yve jumped, staring at Roth and Matt in turn. "How? His father was working on it, but he never solved it."

"Or he never told you," Roth said.

Yve shook his head and glared at Matt. "He's known all this time?"

"He doesn't have the coordinates, but if the data was there on Prospect, it can probably be recovered."

Cruz broke in, coming out of his seat. "So what are you

suggesting? Send this kid on a Displacement Drive ship ten thousand light-years across the galaxy? On the chance that he *might* be right? That we *might* be able to get that data?"

"Yes. On the fastest-reflux drive possible."

"That's the most idiotic plan I've ever—"

"Wait," Congressperson Tomita broke in. "Why are you so vehement about this, Dr. Roth?"

Before he could answer, Yve cut the debate short. "Cadet Lowell is the son of Dr. Oscar Stanford. I assume you recall the nature of Dr. Stanford's research on Prospect?"

Tomita stared at Matt for several long beats. Finally, he sighed. "Send him. And do it fast."

PART THREE

"A good battle plan that you act on today is better than a perfect one tomorrow."

—George S. Patton, General of the Army, United States of America

16

PAST

The UUS *Helios* had that raw look of a new Displacement Drive ship. Where fresh armor didn't cover the surface, construction scaffolding webbed the rocky core. Workers swarmed through the asteroid, welding strong steel reinforcements, adding weapons batteries, and building the decks that would house its crew. This rock was fast being transformed into a fortified platform equal to that of the *Ulysses*.

At the moment, though, its incomplete dock held only a single Hellion, two Cheetah fighters, and a handful of transport shuttles. Matt looked at them uncertainly as their shuttle locked in to its cradle.

Jahl read his mind. "We don't need the defense," he said. "The *Helios* can run faster than anything out there. And, theoretically, even the incomplete armor can take a direct hit from a hundred-meter asteroid and survive."

Regardless of the risk, the *Helios* was what they needed. Brand-new tech meant the ship could recharge its Displacement Drive in only thirty seconds. Displacing 120 times an hour, it could move 2,400 light-years at maximum speed. Prospect was more than fourteen thousand light-years away from Mecha Base, but even that vast distance was only a six-hour trip. They could be out and back in a day, if the data was easily accessible.

Still, Matt wondered, *will that be fast enough?* UNN

showed the entire Universal Union in turmoil. Demonstrations on Eridani demanded the Senate and Prime act, throw everything the Union had at Rayder immediately.

Explanations of the problem of where to strike and the trouble with coordinating such a massive attack didn't go over well with the public. Dr. Roth's biomechanical tech was the magic cure for all their ills. He'd been built up by the press for so many years, they had blind faith that Mecha would save them. Hellions, Demons—they didn't care. Heroes or new cadets—they didn't care about that either. All they knew was they had to act now! The Union seemed to be simply getting in the way of Roth's victory.

It also didn't help that the fringe press had picked up on the HuMax angle and were playing it up for all it was worth. Why did Rayder look the way he did? Was it just a disguise to unsettle them, or was this the start of a HuMax rebirth? *History rewritten? The genocide a failure?* the press asked. Bustling Senators ducked and ran when confronted with questions about the HuMax. The official explanation of the HuMax question was simply silence.

But Matt already knew: somehow, somewhere, HuMax had survived. He had been nose to nose with their leader. His father died because he was in the monster's way.

Public rage had boiled over, and arsonists had already hit the Union Public Hall outside the Senatorial Chambers. The UNN ran bumps of the blazing flames and billowing smoke over the burning questions:

Union Incapacitated?
Military, Strategic Failure?
Have We Been Misled?

At the same time, governors of the Union's new colony worlds began wondering openly about joining the Aliancia or Taikong. Throughout the Union, everyone looked up at the skies nervously, expecting another attack from Rayder at any moment.

But Rayder had returned to the shadows. In the wake of his announcement, he seemed content to sit back and watch the Union tear at itself.

The questions were big and ugly: How long had he been planning his strike? How big of a force did he command? What was his ultimate goal?

Matt shivered. *And this is the man I'm supposed to kill.*

It seemed an impossible task. One man against a super-human with Mecha and the capability to strike at the heart of the Union? He couldn't even work with his teammates well enough to Merge the Demon. They probably wouldn't find the actual coordinates to Rayder's location; the data would be too bit-rotted, too far gone.

"We'll find it," Jahl said quietly to Matt, as they floated down the newly chiseled corridors of the *Helios*. Only a handful of steel pressure doors were in place. Everything else was plasti-sealed rock.

"That's really—"

"Creepy, I know," Jahl said. "But trust the Wunderkind of Hyva. If the data is on Prospect, I'll retrieve it."

"And if it isn't?" Matt wished he'd been able to take Peal too. Hell, he wished Michelle and Soto and Stoll could come as well. But Senator Tomita was adamant: Matt and one data-recovery specialist only. Everyone else had to be prepared to ship out to defend the Union.

"I wish they were here too," Jahl told him.

Matt just smiled back at him and tried to think of absolutely nothing, so Jahl might shut up for a while.

Unlike most Displacement Drive ships, the *Helios'* bridge was buried deep within the heart of the asteroid. Matt and Jahl drifted down the elongated throat of the vessel before they found the bridge near the inner belly of the rock. Inside, the bridge was completely covered in NPP displays. The swirling maelstrom of the protoplanet dominated one side of their POV, while the hulking mass of Mecha Base covered the other. It was like floating into empty space. Matt instinctively flailed and looked for a handgrip.

"Footholds are available near the control consoles," an unfamiliar man said from the center of the room. He was flanked by two familiar faces: Dr. Roth and Yve Perraux. Three pilots wearing interface suits reclined in the very middle of the room, their hands resting lightly on low consoles.

"Captain John Ivers, meet Cadet Matt Lowell and Auxiliary Jahl Khoury," Yve said, when they'd drawn close.

Captain Ivers studied Matt briefly. "So you're going to save the Union?"

Matt made himself nod.

Ivers seemed satisfied. He turned to one of the pilots. "Is everyone on board?"

"Yes, sir."

"Launch for Prospect."

The scene outside changed instantly to a smooth star field. Matt jumped. "You Displaced straight from Mecha Base? Uh, sir?"

Captain Ivers grinned. "Our pilots are good."

"Your pilots are assisted by my bio-interface technology," Dr. Roth said.

"That too," Ivers conceded.

"They're using the interface suit to sense and optimize the next jump," Jahl said, respect resonating in his voice. "It's—what?—potentially a factor about a hundred times more accurate than conventional piloting?"

"About that, yes," Dr. Roth said, allowing Jahl a thin grin. "The challenge isn't simply recharge speed; it's in the calculation and compensation for gravitational fields outside the Displacement Drive ship's microgravity."

The stars changed again, this time more subtly, the star field shifting slightly toward starboard. One nearby sun glowed much brighter than before.

Before anyone got a chance to speak, the stars shifted again. The bright star disappeared from the display. They'd already shot right past it.

"It's a little disconcerting," Jahl said with a nervous smile.

"I'm afraid the *Helios* has few comforts," Captain Ivers said. "There's a storage room with sleep nets and Insta-Paks. Beyond that and the latrines, not much has been built out yet."

"I'll stay here," Matt said.

Ivers nodded, while Jahl left for the storage room. Dr. Roth and Yve remained. Dr. Roth looked out at the shifting stars, his gaze far away. It was telling that he'd come on the trip to Prospect personally. Was he concerned that Rayder had captured his technology? Or did he not trust Matt?

Hours crawled by. Matt thought of sleeping, but his whirring mind couldn't let him off the edge. So many questions. And not just how they were going to defeat Rayder.

I didn't know he'd found it. Yve's words.

I'm sure you recall his research on Prospect. Dr. Roth's words.

This could mean the Union had been looking for Rayder's location all along. No. Not Rayder's location. Rayder had been looking for the same planet too. That's why his father had died.

But why? What was that planet?

Matt had to ask. He floated over to join Yve, who rapidly tucked away his slate. "What's up?" he asked, shifting uncomfortably.

"What was my father looking for?" Matt asked. "What is that planet?"

Yve plastered a sickly grin on his face and drummed his fingers on his slate.

"It's not just Rayder's location. I know that."

Yve looked away. For a long time, it didn't seem like he was going to say anything. Finally, he said, "It's the final HuMax world."

"Final HuMax world?" Matt asked.

"Their grandest world," Yve told him. "The location was lost in the HuMax war. Or buried. Or . . . you don't know how close we came to being wiped out. A lot of the records are simply gone."

Matt nodded, suddenly understanding the implications. If that was the most advanced HuMax world, the technological treasures there would be enormous.

"Did the Union know HuMax were still alive?" Matt pressed.

Yve's face went still and unexpressive.

"Did you know Rayder was HuMax?"

Yve sighed. "I didn't . . . I can't . . ."

"You didn't or you can't?"

Yve shook his head.

"I deserve an explanation," Matt grated.

Yve laid a hand on Matt's shoulder, and for a moment, his face convulsed in sadness. "Yes, you do. Matt, I feel awful about what happened to you, but I'm bound by an oath to the Union. I can't give you your answers."

"Which means yes?" Rage welled in Matt. It made complete sense. The need to hit the Corsairs with an irresistible force; the urgency for Merging the Demon; all the crazy, stupid chances they took. It was all because the Union knew who Rayder was. *What* Rayder was. A Superman who'd survived a genocide and was now bent on the destruction of the Union that had destroyed his race.

Matt changed tack. "How'd you get off Prospect?"

"I told you. The transport—"

Matt clenched his fists and cut Yve off. "The transport I saw destroyed, which somehow conveniently led to a Union Displacement Drive ship that didn't exist, which escaped bombardment by Rayder. Right. Good story."

"I—," Yve began, then caught himself, clamping his jaw tight shut. For a while, the only sound in the bridge was the incessant hum of the ship's antimatter core.

"It wasn't just Rayder," Yve said. "It was a half-dozen Corsair ships, led on by the promise of treasure by Rayder. Rayder turned on them the moment he had what he wanted. He wiped out all of their ships except one."

"Which you shipped out on," Matt whispered.

"I had to. I—"

"You joined the Corsairs?"

"Only to get away. As soon as we hit the Aliancia, I was gone."

Matt gripped the railing hard enough to make his bones creak. *Yve. Part of the Corsairs.*

"The Corsairs aren't a monolithic block," Yve said, stepping away from Matt. "Some are relatively benign—"

"Benign!" Matt yelled, seeing his father crawl, trailing blood, across the expanded-steel deck.

Captain Ivers snapped to attention and came to approach the men. Matt quickly forced himself to relax. Yve had done what he had to do. It was the only way out. Desperate people do what they have to.

"Is everything okay here, cadet?" Ivers said.

"Fine," Matt said.

"Maybe you should wait in the storage room," Ivers told Matt.

"It's okay," Yve said. "He has his reasons."

Ivers studied the two men, then shrugged and drifted back to watch the displays above the pilots.

"I know what I did was wrong," Yve said, softly. "And I know there are shades of gray you don't want to see. But I hope this won't change your dedication to wiping out Rayder, because he—"

Matt bellowed laughter. In the mind's eye of his Perfect Record, Rayder gave the order to kill his father. Like he could ever forget that. Like any shade of gray would change that. No. He knew exactly what he was here for.

"Rayder's going to die," Matt said. "I guarantee that."

From orbit, Prospect was a dusty, yellow-colored ball, striped by formidable ochre mountain ranges. There were no oceans, no lakes, no green oases. Only a thin blue membrane of breathable atmosphere at the horizon indicated that it was a planet with an oxygen-nitrogen atmosphere capable of sustaining life. Even at that, it was tenuous, barely breathable. Matt remembered that some of the

UARL staff had to use supplemental oxygen when they
were out on the surface.

A suitable final world for HuMax, Matt thought, as they
dropped toward the surface in one of the *Helios'* shuttles.
The tiny, four-person craft was completely full: Dr. Roth,
Yve, Matt, and Jahl. Nobody spoke as they descended.

They touched down outside Prospect Advanced Research Labs' surface hangar. Matt swallowed, scenes from
his childhood flickering through his mind. Hiking to the
nearby hills. The constantly shifting sand dunes. The bright
steel of the hangar abraded by the incessant wind.

One of the hangar girders had fallen, and the domed
roof had a broken-backed look. Other than that, it could
have been the day Matt ran screaming out onto the sand
sixteen years ago. The hangar door gaped open, sand cascading into its interior.

Inside the hangar, absolutely nothing had changed. The
blasted and broken Powerloader still slumped against one
wall, with only a coating of dust and corrosion marking the
passage of time. The shuttle still sat open, ready for Matt
and his father to run to its safety. But now the interior was
dark, the batteries long since exhausted.

"Are you all right?" Jahl asked.

Matt nodded, biting his lip.

Jahl went to help Dr. Roth bring the lab's power core
back online. The steel-cage elevator juddered and groaned
as the lighting came on and dim screens showed start-up
routines.

The four men entered the elevator and descended in silence. At the bottom of the shaft, blue-tinged work-lights
glowed, flickering from years of disuse. Long, precisely ma-
chined corridors led off from a domed central space. Along
the sides of some of the hallways, carvings showed scenes
of heroic people lounging against lush landscapes.

As a kid, Matt had never even wondered about the art.
Now it fit. He imagined violet- and yellow-eyed HuMax
thronging through these broad corridors, looking longingly

at their artwork. They had no forests, no seas, no verdant vistas. Was it possible they hadn't chosen to live on the most challenging planets in the Expansion? Had they attacked humanity, in part, as revenge?

Matt led the others down a broad corridor toward his father's lab. Dark rooms gaped off either side. Some were massive and echoing. Work lights cast long shadows in one gigantic space, which had markings like a football field etched in the stone floor. Dark stains hinted that the final game played here hadn't been football.

At his dad's outer lab, Matt stopped and held on to the doorframe for support. He could almost see his father standing there, just like that last day. The only difference was that the screens displayed only a single message, SYSTEM OFFLINE, rather than the diagrams from so long ago.

"Good," Jahl said, pushing past him. "It's a standard Union Datasystems machine. If the data is there, I'll get it."

Jahl sat at the console and muttered into the mike, swiping at the gestural interface.

SYSTEM NOT FOUND, the screen replied. Dr. Roth and Yve exchanged glances.

"No problem," Jahl said, pairing his slate with the system. It displayed a long trail of diagnostic data. "Give me a bit."

Matt made himself walk farther into the room. Beyond the outer lab was a small office with a cubicle maze he used to use for hide-and-seek, and the closed door to his father's inner lab.

Matt went to look into the office cubicles. Dusty desks and dim displays stared back at him. On a table in the center of the space were metallic cylinders and crystal spheres, all physically tagged with their recovery location. HuMax technology. Matt picked up a lightweight sphere. It glowed briefly, and a voice spoke in his head: *Welcome, new user. Please speak registration number.*

"What the hell?" Matt exclaimed, dropping the sphere. It fell and hit the table with a metallic ping.

"Direct mental link," Yve said, making Matt jump. "One of the things the HuMax were way ahead of us on, even with Dr. Roth's interface suits."

"My interface suits are superior in many ways," Dr. Roth said from the other room.

"Their technology was still more advanced than ours," Yve shot back at Dr. Roth.

"As point examples, perhaps," Dr. Roth replied.

"If the HuMax were so advanced, why not use the technology for the Union?" Matt asked, struggling to keep his voice even. With that tech, maybe his father would have survived. Maybe Rayder wouldn't even be a threat!

Yve frowned. "It has as many bad applications as good. In fact, it's widely speculated that tech like this was used to keep the HuMax under control."

"Control by whom?" Matt probed.

"HuMax were closely tracked," Yve replied. "There was a point in time when anyone could bear a HuMax child, once the genetic modifications were well-known and easily applied. Many did. And many were grown in factories."

"The natural result of allowing any mother to pick her child's enhancements. Of course they would choose every one," added Dr. Roth.

Yve nodded. "Or allowing any corporation to grow their superworker, someone to send out to do the tough terraforming work on marginal worlds."

And none of this is in the histories, Matt thought. How much were they really hiding?

More important, why hadn't his father told the Union about the location of the HuMax final world? What did he fear from that revelation?

"We're screwed," Jahl called, from the outer lab. "Maybe."

Matt and Yve went back outside the cubicles, where Jahl was poring over code. Jahl turned to face the three other men.

"Whoever wiped this did an overachieving job—1,024 scrubs at the molecular level. There's nothing left."

"So why's it a maybe?" Yve asked.

"Because we're smarter these days." Jahl paused, as if waiting for someone to complete his sentence. When nobody did, he continued, "We have nanolevel reconstructors. They may be able to rebuild the data structures."

"So get started!" Yve yelped.

"Already started. But they have to scrub through the bit-rot several trillions of times. Sit back; we'll be here for a few hours."

Matt wandered back into the cubicles, back to the door of the sealed lab. This was where his father had hidden through many long days and nights. He put his hand on the door screen, but it just squawked and displayed: NO ADMITTANCE AUTHORIZED. INPUT ALTERNATE ENTRY CODE.

Just like when he was a kid. His father had watched him try to get entry to the lab, punching in every possible combination of numbers on the keypad on the screen.

"Not yet," his dad had told him, before slipping into the lab without him.

But one day, he'd said something strange, something in that passionate voice he got when he was thinking about Matt's mother. "The lab's my heart now, and the key to my heart is a purple flower, a barren red rock, and a hanging hospital gown."

Matt stared at the keypad. *Was that some kind of code?* The keys had only numbers on them, not letters.

Numbers. Like on the photos.

The purple flower was 42. The barren red rock, that had to be 6,342. And a hospital gown, there were a lot of photos with those in them, but there was only one that was hanging alone: 941.

With shaking fingers, Matt keyed in 426342941.

The lab door popped open, dust motes filtering down in the harsh work light.

Matt slipped inside, his heart thundering. His father had hidden some things for only him to find.

The interior of the secure lab was solid stainless steel. Dim purplish lights glowed down from the ceiling. Also projecting from the ceiling were fire-foam sprayers and carbon-rimmed apertures that looked uncomfortably like the business end of a flamethrower.

For sterilization? Matt wondered.

In the middle of the secure lab, on an examination table, hulked a dried black mass. Thickly wrinkled, veined, and cracked with age, it looked more plant than animal. Matt leaned in to inspect it. Coarse, shriveled leaves grew from a thick central stalk, together with rock-hard pods the size of his fist. Matt pulled at one of the leaves, expecting it to crumble into dust, but the plant was more leathery than brittle, mummified by its long entombment in the lab.

"HuMax technology, maybe," Jahl said behind him.

Matt jumped and whirled. "Fuck! You scared the crap out of me."

"Sorry," Jahl said, sliding onto a stool in front of a long, stainless-steel workbench. He poked at the lab tools in front of him, then bent over a screen and turned it on.

"What are you doing?" Matt asked, feeling profoundly uncomfortable. This was his dad's space. Only he was supposed to be in here.

"Then you shoulda closed the door," Jahl told him. "And, yes, I know you really, really, really don't like when I read your mind."

The screen flashed to life, displaying: SYSTEM OFFLINE. RE-SOURCES 100% UTILIZED.

"Sorry. I had to check," Jahl said. "But it looks like the lab system and the exterior system are one and the same. It's running the same reconstruction software."

"What does that mean?"

"It means if the rebuild doesn't work, we really are screwed. We'll know in an hour and ten." He got up off the stool and went back to the outer lab, closing the door behind him with a solid thunk.

Matt poked through the sample drawers and storage cabinets, but the rest of the HuMax artifacts didn't look much different from the ones outside. Matt carefully avoided the direct-mental-interface globes, and he was glad he hadn't picked up the cylinders when he saw they were tagged TOOL/WEAPON.

One of the lab benches had been set up as a desk. A photo of Matt's father's graduating class at Aurora University sat on one side of the desk, next to a smaller image of Matt, and another frame with his mom's photo in it. Matt picked up his dad's photo and looked at it. The man was impossibly young. No older than Matt was at this moment. What had he been like when he was Matt's age?

Matt had to squeeze back tears.

Can I avenge my father? Can I take on an entire race to do it?

On the other side of the desk, a dusty figure lay. Matt started. His old PowerSuit Plus toy. It was cool, because you could use a little slate to control it, walk it across the ground, and make it pick things up. It was one of the reasons he'd saved and saved for the Imp when he was growing up on the *Rock*.

Matt picked it up and turned it over in his hands. His dad must have brought it in here. Had he picked it up absentmindedly on his way into the lab one of his final days?

Matt opened the cargo compartment of the PowerSuit Plus. He'd left something in there, a scrap of plastic. He pulled it out and unfolded it.

There was writing on the plastic. But not his. His father's neat, precise block lettering. It read:

One perfect blue sky, a thousand sparrows, the beach at sunset with a silhouetted sailboat. The first city on Earth, rays through leaves against Eridani sky, bees in a hive; textile weavers on Hyva, a raptor against a full moon, the end of the first road on Prospect. Wine bottles and green grapes against a hillside vineyard, a 1952 Ford, Gantry 99; wild parrots in Brazil, heavy water mining on Jupiteroid world, pills in a green case. Your mother in a pink gown, my lab late at night, sleeping in the chair, our picnic on Prospect.

Matt's Perfect Record flashed each image and its number as he read it. Each complete and unmistakable, each as clear as the day he saw them on his dad's slate.

But the numbers themselves were meaningless. Galactic coordinates were three numbers, standardized by their distance from Earth with the axis of the Milky Way galaxy as an arbitrary north. They'd have long decimals after . . .

Wait.

2848865833233.908296865, 2947956624464.03808585, 385-6863685235.3075080672, if he followed the periods and commas.

Could that be it? The location of the HuMax final world?

On the back of the paper, a single scrawled number: 10,956.

The image of the city behind Rayder. The one Matt had seen during that infamous broadcast.

That was it. Matt wanted to scream with glee. His father had found the final world, and he'd hidden his backup here, with clues only Matt could decipher.

I know where Rayder is.

Matt ran out of the lab, clutching the scrap of plastic. He had to tell everyone. He had found the location.

Except . . . why hadn't his dad told the Union? Why had he gone to all the trouble to hide the information?

But did it matter? He could take the fight to Rayder!

In the outer lab, Jahl sat tensely over his console, while Dr. Roth looked over his shoulder. Yve was nowhere to be seen.

"What about the Displacement Drive ship records?" Dr.

Roth asked Jahl. "Those would be stored locally on the ship."

Jahl shook his head. "The ship Dr. Stanford used, the *Titan*, was lost in an engagement with the Aliancia over a decade ago."

"Then we are at an end," Dr. Roth said, his face emotionless.

Peal looked up at Matt. "We're still screwed," he said. "I can't recover the data. It's too far gone."

Matt grinned, nearly brimming over with elation. "Maybe not." He waved the slip of plastic at them. Dr. Roth took it and squinted at the words.

"I don't understand," Dr. Roth said.

Matt explained his father's old memory games and the numbering scheme they'd used. Roth nodded, rapt.

"Of course. A cipher only you can decode. Brilliant."

Matt nodded.

"So?" Jahl asked. "What are the coordinates? Where's Rayder?"

Matt grinned. "Maybe it's best I tell Colonel Cruz and Congressperson Tomita personally, when we return to Mecha Base."

Thinking, *Because then maybe I can lead the team. Maybe I can meet Rayder face-to-face.*

In a Demon.

The trip back to Mecha Base was uneventful, so Matt slept in the storage room. He half expected to wake to Dr. Roth bending over him, with NPP screens in the background showing the coordinates he held in his head.

But when he woke, it was to the thud and thunder of a bombardment.

Matt flew down to the bridge. Captain Ivers swore over the pilots, while Yve and Dr. Roth watched the 360-degree screens with wide eyes.

They were back at Mecha Base. On one side, the hulking gray asteroid covered their point of view. On the other side, though, the maelstrom was dotted with ships. The lead asteroid was instantly recognizable, even without reading its tag: the heavily armored UUS *Atlas*. The ship Rayder had captured.

Behind the *Atlas* were three other Displacement Drive ships. These were more typical asteroid ships, mainly rock. They sparked as bits of rock and dust scoured their surface.

Nearer Mecha Base, battleships from the *Atlas* grappled with an army of Hellions. The flash of Fireflies and Seekers lit the red-orange dust with a hellish radiance.

Mecha Base was under attack.

Rayder had found them.

17

ASSAULT

Matt stared openmouthed at the battle outside, damning himself for not expecting it. Rayder had captured the *Atlas*, its crew, and the Mecha Corps. He must have scoured the brains of the men and women he held hostage. Of course he'd discover where Mecha Base was—and of course he'd make it his first target.

White-hot explosions painted the bridge of the *Helios* in ghostly light as the battle raged. For the moment, nobody moved, shocked at the enormity of the offensive.

Outside, hundreds of Rayder's battleships advanced on scores of Flight Pack–equipped Hellions. The battleships came fast, in complex, dancing patterns, screaming past the Hellions and firing on them from both sides. The Hellions thrashed and convulsed in the concentrated fire. A handful of battleships accelerated toward Mecha Base, with Hellions in close pursuit. The Hellions fired Seekers at Rayder's battleships, taking out one, two, three at once. But more pressed on.

Another battleship threw on even more acceleration and impacted the giant steel doors of the Hellion dock, warping one out of place. Air gusted out from the dock, crystallizing quickly in the cold of space.

Three Hellions outside the dock turned to fire on the crashed battleship. Behind them, another battleship decelerated fast and fired on the Hellions, sending them scattering. One caught itself deftly on the edge of Mecha Base's armor and reached down to swing its companion out of the line of fire.

The way they moved looked familiar. Matt saw the tags on the *Helios'* NPP: MAJOR G. SOTO and CADET MICHELLE KIND.

My team, he thought. *They're being attacked.*

"Holy hell," Captain Ivers said, breaking the silence. Matt realized it had been only moments since they Displaced in.

Rayder's battleships advanced toward Mecha Base, their complex formations confusing and overcoming the Hellion's maneuverability. More numerous and better-armed, they were winning the fight to board Mecha Base.

But it wasn't all going Rayder's way. As Matt watched, a house-sized mass of the maelstrom hit one of the unar-mored Displacement Drive ships. Dust flew away from all sides of the ship, and a huge gust of boulder-sized rocks and smaller flakes of stone exploded out of the impact crater. The asteroid ship actually slipped sideways under the force of the impact, and the enemy bridge went dark.

Rayder had only one armored ship! That means he's vul-nerable! If we can get to him, if we can use the Demons—

"Send me in!" Matt cried.

"Excuse me?" Captain Ivers asked.

"Sir, I mean, permission to deploy, sir. If I can take a Demon, I can go after Rayder—"

Matt was cut short by public comms from Mecha Base. "*Helios,* withdraw immediately. Repeat: recommend imme-diate withdrawal. Mecha Base is under heavy fire."

"No shit," Ivers said sardonically. "Tell me our weapons are at least functional, pilot."

"Heavy matter coming online, sir," one of the pilots said.

"Sir!" Matt said. "Please!"

"You want to go after that bastard?" Ivers grinned at Matt.

"Sir, yes, sir!"

"Sir, I recommend we withdraw," Yve said, darting forward. "Cadet Lowell has critical information we can't lose!"

Matt groaned. Yve was right. But . . . his father must have had his reasons for not telling the Union.

Matt shot over to Jahl. "Your entangled computing can record, right?"

Jahl nodded.

"Then remember this." Matt rapped out the numbers. "If I don't come back, use your own judgment who you tell it to."

Jahl opened his mouth to speak, but Yve cut him off.

"Sir, I still don't think we can let Cadet Lowell fight. What if there are other codes that only he can solve? We should withdraw now!"

"You want us to lose Mecha Base?" Matt yelled at Yve. "You want us to abandon those pilots out there—like you abandoned my dad?"

Fury sparked in Yve's eyes, but before he could speak, Dr. Roth cut in.

"Is there any possible reason I should authorize your use of a Demon, Cadet Lowell?" Roth sneered. "What can you possibly do, save deliver my latest technology into enemy hands?"

"Yes. Because I'll win this," Matt said, standing firm, even as his eyes slipped to watch his embattled friends.

"I'm sorry. I cannot believe that," Dr. Roth said. "Concur with the liaison's recommendation to withdraw, Captain Ivers."

But Ivers wasn't paying any attention to Dr. Roth. He was watching Matt. Seeing him track the battle outside

"That your team?" Ivers asked, nodding at Michelle and Soto.

"Yes, sir!" Matt snapped.

"Heavy-matter weapons online, sir," one of the pilots said.

Ivers bent over a control panel and keyed in a short sequence. "There's a Hellion in the hangar. It's now yours. Godspeed."

Dr. Roth jumped forward, his eyes wide. "I said, I recommend we withdraw—"

Ivers sneered. "Let me know when they put you in charge of my ship. Pilots, aim and fire at will, concentrating on the unarmored ships."

Matt didn't wait any longer. He threw himself out of the bridge and down the corridors at full speed, found the Hellion and the interface suit within, tore skin getting into it, and dropped into Mesh.

It was strange being in a Hellion again. Like a child's game. Metallic muscles worked beyond the wraparound screens, casting odd, distracting glints, unlike the immersive Demon. Matt breathed the sweat of a dozen pilots, unlike the sanitized, metallic air from a Demon's mask.

The only thing worth feeling was the support cradle the Hellion was locked into. Through it thrummed the oversized fusion heart of the *Helios*, the chant of data between the Displacement Drive and the pilots, the flow of images and messages from Mecha Base and beyond. It was just like his first exercise, when he caught the Corsair fighter in the bay and Merged with it.

Overlays flashed on Matt's POV, showing the current state of the battle. The Mecha had fallen back closer to Mecha Base, but seemed to be holding the battleships at bay. The battleships had to approach in the lee of Mecha Base's armor, so the closer they got to Mecha Base, the more concentrated the fire from the Mecha.

Still, a Hedgehog battleship and a handful of Corsair-captured Taikong fighters had slipped through. They fought against two Mecha at the lower level Hellion dock: Soto and Michelle's Hellions.

A sudden thought came to Matt: *You could Merge with this ship. Just like you did during your first exercise above ground. Displace away. Then Displace down right on top of Rayder. Hit him hard. Crush the* Atlas *and end it.*

Because Rayder had to be there. He wouldn't miss his chance to watch the capture of Mecha Base.

You could end it now.

Michelle and Soto fell back in the battle diagram, hanging at the dangerous edge of Mecha Base's armor.

Merge with the ship. Get Rayder.

"No," Matt said, triggering the external hatch. It opened to reveal the gray rock of Mecha Base. The edge of the Hellion dock was just visible. Beyond that, two Hellions moved. Michelle and Soto.

But you would have your revenge!

"And I will," Matt breathed, jumping hard toward his friends.

Matt went wide of the two Mecha, almost missing the edge of the armor on Mecha Base. He caught and held on as depleted-uranium slugs hammered his Hellion, making him wince. His targeting overlay showed the source of his bombardment: a group of Rayder's men in battle-tech space suits.

Matt launched Fireflies, but the men slipped out of range before they impacted. They were wearing Flight Packs. Matt sorely wished for his own as more slugs hit. He couldn't do much more than hang on the edge of the armor if his Fireflies and Seekers didn't work.

He searched for Michelle and Soto; they were launching Seekers at Rayder's nearest battleship. The big Rhino rocked with the explosions but kept firing at them. Soto lost his grip and Michelle had to grab at him and pull him down back under the edge of the armor.

"Matt!" a familiar voice shouted through Matt's cockpit as Sergeant Stoll's comms icon lit on his screen. "Ah, I mean, Cadet Lowell, report status!"

"Helping my friends," Matt said. "Ma'am."

"Adding you to my control group," Stoll said.

"Matt!" Michelle called. "Did you find it? You shouldn't have come! We're pinned down!"

Matt laughed. "Yes, yes, I shouldn't have, and I can see that."

"Idiot kid," Soto said. "Too bad you don't have a Flight Pack or three. They can't kill us, but we can't knock them out either!"

Matt saw the problem. Fireflies and Seekers were too slow, and there was no way they could use a Zap Gun and fire into the maelstrom. And without the maneuverability of Flight Packs, they were too far away to use their Fusion Handshakes.

Or are we? Matt grinned. It was a terrible idea, but one that might actually work.

Matt jumped off the edge of the armor, aiming for the attacking Rhino. If he was lucky, the Rhino would consider him a valuable capture. If he wasn't, the big ship would simply move out the way, and he'd be headed for a one-way ride into the center of a forming planet.

"Are you crazy?" Michelle screamed.

"Probably!"

The Rhino swelled in front of Matt, its massive, scarred armor resolving into individual plates. The lights of the bridge burned bright white against the brown-red red of the maelstrom. Figures moved on the bridge, silhouetted by the light. Just like that first day at Earth, on *Mercury*, Matt thought. He remembered his promise to the security chief: *No more dumb stunts.* He laughed.

Matt was close enough to see the rivets that held the Rhino together. A port opened on its side, and men in armored space suits jetted out. They'd intercept him in seconds.

Matt hit the Rhino near the bridge and grabbed for something to stop his bounce. His metal fingers found a thruster port and he latched on, his impossibly tough biometal tearing the relatively soft steel alloy of the Rhino.

Depleted-uranium slugs juddered Matt's Hellion, and he almost lost his grip. He grabbed with his other hand, caught the fusion port, and thrust his arm all the way down into it.

Fusion Handshake, he thought.

Pure pleasure welled as his Hellion's arm rang with power. Blue flame exploded from the fusion port, showering Matt's Hellion with molten steel. Fire burned Matt's arm as the Handshake drove deep within the Rhino. Flames billowed out from shattered bridge windows, armored space suits spewed from ruptured ports, and the whole battleship ballooned with the force of Matt's blow.

His arm popped out of the port, gleaming with melted steel. Matt tucked into his legs, then fired out another Fusion Handshake at just the right moment to drive himself back toward Mecha Base.

The scaffolding supporting the armor came up fast. Matt caught it and stopped himself in time to watch Soto and Michelle clean up the remaining men in armored space suits.

When they were done, the three stood under the shattered Hellion dock door. Men inside were setting up heavy weapons, preparing for additional attempts to board. Toward the maelstrom, the battle still raged between Mecha and Rayder's forces.

"Want to finish this?" Matt asked Michelle and Soto.

"One neat stunt, and the cadet gets a big head," Soto said, but his voice was full of admiration.

"It probably won't work against a Displacement Drive ship," Michelle said.

"No. But a Demon will."

Dead silence from the comms for a beat.

"You're proposing—," Soto began.

"We go get the Demons. The dock's only a kilometer or so away."

"We don't have Flight Packs!" Soto said. "It'd take an hour to shuffle over the surface."

"One jump will do it," Matt said.

"And you expect to come down?"

Matt studied the Hellion's gravimetric readouts. He could do it. He had to do it.

"Roth will never go for it," Michelle told him.

"We don't need authorization. We need to finish this battle and win this war."

"So, we die if we don't try, and we might die tryin'," Soto said, chuckling. "Sounds like the sort of day I joined Mecha Corps for."

The three Hellions flew over the surface of Mecha Base in a long, flat trajectory. Barren rock spooled past underneath them as the asteroid fell away.

"What if we don't come down?" Soto asked.

"We will!" Matt ground his teeth as his projected trajectory showed on the screen. They'd jumped off a little hot. Instead of hitting just before the dock, they'd pass over it and land on the far side.

Ahead, wan sunlight glinted off gleaming metal: the Demon dock. It wheeled toward them. Even from a distance, they could see the air lock was closed tight.

Soto muttered a long string of curses as they sailed over the dock. Soto rotated and deftly fired Seekers. Bright light erupted beneath them. The Demon Dock's door went red and billowed outward into vacuum.

"Notify Dr. Roth. We regret to report misfire compromised the Demon dock integrity," Soto said through the comms to Stoll. "Recommend pilots enter Demons to ensure they are not captured."

Matt crawled till he was close enough to grab the rim of the air lock, and he flung himself in. The red-hot metal seared his hands, but he barely felt it. He was focused on the Demons standing ready on the steel grate.

Matt yanked his neural coupling and slammed on his helmet, simultaneously triggering the cockpit release. His cockpit unfolded, voiding its air with a screech. The helmet almost came out of his hands, and he felt the too-familiar tug of vacuum before he got it seated. He jumped out of the cockpit and looked back at Soto and Michelle. Major Soto was already out of his cockpit, wearing his own utility suit. Matt waved him over. The utility suits had no comms, and were good for only a few minutes of air, but they'd have to do.

Michelle's cockpit was still closed. Matt waved at her frantically, trying to pantomime opening the cockpit. Nothing happened as the seconds ticked away.

Shit.

Maybe her release was damaged in the fight. Or maybe she didn't have her utility suit on? Matt jumped off toward Michelle's Hellion. When he reached it, he hesitated at the external emergency release. If she was trapped in the Hellion, she would be screaming for him to open her cockpit, but he wasn't sure if he would even be able to hear her through all the turbulence. And if she didn't have her suit on, she'd be exposed to the vacuum of space if he opened the air lock. Matt knew from grim experience that humans could only withstand a few seconds in vacuum before losing consciousness, and more than a minute was usually fatal.

There wasn't any choice. He had to take the chance. Matt triggered the emergency release.

The cockpit blew open with a blast of air, which crystallized into snow in the cold of space. Michelle sprang out of the cockpit, already wearing her utility suit. She offered Matt a smile, then pushed off toward the Demons. She had been locked in.

The three shot toward the Demons. The dock was deserted, but frantic Auxiliaries loomed outside the viewing windows.

No going back now, Matt thought. It was almost a relief. They were committed. Whatever happened after they got into the Demons would determine their fate.

A chime sounded, and a warning flashed in Matt's utility suit: AIR 0:59 REMAINING. As he watched, it counted down to 0:58.

It would take that long to fly across the dock. He'd be sucking stale air when he arrived at the Demons. Better hope there wasn't any problem getting inside.

Matt's warning chime sounded as he drew near the Demon. The soft hiss of the recycler stopped. There was no immediate change in his air, but he knew it wouldn't be long before he breathed nothing but carbon dioxide.

Matt dove for the safety of the Demon's interior. He tore off his helmet, plugged into the neural connector, snugged on the mask. Magnetorheological gel flooded the chamber. His utility suit gave a tiny little gasp and died when the fluid reached its neck. Matt waited impatiently as the fluid ran over his face, into his hair, past the top of his head.

Matt's mask lit and his suit went active. Matt's heart soared with the thrill of Mesh.

"Michelle?" Matt asked.

"I'm in," she said. "Meshing."

Matt grinned. It was almost as if he could see the future. They weren't going to die in their Demons today. They wouldn't end their time in the core of a collapsing planet. They were meant for the Demons. The three of them. They'd do it.

Mesh high, Matt told himself.

But he knew it wasn't just that.

"Let's go!" he yelled.

The three Demons blasted into the theater of battle.

The Hellions close to Mecha Base were being pressed hard by Rayder's fast-moving battleships. Farther off, only a single Displacement Drive ship remained: the armored *Atlas*.

That's where Rayder is, Matt thought. He thrust forward as Michelle and Soto joined him.

They shot through the Hellion front line. Missiles flashed from the battleships, flicker-fast, to strike the Demons. Matt groaned and Soto and Michelle rocked back with the force of the explosions. Hellions surged forward through the parting the three had created, landing on the Rhinos and Hedgehogs and clawing at their bridges. Atmosphere voided from a handful of battleships as they tumbled out of control.

More fire converged on the Demons as Rayder's battleships gathered like a flock of metallic vultures around the giant Mecha. Matt raised an arm to protect his sensor array and unleashed Seekers at a dozen ships. Eruptions of gas and sparks flared as ships were directly hit.

But the battleships kept coming. More missiles flared on his backside, bringing more acid-dipped pain. A warning flashed on Matt's screen:

THRUSTER ARRAY 3 REGENERATING.

His forward momentum slowed. He thrust out toward the churning maelstrom, where the battleships dared not go.

Michelle screamed.

"What's wrong?" Matt yelled, turning around.

"Lost visuals! Sensors!" She cried out as a heavy crunch reverberated through the comms.

Matt reversed course and dived down toward the melee, where Soto grappled with a huge Rhino-class battleship and Michelle was enveloped by blasts. His Demon was sluggish, its regeneration counter dutifully counting down the seconds to full thrust: 9, 8, 7 —

A Hedgehog heavy cruiser, deadly and sleek, accelerated toward Michelle. Its forward cannon crackled with energy, ready to fire.

Matt pushed harder. A dozen red tags flared in his POV as his remaining thruster went past its rated power. Through the interface suit, he felt the thruster begin to soften and deform as the metal glowed orange hot.

But he leapt forward just enough to catch Michelle before the Hedgehog fired. Its plasma bolt cut a clean line behind him, dispatching a handful of cruisers and battleships instantly.

"What's happening?" Michelle yelled. Through the Demon, he was able to feel her angry thoughts: *Asshole! Why's he doing this? I don't need help!* She had no idea how close she'd come to being annihilated.

"Sorry," Matt said.

"I had it!" But sudden doubt flowed through their neural connection. She was seeing the battle from Matt's point of view. Matt felt her stomach turn over queasily. She shoved out of his Demon's embrace.

Soto zoomed up into the maelstrom to join them. "Thank the man, Cadet Kind," he said.

Plasma beams lanced at the Demons from the battlefield, striking Soto a glancing blow. He grunted as he spun in place, then caught his spin with his thrusters. He tensed to make a leap down into the battle.

"No! Go after the *Atlas*!" Matt yelled. "Rayder's there!"

"Yeah," Major Soto breathed, his voice fuzzy with Mesh high.

Something whizzed past Matt, dark and fast. Major Soto's Demon was suddenly not there. A choked scream came over the comms. Matt had a glimpse of something moving away from them, very fast, down into the mud.

"Major!" Matt yelled.

Another dark thing passed by Matt, close enough for him to feel its heat as it passed. His screens showed the trajectory: it was coming from the *Atlas*.

"Heavy-matter gun!" Sergeant Stoll yelled. "Disperse!"

Matt and Michelle thrust hard in opposite directions, as Soto's pained voice came through the comms. "Fuck me!" he said.

"Are you all right, sir?" Matt said.

"Regeneration in fifty-six seconds. Thrusters unreliable. Can someone pick me up before I get crushed by one of these asteroids?"

"Coming, sir," Michelle said, and jetted down toward the core of the protoplanet.

Beneath him, the battle between Rayder's battleships and Mecha Base's Hellions suddenly convulsed, twisting into fantastic new shapes. Dark lines cut through the fray toward Mecha Base. Battleships and Hellions vaporized, spewing orange flame through the field of white-hot explosions. Gray flowers of dust, rock, and steel erupted from Mecha Base, rocking the gigantic asteroid.

On-screen, tags showed heavy-matter fire from the *Atlas* slicing through the battle and striking Mecha Base. Rayder was firing through his own men.

More heavy-matter fire sliced through the battlefield, impacting on the *Helios*. The giant ship canted and veered to one side, grinding against the side of Mecha Base in a soundless cataclysm.

Captain Cruz's bridge blew inward in a blue-white beam of a fusion cannon.

"Cadet Lowell, fall back with Hellions and support Mecha Base!" Sergeant Stoll yelled.

No. That's wrong. The Hellions were making short work of Rayder's remaining battleships, now that he'd decided to sacrifice them with a direct assault. The problem was the *Atlas*. It's heavy-matter gun was pounding everything to ruin.

He had to stop it. Now.

"Cadet Lowell!"

"Suggest alternate strategy," Matt rapped out. "Permission to use Zap Gun, ma'am!"

"Permission not granted! Return to Mecha Base!"

Matt's heart sank and blind despair washed over him, the feeling amplified by his Mesh. How did they expect him to take out that ship without the Zap Gun?

Soto's and Michelle's Demons came flashing up out of the mud to join Matt.

"Permission granted," a new voice said. Colonel Cruz's comms icon flared the life. "Take him out, cadet! Damn the consequences!

"Now we get Rayder!" Matt yelled, thrusting toward the *Atlas*.

"With you a hundred percent!" Michelle shouted, following.

"Fat ladies singing now!" Soto blurted, joining the team.

Matt grinned so hard it hurt, and pulled the glowing Zap

Gun out of his thigh holster in one smooth movement. The gun vibrated with power, seeming to sing to one small part of his mind—the part that chanted, *Kill. Destroy. End it. Finish him.*

Next to him, Soto and Michelle unlimbered their Zap Guns too.

But this was his.

Matt surged forward, accelerating ahead of his companions. He raised the Zap Gun. The *Atlas* ballooned in size.

His screens screamed:

TARGETING LOCK

Matt fired. Pure power hammered down his arm and into the gun. Blinding radiance exploded ahead of him. Heavy-matter rounds vaporized like firecrackers in the antimatter annihilation.

The *Atlas* disappeared. One second it was there, lit bright gray-white in the flare of his Zap Gun. Then it was gone.

Displaced. Rayder had run.

Matt flew through empty space where the *Atlas* had just been, screaming in frustration.

18

HOME

Matt, Michelle, and Major Soto stood stiffly in Colonel Cruz's temporary quarters, where Congressperson Tomita, Dr. Roth, and Captain Ivers glared down from hastily arranged wall screens.

The whistle of escaping air still came from the corridors of Mecha Base. It had taken a real beating. Auxiliaries swarmed everywhere, patching leaks and installing emergency air locks on the more damaged sections of the base.

"Total disaster!" Congressperson Tomita yelled, his face red-purple. "That's what this is. Don't try to sugarcoat it."

"Thanks to the efforts of all our forces, and the extraordinary contributions of these three corps, we saved Mecha Base. Hardly a total disaster." Colonel Cruz said.

Tomita softened. "Bravery should be recognized and encouraged. However, it doesn't change this outcome."

"We'll relocate the base—," Colonel Cruz began.

"To where?" Tomita thundered, cutting off Cruz. "This was the impossible location. Impossible to imagine, impossible to find, impossible to assault. And we nearly lost it today!"

"Rayder was significantly handicapped by the maelstrom," Dr. Roth said. "He was only able to bring in a single armored Displacement Drive ship. The others had to withdraw, which gave us a competitive advantage."

Tomita glared at Dr. Roth, blowing out a big breath.

"Over the past decade, we've provided trillions of Union Units in funding for your cadet-destroying Mecha—"

"And the return has been—," Roth began.

"I will finish!" Tomita thundered. "And you will hear me! We have funded everything you asked. Three generations of BioMecha. A hidden training facility on Earth—a veritable underground city. The most remote and secure base of operations ever imagined by the Union, maintained at great cost in a condensing planet. All for nothing! Net result: you were found and nearly taken over by a single man in a single Displacement Drive ship."

"Rayder is hardly a man, and the *Atlas* is hardly a single Displacement Drive ship. If you consider Rayder's captured battleships and—"

"If you consider how big the rest of Rayder's forces are! If you consider his next move will likely be to drop an asteroid or two on Mecha Base, like he did on Geos!"

Roth fell silent, looking away from the camera. Cruz's jaw worked, but he said nothing.

"I'm shutting it down," Tomita said.

"What?" Dr. Roth asked.

"All of it. Mecha Base. Mecha Training Camp. Mecha Corps."

All the color drained out of Roth's face. "You can't do that," he whispered.

"Not unilaterally," Congressperson Tomita admitted. "But I believe I can swing it. We need to stop wasting our time on fairy-tale technologies that simply don't work."

"Sir, we could follow Rayder and finish the job, sir!" Matt blurted. He couldn't hold it in anymore.

Tomita grimaced. "Your HuMax final-world coordinates? Another fairy tale?"

"It's worth pursuing, sir," Yve said, joining Dr. Roth. "Dr. Stanford was closest to that division of HuMax research."

"Even if true, we'd never prevail against Rayder at the HuMax world," Tomita said.

"You seem very confident of that," Dr. Roth said.

"Of course! Do you know what the HuMax achieved? Have you seen what they did . . ." Tomita trailed off, looking suddenly embarrassed.

"The Union seems to know an awful lot about the HuMax," Cruz broke in. "But I've never been enlightened."

Dr. Roth laughed, a harsh, mechanical sound. "They know everything," he said softly.

"Dr. Roth, I warn you—," Tomita said.

Roth nodded. "Yes, I know, speak now or speak never again. It is always that way with the HuMax."

Silence fell over the room. For a while, the only sound was the whistle of air escaping into space.

"I don't care," Matt said. "We can take him."

"We'll finish it," Michelle added.

"Send us after Rayder," Soto said.

"Pure insanity," Tomita said. "You have no idea what you're up against!"

"No," Dr. Roth said. "It is pure insanity not to try to finish Rayder now."

"Dr. Roth, you pursue your own agenda, not the Union's!" Tomita barked.

Roth smiled. "I thought that the final destruction of the HuMax survivors and their descendants was the entire point of the Union."

Tomita's face went deadly still. "Dr. Roth, you speak treason."

Roth shook his head. "I have nothing but devotion for the Union." He looked around at everyone, as if daring them to argue. Then he started shrugging off his coat.

"What are you doing?" Tomita asked.

"Demonstrating my loyalty." He unbuttoned his dress shirt and peeled off his undershirt.

Gasps came from both the video and from the room.

Shining metallic ridges rose out of Dr. Roth's skin. Gleaming veins spread from his chest to his sides, weaving together in a meshwork at his shoulders and arms. Tiny ports shining with gold ran down his sternum. A polished jewel was set into the center of his chest.

"What have you done to yourself?" Tomita breathed.

"I have simply installed the components necessary to complete advanced biomechanical integration. It is part of my work. For the Union."

Matt was simultaneously revolted and fascinated. So that was why Roth could use Hellions, Demons—any Mecha—and suffer no ill effects.

Would I do that? Matt wondered. But he already knew the answer: *To get Rayder, yes.*

Nobody said anything. Congressperson Tomita's image slid sideways and dissolved in bit-rot before coming back solid.

"I propose we allow the Mecha Corps to have their shot at Rayder," Dr. Roth said.

"Have you calculated the chance of a three-Demon Merge standing against—"

Roth laughed. "This team has not yet even achieved a Merge. But they've already accomplished impossible things."

I can do things nobody else can, Matt thought, smiling.

"Seems like an excellent plan to me," Cruz said.

Captain Ivers nodded. "I'll be the taxi service."

Tomita glared from one man to another. "I will still lobby for the end of the Mecha program!"

"But you won't achieve that this afternoon," Cruz told him. He turned to the cadets and Soto, his eyes sparkling. "Get him. Get Rayder. No matter what it takes. Those are your orders."

Matt's heart leapt so high, he didn't think he'd be able to speak. But he shouted, "Yes, sir!" in unison with Michelle and Soto.

Rayder, you die today.

Matt's, Michelle's, and Major Soto's Demons clung to the *Helios*' exposed scaffolding. The *Helios*' unfinished Mecha dock hadn't been large enough to hold them, so they had to ride on the skin of the armored ship.

"Isn't this dangerous?" Michelle asked, her comms icon flaring. "I've heard that if the Displacement field goes unstable—"

Matt barked a laugh, cutting her off. The irony. He remembered all too well wanting to lie out on the surface of UUS *Ulysses* with her and watch the stars change. Now he'd get his chance, as soon as they were under way from Mecha Base.

"Old wives' tale," Major Soto said. "We're completely safe. Just don't go on a jump before we Displace."

"Yep," Matt said. "No problem."

"Uh-huh." Michelle didn't sound very sure.

"I've done it a thousand times in a space suit," Matt told her. "I did it on my way to Earth."

"You did?" Michelle sounded stunned.

Matt nodded. "It's really nothing to worry about."

Michelle's comms icon remained silent. Matt searched for words to reassure her, but with his heart pumping double time in anticipation of meeting Rayder, he couldn't think of anything

Near Mecha Base, the UUS *Cerberus* powered toward the twisted wreckage of the Demon Dock. Probably to take Dr. Roth and Yve back to the Union. They'd shuttled out before Matt, Michelle, and Soto had arrived on the *Helios*.

"First Displacement in ten," Captain Ivers said, his comms icon lighting.

Matt's talons gripped the steel girder involuntarily tighter, scarring the pristine metal. He made himself relax. The girder groaned, and Michelle's Demon turned its visor toward him, as if amused.

"Displace," Captain Ivers said.

Suddenly, they were out in open space. Michelle gasped. Matt grinned. It was almost as good as being on the surface, lying out in nothing but a space suit. He wanted to reach out and take her hand, but he kept his talons locked on the scaffolding.

Another Displacement. Another. Silence stretched between the three Demonriders. They'd be outside for well over an hour—it was 155 Displacements to the HuMax final world.

"You really think we can do it?" Major Soto said, his voice echoing and hollow.

"Do what?" Matt asked.

"Take out Rayder."

"Of course!" Matt said. He was amazed Soto had even asked. Soto, the veteran of the biggest Mecha engagements out there. Always in control, always strong and confident. The Hellion pilot who'd mastered the Demon against all odds.

Silence from Soto. As the Displacements ticked away, Soto's words grew like a cancer in Matt. Maybe he was right to ask. They'd never even tried to Merge with Soto. And even if they Merged, it was only a third-order configuration, not a fourth-order one. They were missing a fourth pilot. Would they have enough power to overcome Rayder?

Matt shivered, suddenly ill at ease.

Mesh feedback, he thought. *Amplifying my emotions.* But knowing that didn't help.

"We can only do our best," Michelle said. But her voice was uncertain too.

"We'll do it," Matt said. "We've done the impossible. We'll do it again."

"You've done the impossible," Michelle mumbled. "Not us."

"We don't know what we're getting into." Soto's voice quavered.

Matt searched for a way to bring the team back, but Captain Ivers cut in before he could say anything.

"I'm betting you can do it," Ivers said.

Silence from the Demonriders, but Matt sensed the chance to change the mood. "How much, sir?" he said.

"How much what?" the captain replied.

"How much will you bet?"

Ivers guffawed. "Five units."

Matt laughed, and Michelle and Soto joined him. Suddenly, the mood didn't seem so oppressive.

"That's not much," Michelle told Ivers.

"When you do this, you won't need my pocket change," Ivers shot back. "You'll be the biggest heroes the Union has ever known."

More laughter echoed through the Mecha; then everyone dropped into comfortable silence for a time.

Space enveloped them in its glory. Every star like a perfect pinprick in velvet. The shining alloy of the *Helios'* armor, lit only by the distant stars. Ahead of them, a vague red-purple smear grew slightly larger. A nebula like a black eye glowering down at them.

What waited for them there? Would they Displace into the middle of a fleet, charged and ready to crush them?

Matt set his comms to PRIVATE: CADET M. LOWELL → CAPTAIN J. IVERS.

"How much do you know about the HuMax final world, sir?" Matt asked.

Iver's comms icon lit, but he hesitated before he spoke. "Not much, unfortunately."

"How much does the Union know, Captain?"

Another pause from Ivers. "A hell of a lot more than I. I knew the Union and the HuMax are intertwined. But that's about it. Tomita surely has his reasons why he doesn't want you to go. But I don't know what they are."

The Union and the HuMax are intertwined. Matt shivered. How much so? What did that mean? A cold hand clutched his heart.

But he couldn't think about that now. He had to stay focused.

Matt's Perfect Record unreeled the vision of his father's death once again. Matt squeezed his eyes shut against the image of Rayder's thin, cruel smile as he said those final words. *Courage must have its reward.*

No. Obsession would have its reward. Obsession with revenge had set him on this course. Everything else was an excuse. His life had been folded into a single purpose, like a paper airplane. He'd launched himself on a singular mission, and today it would pay off.

Matt breathed, deep and ragged, as he imagined Rayder cowering under his Demon. Only this time, it wasn't courage that would have its reward. Evil would have its reckoning, and the payoff would be death.

And when that was done, he could finally do . . . whatever it was he wanted to do.

What do I want to do? Matt wondered.

They were deep in the nebula now. Entire swatches of stars were masked by its black-purple tentacles. A single blue-white sun lay before them, little more than a bright star, like Earth's sun as seen from the orbit of Saturn.

Thirty seconds to final Displacement.

"So what's the plan?" Soto asked.

Matt started. Soto was the leader. *Isn't he?* It didn't make sense that they were looking at him to lead.

Or did it?

Act like a leader, he told himself.

"Kill Rayder," he said, finally, low and rough. "Go home."

Soto chuckled. "Simple. But I can go with that."

"So can I," Michelle breathed.

Matt counted down the seconds to the final Displacement, his heart hammering double time.

Two. One. Zero.

They Displaced.

The *Helios* snapped into existence over a world painted in blue-tinted darkness. A white dwarf sun hung close and huge, larger than earth's moon. Solar storms and gray-black pockets of magnetic flux writhed on its surface. Matt's radiation readings wavered at levels twenty times higher than long-term human tolerance.

Human tolerance, Matt thought. Not HuMax tolerance. Their carefully designed genetic backup and repair system made them relatively immune to radiation, unless the exposure was massive. They couldn't walk into a nuclear reactor or survive a nearby atomic blast, but the radiation levels of this system were well within their comfort zone.

This system. The Demon's star charts had refused to give it a name or even a numeric descriptor. The overlays on his POV remained stubbornly set at LOCATION: UNKNOWN (0.0,0.0,0.0) (JOTUNHEIM).

Matt's Perfect Record brought back a single line from an Ancient Human History lecture. Jotunheim was the land of the giants in Norse mythology. It was also one of the places where Ragnarok, the end of the world, would be ushered in.

It's an appropriate name, Matt thought. The HuMax were giants in their own right, and they almost brought about the end of the human race.

The *Helios* rocked hard.

"We're under fire!" Major Soto yelled.

"No! My screens are clear!" Matt said, scanning the sky. The *Helios'* sensors confirmed: NO UNFRIENDLIES IN THE AREA.

Another tremor shook the huge Displacement Drive ship. Michelle scrabbled for purchase on the scaffolding.

And still his screens were clear. "What the hell!" Matt cried.

"Gravity waves," Michelle said grimly. "Look at the system diagram."

Matt did. And gasped. If Mecha Base was bedlam, Jotunheim was beyond insanity. Its white dwarf sun orbited a micro–black hole. Or perhaps a better way to put it was that the black hole was slowly eating the entire system. The sun and its single planet whirled around it like marbles circling a drain. The black hole hungrily drew in solar wind, hydrogen atoms, and photon flux into its depthless maw.

The black hole actually bent the light from the sun. It was that close. In a few years, or a few hundred, the sun would lose its battle with the black hole, and it would disappear forever.

Why would anyone choose to live here? Matt thought, even as he realized, *Maybe they didn't.* Even the HuMax would have no desire to live on such a desolate rock. But their creators would want to test their limits. To see what they could withstand.

What better place than a system wracked by gravity waves, irradiated with Cherenkov radiation, and doomed to die in a handful of years. Matt could almost imagine what had gone through their minds: *If it doesn't work, it's self-disposing. Gone. As if it never occurred.*

And in that moment, Matt felt something almost like sympathy for the HuMax. Like Stoll and like him, they hadn't chosen their genes. They'd been made. They'd been used like pawns in a much larger game.

But they'd also attacked their creators.

Another gravity wave hit the *Helios*. Matt's comms icon lit: CAPTAIN J. IVERS.

"Who's attacking us?" Captain Ivers asked.

"We're not under attack," Matt told him. "It's gravity waves from the sun."

"Where's Rayder?" Ivers asked. "The planet's a cinder."

The *Helios'* sensors fed him images of Jotunheim, the system's single planet. It was a hell of freezing plains and boiling lakes, alternating with jagged, kilometers-high mountain ranges. Deep fissures revealed angry red magma, venting sulfuric acid clouds.

A deep-sensor diagram told the story: Jotunheim, torn between the gravitational pull of the sun and the black hole and wracked by gravity waves, was at the very edge of its structural integrity. The entire core was molten and ready to erupt over the surface at any moment. The atmosphere itself was hardly breathable, at least by normal humans; with several percent carbon dioxide, huge amounts of ozone and carbon monoxide, and a soup of sulfuric aerosols, it would kill them in hours.

But at the same time, the planet was also covered with life. Strange, twisting black plants that tracked the feeble sun with mirror-coated leaves, focusing the pale white light into something that could sustain life. The plants coiled over the peaks and out of the atmosphere into raw space. They snaked along the frozen plains. They writhed in the boiling lakes.

Like the plant in my father's lab, Matt thought, wondering what they were. Why had his father brought one back? What magic technology did they contain?

And then there was the city. The HuMax city. Situated in a deep, dark crater and pounded to ruins by the long-ago war, it was still grand and beautiful. Rayder's broadcast had given no sense of scale. The largest buildings towered more than two kilometers into the sky, stubbornly refusing to disintegrate despite the tremors and gravity waves. The arched walkways connecting them stood a kilometer high, with not a guardrail in sight. The colossal statue of a man and woman reaching toward the stars was itself more than a thousand meters high. It shamed humankind's most monumental architecture.

And the city still lived. Green-white light pulsed from the buildings, painting the broad avenues a sickly mint color. Rayder's base? Or something left from hundreds of years ago, still working after all these years?

"Screens are still clear," Captain Ivers said.

"He'll be here," Matt growled.

But the system remained silent. There was nothing there. Was it possible Rayder had fled?

Suddenly, Matt's screens lit with brilliant icons and screaming yellow tags. One, two, three, four, five, six, ten, twelve Displacement Drive ships appeared simultaneously, in a perfect ring around the *Helios*.

Then, a moment later, a thirteenth Displacement Drive ship appeared. UUS *Atlas*.

"Displacement detected! Ship de—multiple ships detected! Heavy-matter weapons lock!" shouted the babble behind Captain Ivers' comms icon.

Battleships and cruisers poured out of the Displacement Drive ships. Matt's screens became a cloud of yellow and red tags, like a swarm of bees in the *Rock*'s gardens.

"Heavy-matter gunners, fire at will!" Captain Ivers said. The *Helios* thudded with the force of the heavy-matter gun.

"Orders?" Soto snapped on the public channel.

That's right. They were waiting for him. Matt's blood boiled. This was it. This was his time—

BOOM! Brilliant light flashed all around them. Armor, girders, and boulder-sized rocks flew from the surface of the *Helios*. Antimatter-annihilation beams flashed, tracing molten lines on the *Helios*' armor. Apparently Rayder didn't have any reservations about using his own version of the Zap Gun.

The *Helios* leapt violently, throwing Matt off the surface. The only chance they had lay in getting out of range of the antimatter beams.

"Shelter!" Matt yelled. "Get in back of the ship!"

He lit thrusters and dove for the lee of the ship, Michelle and Soto close at his heels. But there was no shelter. Metal melted and buckled under the brilliant onslaught of antimatter energy. The *Helios*' only battleship nosed out of the tiny dock, its front section disappearing in the blaze.

"Displace!" Matt shouted. "Get out of here!"

But from Captain Iver's comms, there was only static.

Michelle and Major Soto caught up with Matt, off to one side of the flaming *Helios*.

"Why aren't they shooting at us?" Michelle asked.

"They're cutting us off," Matt said. If Rayder wanted to capture the Demons, he had to disable the *Helios*, so they had no chance of escape.

As if on cue, the antimatter weapons stopped firing. The *Helios* slowly tumbled, red and smoking.

"Heavy-matter weapons disabled," Captain Ivers' voice came through the comms, ragged with emotion. "Deep-sensor arrays damaged. Cannot Displace."

As Matt watched, a Corsair battleship nosed up to one of the shattered docks. Space-suited troops poured out of it.

"You're being boarded," Matt told him.

"We'll fight them off!" Ivers said. "You go take care of Rayder!"

"Yes, sir!" Matt said.

"Acknowledged, sir," Michelle said, her voice thick with emotion.

"Immediately, sir!" Soto snapped.

ANTIMATTER WEAPONS LOCK

Matt's screens screamed at him.

Matt thrust away from the *Helios*, twisting and turning at lightning speed. Even submersed in the magnetorheological fluid, his vision went alternately dark and red from the g-forces, and his space suit bit painfully into his body. Michelle and Soto were two flickering blips close behind him.

But the ANTIMATTER WEAPONS LOCK didn't drop on the display.

Matt pushed his Demon even harder. It transformed from its Mecha shape to its streamlined spaceship form, then into a slim arrow of metal flaring into the void. G-forces slammed him into a netherworld between consciousness and insensibility, and he cried out from the pain. His world collapsed to a tiny tunnel of vision, fixed firmly on that one tag.

But even here, at the edge of his capability, it remained:

ANTIMATTER WEAPONS LOCK.

Matt's battered brain knew a moment of pure defeat. Rayder's troops could blast their Mecha to atoms at any moment.

A glimmer of hope: so why didn't he?

Matt managed a grim smile through the battering pain. Of course. It was all about the Demons. Rayder wanted them, no matter the cost. He wouldn't simply blast them out of the sky. He'd do anything to capture them intact.

But what would Rayder do?

A flicker of movement, lightning fast. Matt didn't even have time to glance at it before—

Bang! The pilot chamber rang like a bell, and Matt grunted with the shock of a physical blow. Through the interface suit, he felt the chill touch of long, bladelike talons. There was a dark gray, quicksilver shape clinging to him: a Hellion.

Matt almost laughed. Rayder's captured Hellions. But Hellions against Demons was like pitting slingshots against atomic weapons. Matt's Demon transformed back into a humanoid Mecha shape, and he reached out to swat it aside.

The Hellion zipped out of reach, so fast it actually seemed to disappear. Matt's eyes couldn't track it. Matt grabbed at it again, and it blurred away from his hands. He never even got near it. The thing was insanely fast. Faster than any Hellion he'd ever seen before.

"Rayder's released the limiters," Major Soto said, his voice thin and strained.

"What does that mean?" Matt yelled, as the Hellion continued to evade his grasp.

"With no limiters, Hellions are blazing fast. But they were so addictive, we could never use them that way."

Matt grabbed at the Hellion with both hands. It was like trying to catch a dragonfly. Every time he came at the thing, it jumped effortlessly out of his way. Matt thrust back, then swatted as it came at him. The Hellion grabbed onto his hand, its claws cutting into Matt's biometallic flesh.

Explosive pain struck Matt's arm. A shock wave enveloped Matt's hand, and his Demon's fingers blew off into space. The dreaded REGENERATING clock began counting down: 800, 799, 798 . . .

"What was that?" Matt yelled.

"Fusion Handshake," Major Soto said. "But residuals show it using heavy matter. Gives it a ton more power. Nice trick."

"Nice?" Matt said, as the pain ebbed. The Hellion scrambled up his arm and wrapped around his helmet. Its hands glowed. The damn thing was going to Fusion Handshake his head right off!

Matt scrabbled at it with his one good hand, but it twisted its body out of the way.

Matt's vision went completely white as the pilot's chamber rocked with the force of an explosion. An overlay showed Seekers coming from Michelle's Demon and intersecting the Hellion. It fell away from Matt's head as the brilliant blue flare of its Fusion Handshake sent him reeling. Matt's screens went dark and pixilated for an instant, then snapped back to full clarity. It hadn't blown his head off! He could still see!

"Thanks, Michelle!" he called.

Two more Hellions blurred up to Matt. They latched on to his leg and triggered their Fusion Handshakes. Pain rocketed up his body, and his leg fell limp. His first REGENERATING clock was joined by another countdown:

REGENERATING (LEFT LEG): 200, 199, 198 . . .

Through the pain, Matt saw the same thing happening to both Michelle and Major Soto. Hellions swarmed their bodies, triggering blue-white shock waves. Michelle's arm flashed orange, then fell useless like Matt's leg. She thrashed at the Hellions, but they simply scrambled away. She triggered more Seekers, enveloping herself in brilliant explosions. Her Demon rocked with the blows, as the Hellions dodged the missiles. She was hurting herself more than the Hellions.

Soto's Demon disappeared in a cloud of Firefly explosions, but the Hellions that surrounded him just jumped out of the expanding cloud before descending on him again.

One of the super-Hellions wrapped itself around Michelle's visor. Matt screamed and charged, holding his Mecha's arms out and triggering his own Fusion Handshake. The thrill of power surged through his arms as the shock wave blew the Hellion off of Michelle's head.

The Hellion only tumbled a moment before recovering and coming back to the fight. It joined two others and came at Matt. Before he could trigger the Fusion Handshake, two had latched on to his arm and a third had covered his head. And he wasn't the only one in trouble. Another super-Hellion took Michelle's good arm, and Major Soto was still beating at the ones on him.

Major Soto fired a cloud of Fireflies and Seekers at both Michelle and Matt. The super-Hellions spun away, overwhelmed by the sheer barrage of weapons. One Seeker must have found its target, because a Hellion was shattered, twitching, its pilot's chamber venting gas and its left arm missing.

The Demons had a moment now to take stock. Soto's voice cut in over the comms. "Out of ammo. Regenerating."

Matt looked at his own stores of Fireflies and Seekers. He was running less than 20 percent, and the regeneration time stretched out into long thousands of seconds.

"Michelle?"

"Thirty-seven and thirty, Fireflies and Seekers," she rasped out.

Matt clenched his fists and groaned. He'd never thought their weapons were expendable. Like a stupid kid raised on videos where the brave Union heroes never ran out of ammo, and the Corsairs were always terrible shots.

And they had no real chance during training to run up against Mecha limits. If they'd gone through the full Training Camp, if they'd had more practice time, maybe they would have known. Instead, they were out here, unsupported and alone, against the most powerful Corsair fighting force in the universe.

The super-Hellions came at them again like shooting stars, so fast Matt almost couldn't follow them. Their swept-up visors reflected the dead gray light of the white dwarf sun, glittering like jewels on velvet.

We are going to lose. To Hellions.

Unless. Matt grinned. There was one chance. Matt hit his thrusters hard and grabbed Michelle with his good arm as they passed. Michelle's Demon tensed, but she got in only a single yelp before Matt reversed course and aimed at Major Soto.

"What the hell are you doing?" she asked, as Matt brought all three Mecha together.

"Merge," he said.

Michelle's terrified thoughts sped through his mind. *No, no. Crazy, never worked. Unstable. The major isn't ready.*

And yet she reached out to touch Major Soto, completing the circuit. The major's terrified thoughts added to the cacophony: *No, can't work. Won't work. Not now!*

The Hellions hit them like bullets and scrabbled over them like roaches, looking for the best places to destroy. One wrapped around Matt's visor. They had only moments to—

Merge, Matt thought.

Matt dove into a bottomless gray space that smelled of dust and prickled like static. Thoughts battered his consciousness as the distant explosions of the Hellions' Fusion Handshake echoed off his biometallic skin.

First, Michelle. She was back at her home on Earth. Mom was plugged into the global net. Dad was passed out on the back porch, looking across the swamp at a golden sunset through black, moss-hung trees. Her bag sat beside her, and the dying echoes of her voice told the tale: she'd just said good-bye. But this wasn't her departure for training camp. This was the first time she'd left. This was when she'd hitched over the heaved roads to Orlando. Thirty miles on the back of a truck, to end up in a crumbling city of hopeless kids slumped over games in grease-stained diners that hadn't changed in a hundred years. Walking into the recruiting center for the Displacement hospitality trade. Then walking out. Going back home defeated. Her parents never noticed she'd left. And lying awake that entire night, knowing, *I won't end up here. I'll be the first. I'll be a Mecha pilot. That's my only chance.*

And I am here now, Michelle thought, her mind kaleidoscoping through their days at training camp, the rush of first Mesh in the Hellion, the first dizzying look at Mecha Base, Ash's death, their escape from the maelstrom. Respect and love, desire and hate colored reflections of Kyle's face. And Matt's face as well.

It's all right. Time to Merge, he told her.

Hurting, Major Soto thought. But the thought was fleeting. Major Soto's memories were much more immediate. His first time in the Demon, the time when it tried to rip him out of its chest. The amazing feeling, the amazing feeling of Mesh as it should be. But also the pain like a dagger in his heart. Cutting out what he was. He'd lost a huge piece of his memories on that day. They'd simply been ripped out of his head. Major Soto's mind was an echoing room, furnished in sparse determination.

But I will do this, Soto thought, sudden and strong. He reached out to Matt. Matt took his hand.

Searing static exploded in their minds. For a moment they simply ceased to be. No thought. No desire. No need. Just blinding static and unending pain.

He realized Michelle and Major Soto were screaming alongside him. The brilliant light of reality was close, so close.

Just a little more, he thought.

Gathering their strength, they shoved upward toward the light. Their skin flayed from his body in his mind's eye. Tendons and muscles tore to shreds. His organs streamed out behind him.

Not much longer, not much longer, Matt's mind chanted madly.

We can make it, Michelle thought.
Together, Soto thought.
Together, they said again in unison.

For endless moments of time, Matt saw everything as if from outside himself. He watched as the three Demons flowed together, forming a gleaming, seamless red ball. The Hellions' Fusion Handshakes bounced off the smooth sphere, causing only tiny ripples in its surface.

The Hellions unleashed a fury of Seekers and Fireflies. Their impacts were tiny vibrations, faraway and unimportant. They didn't even scratch the perfect surface of the Merged Demon. The Hellions paused in defeat, then withdrew to observe the sphere.

The Merged Demon took form. The sphere elongated and streamlined to form the sleek space shark they'd glimpsed in the first Demon Merge. It fired maneuvering thrusters to face the waiting super-Hellions.

Before the Hellions could react, they transformed again. Arms cleaved from the merged body. Its tail thrusters split to become legs. A head and up-slanted visor grew from its front section. Veins of orange fusion power glowed all over it body as the transformation continued. Arms bulked out with biomechanical muscle. Legs elongated and gained form. Thrusters appeared on the Merged Demon's back, exhaling wavering heat and white fusion exhaust.

The Merged Demon's form locked down with a shock Matt felt all the way to the core of his body. He had one last glimpse of it in his all-seeing point of view: a towering red statue of cruelly perfect curves, streamlined beyond measure, striated with muscle that glowed bright orange with power.

Matt opened his eyes. His body thrummed with energy, as if it were filled with the furious power of the Merged Demon. The super-Hellions weren't even worth considering. Rayder was only a minor distraction. Matt, Michelle, and Soto were all-powerful, gods themselves.

To one side of Matt lay Michelle, suspended in her interface suit. Her hair floated free in the magnetorheological
fluid, like a halo. Her face was covered by the opaque mask,
but he knew she was smiling at him. She felt it too. This was
it. This was all. They couldn't lose.

To Matt's other side was Major Soto. Like Michelle, his
face was covered. But Matt knew he wore the same crazy
grin. The rictus of power.

Super-Hellions swarmed toward them. Matt raised an
arm and brushed them off effortlessly. No longer did the
super-Hellions blur with speed. They seemed slow, lumber-
ing. How could he have ever thought them fast?

Matt batted the super-Hellions away as fast as they
came. Or was it Major Soto? He didn't know where he
ended and Soto began. Or was it Michelle who thought,
Nice, nice, very nice, as they plucked the Hellions off their
Merged Demon?

ANTIMATTER WEAPONS LOCKED flashed a warning in Matt/
Michelle/Soto's POV.

Blinding light lanced at them from Rayder's Displacement Drive ship. Their Mecha hands came up instantly,
triggering a Fusion Handshake like a shield. The antimatter
annihilation passed over them without effect.

In the wake of the explosion, Rayder's battleships came
at them, a thousand dark gray, purposeful ships bristling
with weapons and humming with death. There were hulking Union Rhinos, graceful Taikong Shui Niu and swift
Aliancia Caballos. It was a force that could tear an independent Displacement Drive ship apart in seconds, a force
to occupy a planet. The Merged Demon, even in its glory,
was a glowing pinprick against the coming storm.

Matt/Michelle/Soto crossed their Mecha's arms in front
of themselves. The arms transformed and stretched hundreds of meters in length. Fusion ports opened on their
sides, forming a glowing orange X like a shield.

This is the X weapon, Matt suddenly knew. They hadn't
even had to think about activating it. It had just happened.

"Stop now, and you'll live," Matt/Michelle/Soto said, transmitting on all frequencies. "Continue and die."

The Corsair battleships didn't slow.

Matt/Michelle/Soto reached out. Their elongated arms stretched even farther to slice into the cloud of oncoming battleships. Their arms became only molecules thick, barely containing the radiant orange death within. Fusion ports spat fire into the cloud in all directions.

Where their arms passed, battleships and fighters flashed to vapor and destroyers wilted. Entire sides of ships disappeared, spilling Corsairs into empty space. Blackened hunks of steel and glass tumbled out of the sky, and the enemy's remains pattered the skin of the Merged Demon like hail.

When the clouds of destruction parted, a handful of Corsair battleships turned tail and jetted away. Their drives were like white stars of victory.

Matt's heart hammered in time with Michelle's and Soto's. A breathtaking surge of pure exhilaration passed through the trio. They'd done it! They'd turned the Corsairs back! Now all they had to do was—

HEAVY-MATTER WEAPON LOCKED, their screens screamed.

Their world rang like a bell. Matt/Michelle/Soto rocked back, screaming. When they came to and stopped their spin, the overlays showed what had happened: they'd just been hit by a series of heavy-matter weapons from Rayder's Displacement Drive ships.

Pushing their thrusters past redline, they shot at the Displacement Drive ship. Their arms reached out, clearing the few remaining fighters and battleships out of their way. They hit the Displacement Drive ship like a hammer and it rang like a bell. The Merged Demon grappled with the giant ship, like Atlas lifting his globe. Matt/Michelle/Soto reached in through an open dock, pushing aside corridors, drilling through rock, probing deep to the core of the ship, where the Displacement Drive's fusion core beat like a heart.

They squeezed. Flame erupted from every port on the

Displacement Drive ship. Fissures opened in its surface. A deep rumbling built toward a crescendo.

Matt/Michelle/Soto leapt off the Displacement Drive ship, just ahead of the expanding explosion. House-sized chunks of rock and twisted steel ricocheted off the Merged Demon's hide, but the pain was distant, unimportant. Matt/ Michelle/Soto turned to watch the expanding ball of gas, laughing at the insane power of the Merged Demon. They'd just crushed a Displacement Drive ship like a kid would crumple a piece of paper.

Matt/Michelle/Soto shared a moment of pure exhilaration. *This was what we've been striving for.* An irresistible force, one that no Corsair could stand against.

HEAVY-MATTER WEAPONS LOCKED, their screen said. A vector traced a line to two, three, more Displacement Drive ships.

Matt/Michelle/Soto turned to face the ships just as they fired. The Merged Demon instantly triggered a Fusion Handshake as it shot toward the two ships. On their armored sides, docks slid closed and weapons retracted behind protective shutters.

Closing up? That meant the Displacement Drive ships were getting ready to Displace. Sometime in the next few minutes, Rayder's forces would simply disappear. And if the ships got away, they'd lost. Rayder would simply regroup again and hit the Union harder.

Matt/Michelle/Soto slammed a hand into an armored dock. The dock doors exploded inward, exhaling a single white puff of atmosphere. The Merged Demon's hand flowed into the ship. This time, they didn't immediately crush the enemy. Matt guided them toward the bridge, where Rayder's information systems were located.

Merge, Matt thought, and the Demon's hand became one with the Displacement Drive ship's systems.

Data flowed into them. Rayder's orders. Details of what he'd done to the Hellions to unbuffer their neural interfaces and release all the limitations on their operation. The mind control that held Kyle and the other pilots in its iron grip. Relief poured off Michelle, but at the same time, there was an undercurrent of doubt. *What has happened between us?* she wondered. *What has Rayder changed in Kyle?*

But there was more data. So much more. Gigantic chunks of seemingly magic technology. Mature nanotechnology. Precise control of genetics, to the point of building completely synthetic organisms. Communications systems that acted directly on the human brain, with no electronic intermediaries. Matt gasped at the expanse of it all. What had they lost in the HuMax war?

But there was no time to dwell on that. Milliseconds were ticking away. Soon Rayder's ships would Displace away, and all would be lost.

Matt/Michelle/Soto triggered the Displacement Drive ship's thrusters, driving it into the nearest of Rayder's giant battleships. The Merged Demon reached through a closing port into the antimatter heart of the battleship.

This time, they didn't crush it. They grabbed the antimatter core of the Displacement Drive ship and took it into themselves. Absorbing its power. Absorbing the very metal of the Displacement Drive ship. The ship shriveled like a deflating balloon. The Merged Demon surged in size and power. It glowed, blindingly luminescent orange against the blackness of space.

ANTIMATTER WEAPONS LOCKED showed on their screens.

HEAVY-MATTER WEAPONS LOCKED followed close behind.

A half-dozen tags showed weapons tracking them from the handful of open ports on Rayder's Displacement Drive battleships. Rayder would sacrifice those weapons as they Displaced, for one last shot at the Merged Demon.

Which meant they only had seconds left.

Matt/Michelle/Soto gathered the antimatter power inside the Demon, concentrating it down to a point of pure radiance.

Now, they thought.

Arms of pure light shot out of the Merged Demon and

plunged into Rayder's nearby Displacement Drive ships. From there, they gathered brilliance and lanced quickly from ship to ship. Glowing arms of power embraced eleven of the most powerful battleships in the universe. Data coursed into the Merged Demon; they had total control. Rayder's forces weren't going anywhere.

Except one ship: the *Atlas*. Far away. So far. Matt/Michelle/Soto gathered their strength and flung their X weapon at the *Atlas*. But even with the power of eleven antimatter drives in their control, they couldn't reach it.

Shit! Matt ground his teeth. He imagined Rayder's laughter echoing in the cockpit.

It's all right, Michelle told him. *We have his fleet.*

Yes. Time to end it, Soto thought.

But they didn't understand! They couldn't just let Rayder go! He'd chase Rayder to the end of the universe—

You will, Michelle told him.

"That's next," Soto said out loud.

Rayder's fleet of Displacement Drive ships was slipping out of their grasp. Their teams of programmers were systematically building walls around their most important information nodes. If they didn't do something soon, they'd gain control of their Displacement Drives and disappear.

"Surrender now!" Matt/Michelle/Soto said. The words echoed through every hall of the Displacement Drive armada, on every transmission, through every speaker.

But in all the ships, both human and HuMax eyes looked up and sneered as they redoubled their efforts to throw off the Demon's control.

HuMax eyes? Matt started. There were more HuMax than Rayder? Yes. Dozens. Hundreds. The HuMax were still alive.

They closed all of their hands at once.

Around them, eleven violent orange flowers blossomed in space. Fragments of asteroid and sheets of steel armor cascaded through space. Bits of the Displacement Drive ships pattered off them like rain. The Merged Demon shrank back to its original form.

Rayder's fleet was destroyed! And the Merged Demon was the only force that could have done it. Matt/Michelle/Soto radiated contented fulfillment.

Far off, only a single Displacement Drive ship remained. The *Atlas*. Rayder's ship.

"Let's get him," Matt grated.

Matt/Michelle/Soto thrust at Rayder's ship, using all their power. This was it. This was the end. Matt screamed soundlessly in his mask, electrified with glee.

And yet ... why isn't Rayder firing? Matt wondered. But it was a tiny thought, pushed far back in the dark recesses of his mind. It didn't matter. Maybe Rayder thought he could Displace away. Maybe he just wanted to give them pause by holding back. Just as he'd held back with the power of life and death a decade and a half ago.

Matt/Michelle/Soto reached out as they rocketed toward Rayder's flagship. Their arms transformed into gleaming red spikes. Matt grinned, imagining Rayder's flagship shattering into a million pieces.

In a flash, they were there. The Merged Demon's spikes drove into the ship's armor, punching deep within. For a moment, Matt/Michelle/Soto felt everything within the flagship. The digital heart of Rayder's computers. The data he'd hidden from the rest of the Corsairs: huge reams of information gleaned from the ruins of the HuMax city, the complete template of the HuMax genome, the grand search that had driven the Expansion, even the Union's involvement in —

Look out! Michelle screamed, sharp and urgent. Four super-Hellions rocketed around from in back of the Displacement Drive ship, their Zap Guns at ready. Intense beams flared from their barrels, blotting out all vision.

Matt, Michelle, and Soto screamed, the sound reverberating as the Merged Demon's biometallic skin took intense fire. Red warning tags flared all over Matt's POV, and the dreaded REGENERATING text showed. But this time, the numbers flashed up: 45, 55, 65 SECONDS TO COMPLETION.

Matt/Michelle/Soto thrust one arm desperately deep into the ship, reaching for the antimatter core. That was the only way they'd fight off the Hellion siege.

But instead of the comforting warmth of the ship's antimatter core, they found something else. A new control, hastily added to the generator. A control that could turn the ship into an antimatter bomb.

Suddenly, Matt saw the whole picture. Rayder wasn't a showoff. He was a pragmatist. Try to capture the Demon with his remaining Hellions, but if that didn't work—

—destroy the Demon at all costs.

Matt/Michelle/Soto pulled back from the flagship in a flash, lighting thrusters and rocketing away from the ship.

Behind them, annihilation erupted from Rayder's flagship, enveloping Matt/Michelle/Soto in a wave of actinic fury.

The skin of the Merged Demon peeled back and burned away, revealing shining metallic muscles. The muscles glowed red with heat and began to melt. The visor went black before flickering back to a black-and-white, low-resolution display.

The pain was like being thrown naked into hot oil. Every nerve exploded with agony. It was so far beyond anything Matt had ever felt, he didn't even hear his own ear-piercing wails.

When it passed, the Demon hung, uncontrolled for long moments, slowly tumbling away from Rayder's flagship.

MOVE, Major Soto thought through the pain.

Matt and Michelle jerked back to attention. Only two small segments of their visual sensors still functioned. The rest flickered or were blank.

But it was enough to see the five Hellions. Four of them were scorched and twisting. One was pristine, untouched by the blast.

Rayder, Matt thought.

The single Hellion flashed at them, lightning quick, two Zap Guns held in both hands. The barrels glowed deadly blue as the Zap Guns prepared to fire.

Matt/Michelle/Soto's world shattered into a billion pieces. It was beyond pain. The Merged Demon's talons crisped and burned away like matches. Biometallic muscle glowed yellow-white and ran like water. The last of their skin seared away. Red warning tags swarmed in their screen, over a display where only a few thousand pixels flickered. REGENERATING indices filled half the screen. They counted down from 9,500 seconds.

Run, Matt thought.

Thrusters sputtering, the Merged Demon turned away from the Hellion. It jagged to one side to avoid a Zap Gun burst, but a perfectly timed shot from the other gun sent the Merged Demon tumbling.

Matt/Michelle/Soto fired their remaining thrusters, trying for an erratic and unpredictable path. Rayder had sacrificed the entire *Atlas* to get a shot at them. Now he was out for his own retribution.

"Down," Matt croaked, and thrust the Demon toward the dead planet.

Matt could almost hear Rayder's harsh laughter. Anger, white-hot and wicked fast, surged in his mind. Matt scrabbled for his own Zap Gun, but the door wasn't just jammed; it didn't exist anymore.

"Too much damage for normal transformation," Soto said, reading Matt's mind. "We can't even unMerge."

Matt groaned in frustration. If he could only get a shot!

Sudden insight bloomed. There was a way he could shoot the Zap Gun.

"You're crazy," Michelle said.

No, I'm not, Matt thought. If he fired the Zap Gun in place—in its hip holster—the beam would cleave right through the biometal. All he had to do was to get his leg lined up with Rayder—

"You'll blow our leg off!" Soto said.

Do you have another option? Matt thought, disabling interlocks and rerouting controls for the Zap Gun.

No, Soto admitted.

Let's hope we can regenerate, Michelle thought.

Burn that bridge later, Matt thought. The Merged Demon's leg exploded in a cascade of white-hot biometal. The brilliant Zap Gun beam speared inky-red space.

It intersected with the Hellion. Its arm and shoulder went red-hot and flashed to vapor. The Hellion thrashed, trying to get away. Half its visor disappeared.

Matt grinned so hard, it hurt. He could almost hear Rayder's screams.

The Hellion's thrusters went ultraviolet-overload and the dark-quicksilver Mecha leapt away in an uncontrolled spin. But it wasn't dead. The pilot's chamber was still intact.

They tried to get another shot, but they'd hit atmosphere; buffeting made targeting with the Zap Gun impossible.

The Hellion fell out of their view, as the biometal heated in the atmospheric plunge.

"Now what?" Soto asked.

"We figure out how to land," Matt said, watching the HuMax city swell quickly below them. "And quick."

19

HUNT

The Merged Demon lay scattered down the broad avenue of the twisted HuMax city. The white dwarf sun, low on the horizon, slashed alternating gray highlights and pitch-black shadow on the Demon's carbon-scarred red metal.

The suspension gel had vaporized from the pilot's chamber, but their view masks still worked. Matt held his in one hand and watched the bad news mount:

MAJOR SYSTEMS COMPROMISED: MOBILITY, STABILITY, SENSORS, WEAPONS, PILOT SUPPORT.
BIOMETAL MASS LOSS: 26%
ENERGY SYSTEMS IMPACTED: OUTPUT 33% NOMINAL

"It could be worse," Soto said.

Matt nodded, but said nothing. He took off his view mask to look around. Through a fissure in the pilot's chamber, the foul air of the HuMax world seeped, making him cough.

"Yeah, we could be dead," Michelle added.

"But we're not," Matt said. And neither was Rayder. Rayder was down here in the city, as shattered as they were. Maybe worse.

Maybe dead, Matt thought.

But probably not, whispered a little voice. *He's doing the same thing as you. Regenerating. Or else he'd be raining fire on you right now.*

A loud chime came from within the Merged Demon, and the biometallic muscles surrounding the pilot's chamber twitched. Matt's face screen blinked bright red. He held it up to look inside.

RADICAL REGENERATION NECESSARY
PILOTS EXIT MECHA

The pilot's chamber opened with a loud groan. One petal of the iris hung up, halfway open, on the deformed entrance. Hot air, stinking of sulfur, poured in.

"Fucking hell!" Michelle barked, coughing.

"Pull up your hood," Soto said, grabbing at the back of his utility suit.

"No air!" Michelle coughed.

Soto fastened his hood in place and blew out a big breath. "It'll draw air from outside and purify it. Somewhat."

Matt pulled up his hood, fastened it, and took a deep breath. The thin, hot air still stank and hurt his throat, but it was better, more breathable with the suit.

"Pilots exit cockpit," a voice sounded through the Mecha. "Radical regeneration beginning."

Soto dropped to the ground and searched frantically on the floor of the pilot's chamber, as the Mecha began to convulse.

"What are you doing?" Matt yelled.

"Survival kit!" Soto yelled back. "Pistols!"

Aha. Matt dropped to his knees and helped search. In a small compartment was a single survival kit, including a mini needle-gun pistol.

"Pilots exit cockpit immediately," the voice boomed, and the Merged Demon convulsed.

"It'll have to do," Soto said, scrambling out of the cockpit. Matt and Michelle followed, sliding down the scarred metal to stand on the broad avenue.

From the ground, the HuMax city was monstrous, inhuman in its proportion. The architecture soared with a simple grace and unity of form that Matt had only seen on Aurora, and even then only in a tiny part of the newest cities. Here, even the low, utilitarian buildings boasted subtle curves and angles that enhanced their forms, and blended seamlessly with the city's overall motif. But the scale was huge, out of proportion. The avenue, if intended for cars, was fully twelve lanes wide, but there were no markings on its glass-smooth surface. Had pedestrians once promenaded down this immense thoroughfare? It wasn't a city for humans. There was no warmth, no spaces for living. It was a city of nothing but monuments and relics.

Still, even half-shattered and carbon-burned, the crystalline beauty and immense scale once again made Matt wonder, *What have we lost?*

The Merged Demon gave a great groan and convulsed. Its arms folded up tight against its body, flowing into it. Its legs tucked underneath itself, and its visor descended into the crushed torso. Red scaffolding grew swiftly over its carbon-blackened craters, but then crept more slowly, its edges glittering with new bright metal.

"How long do we have?" Matt asked.

Soto shook his head. "I don't know. I've never seen a Mecha take such a big hit."

"Will it be able to regenerate, you think?" Michelle asked.

"I don't know." Soto sighed. "Radical regeneration. I've never seen that. It makes sense, though. Make something new out of what you've got left."

"It might," Matt said, remembering the Mecha records. Appendix C. "But who knows what it'll turn into."

Soto shrugged, his own expression clamped into a grim frown.

"How long can we survive? If it doesn't fix itself?" Her voiced trailed off in a fit of coughing.

"It doesn't matter," Soto said, his voice expressionless. "Rayder will come for us before our lungs rot or we die of radiation poisoning."

"He may not even be alive," Michelle said.

"You really believe that?" Matt asked.

Michelle shook her head, looking away.

Soto looked up at the sky. "Even if Rayder is dead, there are still Hellions up there. They weren't hit that hard. They'll regenerate. And we don't know about the *Helios*; we can only assume it's Corsair-held."

"So what do we do?" Michelle asked.

"Wait. Hope this thing turns into something that'll get us to orbit. Hope Rayder doesn't get to us first. Hope we can overcome the Corsairs on the *Helios*."

"That's a lot of hoping," Michelle said, trying for a smile.

"If you have a better plan, let me know."

"We could go after Rayder," Matt said.

Both of his companions turned to stare at him.

"He's out there," Matt told them, scanning the city. "We know he crashed. Maybe worse than us. We can find him and take him out first."

"I knew there was a reason I liked you," Soto said. "You don't stop."

"We don't stop. We're a team. We don't need his Mecha to finish this mission."

And if he isn't alive, I can see the body. I can put that in my Perfect Record and replay that every day my childhood comes back to haunt.

"You hate him so much," Michelle said.

"Who?" Matt asked.

"Rayder. He's your life. He's all you see."

She was right. Rayder had forged him, as surely as a father forges a son. He'd wrapped his whole life around his revenge.

"Determination and death. You're nothing else," she told Matt.

Matt shook his head. He wanted to contradict her. He tried to imagine a future where he didn't have to chase his ghosts, a future with Michelle.

The silence stretched out. The empty city around them suddenly seemed like ultimate desolation, despite its beauty. Knife-edged shadows separated the city into shades of bright white and pure black, while the pale sun slowly fell toward the horizon. A gravity wave hit with a long, rolling rumble. The building to their side folded in on itself and collapsed, showering them with clouds of dust.

"Have you ever been at a point where you're sure it won't work out, but you've pulled it off in the end?" Matt asked.

Major Soto chimed in. "Yeah. First deployment on Deseret. Crazy Corsairs had us surrounded, pinned down. Just two Mecha, two Imps. They had a fleet of Taikong tanks. Like, seventy of the damn things. Like they were having a sale at the Union-Mart." Soto let himself laugh. "Nobody coming to get us either. It was a pop-and-drop, 'cause there were Corsairs in orbit too."

Soto told them of looking across the wastes at sure death, flailing as his Mecha was struck by artillery from all sides. Back to back with his partner, Soto saw the future: both of them dead, burning, in a dumpy adobe town on a dry frontier world. It was that vision, that moment, that prompted his charge through the tank brigade. Somehow he'd avoided the worst of the shells. And at their back, he'd been able to cut them to ribbons with Fireflies before the tanks had a chance to turn around.

In that moment, there was a tiny bit of hope.

"What about you, Michelle?" Matt said.

Michelle nodded. "Yeah. Vector math. Mecha piloting is lots of vector math, at an almost instinctual level."

She told them about school. Michelle had excelled at almost everything, both physical and mental. She'd breezed through calculus and the lower maths, but vectors and differentials—they eluded her. She could sit down and crunch out an answer, but it wasn't easy. It certainly wasn't effortless. She sweated at every test, frantically scrawling equations as the seconds ticked down to zero. At night, while her friends were out partying or seeing their boy-friends or working and pulling down decent money, she worked into the early morning on matrices and differen-tials. She had to ignore the tick of rocks on her window as another hopeful classmate tried to get her attention. She had to pinch herself awake in class more times than she could count. She had to say no to everything.

Yet the equations still danced out of reach. She couldn't get them. Not on the level of a Mecha pilot.

Until that one day. The final. The one that was transmit-ted to the Union Academic Records. She knew she'd mud-dle through, but there was no way she'd be in the top tier. She went to bed early that night and dreamed of equations. She woke late, almost late enough to miss the test. She ran through the hallways of school, her hair unwashed, her teeth unbrushed, to get to her seat the moment the starting chime sounded.

And . . . it was magic. The knowledge that had eluded her was simply there. She could look at the vectors and know the solutions instantly. She giggled as she wrote the answers down, her stylus flying across the screen.

"And we'll do that here," Matt said.

"What about you?" Michelle asked. "When did you do the impossible?"

Matt smiled, thinking about his flight across the surface of UUS *Mercury*, of his first disastrous-but-amazing exer-cise, of fighting his way out of Mecha Base.

"Every day I can," he told her.

Major Soto chuckled, and Michelle grinned.

A flicker of movement over the top of the fallen Demon caught Matt's attention. He squinted and looked up. Some-thing like a polished chrome balloon peeked out over the chest of the Mecha. It bobbed slightly.

The silver bubble came up over the top of the Mecha,

walking on six spindly steel legs. One of the legs hung at a contorted angle, and corrosion splotched the sphere's silvery surface. It was completely featureless except for a single black spot on its face, which swiveled toward them.

Matt shoved Soto out of the way and leapt to put his body between the sphere and Michelle. Soto yelled and Michelle opened her mouth to say something when the sphere started firing. Sharp reports echoed off the hard buildings of the empty city, and rounds ricocheted from the smooth surface of the avenue where Matt had just stood.

Soto grabbed the needle pistol out of the survival kit, sighted, and squeezed off two quick shots. The first spun the silver ball around. The second pierced it. It fell behind the Mecha, hitting the ground with a metallic crash.

"What the hell was that?" Matt spat.

Soto frowned. "I don't know. Automated sentry of some kind? Who knows what they used in the war. All we can do is hope—"

Three more sentries popped over the edge of the Mecha, their gun ports swiveling to target the three Demonriders.

"—that there ain't more of them," Soto finished.

Soto squeezed off three more shots and all three sentries fell, smoking. "Now, we just gotta hope—"

A dozen sentries peeked over the edge of the Mecha, surveying the scene more cautiously than their predecessors.

"How many rounds in that gun?" Michelle asked.

"We started with a hundred," Soto told her.

The sentries came over the Mecha. Others appeared at their back. Gun ports swiveled to target.

"Run!" Soto yelled, firing as he backpedaled from the horde.

The three Demonriders ran deep into the city of Jotunheim, dodging broad avenues that offered no coverage, squeezing through cracks in the monumental buildings, racing through indoor plazas centered around long-dry fountains and monumental arches, past piles of bones scattered like twigs.

Soto kept up covering fire, but the horde of sentries only grew. Now there were at least fifty of the things coming after them, creaking along on corroded joints, rushing forward on twisted, needle-sharp claws. Their guns spat in a continuous patter, but most shots went wide after hundreds of years without maintenance.

"We need a strategy!" Matt yelled.

"I'm open to suggestions!" Soto yelled back.

Matt gritted his teeth. He didn't have any good ideas. The toxic air tore at his lungs even through the suit's filters. He wasn't thinking straight. Everything was becoming more and more a blur. Jotunheim was a city of rubble and ghosts, dreaming under a purple-black sky. The wan sun sat on the edge of the horizon, bloated by atmospheric distortion and painted in alien shades of blue and teal. Green-white light sparked and brightened within the buildings as the natural light faded.

"Funnel them down," Michelle said between gasps of breath. "Find . . . narrow fissure . . . wait for them."

"Worth a try," Soto said.

They snaked through a long ravine where two buildings had slumped together. When they were through, Soto turned to target the exit.

Soon the first sentry came scrabbling through. Soto waited until it was out and a companion had joined it. Then he shot precisely, taking out both at once.

"Yeah!" Michelle said.

"You two go," Soto said. "Hide."

"No way," Matt said, as more sentries came through the fissure.

"Go!" Soto yelled.

"Not a chance. We'll throw rocks if we have to," Michelle said.

Soto shot the next two sentries. More crowded behind

them. "This won't work. Thirty-two rounds left. We need a better plan."

"Gotta get back to the Mecha," Matt said. "If the regeneration is complete, at least we'll have armor."

Overhead, a scream of fusion exhaust echoed. Matt looked up. A quicksilver Hellion wearing a Flight Pack passed down one of the avenues a few blocks over. Its visor pointed down.

Michelle's head snapped up. She saw the Hellion and went white. Soto glanced up from firing, did a double take, and swallowed. A deep chill gripped Matt.

Rayder—or, more likely, one of his men—was back. Scanning the city. For them.

"Back to the Mecha!" Matt said, and ran once more.

Matt's breath tore his throat like a knife as they rounded the corner onto the wide avenue where the Merged Demon lay. The sentries—more than a hundred of them now—ticked and clicked along only a hundred meters behind them, their corroded legs beating an irregular rhythm of menace.

Michelle gasped and stumbled, racked with coughs. Matt pulled her up and struggled for more speed.

Then he saw the Merged Demon. Or, rather, what it had become. It wasn't a Demon anymore.

Bits of the Demon's carbon-scarred red biometal still lay scattered along the boulevard, abandoned in the regeneration process. In the middle of the Demon remnants, something stirred. Shining bright, mirrored chrome, the new Demon was much smaller—only about the size of a Hellion. Bristling with spikes and covered with irregular splotches of fusion ports, it wasn't even symmetrical. Its left arm was huge, bulky with corded metallic muscle. Its right arm was slim and tiny, tapering down to slim claws. Its visor was a dark V, set askew on a face clamped in grim determination.

Matt shivered. It was like a living thing, struggling desperately to stay alive. Was the static-dusty presence he felt in Mesh real? Was it sentient?

And how had Dr. Roth developed it, if it wasn't related to HuMax technology?

The new Demon groaned and twitched as regeneration progressed. Matt glanced involuntarily at Soto, who looked back with frightened eyes.

None of the trio spared a word as they raced up to the new Demon. If it wasn't functional, they were done. Everything was over. They'd die on this lost HuMax world.

As they made it to the big Mecha, Michelle gave another involuntary cry and pointed up at its chest, where a cockpit iris opened.

Matt's heart leapt. Maybe there was a chance!

The three scrambled up the side of the Demon and threw themselves in the cockpit. Michelle went in first, the fastest of the three. Matt came next. It was a tiny space, barely big enough for three pilots. Michelle cursed and shoved him off her, just in time for Soto to come down on top of both of them.

The ticking of the sentries' talons was loud inside the cockpit. A single claw peeked over the edge of the opening.

"Close the hatch!" Michelle yelled, but nothing happened.

Matt tore off his utility suit hood, grabbed one of the three interface cables, and socketed it into his suit. The Mecha's pain of regeneration flowed through him, and Matt groaned as he thought: *CLOSE HATCH!*

The Demon's pilot's chamber quickly closed, severing two of the sentry's spikes. Suddenly they were in perfect darkness.

"Where are the view masks?" Michelle asked.

Matt felt around, found one, and handed it to her. "Here. Plug in."

They all found their masks and plugged in. Matt's, Michelle's, and Soto's thoughts cascaded over the Mecha's pain. *Why is it hurting? Because it's still regenerating. Will it fly?*

"First things first," Matt said.

Matt/Michelle/Soto brushed away the sentries with their

small arm. It moved jerkily, like a cadet's first time in a Mecha, and sent waves of pain back through the neural interface. But the sentries scattered from the blow.

"It's clumsy," Soto said.

Not good, Michelle thought.

Together, they got the regenerated Demon to its feet, where it swayed drunkenly. One leg seemed to be slightly longer than the other. They took some practice steps, wincing at the agony. Red icons flared in their POV:

MERGE REINTEGRATION: PARTIAL 3RD ORDER
INTERNAL SYSTEMS ASSIMILATION: INCOMPLETE
TIME TO FULL REGENERATION: UNAVAILABLE

Wonderful, Matt thought.

Matt/Michelle/Soto fired thrusters. The regenerated Demon skated down the avenue toward the heart of the city, jagging this way and that in the unpredictable thrust. They tried to leap upward, but managed only a shallow, headlong flight. The Mecha crashed face-first into a hundred-meter-tall tower, which showered mirrored glass fragments down on them.

"Ouch," Matt groaned.

"It needs more time," Michelle said.

We hope, Soto thought.

Brilliance fell from the sky, exploding all around the regenerated Demon. Matt/Michelle/Soto staggered back from the force of the explosions. Their visuals lit with new tags: a Hellion directly above them, firing Seekers.

Matt/Michelle/Soto tried to launch their own Seekers, but the screen showed only one crimson warning:

WEAPONS SYSTEMS OFFLINE:
REGENERATION STATUS UNAVAILABLE

No weapons! The Hellions could sit back and slice them to pieces.

The trio shoved off the building and managed a shambling run down the street. Nearer the heart of the city, buildings rose like walls, some leaning at crazy angles to touch each other. Maybe they could find shelter somewhere until the weapons regenerated.

More Hellions fell from the sky, raining Fireflies and Seekers. Talons flashed out of the blinding explosions, slicing the Demon's biometallic skin. Matt/Michelle/Soto yelled in pain as barbs sunk deep within them.

The regenerated Demon stumbled back, striking a three-hundred-meter tall tower. Twisted steel groaned as the spire slumped against another building. Clouds of glittering crystalline dust rose around the Mecha. All five of them. Rayder's entire force.

Four of them were in good shape. The fifth was twisted and broken, one arm gone; the other arm was deeply scarred, exposing shredded biometallic muscle. Its visor was sheared completely off, and a man's head was visible through the shredded pilot's chamber.

A man? Matt looked closer. The Demon's sensory enhancement shot his POV forward, and he could see the pilot clearly.

Rayder.

Matt screamed in rage, forcing the Demon to charge on Rayder. A Hellion flashed out of the cloud and grabbed the Demon's visor, triggering a Fusion Handshake. A quarter of their vision disappeared in searing light. Another Hellion scrambled in place, its hands reaching for the Demon's neck. Matt/Michelle/Soto struck it off at the last moment. It bounced off a building, cat quick, and came at them again.

The Hellions charged the Demon. It was like a scene out of purgatory: massive, battle-scarred ruins and endless flames, against which giants battled.

The Hellions were on them again. Talons sliced deep.

Fusion Handshakes rocked them. Matt/Michelle/Soto flailed and rolled, trying to drive them off.

But the Hellions were fast. Too fast. They drove the Demon to the center of the city. Kilometers-high buildings rose like canyon walls all around them, punctuated by pylons of glowing, green-veined metal. In Matt's POV, the pylons emitted strong electromagnetic waves, perhaps part of the city's still-working power system.

But there was no time to dwell on that. The Hellions came at them again. Biometallic flesh burned away and raw muscles glittered from the open wounds. Matt/Michelle/Soto convulsed, and the Demon shook with them.

Matt had a sudden vision of their future: torn and broken, lying at the center of the grand HuMax city, another treasure for Rayder to plunder.

No! Matt's rage exploded like a nuclear furnace. He wouldn't let that happen.

And he knew exactly what he had to do.

You're insane, Michelle thought.

Yes, he is, Soto thought. *Let's fucking do it.*

They rocketed the Demon at the nearest pylon, embracing it with a lopsided hug. Their own talons dug deep into the metal.

Now, if it's part of a power system, and if it's smart enough . . . all intelligence yearns for Merge, Matt thought.

The babble of the city's systems coursed through their Demon. Mindless routines, done over and over until failure. Historical records of the founding. Surveillance video of empty plazas, dead skies, as the city slowly crumbled over the years. Calculation and assessment of the environment, as it slid closer to unlivability. Incredible images of HuMax flying as gods under the purple sky. The sound and fury of the Human–HuMax War.

And power. So much power. More than he ever expected. This wasn't a dim nuclear heart pulsing its last beats. This was raw, unlimited power drawn from the molten core of the planet itself.

Matt/Michelle/Soto reached for it—and became the city.

Suddenly they were everywhere. Every functional surveillance camera fed images to their minds. Every working node of the city's power system waited at their will.

The Demon flowed into the city. Veins of biometal snaked down the pylon and through the streets, scarring their mirror-smooth surfaces. Ropes of power coursed up the buildings and deep down to the city's core.

Matt/Michelle/Soto took the power into themselves. And then, in a concussive rush, gave it back.

NOW, Matt/Michelle/Soto thought.

Green fissures formed on the deserted avenues of the city as razor-sharp spears of silvery biometal erupted all around the Hellions. The spears shot at the Hellions simultaneously, moving so fast, no human eye could track them. Only vector traces in the trio's goggles showed their trajectories.

Three of the Hellions were immediately impaled against the side of HuMax buildings. Spikes drilled deep into their arms, legs, and visors, until they hung limp. Tags indicated that the pilots were still alive.

Matt/Michelle/Soto felt the Hellion's pilot's thoughts. Single-minded in their dedication to Rayder. However, beneath that, good men and women who just wanted to be released from the mind control. The Union's Mecha pilots were still in there.

None of the three were Kyle, though. Michelle's waves of worry cascaded through Matt and Soto's minds. But at the same time, she thought grimly, *Let's finish this.*

Two Hellions fled. Matt/Michelle/Soto's spears followed, snaking through the avenues of the city at dizzying speed. Matt's POV blurred and went incoherent as it leapt from camera to camera. He had no idea where he was. But at the moment, it didn't matter. The intense pleasure of chasing Rayder's mind-controlled goons, moving without thinking, was enough.

Their spears struck the rearmost Hellion, shearing off its

legs. It tumbled to a stop in a cloud of dust, at the edge of an open space full of vegetation. More spears of city bio-metal impaled its arms, holding the struggling Mecha down.

And in that moment, a sudden thought, familiar and intense:

Kill me.

Kyle.

Flashes of memory hit them: Kyle's capture. The mind-control crown, the terror of nanonetworks in his brain. But a small part of him still fought on.

We'll help you, Michelle thought through her tears.

No help! Just kill me! Kyle's thoughts bounced between mindless devotion to Rayder and his true rage.

"We'll cure you," Michelle sobbed, out loud.

But the only thing they could do was hold him down as they went after the final Demon. Rayder.

Rayder's Hellion shot down a broad shaft set in the middle of an industrial-looking area of the city, filled with shattered, low buildings that exposed complex mechanisms within.

Spears followed the last Hellion. But the shaft pierced deep into the planet. Without a source of power and intelligence, the shards grew thin and weak and fell away.

Rayder's Hellion disappeared into the hot darkness.

20

RETRIBUTION

Matt screamed in frustration, struggling to pull away from the pylon. *I'll chase Rayder down! I'll finish this!*

"You can't!" Michelle yelled. "We have to hold the Hellions!"

Matt sagged. She was right. They couldn't go after Rayder. They had to hold the Hellions down until they could get the pilots out.

They do, Matt thought. *Not you.*

Fear from Michelle and Soto spiked through the Demon as they read his thoughts. *You can't unMerge now!* Michelle screamed in his mind.

But she was wrong. He could. Matt saw every system in the regenerated Demon humming easily under the control of Michelle and Soto. They'd mastered it. They didn't need him.

Matt pulled against the side of the Demon, thinking, *UnMerge.*

The Demon's side stretched, twisting into a new form. An arm rose out of the silvery biometal, forming into talons as they watched. The edge of a visor peeked out.

Don't leave me, Michelle thought, radiating fear.

I'll be back, Matt told her.

The pilot's chamber convulsed, and Matt felt himself moving away from Michelle and Soto. Soon he was alone in his own smooth, biometallic cockpit.

A tiny Mecha stood beside the regenerated Demon, its bright chrome surface reflecting the monumental architecture of the alien city. Only four meters tall, it was a little more in size and girth than a PowerSuit.

Inside, Matt's view screen showed:

NEW CONFIGURATION ACCEPTED: MESH STABLE
COMMUNICATIONS: ENABLED
SENSORS: BASIC
WEAPONS SYSTEMS: NOT AVAILABLE

Matt grinned. A tiny, unarmed Mecha versus a half-smashed Hellion? That would have to be enough.

"You crazy man," Soto said, his comms icon lighting. "You really won't stop."

"How are you two doing?" Matt asked.

"Good," Michelle said. "We'll be fine."

Matt took off down the avenue toward the edge of the city. The mini Demon handled better than the reconstructed one, but it was still a little shaky.

"Make sure you come back!" Michelle shouted after him.

"I told you I would," Matt said. But deep down, that little voice asked, *Will you? What if that's the price to destroy Rayder?*

"See you both soon," he added.

Matt rushed through the streets, following the Merged Demon's spears. They led him to the industrial section and the yawning chasm. Up close, it was huge—at least fifty meters across. It descended into pitch-darkness.

Matt flung himself into it, like a pebble down a well. Rough rock walls rushed past him as he gathered speed, slowly disappearing into the darkness. Suddenly, Matt had a terrible thought: *What if my thrusters don't work?*

He tumbled to orient the Mecha, then fired his rear thrusters. They came on with sputtering flares, but it was enough to slow him and light his way.

The hole above shrank to a faint purple pinprick as he descended. At the same time, the rock walls changed. They began to glow red with heat. Veins of orange stone snaked down the walls. *Magma?* The outside temperature had risen to seventy degrees Celsius. Rayder, exposed in the cockpit, must be frying.

Boom! Matt struck a rock outcropping and tumbled, his vision wheeling.

Below him was another ledge and a deep alcove, filled with complex machinery and screens. In front of the machines crouched a trashed Hellion.

Rayder.

Matt spun in midair, hitting his thrusters full-on. He hit the ledge hard enough to send dust flying in the air. Shards of stone fell down on him. He ran at Rayder, who had just started to turn from his console.

Rayder dodged at the last moment and Matt crashed into the console, sending sparks flying. For a moment, he felt everything in the gigantic control system, the mother of the city's own power grid. HuMax had been burrowing deep into the molten core of their world for hundreds of years. Adding nuclear generators. Carefully placing . . .

A Displacement Drive.

Rayder was trying to Displace the entire planet?

Rayder's good arm flickered out, too fast to see, and caught Matt's mini Demon by the neck in a viselike grip. Matt squealed as Rayder yanked him off the ground and brought him close to his face for examination.

That face. Those yellow and violet eyes, as cold and dead as he remembered them as Rayder stood over his fallen father. Red rage blotted out Matt's vision. He lashed out furiously at Rayder, but the man held him fast.

Merge, Matt thought. But nothing happened. Rayder's Hellion might as well have been stone. He couldn't even feel Rayder's thoughts!

Rayder held the mini Demon carefully away from his body. A knife-thin smile grew on his features.

"You're a persistent fighter, corpsman," Rayder said. "Let's see who you are."

Open, he thought.

The mini Demon unfolded like a flower. Baking heat hit Matt like a hammer, but he pulled his face mask off. To see Rayder with his own eyes.

Rayder looked at him calmly, without recognition.

"Fifteen years ago," Matt said. "Prospect."

Rayder threw back his head and laughed. "The child. *Bravery must have its reward.* But I'm afraid the reward is only death delayed."

Rayder walked to the edge of the pit and dangled the mini Demon over its side. Corrosive gas stung Matt's eyes, making him tear up. His whole body was cooking. He tried to close the hatch, but the Mecha didn't respond to his command.

Rayder? Is Rayder in my systems?

A creeping coldness came over him. Yes. Rayder was in his Demon. Merging. Pulling out data.

"Who do you think created the HuMax, child?" Rayder asked. "None other than your perfect Union."

Matt rocked back in shock. That couldn't be true! The Union was created out of the rubble of war and desperation to destroy the HuMax! They'd risen to turn the tide of the Human–HuMax War! They—

"Have been chasing us down for a century and a half," Rayder said. "And studying us. Why did I strike Geos, and why was your news so silent? We were freeing our comrades—that's why."

Matt hung openmouthed. Could it be true? Was the bombardment an excuse to release HuMax prisoners? Or, worse, lab subjects?

But in the back of Rayder's mind, something coiled. Something dark. He hated all humans. And it wasn't just revenge. It was an all-consuming insanity that wouldn't be satisfied until humanity was extinct. But he wanted to study Matt. Matt's Merge capability was better than any

Rayder had imagined. But once Rayder knew the secret—

I'm in his mind now, Matt realized.

From Rayder, a sudden pulse of panic. Matt didn't hesitate a microsecond. He reached out hard, thinking, *Merge!*

The two Mecha melted together. The resulting black-chrome sculpture toppled into the abyss. Toxic gases welled up at them as the temperature rose. None of Matt's systems responded to his thoughts.

No time for finesse. *UnMerge!* Matt screamed in his mind.

The two Mecha melted back to their original forms. Matt's hatch slapped closed and he snugged the face mask into place. Rayder tumbled next to him, slumped half out of his Mecha, seemingly inert.

Pressure and temperature rose rapidly, and Matt's antimatter core was finally blinking its low-energy warning.

He had no choice. Matt fired thrusters and headed toward the surface.

Watching Rayder spiral down.

Back in the city, Matt found Michelle and Soto's part of the reconstructed Demon still Merged with the city. Its visor swiveled to watch him approach. His comms flickered to live, showing Michelle's icon.

"You made it!" she cried.

"What about Rayder?" Soto asked.

"Dead," Matt said. *Or at least I hope so.*

"Congratulations," Soto said.

Matt nodded but said nothing. Victory didn't feel, well, like he expected it would. *Your father's killer is dead,* he told himself. *You should be ecstatic.*

But there were too many other questions.

"Now all we have to do is get off this rock," Soto said. "From what I can tell, the thrusters should be up to it, but how do we drag the Hellions back with us?"

"Merge with them," Matt said.

"But what about the *Helios*?" Michelle asked. "It was boarded."

"We'll deal with that when we're there," Soto told her.

The three Merged into the fully reconstructed Demon configuration. Red and yellow warnings still scrolled on their screens, but the thrusters appeared to be almost fully regenerated.

More magic, Matt thought.

"What?" Michelle asked.

"Nothing."

One by one, they Merged with Rayder's captured Hellions. The mind-controlled pilots' thoughts buzzed in their heads like angry bees. But it wasn't enough to challenge their control.

Up to orbit, the thrusters were a little unstable, but Matt/Michelle/Soto were able to maintain their attitude and direction.

The icon for the UUS *Helios* appeared in their view masks. It was still there, at least. As they drew near, they could see a Hellion crouching near its hangar doors. The Hellion raised its head to look at them, then grabbed for its Zap Gun.

But they'd destroyed or captured all of Rayder's Hellions. Which meant this was the one from the *Helios*. The one Matt had used. So either it was captured or—

"Captain Ivers!" Matt barked. "It's us! If you're in control of the *Helios*, please answer!"

Ivers' comms icon immediately flashed to life. "What the hell did you guys turn into?"

Matt/Michelle/Soto all grinned, imagining what the lopsided, reconstructed Demon, now half-Merged with a bunch of Hellions, must look like on Ivers' screen.

"We don't know yet, sir," Soto said. "Are you secure? Can you share your bridge surveillance with us?"

"Good man. Don't trust—verify. I think someone said that a long time ago." A video feed from the *Helios*' bridge came on. It showed Ivers and two pilots in interface suits reclining behind him. The third pilot's seat was empty, as was the rest of the bridge. "They were tough buggers, but Sam cleared them out." He nodded at the empty pilot's chair.

Matt started. "Your pilots are Mecha Corps?"

Ivers nodded. "Where else? They have the interface-suit experience."

The Hellion outside the dock lowered its Zap Gun and returned it to its holster. Still, Matt felt gnawing unease. Using Mecha tech in Displacement Drive ships meant Dr. Roth's technology was spreading. He was consolidating more power. *What does that mean?* Another question to be answered.

Damn it, life after Rayder is supposed to be simple! Matt thought.

"Life is never simple," Soto said out loud, as waves of amusement radiated from Michelle. Matt swallowed. He'd forgotten about sharing his thoughts.

"What happened with Rayder?" Captain Ivers asked.

"Killed, sir," Soto said, before Matt could speak.

Ivers smiled. "Good deal. Now let's get you guys home."

21

REWARD

Despite their triumph, it was a chilly reception back at Mecha Base. Matt, Michelle, and Major Soto were immediately marched up to the debriefing room by armed Auxiliaries, past swarms of repair crews still working on the compromised base. The atmospheric leaks had been silenced, but most of the slit windows were still covered in opaque foam. Large impacts from the maelstrom shuddered through the base, making the construction dust dance in the bright work lights.

Matt walked through the hallways in a daze, his Velcro soles heavy on the utility carpet. He hadn't slept since before they left. Their unMerge and return to the *Helios* was a blur, as was their last brief battle with the Corsairs. Michelle and Soto had done most of that. He'd still been in a daze, thinking, *Rayder is dead.*

I hope Rayder is dead.

No. It was unthinkable. There was no way he could possibly survive. He'd fallen into the molten core of Jotunheim and been consumed. That was the only possible ending.

Like the histories? Matt thought. *The ones with the valiant and innocent Union fighting the HuMax scourge?*

Who did you think created us? Rayder's voice echoed in his mind.

No. How could he even consider the word of a HuMax monster, the man who so casually killed his father?

But if his race was being used by the Union and his father had been part of the research . . .

Matt shook his head. "No," he breathed.

Michelle looked at him. "No, what?"

"Nothing."

She nodded, but kept studying his face for a long time. He felt her gaze hot on his cheek.

You should be happy, he told himself. *You're free.*

In the meeting room, Dr. Roth, Yve Perraux, and Colonel Cruz flanked a jumpy FTL display that framed Congressperson Tomita and a woman. Someone very familiar.

Kathlin Haal, the Union's Prime.

Matt started and stood rigidly at attention. Major Soto and Michelle snapped off salutes.

"Ms. Prime!" Michelle breathed.

"At ease, corps," Prime Haal said.

"It's an honor, ma'am," Major Soto.

"No, it's my honor, corpspersons. Thanks to you, we are rid of the Union's most significant enemy." Still, despite her praise, her expression didn't change a millimeter.

"But . . ." Matt started.

Prime Haal nodded. "Yes. You're a very perceptive young man. As well as talented." For several long moments, her severe gray eyes stared straight at Matt.

The FTL transmission slid into bi-trot before Prime Haal continued. ". . . sure you're familiar with the phrase, 'I have good news, and I have bad news.' "

"Yes, ma'am," the three said in unison.

Prime Haal sighed. "This is by far the worst part of my job. But, in this case, I believe the good and bad to be fairly balanced, something I hope the Union can always strive for."

Good and bad in balance. Matt remembered Rayder's words, but clamped his jaw to keep from saying anything.

"First, the bad. We are unable to publically recognize your contributions, corpspersons. This expedition was so, well . . . off book and off scale, there will be no medals."

Soto nodded, his jaw set hard. Matt blew out a breath. If that was the end of it, he was fine.

"Next, the good. Despite our lack of public recognition, you have my assurance that your value will not be overlooked, and you will be awarded the achievement of Demonrider, as recommended by Dr. Roth."

Tomita stirred unhappily in the background. Haal shot him a glance before continuing. "This brings me to my last decision. Congressperson Tomita has brought to my attention details of the security failure of the BioMecha program, despite the rich budget allotted for such purposes. He has valid points and concerns. Despite this, I will not immediately close the BioMecha program, as he recommends. However, additional Union oversight will be provided to ensure security. Mr. Perraux will be relieved of his assignment, in favor of a team composed of Union Army Intelligence personnel."

Yve's mouth shot open, but no words came out. He was being downgraded, and Matt couldn't suppress a tiny bit of satisfaction. Yve was a politician, a compromiser. And the days of playing it safe were over.

"Oversight!" Dr. Roth snapped. "We have gone beyond the beyond to assure security. You cannot compare the situation with Rayder—"

"Yes, I can!" Prime Haal thundered over him. "You are fully briefed and apprised of all Union treaties, threats, and campaigns. We expect you to plan for them. If you cannot, the Union will plan for you."

"I will not simply open my private facilities to your thugs!"

"Yes, you will," Prime Haal said. "If you wish to remain the sole biomechanical contractor to the Union."

"There are no other contractors!" Dr. Roth said. "My technology is proprietary. No research institution is even close to duplicating it."

Haal gave Dr. Roth a knife-edged smile. "What need do we have of duplication when we have battleships and antimatter weapons? Doctor, please let's not make this ugly."

Roth slammed a fist down on the desk, his jaw working, but he said nothing out loud.

"If that is clear, then my business here is at an end," Prime Haal said. "Corpspersons, thank you again. You're a credit to the Union. I only wish we could recognize it."

You can't, Matt thought. *Because then the truth would come out.* Where they fought. What they fought. What the Union doesn't want anyone to know.

The Union was run by the same people responsible for losing control of the HuMax in the first place.

He clenched his fists until his knuckles went white. Prime Haal and Congressperson Tomita winked off.

Colonel Cruz sat up straighter. "Corpspersons, we will have a small graduation ceremony for you tomorrow." Then his expression softened.

"Thank you," he told them. "Even if I can never say it in public, you are the heroes of the Union."

"It was our honor, sir," Major Soto said.

"Thank you, sir," Michelle added.

When they left, Michelle split off from the group to go down to the infirmary, where doctors still worked on the four mind-controlled Mecha pilots. Matt watched her go, then followed Dr. Roth down a different set of passages.

He caught up with Dr. Roth at the entrance to his lab. Roth turned around with a deep frown of annoyance.

"What do you want, cadet?"

"Did the Union create the HuMax?"

Roth's eyes widened a fraction, and he said nothing for a long time. Finally his expression softened to neutrality. "The Union has many agendas, not all of which are visible."

"But did they?" Matt asked. "Have they been experimenting on the HuMax?"

Roth pursed his lips. "There are living HuMax who would see us all annihilated. That's what matters."

"Are they monsters?"

"Are we monsters?" Roth asked, and turned back to his door. "Now, if you will excuse me, cadet."

Matt said nothing, his mind whirling. *The Union has many agendas,* he thought. But what was Dr. Roth's agenda? What was his goal? And how had he developed that near-magic Mecha technology? They'd seen nothing like that even in the HuMax city. Rayder himself didn't know where it came from.

But there was one more question he could ask Roth, one more important than any other.

"Who made me?" Matt asked. "What am I?"

Roth turned from the door to offer a sardonic smile. "Not HuMax," he said, and slipped into his lab.

Their ceremony was in the Hellion Dock, the same setup as Kyle's send-off. Ranked Hellions stood behind the stage. The thing the Demon had become had been taken to Dr. Roth's lab, so the Hellions had to suffice. Matt couldn't help but look up at them and think, *Let me in.*

He was hooked. And that was perfectly fine.

Across the way from the docks, the lights of the Decompression Lounge shone. Silhouettes told of silent observers of their ceremony, but the actual audience was sparse: Peal, Jahl, Stoll, and Kyle. Kyle still looked fuzzy from the drugs, draped almost bonelessly on his seat, but the doctors said he'd be fine, Michelle told them. Maybe a little too brightly.

Kyle waved at Matt and offered a wan smile. Matt waved back and forced a grin. There was no need for them to be rivals. There was nothing left of the man.

And his feelings for Michelle? He could accept them now. He wanted to be with her, to tell her he loved her, but he had no idea when the time would come. Or if it would come at all.

"Attention, cadets and corps!" Colonel Cruz barked out, taking the podium at the front of the stage.

Matt, Michelle, and Soto each wore new, crisp, blue dress uniforms. Matt tugged at the too-tight collar and kept his eyes to the front, joy and uncertainty fighting in his mind.

Cruz called Major Soto's name first. Soto walked slowly

and purposefully to face the older man. Colonel Cruz studied Soto's face for long moments. Finally, he sighed and said, "For overall valor and capability, I award you the achievement of Demonrider, Major Soto."

Cruz continued. "There will be no increase in your rank, as this is an achievement not tied to any campaign."

Soto nodded. "I understand, sir. Thank you, sir." He stepped back into line.

"Next, Michelle Kind," Cruz said.

Michelle gave Matt one last glance, then moved to stand rigidly in front of Colonel Cruz.

"For overall capability and heroism, I certify the completion of your Mecha Corps training, Private Michelle Kind. You will take the new rank of captain, and wear the achievement of Demonrider."

Michelle nodded calmly, but her voice choked as she said, "Thank you, sir."

Matt finally stood in front of Cruz. The older man's eyes narrowed down on him like lasers.

"For exceptional capability in all classes of Mecha, I certify the completion of your Mecha Corps training, Cadet Matt Lowell. You will take the rank of captain, and wear the achievement of Demonrider."

"Understood, sir," Matt said.

Cruz just nodded. Then he held out a hand, stopping Matt before he could turn away. "Thank you again. And keep it up."

Matt bowed to Cruz humbly. "I'll do my best, sir." He went back to stand in line with the others.

"May I present to you our newest Mecha Corps," Colonel Cruz said.

Scattered applause came from the tiny audience, echoing loud in the large dock.

They gathered at the Decompression Lounge afterward. The Mecha pilots at the bar glared at them and left. Matt sat at a table near the window, not yet knowing how to feel. How would it work out with Dr. Roth?

How about Michelle?

Michelle talked with Kyle for a while. Kyle leaned over the table toward her, but she rocked back, aloof. They circled each other like the opposing poles of a magnet.

Matt sat alone in his own thoughts. So many questions, and so few answers. So many agendas, so many players. His future stretched out in front of him like a rutted country road disappearing into pea-soup fog.

It wasn't supposed to be like this, he thought. *Kill Rayder, and then everything would be clear. No more obstacles. Get on with your life.*

Except, Matt realized, he never really knew what his life was. His future was as cloudy and confused as ever, because he'd never thought past that one goal.

Matt sighed. He was empty, echoing. What would fill him up besides the Mecha?

Toward the end of the evening, Michelle came to sit next to Matt.

"Now what?" she asked.

Matt barked sudden laughter. "You too?"

"You too, what?"

"I was just thinking, *What the hell do I do now?*"

Michelle's gaze bounced down to the table. "You killed Rayder, right?"

Matt nodded. *At least I hope so,* he thought.

"How do you follow that?" Michelle breathed.

"First Mecha Corps from Earth," Matt said. "How do you follow that?"

They both laughed. It was a brittle, uncomfortable sound.

"Save the universe," Matt said, after a time.

"From what?" Michelle said. Her tone was light, but her eyes were haunted. Maybe putting it all together. The Union and the HuMax.

Matt sighed. "Whatever it needs saving from."

Michelle nodded and reached out to take his hand. He squeezed it softly. He imagined the feel of her lips on his.

But it wasn't time for that. She watched his face warily, as if expecting him to lean over the table and try again.

"Seems a tall order," Michelle said, after a time.

"We'll do it."

Michelle grinned. "How?"

"However we need to."

Michelle laughed. "Somehow I knew you'd say that." She squeezed his hand, content to let him hold it for a while. Her smile was bright and full of promise.

It wasn't much.

But it was enough.

ABOUT THE AUTHOR

Brett Patton, in the words of a friend, "was watching Evangelion while you were reading Heinlein." Actually, don't tell anybody, but he was doing both. And actually, don't tell anyone, but he's also taking liberties with the quote. He's been writing fun, action-oriented science fiction for years, but this is his first published novel. He lives with his wife, Lisa, in Los Angeles, where he is sometimes asked to consult on "rubber science" for various science fiction movies. Visit him at his Web site: www.brettpatton.com

THE ULTIMATE IN
SCIENCE FICTION AND FANTASY!

From magical tales of distant worlds to stories of
technological advances beyond the grasp of man, Penguin has
everything you need to stretch your imagination to its limits.

penguin.com/scififantasy

ACE

Get the latest information on favorites like
William Gibson, Ilona Andrews, Jack Campbell,
Ursula K. Le Guin, Sharon Shinn, Charlaine Harris,
Patricia Briggs, and Marjorie M. Liu,
as well as updates on the best new authors.

ROC

Escape with Jim Butcher, Harry Turtledove, Anne Bishop,
S.M. Stirling, Simon R. Green, E.E. Knight, Kat Richardson,
Rachel Caine, and many others—plus news on the
latest and hottest in science fiction and fantasy.

DAW

Patrick Rothfuss, Seanan McGuire, Mercedes Lackey,
Kristen Britain, Tanya Huff, Tad Williams, C.J. Cherryh,
and many more—DAW has something to satisfy the
cravings of any science fiction and fantasy lover.

*Get the best of science fiction and fantasy
at your fingertips!*

R0064